The Christmas Story Book

The Christmas Story Book

Collected by Ineke Verschuren

Floris Books

This collection first published in Dutch
© 1986 Christofoor, Zeist

This collection first published in English in 1988 by Floris Books
Third impression 1995
English version © 1988 Floris Books, Edinburgh

British Library CIP Data available

ISBN 0-86315-077-2

Printed in Great Britain
by Redwood Books, Trowbridge, Wilts

Contents

From Christmas to Epiphany

Advent

Why God Created Man

Dan Lindholm

God created the world and all that it contains, from the tiniest worm in the earth to the crown of creation: Man.

The angels watched and wondered about it. One thing in particular seemed incomprehensible to them; why had God created man? But however much they pondered it remained a riddle for them. They thought that God did not need mankind down there on the earth after he had the heavens full of angels. They discussed it among themselves and eventually agreed to ask God himself. One of the smallest angels took courage, stood before the Lord's throne and asked, "Heavenly Father, your house is full of great and little angels. Why then did you create Man?"

When God the Father heard that, he called: "Gather together, heavenly host."

Then he bent down to the earth, plucked a red rose which had just opened. "Look," he said to the angels, "Who can tell me what I have here in my hand?"

But none of all the countless angels knew what God was holding in his hand. In silence they stood round his throne and did not know what answer to give.

God the Father then spoke: "I have created Man so that there may be a creature in the world who *knows* what God the Father has created."

The Betrothal of Joseph and Mary

From the Protevangelium of James

After Joachim and Anna had waited for a long time for the birth of a child and Joachim had withdrawn into the desert in shame, an angel of the Lord came to Anna and said: "Anna, Anna, the Lord has heard your prayer. You shall conceive and bear, and your offspring shall be spoken of in the whole world."

And Anna said: "As the Lord my God lives, if I bear a child, whether male or female, I will bring it as a gift to the Lord my God, and it shall serve him all the days of its life."

And behold, there came two messengers, who said to her: "Behold, Joachim you husband is coming with his flocks; for an angel of the Lord came down to him and said to him: 'Joachim, Joachim, the Lord God has heard your prayer. Go down; behold, your wife Anna shall conceive'."

And Joachim went down and called his herdsmen and said: "Bring me ten lambs without blemish; they shall belong to the Lord my God. And bring me twelve tender calves for the priests and elders, and a hundred kids for the whole people."

And Joachim came with his flocks, and Anna stood at the gate and saw Joachim coming and ran immediately and hung on his neck, saying: "Now I know that the Lord God has greatly blessed me; for behold the widow is no longer a widow, and I, who was childless, shall conceive."

And Joachim rested the first day in his house.

And when the time was fulfilled a girl was born, and Anna called her Mary. When the child was three years old her parents brought her to the Temple of the Lord, to fulfil the promise which they made.

When she was twelve years old, there took place a council of the priests, saying: "Behold, Mary has become twelve years old in the Temple of the Lord. What then shall we do with her?" And they said to the high priest: "Stand at the altar of the Lord; enter and pray concerning her, and what the Lord shall reveal to you we will do."

And the high priest went into the Holy of Holies and prayed concerning her. And behold, an angel of the Lord suddenly stood before him and said to him: "Go out and assemble the widowers of the people, who shall each bring a rod, and to whomsoever the Lord shall give a sign, his wife she shall be."

And the heralds went forth and spread out through all the country round about Judea; the trumpet sounded, and all ran to it.

And Joseph threw down his axe and went out to meet them. And when they gathered together, they took the rods and went to the high priest. He took the rods of all and entered the Temple and prayed. When he had finished the prayer he took the rods, and went out again and gave them to the widowers: but there was no sign on them.

Joseph received the last rod, and behold, a dove came out of the rod and flew on to Joseph's head. And the priest said to Joseph: "Joseph, to you has fallen the good fortune to receive the virgin of the Lord; take her under your care."

And Joseph was afraid, and took her under his care.

The Search for the Secret King

Eberhard Kurras

Not so very long ago there was a country which was the biggest in the world, for it had conquered nearly all the other countries. It had become not only very famous but also very rich, and its inhabitants had to admit that there was scarcely anything to mar their good fortune.

One day a very strange illness broke out in that country. At first it attacked only a few people, then more and more people were affected until finally it became an epidemic. The symptoms were a curious kind of paralysis. People who succumbed to it could no longer move, soon they could not speak and finally they could not think. The inhabitants were deeply perplexed because the evil had come upon them in the time of their greatest prosperity.

As the illness spread and took hold of the most important people, the king finally called his counsellors together and consulted with them, what was to be done in this predicament. But the counsellors could think of nothing beyond what the doctors had already tried. In the end they proposed to the king that he should send out a proclamation throughout the kingdom that if anyone knew what should be done he should present himself immediately.

The king did this, and after a time a very old shepherd appeared at the palace. He gave the king unexpected advice. He said: "In this extremity only one thing can help you. Send your daughter to the Secret King and he will give you what you need."

The king did not like what he was told at all. He just did not want to send his very own daughter all by herself out into the world to an unknown king, especially to one who was also a Secret king. But when he became ill himself he decided after all to follow the shepherd's advice.

So the young princess went out to look for the Secret King. She did not know where he lived, nor did she know the way, but she was filled with the ardent desire to find him and to help the people. She wandered on from morning till night and had still not found him, and as she had not achieved anything by the end of the day she resolved not to seek lodging for the night, but to remain in the open lest she should miss seeing a sign. So she climbed to the top of a hill and stayed there all night.

She now saw that an endless sky of deepest blue formed a vault above her. Never had she seen the sky like that. She gazed at it steadfastly for a long time and gave herself up to the exalted vision. She felt herself growing freer and greater and she felt that she could understand many mysteries of the world. Then she fell fast asleep.

When she awoke next morning she noticed to her astonishment that she was wrapped in a wonderful dark blue cloak. She arose and went on her way. She met many people who needed her help, some of them cursing her. The king's daughter did everything required without complaining or growing angry. Then she was approached by a woman who had hardly any clothing on and who begged her for something warm to wear. The king's daughter gave the woman her own clothes, for she still had her blue cloak. However, when she looked down she saw that she was wearing a new robe that was shining in the most beautiful red.

As she went on the following day she encountered many obstacles. The paths became harder and harder, and her strength began to fail. Only her determination remained steadfastly fixed on her goal. She came to an upland meadow with magnificent leafy trees bearing glistening fruit. Exhausted, she sat down under the largest tree, but as she was sitting there thinking, "If only my strength could match my determination!" the huge tree began to shake and shake and two lovely warm golden shoes fell down. When the king's daughter put on the shoes she felt her limbs flowing with a strength such as she had never felt before. Then she was able to go on.

On the fourth day the path descended and gradually led into the inside of the earth. First she was surrounded by terrifying darkness, then it became lighter and lighter, and at last she was bathed in an indescribably soft light. It seemed to her that she had come into the very heart of the earth. In the middle of the space stood a throne and on it sat a youthful king shining like a gentle sun. Round him stood the spirits of Nature, the leaders of mankind and the highest of the angels. The king's daughter knew now that she had reached the end of her journey.

15

The king on the throne looked at the maiden and saw what she was wearing: the blue cloak, the red robe and the golden shoes. He now spoke to her: "I see that you are worthy to receive the healing gift and bring it to mankind," and he gave her a golden bowl filled with sparkling water and bade her drink. Then he told her to take it to the people and to tell them about the Secret King. Whoever believed her would be allowed to drink and would be cured of the illness.

The king's daughter took the bowl and journeyed back into the land of men. When she told the people about whom she had met, most of them did not believe that there was a Secret king. But the others did believe, drank from the golden bowl and were cured of their mysterious illness.

In this way many have received new life. Many more will come too when they open their hearts to the tidings that there is a secret king who guards and bestows the water of life. He dwells amongst us and waits.

The Legend of Santa Lucia's Day

Selma Lagerlöf

Many hundreds of years ago there lived in the southern part of Värmland a rich and covetous old woman called Lady Rangela. She owned a castle, or rather it was a fortified manor, at the narrow entrance of a long bay which ran deep inland off Lake Väner. She had built a bridge over this narrow entrance, and this bridge could be drawn up like a drawbridge over a moat. At the bridge Lady Rangela kept a strong guard who would lower the bridge for those wayfarers who agreed to pay the bridge-toll which she demanded, but for those who were too poor or who otherwise refused to pay the bridge remained drawn up. As there was no ferry these last wayfarers had to go right round the bay, a detour of several leagues.

When Lady Rangela began to exact toll from wayfarers in this way it caused much discontent, and probably the sturdy farmers who were her neighbours would have long since forced her to give them free passage if she had not had a powerful friend and protector in Lord Eskil of Börtsholm whose domains marched with her own. This Lord Eskil who lived in a real castle with walls and towers, who was so rich that his whole lands comprised a whole härad or county, who had a retinue of sixty armed followers when he rode through the country, and who moreover was a valued counsellor of the king, was not only a good friend of Lady Rangela, but she had succeeded in making him her son-in-law, and so it was quite natural that no one dared interfere with the activities of the avaricious woman.

Year after year Lady Rangela kept up this practice without opposition when something happened to cause her grave misgivings. Quite suddenly her poor daughter, Lord Eskil's wife, died, and Lady Rangela told herself that a man like Lord Eskil with eight children who were still minors and a household like a king's would soon marry again, especially as he was not so very old. But if the new wife were to be hostile to Lady Rangela this could be very detrimental to her, for it was almost more necessary for her to be on good terms with the Lady of Börtsholm than with the lord himself, as Lord Eskil who had to undertake many great affairs was constantly journeying, and while he was away it fell to his wife to order the life of the castle and its domains.

Lady Rangela weighed up the matter carefully and once the funeral was over she rode over one day to Börtsholm and sought out Lord Eskil in his private room. She led the conversation to his eight children and to the care which they needed, to his countless servants who had to be supervised, fed and clothed, to his great banquets which were attended often by kings and princes, to the great revenues of his herds, fields, hunting grounds, his beehives, his hop-gardens, his fishing, all of which had to be reckoned up and accounted for in the great house; indeed, of everything which his wife had had to administer, and in this way conjured up a frightening picture of the great difficulties which loomed up before him after the death of his wife.

Lord Eskil listened with the respect due to a mother-in-law, but with a certain misgiving. He was thinking that all this might mean that Lady Rangela was offering to take charge of the running of Börtsholm, and he had to confess that this old woman with her double chin and her hooked nose, her rough voice and her peasant greed would not be a very pleasant company in his house.

"My dear Lord Eskil," Lady Rangela went on, who was perhaps not unaware of the effect of her speech. "I know that you have the opportunity to make a very advantageous marriage, but I know too that you are rich enough to consider the well-being of your children before the dowry and inheritance that such a marriage might bring, and so I should like to suggest that you choose one of my daughter's young cousins as her successor."

Lord Eskil's face cleared visibly when he heard that it was a young relation which his mother-in-law was recommending, and she proceeded with greater confidence to persuade him to marry Lucia, the daughter of her brother, the high judge Sten Folkesson. Lucia would be just nineteen on Santa Lucia's day. Up till then she had been brought up by the pious nuns in the Cloister of Riseberga and had not only been educated in good manners, habits and strict piety, but she had also learnt in the great nunnery's household how to run a lordly establishment.

"If youth and poverty are no disadvantage to her," said Lady Rangela, "You should choose her. I know that my departed daughter would trust the care of her children to her with an easy heart. She will not need to return from the grave like Lady Dyrit of Örehus if you give them their cousin as stepmother."

Lord Eskil, who never had time to think of his own affairs, was very grateful to Lady Rangela for suggesting such a suitable match for him. To be sure he asked for a week to consider the matter, but already on the second day he gave Lady Rangela full powers to take the matter in hand for him. As soon as it was seemly, preparations were put in hand, and the wedding was celebrated so that the young lady was able to enter Börtsholm in the early spring some months after she had completed her eighteenth year.

When Lady Rangela considered how much her niece owed her because she had made her the lady of such a rich and splendid castle, she felt even more assured than when her own daughter ruled there. In her joy she raised the toll on her bridge by a few pennies and strictly forbad her neighbours to help travellers across the narrows by boat so that no one might escape the bridge dues.

Now it happened that one fine spring morning after Lady Lucia had been living in Börtsholm for some months that a train of sick pilgrims who were on their way to the Holy Trinity Well in the village of Sätra in Västmanland, asked to be allowed over the bridge. These people who had gone on their pilgrimage in the hope of regaining their health were accustomed to have their journey eased and helped by all who dwelt along their way, and it often happened that they received money rather than having to spend it.

Nevertheless Lady Rangela's guards on the bridge had meanwhile received strict orders not to show any indulgence, least of all to this kind of wayfarer, for she suspected also that they were not as sick as they made themselves out to be, and simply went wandering round the countryside out of sheer laziness.

When the sick people saw that they were refused passage they raised an unheard of lamentation. The lame and crippled pointed to their limbs and asked how could anyone be so hard-hearted as to increase their pilgrimage by at least a whole day. The blind fell on their knees and tried to feel their way to the bridge-guards in order to kiss their hands while some of the friends and relations of the sick people who were helping them on their journey turned their pockets and purses inside out to show the guards that they really were empty.

But the guards stood there unmoved, and the despair of the unfortunate ones knew no bounds, when to their good fortune the Lady of Börtsholm accompanied by her stepchildren was being rowed over the strait.

When she heard the noise she hastened to the commotion and as soon as she found out the cause she called out: "This is very easily remedied. Let the children go ashore for a while and visit their grandmother, Lady Rangela, and meanwhile I shall have these sick travellers rowed over the water."

The guards as well as the children who knew that it was dangerous to thwart Lady Rangela in the matter of her precious bridge toll, tried to warn the young lady by signs and looks but she noticed nothing, or perhaps did not wish to take any notice. In everything this young lady was the very opposite of her aunt, Lady Rangela. Ever since her earliest childhood she had loved and honoured the canonized Sicilian maiden Lucia who was her patron saint, and had borne her faithfully in her heart as her example. In return the saint had filled all her being with light and warmth and this showed in her appearance which was of shimmering transparency and delicacy, so that one almost feared to touch her.

With many a friendly word to the sick people she now had them ferried over the narrows, and when the last of the crowd had been landed on the other shore she left them while they all heaped such blessings on her that if such gifts were to weigh their worth they would have sunk her boat before it could have been rowed back across the narrows.

Certainly she was going to need blessings and good wishes from now on, for her aunt, Lady Rangela, began to fear that she would not be supported by her niece, and she rued bitterly that she had made her Lord Eskil's wife. She who had so lightly raised the poor maiden now decided that before the latter should do her any more harm she would tear her down from her high position and cast her back into her former insignificance.

In order however to be able the better to strike at her niece she concealed her evil intentions and visited her often in Börtsholm. There she did her best to sow discontent between the people of the castle and the young mistress, so that the latter would grow tired of her position. But to her great astonishment in this she failed completely. This was partly because in spite of her youth Lady Lucia knew how to keep her house in splendid order, but the true reason was that both children and servants seemed to notice that the new chatelaine was under a powerful heavenly protection who punished her opponents and who brought unexpected advantages to those who served her well and willingly.

Lady Rangela soon realized that she could not achieve anything in this way, but she did not wish to give up hope before she had made an attempt with Lord Eskil. That summer however he stayed mostly at the king's court, kept there by long and difficult negotiations. If he did come home for a few days he devoted his time mostly to the stewards and huntsmen. To the female inhabitants of Börtsholm he only gave scant attention, and even when Lady Rangela came on a visit he kept away, so that she never succeeded in seeing him alone.

One fine summer's day when Lord Eskil was at Börtsholm and was just sitting in his private room in consultation with his equerry the castle echoed from such loud screams that he broke off his talk with the equerry and rushed out to see what was happening.

There he found his mother-in-law, Lady Rangela sitting on her horse in front of the castle gates screaming worse than a screech-owl.

"It's your poor children, Lord Eskil," she shrieked, "they are in danger of drowning. This morning they were rowed over to my shore but on the way home their boat must have filled with water. I saw from my home how badly it was going with them and I have ridden here straightaway to warn you. And I say too, even though your wife is my

own brother's daughter it was wrong of her to let the children go off in such a flimsy boat. That really looks like a stepmother's doing."

Lord Eskil quickly asked in what direction the children had gone and then rushed off to the landing stage followed by the equerry. They had not gone far however before they saw Lady Lucia with all the children coming up the steep path that led from the lake to Börtsholm.

The young chatelaine had not gone with the children on their excursion this time but had stayed at home to attend to her affairs. But it was as if she had received a warning from her mighty heavenly protectress who watched over her, for suddenly she left the castle to go and look for them. Then she saw how they were trying to attract attention from the shore by shouting and waving their arms, so she hastened out to them in her own boat and succeeded in the nick of time in rescuing them off their sinking boat and taking them into her own one.

As Lady Lucia and her step-children were coming up the path from the shore she was so engaged in asking them how they had got into such straits, and the latter were so busy telling her about it that they never noticed Lord Eskil coming towards them. Now, because he had become somewhat wary because of Lady Rangela's hint of a step-mother's malice he swiftly signed to his equerry and they hid behind the wild rosebushes that almost completely covered the hill above the shore on which Börtsholm stood.

So Lord Eskil was able to hear how the children were telling Lady Lucia that they had left home in a good boat, but while they were visiting Lady Rangela their boat had been exchanged for an old bad one. They had only noticed the change when they were far out on the lake and the water had begun to pour in on all sides, and they would surely have been drowned if their dear lady mother had not come so quickly to their rescue.

It appeared that Lady Lucia now had an inkling of what was the truth concerning the exchange of the boats, for she turned deathly pale in the middle of the ascent, her eyes full of tears and her hands pressed to her heart. The children pressed round her to reassure her. They told her that they had escaped unscathed from the danger, but she remained motionless, devoid of strength.

Then the two elder stepchildren, two strong boys of fourteen and fifteen put their hands together to make a chair and so they carried her up the steep path while the younger ones followed laughing and clapping their hands.

While the little party went triumphantly on their way between the blossoming roses back to Börtsholm, Lord Eskil remained there deep in thought watching his wife and children. The young woman appeared to him so winsome and strangely radiant as she was borne past him, and perhaps he was wishing that age and dignity would have allowed him to take her in his arms and carry her into the castle.

Perhaps too Lord Eskil was thinking at that moment, how little happiness and how many afflictions were heaped upon him in the service of his high sovereign, while perhaps here at his own hearth peace and joy awaited him. At least that day he did not shut himself up in his room, but spent his time in conversation with his wife and watching the children at play.

Lady Rangela however saw all this to her great discomfort and left Börtsholm as quickly as decency would allow. But because no one dared to suspect her of endangering the lives of her grandchildren in order to bring Lady Lucia into disfavour with her lord and master, the friendly relations was not broken off, and she was able to continue with her efforts to dislodge the young chatelaine from her high position.

For a long time it appeared that all the attempts of the old woman were doomed to failure, for Lady Lucia's heart of goodness and her unimpeachable behaviour together with the help of her heavenly patron saint made her unassailable against all attacks. But towards autumn to Lady Rangela's great joy her niece undertook something of which Lord Eskil assuredly would not approve.

That year the harvest at Börtsholm had proved so abundant that it far exceeded the previous year and indeed all the years as far back as people could remember. Likewise the game and the fish yielded twice as much as usual. The beehives were flowing over with honey and wax, and the hop-fields were laden with hops. The cows gave milk to overflowing, the wool of the sheep was as long as grass, and the pigs had eaten themselves so fat that they could hardly move. All who lived in the castle noticed this rich blessing and they did not hesitate to say that it came upon them because of Lady Lucia.

But while everyone in Börtsholm were busy garnering in the year's yield and reckoning it all up, there appeared a great number of people in distress who had all come from the east or north-east shore of the great Lake Väner. With many tears and piteous gestures they recounted how the whole region from where they came had been overrun by a marauding army host which had passed through burning and plundering. The soldiers had been so vile that they had even set fire to the corn

23

which had not yet been harvested, and they had driven off all the cattle. Those inhabitants who had escaped with their lives would now have to spend the winter without a roof over their heads and without any provisions. Some had gone a-begging, others lay up in the woods hiding, yet others were wandering about the burnt out ruins incapable of undertaking any work, but only lamenting their loss.

When Lady lucia heard these tales, she was saddened by the sight of all the provisions laid up in Börtsholm. Finally the thought of the starving people on the other side of the lake became so overwhelming that she could hardly let the least morsel touch her lips.

Every day she kept thinking of the stories which she had heard in the nunnery about holy men and women who had allowed themselves to be stripped to their bare bodies of clothing to help the poor and needy. Above all she remembered her own patron saint, Santa Lucia of Syracuse, who out of compassion for a pagan youth who had fallen in love with her because of her beautiful eyes, had even gone so far as to tear her eyes out of their sockets and had given them to him all bleeding and sightless, in order to cure him of his love for the Christian virgin who could not belong to him. The young lady tormented herself extremely when she remembered this, and she felt great contempt for herself in that she had heard of so much distress without making a serious attempt to allay it.

While she was thus racked by these thoughts a message was brought from Lord Eskil that he had to travel to Norway on a mission of the king's and was not to be expected home before Christmas. But then he would not only be accompanied by his sixty men, but also by a great following of kinsfolk and friends, and so he wished to warn Lady Lucia to be ready for a prolonged period of hospitality.

On the same day that Lady Lucia learned that her husband would not be returning in the autumn she set about tackling the distress which had so long tortured her. She commanded all her people to bring all the provisions that had been stored up in Börtsholm down to the shore. In this way all the winter provender of the castle was loaded on to boats and barges, certainly to the great astonishment of the inmates of the castle.

Once all the cellars and storerooms had been thoroughly emptied, Lady Lucia, accompanied by her children, her men-servants and maids went on board a well-manned ship, and while she left behind only a few old guards in Börtsholm to whom she entrusted the keeping of the castle, she had herself rowed out with all her stores across the great lake which stretched before her, boundless as the sea.

There are many tales handed down from olden times about this voyage of Lady Lucia. Thus it is told that that part of the shore of Lake Väner where the enemy had harried the worst was almost deserted when Lady Lucia arrived there, and that she had sadly searched for any sign of life or movement, but no smoke rose to the sky, no cock crowed, no cattle lowed.

Nevertheless there was an old priest called Master Kolbjörn still living in his parish. He had not followed his flock who had fled from their ruined houses, because he had the sacristy and the church full of wounded. He had stayed with them, binding up their wounds, and sharing with them what he could call his own, without granting himself either food or rest. Thus he was so faint that he felt that he was near death. On one of the darkest autumn days, when heavy clouds rolled down upon the lake, when the water rolled in black waves to the shore, and the gloom of nature made all the hopelessness and distress seem worse, Master Kolbjörn, who could no longer say mass, went out to pull the bell-rope of his church to call down God's blessing on his extremity. And behold, hardly had the first peels sounded when a little fleet of boats and barges came rowing towards the land. Out of one ship stepped a beautiful young woman with a face shining with light. Before her went eight glorious children, and after her came a long line of servants bearing all kinds of provisions: whole roasted calves and sheep, long spits laden with loaves, barrels of ale and sacks of flour. Help had come at the last moment, as if by a miracle.

Not far from Master Kolbjörn's church, on a headland, that ran out sharply into the lake and was called Saxudden (the Scissor Point) there stood an ancient farmstead. It was burnt down and plundered now, but its owner, a man of seventy, loved the farmstead so much that he could not bear to leave it. With him had remained his old wife, a little grandson and a granddaughter. They had managed to keep alive by fishing, but one night a storm had carried away their gear, and since then they had sat among the ruins waiting for death by starvation. While they were thus waiting, the farmer thought of his dog which lay there with them patiently pining away. The farmer seized a cudgel and with his last strength struck at the dog to drive it away, for he did not wish the dog to die for something which it could not help. But with the blow the dog howled loudly and ran away. All night it strayed round the farm howling. Far out on the lake it was heard and before day-break Lady Lucia rowed towards the land guided by the noise and so brought help.

Further off there was a little house surrounded by a wall where holy women dwelled. They had sworn to God never to leave it. The soldiers had shown some consideration to these pious sisters and had not harmed them or their house though they had despoiled them of all their winter provisions. The only thing that the sisters had been allowed to keep was a dovecote full of doves, and these they had killed one by one until there was only one left. But this dove was very tame, and the pious women loved it so much that they did not wish to prolong their own lives by eating it, so they had opened the dovecote to give the dove its freedom. The white dove first rose high up into the sky, but then flew down again and settled on the ridge of the roof. When Lady Lucia was rowing along by the shore looking out for anyone who might need help, she saw the dove, and realized that where the dove was there must also be people. So she landed and gave the pious women as much food as they needed to live through the winter.

Further south along the shore of Lake Väner there had been a little market-town, which now also had been plundered and lay in ashes. The only thing left were the wharves where the ships used to tie up. Under these piers a man called Lasse the merchant had hidden with his wife when the town was being destroyed, and while all the fighting was going on above she had given birth to a child. But since then she had been so very ill that she could not flee, and her husband had stayed with her. But now their distress was very great and all day and every day the wife begged her husband to think of himself and to leave her to her fate. This he would not do, so one night she tried to creep out of her hiding-place and slip into the water, for she thought that once she and her child were dead he would flee and so save his life. But the child cried loudly in the cold water and the man woke up. He brought them both ashore, but the child had taken such fright that it yelled all night. Its cry was borne over the water and brought the ready helper who had been rowing over the lake on constant look-out.

As long as she had gifts to give, Lady Lucia sailed along the shore of Lake Väner, and on this voyage she felt her heart as happy and light as never before. For just as there is nothing harder than to stay still and inactive when one hears of a stranger's grave misfortune, so too the greatest happiness and the sweetest repose comes to him who is able to help another, even if it is only the least little bit. So she felt this relief and joy without the least premonition that anything evil might be in store for her, when on the eve of Santa Lucia she returned late in the evening to Börtsholm. At supper which consisted of nothing more than some bowls of milk she talked with her companions about the lovely journey which they had made together, and all agreed that they had never known such joyful days.

"But now a time of hard work lies before us," she went on, "we cannot celebrate Santa Lucia's Day with feasting as in former years. We must set to without stint to brew and to bake, to slaughter so that we may have the Christmas feast ready for Lord Eskil's homecoming."

This the young lady was able to say without the least anxiety for she knew that her cow-sheds, her barns and her storehouses were full of God's good gifts, even though at the moment there was nothing ready wherewith to feed people.

Even though the journey had been so happy all who had taken part were very tired and went to bed early. Hardly had Lady Lucia closed her eyes in slumber however, before there sounded the tramp of horses, the rattling of arms, and loud shouts in front of the castle. The castle gates swung open creaking on their hinges and the stones of the courtyard rang with the sound of hurrying feet.

Lady Lucia realized that Lord Eskil had returned with his horsemen. Quickly she sprang out of bed to go to meet him. After hastily donning her clothes, she rushed out on to the balcony to reach the stairs which led down into the courtyard. But she got no further than the topmost step, for Lord Eskil already stood halfway up on his way to her room. A torch-bearer went before him and in its light Lady Lucia thought she saw Lord Eskil's face set with a terrible anger. For a moment she hoped that it was the red smoky light of the torch that made his face so dark and threatening but when she saw that children and servants with miserable and downcast looks fell back before him, she realized that her husband had come home full of wrath, ready to hold justice and award punishment.

While Lady Lucia stood thus looking down at Lord Eskil, he saw her, and with growing fear she noticed that he was smiling grimly.

"Are you coming now, noble mistress, to regale me with a welcoming meal?" he mocked, "but this time your dear efforts are in vain, for I and my men have supped with your kinswoman Lady Rangela. But tomorrow," he added, and now anger overcame him, so that he struck the bannister with his hand, "we expect that in honour of your patron saint Santa Lucia you will serve us with such a good breakfast as befits

this house, nor must you forget to place before me at the first cock-crow my morning draught.''

Not one word could the young chatelaine utter in reply. Exactly as in the summer before when it first dawned on her that Lady Rangela had been working to her undoing she stood stock still with her hands pressed against her heart, her eyes full of tears. She could not but realize now that it must have been Lady Rangela who had called Lord Eskil home before time and had worked him up telling him what Lady Lucia had been doing with his goods.

Lord Eskil went up a few more steps without being in the least moved to compassion by his wife's fear. There he bent over her and said with a terrible voice: "By the Cross of Our Saviour, Lady Lucia, mark this well, if I do not like this breakfast, you will rue it all the days of your life!"

With that he laid his hand heavily on his wife's shoulder and thrust her before him into the bed-chamber.

As she walked into the bedchamber it seemed to Lady Lucia that something which in some unaccountable fashion had been hidden from her was now suddenly revealed to her. She realized that she had acted high-handedly and thoughtlessly, and that Lord Eskil might well have good reason to be angry at her having thus disposed of his possessions without asking him. She tried now that they were alone to tell him this penitently and to beg him forgiveness for her youthful thoughtlessness, but he did not allow her to speak.

"Go to bed now, Lady Lucia," he said, "and take care not to rise before the usual time! If your morning draught and your welcoming meal are not to my satisfaction you will have to walk a road for which you will need all your strength."

With this answer she had to be content although it only increased her anxiety. and we can understand that for the whole of that night she did not sleep a wink. She lay there and thought about what her husband had said to her, and the more she pondered on his words, the clearer it became to her that he had hung a heavy threat over her. To be sure he had determined that he would not condemn her until he had seen for himself whether she had acted as wrongly as Lady Rangela must have maintained. But if she were incapable of entertaining him as he had desired it was certain that a terrible punishment awaited her. The least would be that she would be declared unworthy to remain his wife, and that she would be sent home to her parents: but from the last words which he had said she surmised that he would further condemn her to run the gauntlet between his retainers like a common thief.

When at last she reached the conviction that this was what was to happen — and indeed this was the case, for Lady Rangela had roused Lord Eskil to a mad fury — she began to tremble, and her teeth chattered and she thought that she was about to die. She knew that she must use the hours of the night to find help and an expedient, but her great horror paralysed her so much that she lay there motionless.

"How on earth will it be possible for me to feed my lord and his sixty men tomorrow morning?" she thought in her despair, "I might just as well lie still until the misfortune overtakes me."

The only thing that she could do for her deliverance was hour after hour to send fervent prayers up to Santa Lucia of Syracuse.

"O Santa Lucia, my guardian mother," she prayed, "tomorrow is the day on which thou suffered the death of a martyr, and entered the paradise of heaven. Remember how dark and hard and cold it is to live upon earth. Come to me in this night and lead me hence with thee. Come and close my eyes in the sleep of death. Thou knowest that this is my only escape from dishonour and ignoble punishment."

While she was thus invoking the aid of Santa Lucia, the hours of the night passed and the awful morning approached. Much earlier than she had expected the first cock crowed; the men who looked after the cows walked across the courtyard to their work, and the horses in their stables stood up with a clatter.

"Now Lord Eskil will awake," she thought. "Now he will soon command me to fetch his morning draught, and then I must confess that I have acted so foolishly that I possess neither beer nor mead to warm for him."

At that moment of the greatest danger for the young chatelaine her heavenly friend, Santa Lucia, could no longer restrain her desire to help her protégée who after all had only erred through too great a compassion. The earthly body of the saint which had rested for hundreds of years in the narrow vaults of the catacombs of Syracuse, suddenly was filled with the living spirit, and the saint took on again her earthly beauty and the use of her limbs, wrapped herself in a garment woven of starlight, and went out again into that world where she had once suffered and loved.

Only a few moments later the astonished watchman in the tower above the gate of Börtsholm saw the nocturnal wonder of a fireball rising far in the south. It flew through space so quickly that the eye could scarcely follow its flight, came straight to Börtsholm, passing so close to the watchman that it almost touched him, and vanished. But on this globe of fire, or so at least it seemed to the watchman, a beautiful maiden was borne along, the tips of her toes just touching it, and her arms raised aloft, while all the time she played and danced upon this glowing chariot.

Almost at the same moment Lady Lucia, lying awake in fear and trembling, saw a shimmer shining through a crack in the door of the bed-chamber. Then as the door itself opened immediately, to her astonishment and joy a beautiful maiden clad in robes as white as starlight entered the room. Her long black hair was bound with a tendril, but this tendril bore not common leaves and flowers but twinkling little stars, which lit up the whole room, and yet it seemed to Lady Lucia that they were nothing in comparison to the eyes of the delightful stranger, for they were not only shining with the clearest gleam, but sent forth heavenly love and compassion.

In her hand the stranger maiden carried a large copper jug, from which the mild aroma of a noble grape juice wafted up, and with this jug she glided through the room to Lord Eskil, poured some of the wine into a smaller vessel and offered it to him to drink.

Lord Eskil who had slept well, woke up when the ray of light fell on his eyelids, and he put the vessel to his lips. In his half-wakening state he hardly realized more of the miracle than that the wine which had been offered to him tasted very good, and he emptied the vessel to the last drop.

But that wine that could not have been anything else but the noble malmsey, the fame of the South and the crown of all wines, was so sleep-inducing, that he had scarcely emptied the vessel before he fell back asleep in bed. At the same moment the beautiful holy maiden glided out of the room, leaving Lady Lucia in a state of trembling astonishment and fresh hope.

The illustrious benefactress however did not stop short at attending only upon Lord Eskil. On the dark cold winter morning she walked through the dim halls of the Swedish castle, and she offered a draught of the joy-bringing wine from the South to every slumbering warrior.

All who drank thought that they had tasted celestial bliss. Nor did they remain awake but fell straightway into a sleep filled with dreams of fields of eternal summer and sun.

No sooner had the marvellous apparition disappeared but the fear and helplessness which had weighed all night upon Lady Lucia vanished completely. She dressed swiftly and called all the people of the house to work.

All that long winter's morning they were busy preparing Lord Eskil's welcoming feast. Young calves, pigs, geese and hens were quickly prepared. Dough was set to rise, fires lit under the roasting spits and under the baking ovens, charcoal fanned, turnips were peeled and honey-cakes baked for dessert.

The tables in the banqueting hall were covered with cloths, the costly wax-candles unpacked from the deep chests, and on the benches blue feather-cushions and tapestries were spread.

While all these preparations were in progress the Lord of the Castle and his men slept on. When Lord Eskil finally woke up, he saw by the sun that it was now midday. He wondered not only that he had slept so long, but also and perhaps more, that he had slept away the vexation which had so consumed him the evening before. In his morning dreams his wife had appeared to him in great gentleness and sweetness and he wondered at himself that he had been tempted to condemn her to a hard and ignominious punishment.

"Perhaps it is not as bad as Lady Rangela made out," he thought. "Of course I cannot keep her as my wife if she has squandered all my goods, and it may be enough to send her back to her parents without further punishment."

When he came out of his bed-chamber, he was met by his eight children who led him to the banqueting-hall. There his men were already sitting on the benches, waiting impatiently for him to appear, so that they could start the feast, for the tables in front of them were laden with all kinds of wonderful fare.

Without showing the least fear Lady Lucia sat down beside her husband; but she was not completely free of anxiety, for even though she had been able to produce a meal in haste, she was quite without beer and mead, which could not be produced so quickly. And she doubted rather whether Lord Eskil would feel himself well looked after at a breakfast where there was no ale or beer.

Then she noticed on the table the great copper jug which the holy maiden had brought. It stood there filled to the brim with fragrant wine. Again she felt the greatest joy at the protection of her compassionate saint, and she poured out some wine for Lord Eskil while she told him how it had come to Börtsholm. He listened with the greatest astonishment.

When Lord Eskil had tasted the wine which this time was not sleep-bringing but had a refreshing and ennobling effect, Lady Lucia took courage and told him about her voyage. At first Lord Eskil sat there very gravely, but when she told him about the parson, Master Kolbjörn, he cried, "Master Kolbjörn is my good friend, Lady Lucia, I am heartily glad that you were able to help him."

In the same way it turned out, that the farmer in Saxudden had been Lord Eskil's companion on many campaigns, and that among the pious women he had a kinswoman, and that Lasse the merchant in the market-town had been in the habit of obtaining for him clothing and weapons from abroad. Long before Lady Lucia had finished her story,

Lord Eskil was not only ready to pardon her but he was heartily grateful to her for having helped so many of his friends.

But the fear that Lady Lucia had felt in the night came back to her, and her voice trembled when she finally said: "Now it seems to me myself, my dear lord, that I have done very wrong in giving away your goods without having asked you. But I beg you to consider my youth and inexperience and to forgive me on that account."

When Lady Lucia had said this, and Lord Eskil now realized that his wife was so virtuous that one of the angels of heaven had taken on her earthly form again in order to help her, and when he further considered that he — who would be taken for a wise, discerning man, — had suspected her, and had been about to vent his wrath on her, he felt so much shame in his heart, that he lowered his eyes and was incapable of answering her a word.

When Lady Lucia saw him sitting silent with bowed head her fear returned, and she wanted rather to flee from her seat weeping. But then, unseen by all, the compassionate Santa Lucia entered, bent over the young woman, and whispered into her ear what she should say now. And these words were those which lady Lucia had wished to say but without the heavenly encouragement she would not have dared because of her own shyness.

"*One* more thing, my dear lord and husband, I would ask you," she said, "and that is that you would stay more at home. Then I should never be tempted to act against your will, and then I could show you all the love which I feel towards you, so that no one might ever come between us."

When these words were spoken, they went right to Lord Eskil's heart. He raised his head, and the great joy which he felt drove away his shame.

Just as he was about to give his wife a most loving answer one of Lady Rangela's stewards came rushing into the banqueting hall. Hastily he told how Lady Rangela had set off early to come to Börtsholm in order to be present in time for Lady Lucia's punishment. But on the way she had come upon several farmers who had long hated her because of the bridge toll, and, when in the darkness of the early morning these met her accompanied by only one servant, they chased the latter away, then they tore Lady Rangela from her horse and killed her ignominiously.

Now Lady Rangela's steward was searching for the murderers, and he asked Lord Eskil to send out men to take part in the search.

Then Lord Eskil stood up and spoke with a loud stern voice: "It would appear that it would be most seemly if I gave an answer to my wife's request, but before I do this, I will settle with Lady Rangela. And now I say, as far as I am concerned, she may lie there unavenged, nor will I ever send out my men on blood-revenge for her, for I do firmly believe that her own deeds have brought this upon her."

When that had been said he turned to Lady Lucia and now his voice was so soft that all were amazed at the gentleness of his tone.

"But now I will say to my dear chatelaine, that I do heartily forgive her, just as I hope that she will pardon my vehemence. And because it is her wish, I shall petition the king to choose another to be his counsellor, for now I wish to enter the service of two noble ladies. One is my wife, and the other is Santa Lucia of Syracuse, for whom I shall set up altars in all the churches and chapels of my lands, beseeching her to keep alive and burning within us who suffer in the cold of the North that spark and guiding star of the soul which is called compassion."

On the thirteenth of December in the early morning hour, when cold and darkness holds sway over Värmland, still in my childhood Santa Lucia of Syracuse came into all the houses which lay scattered between the mountains of Norway and the River Gullspång that flows into Lake Väner. She still wore, at least in the eyes of the little children, a garment white with starlight, she had in her hair a green wreath lit with burning flowers of light, and she always woke those asleep with a warm fragrant drink from her copper jug.

In those days I never saw a more lovely sight than when the door opened and she came into the darkness of the room. And I wish that she would never cease to show herself in the homes of Värmland. For she is the light, that overcomes the darkness, she is the legend that overcomes oblivion, she is the warmth of heart, that makes the frozen countryside lovely and sunny in the midst of the hard winter.

Andrey

Gerhard Klein

We understood each other right from the very first day when I came as overseer to the estate in Lower Bavaria in the last year of the war. I had only one German worker, old Joseph, the tractor-driver. The others were a real mixture of European nations. For the woods I had two Frenchmen, excellent foresters from the Ardennes; with the horses was a Serb; in the byre a big Polish family; and for shawing turnips and haymaking there came parties of Russian prisoners-of-war lent to us by the sugar factory. Then there was Andrey and his Babushka, maid of all work. I wonder how they are now over there on the broad prairies of Canada. Perhaps it reminds them of the wide steppes of their homeland which they had to leave.

The first time that I looked into Andrey's clear blue eyes was when I went to see him on the midden. No one could shake the dung out and set it up as lovingly as he. To be sure it was something new for him that dung was to be treated carefully as something precious, to be covered with earth and built up into a proper compost-heap; but now that work was his pride. There he stood barefoot on the steaming dunghill, working away steadily, not like the others who suddenly would start working frantically when they saw the boss approaching. A word of praise made him look up and his look went straight to my heart: goodness and sadness, peace and equanimity — all this spoke in his gaze.

But he only nodded in a friendly way and went on working. He hardly ever spoke. When he did I was surprised at the passable fluency of his German.

It so happened that I was able to give the old couple a little room to themselves, for I soon noticed how they suffered living closely together with the others. They kept this room meticulously clean. In one corner they had a little cross like those Russians usually wear on their breast. This cross was hung over a piece of cardboard covered with white paper, and always in front of it stood flowers in an old food tin.

I knew that Andrey was the only honest man on the whole estate. During that time of scarcity everyone stole what he needed, and it was a nuisance that we had to keep as much as possible under lock and key. In one respect only did Andrey deviate from his strict honesty, and that he did with my tacit acquiescence. Because of the frequent air-raids the electricity often failed, so candles had to be ready at hand in the stable. Andrey who helped with the horses and especially with the foals knew where I put the candles. They were used up remarkably quickly. I guessed why and let it be.

We came into conversation for the first time in the late autumn when we were getting in the sugar-beet. We were hard pressed as frost threatened to overtake us. Everyone had to lend a hand. All the Poles were out at it too. Evening was coming on but the people seemed to be oddly bewitched. They kept on chattering excitedly and looking up at the sky, I thought at first that they were afraid of low-flying aircraft which sometimes shot at people working in the fields. Only Andrey and his Babushka went on working steadily, their knives flashing while the shaws fell in one heap and the beetroots on the other. It is impossible for me to set down Andrey's marvellous manner of speaking.

When I came up to him he looked up sideways, his eyes a-twinkle, while he pointed at the Poles and then tapped his forehead: "Master, do not worry, they are stupid and godless. They think the sun will hop and go round the sky as it sets and the Mother of God will appear. That is the sign that the war will soon be over. But what's the use of the war being over and people remain bad? A new war will then come soon. People look outwards. They should look inwards. That would be better."

And he went on working steadily.

I went on my way thoughtfully. What a man! How different from those Russians trained in dialectics who had been in the Red Army and with whom I had often conversed.

But Andrey was often able to help me without words, with a gesture of greeting, with a look or shake of the head, when I crossed the farmyard full of cares.

Once I had to go into town to buy seed at the co-operative. I wanted to get something nice for Andrey, but there was nothing to be had.

Then in a second-hand shop I saw a Russian icon. Perhaps a soldier had sent it home. I bought it and put it in my pocket.

I was very happy on the homeward journey. I was quite filled with the picture of Elijah going up to heaven in the chariot of fire and casting his mantle down upon Elisha who was ploughing below.

When I arrived Andrey came briskly to take the horse and trap from me. I took the picture out of my pocket and said: "I got this for you. I hope it will give you both joy."

He unwrapped it, turned pale, crossed himself reverently and vanished. I was quite taken aback and sat perplexed in the trap. Finally I had to unharness the horse myself. Very soon however Andrey reappeared looking embarrassed, seized my hand and kissed it while the tears flowed down his cheeks. He could not speak.

That evening I left a whole bundle of candles in the stable. They had all disappeared the next day.

Advent came. St Nicholas' Day fell on a Sunday. For days I had seen Babushka washing and cleaning. She had brought out the little table and the two stools into the courtyard and scrubbed them clean. She filled the palliasses with fresh straw. Something was on the go.

On the Saturday after work was finished they both came to me, stood shyly at the door, and finally Andrey managed to say: "Would his excellency the factor not be offended, but would he do them the honour of coming to them for the Festival of St Nicholas on the morrow?"

I accepted and arranged for them to receive a larger loaf of the white bread which, contrary to regulations, we baked for our people, and I told Andrey that I should bring a bottle of wine with me which I had been given as a present. But I had a request. He should tell me how he had got here. He said that he would and both of them went off radiantly happy.

I shall never forget that winter's evening. In a corner, surrounded by green branches, the icon shone in the light of many candles. Over the table was spread a white shirt — the poor couple had nothing else. The bread was lying on a tin plate, and instead of glasses there were mugs.

I hardly dared enter, the atmosphere in the little room was so solemnly festive.

After a long Russian prayer we sat down.

Then he began his story. He told about the remote village in the forest, about his grandfather's hut to which he had fled after the revolution, about the war coming nearer and nearer. They wanted to stay where they were. What could happen to poor peasants? The Jews of the village, who had a little congregation with a synagogue, had fled. Only the rabbi, Old Abraham, did not want to leave. The graves of his ancestors and children were there, and there he wished to die.

"The hut lay off the beaten track, but the Germans might come after all. We forced him then to hide in the forest, where we had store-rooms in the earth. We made one habitable for him and brought him food every few days. We thought the war might soon be over and he could come back to his house. We often heard him praying aloud when we were in the forest.

"But he grew sadder and weaker. Once I asked him what was the matter. He said, 'How can I live when I cannot serve my God? If only I could worthily receive the Holy Bride, the sabbath, once more — but here it cannot be.' I saw that his whole heart was set on this. I told him that now it grew dark early and that there had been no more Germans in the village. I told him to come to my hut in the forest once evening had fallen. What should I have ready for him?

"He asked for seven candles, a loaf of bread and some wine.

"That is how it was. I had the meal ready in a back-room, everything laid out as it is here. The candles were lit, and our Holy Elijah hung in a corner, just as it is here. Then he came with his flowing white beard. He looked like Abraham himself when he invited the Angel of God to eat with him. Abraham opened the shutters of the window which we had closed so carefully.

" 'How,' he asked reproachfully, 'can the Holy Prophet who is always wandering over the earth to prepare the coming of the Messiah be able to see that here the Holy Sabbath is being celebrated? Lay another plate and cup for him so that he may see that we are expecting him. And do not bar the door.'

"We could not gainsay him. Then he began to sing, his body rocking to and fro, with his eyes closed and a rapt expression on his face.

"I implored God and all the saints to protect us. Even though Abraham was not a Christian it was certainly no sin to help him before his death so that he might serve God in his own way. Then we sat at the meal and he told us about long bygone times.

"Suddenly all around we heard vehicle engines and shouts. I knew right away it was the Germans coming to search the village.

"The old man did not seem to notice. He began his singing again. There was a loud knock on the door of the house. We sat petrified. Heavy footsteps sounded through the hut. The door of the room burst open and there was a soldier with a full beard covered with frost. He was an oldish man. He held his gun ready to shoot. Old father Abraham stood up courteously and with a great open gesture pointed to the empty chair and the place already laid at the table. Our hearts stood still. What was going to happen?

"Oh, the angels were there. The German leaned his rifle against the wall. He looked steadfastly at the candles and the picture. He sat down, he drank the cup of wine (an officer had given me the bottle when he was billeted on us) and ate of the bread. He crossed himself, wiped his mouth, bowed to the old man and went out, closing the door behind him, and all was quiet. The candles burned down. The old man prayed aloud. It was a psalm no doubt. We took him back to his underground house.

"Master how happy we were when you brought us the picture. We are so grateful! Now we have the angel again to protect us."

When I questioned Andrey further I learned that someone had betrayed them and that the Germans came again and forced him to lead them into the forest. There they found the old man dead. His face was lit with a shimmer of bliss.

"But they took us, and that is why we are here."

Our candles too were burning low. I was able to tell Andrey and his wife that I was really a priest by profession, and now I wished to say a blessing for Old Abraham, for the whole sick and wounded world.

I went away from that little wobbly table in the room as from an altar.

I went back through the snow-covered farmyard. The moon stood high above the forest. I looked back at the tiny window of the room and I thought of the singer who was not able to bear the suffering and darkness of the First World War and who died in it, a singer who knew the shadows and the pain as deeply as anyone — Georg Trakl who bequeathed to us this song which I now sang to myself, the Song of a Winter Evening.

> When the snow falls at the window
> And the vesper-bell is ringing,
> For many guests is set the table
> And the house in order stands.
> Many a wandering pilgrim comes
> On dark paths to reach the door;
> Blossoms gold the tree of grace

Drawing sap cool from the earth.
Wayfarer, in peace now enter
Though pain the threshold turned to stone,
See in purity is shining
On the table bread and wine.

Blind Peter

Gerhard Klein

After a long journey across broad plains, through dense forests, over the great rivers that flow to the North, I arrived at the lonely manor farm in East Prussia. It was evening now and I felt apprehensive. Here in the East everything was different. The great expanses seem to draw you on and on.

Sunday morning brought a quick tour of the stables, cowsheds and barns. Driving to church in the trap enabled me to get to know the extensive fields and paddocks belonging to the manor. Suddenly my attention was diverted from the landowner's friendly explanations. On the road in front of us appeared three dark figures, remarkable even at that first glimpse. On the left was a tall thin man constantly gesticulating, on the right a man walking crabwise leaning on a stick, his left leg lame, and in the middle a small round very agile old man. All three were in their black Sunday coats.

"Now you can meet our three holy kings," said the landowner. We offered them a lift in the back of the trap and took them to church. The lively conversation of the three became silent in the presence of their lord and master. As it turned out I was to have much to do with them.

The first tall man was our compost-master. The wonderful thing about these big East Prussian estates was that every individual, even those with severe handicaps, could be integrated into the life of the farm. Joseph was deaf and dumb, but he could lip-read very well, and the landowner had hit on the right thing when he put him in charge of all the dung and compost heaps.

You could then see him going across the fields with a little wooden box under his arm, a thick rod with an iron ferrule and a cross-piece on top which he used as a measuring stick. If you came upon him at one of the dung-heaps set up in the fields, with great dignity he would show

you the deep holes which he had bored in the heap at exact intervals. He would then take the preparations out of the box, and his extremely lively gestures tried to make clear to you, now comes the oak-bark, then dandelion and milfoil, and so one after the other the various herbs until at last he took out the bottle of valerian which he sprayed over the top of the dung-heap.

I could see how deeply Joseph felt the importance of his task. If he happened to come across one of our Russian prisoners not turning over one of the dung-heaps properly he would become almost angry and take the fork from him and show him how to do it. This he could do in exemplary fashion as shown by the long rows of heaps behind the stables and cow-sheds. These heaps were well mixed with earth and covered over looking like grave-mounds. When the cowmen wheeled out the dung and tipped it out it was another of Joseph's jobs to set it up properly. Then there would always be some half serious, half joking altercations between him and his fellow king, bent Joseph.

The latter had got his stiff leg in the First World War. He was practically married to Liese, a very old horse which could still do light work however, for we did not like to take a faithful animal of long service to the knackers, and did not grudge him his fodder. The two of them took the milk round, and unloaded little cartloads of earth where Joseph did not want it.

But for me the most important of the trio was the third. He was ancient. No one knew how old. I reckoned he was over ninety. Blind Peter had grown up on the estate. He lived in a lone cottage at the edge of the forest. All day long he was on the move, finding his way without any trouble for he knew every stone, every tree, every fence. He was respected by everyone. He was reputed to know more than other people, above all he could hear things no one else could. I learned a lot from him. It could happen that he would suddenly appear beside me on the way home in the evening while I was planning the work for the next day.

"Well, Inspector," he said once, "What are you thinking of doing tomorrow?" It was a calm winter's evening, overcast and quite mild.

"I think we'll drive into the forest with all our forty Russians and root out some tree stumps, we need wood for our people."

"Well," he said, "It's no good."

That was a warning to take heed of and think up some other work. During the night a terrible storm broke out. Next day all the sunken roads were snowed up. Even though the snow did not lie so deep on the fields the wind had blown it into deep drifts in places, and we had to keep all the Russians shovelling snow to clear the roads. This we had to do for the army.

Another time I remember we were all sitting comfortably at coffee when the head ploughman came rushing in with the news: "The horses have broken out of the paddock and have got into the turnip field."

I had the man mounted on one of the coach-horses which was in the stables, gathered together all available hands, and then we went out to round up the horses. But the twenty-eight work-horses only made fools of us. We tried to surround them but all they did was to whinny mockingly and rush off into another corner. We were fairly out of breath and darkness was falling. Suddenly I noticed how they pricked up their ears and looked in one direction. Far away a small figure could be seen silhouetted against the evening sky. It was blind Peter, calling the horses together with short authoritative, but not very loud cries that sounded like spells, and they quietly followed him back to the farmyard.

Shortly before my arrival Peter's wife had died, and I was worried how he would manage on his own. Sometimes I would send him one of the Polish girls to help him tidy up, but he kept most of it in order himself. One morning he came to collect his milk and said, "Inspector, I need more milk now."

"It's good, Peter, that you're drinking milk. Milk's good for everybody."

He looked at me quite blankly, if one can say that of a blind person.

"But Inspector I need the milk only for the porridge. For drinking schnapps is good. But we're now more people. And when you're going to town, buy a pair of shoes for a boy of six or seven, and some good sewing gear; I've got plenty of old clothes to be altered."

Then he undid his handkerchief, took out some coins and left me standing. I soon met him again and slowly got out of him what had happened. He had been sitting peacefully in his room smoking his pipe. Night had fallen when he heard a noise at the door. He called, no one answered, he opened the door, and there lying on the doorstep he could feel there was a woman. He brought her in and she had a boy with her. Now all our old people over there in the East could speak a little Polish because every year Polish workers used to come for the harvest. He managed to get out of the woman that because of partisans there had been a punitive expedition to her village. She and her son were the only survivors: all the men, women, children and old people had been massacred, and the village set on fire. Terrified out of her senses she had fled, always westward. Compassionate people had given her something to eat here and there.

I myself went to see the woman as I was in charge of all that went on in the estate. The boy had large, frightened eyes. As a matter of course Blind Peter had taken the matter in hand and had told her she could stay with him. She hardly spoke but she gratefully took on the work and so there was suddenly a family in the house again. She was able to work half days for us and so earn the bare necessities for herself and the child. A wonderful, almost tender relationship sprang up between the boy, Marek, and the old man. The boy ran after him everywhere like a little dog and brought him all sorts of things. The blind man felt each thing and told the boy what kind of flower, stone, or animal it was. In the evenings they would sit together and the old man taught the boy. Sometimes I went over and listened. Blind Peter was one of those rare people who knew the whole Bible off by heart. But how alive his telling could be. Sometimes ancient sagas and fairy tales were told, and he also spoke of dwarfs and nixies. When the blind man spoke about the dwarfs, describing exactly how they looked and where they lived, that they really did have a king, then I could not help thinking: he knows them, he really can see them.

From time to time old Peter would warn little Marek very earnestly never to go to the Black Pool. Marek had to promise that he would never do that. Old Peter then would tell about a nixie that lived in that pool. Especially when the moon was full she would appear, but you had to beware of her. He described how beautiful she was, and you had the uncanny feeling that he knew her very well. Then it occurred to me that one place on the whole estate where I had never met Peter was at that Black Pool whereas he wandered about everywhere else. I asked some of our other old people, the smith and the wheelwright, whether they knew anything about it; but the people over there are very reticent especially towards an newcomer. Nevertheless I was able to gather from their hints that the Black Pool had played a particular part in Peter's life. I figured out that it could well have been where he used to go poaching and that he had been involved in a scuffle. I could never get out of him how he had become blind. But there seemed to be a connection there.

Once during Advent I went to his little house again. I looked in through the low window, and saw the three sitting in the candle-light while the old man was teaching the boy an Advent song. I can still hear today the thin old man's voice and the boy's strong singing. Later I looked up the song and I should like to set forth the first and last lines.

> Lord Jesus Christ, Son of God.
> Thou who from high heaven's throne
> Hast descended to the world
> To work our weal.
> Help us live right worthily
> And blissful die in thee,

That we may love and praise thee
Here in time and there eternally.

That evening I did not go in, but quietly took myself home, touched by the peace which emanated from this poor cottage in the midst of all the confusion of the dreadful war.

And now I come to the night about which I really want to tell. It had been a very still winter's day with the evening sun shining yellow through the clouds. The birch-trees stood in the frost, their silver stems draped in their slender branches and twigs. We had cleared the ditches and set up the soil from them as compost. I had retired to my room earlier than usual, for the winter evenings are the countryman's wages for the toil of the year. Suddenly I heard, not a knocking, but a thundering at my door. Half suffocated calls and screams: "Mr Inspector, Mr Inspector!"

It was Maryusha, tears coursing down her cheeks, her hair all wild, shouting: "Marek gone, Peter gone, everybody gone, don't know where."

She had been in the farmhouse all day helping with the Christmas baking. Of course the situation was unusual. Something could have happened to the old man, he could have fainted or he could have broken a leg, but that the boy should also have disappeared was serious. So everyone was rounded up, the Russians out of the bunkers, lanterns got ready, a sledge harnessed and off we went on the search. We fanned out in all directions. We called, no answer. We looked for tracks in the snow, nothing to be seen. The mother grew more and more frantic. Suddenly, I do not know how, I thought of the Black Pool. So we set off towards the woods where the pool was and soon I saw the glow of a fire. That was remarkable in the middle of the night. We came nearer and nearer and stood as if turned to stone. Had we not been imagining the most terrible things, filled with fear that something awful had happened? Now we came upon something we could never have dreamed of, and we did not know whether to laugh or cry.

In the woods was one of those bark huts used as a shelter for the woodsmen with a smoke hole in the roof and a hearth for a fire on the floor. There in front of a merrily blazing fire old Peter was sitting on a block of wood with his shirt sleeves rolled up and on his lap a big bundle which turned out to be the boy wrapped in the old man's long coat. Inside the hut the boy's clothes lay spread out to dry on a heap of wood.

"Sh," said Peter, "he's asleep. It's good that you've come Inspector, for he was here up till just now."

"He? Who do you mean, he?" I asked, quite puzzled.

"Who do I mean?" he said indignantly, "Why, he of course."

I shook my head. It really was not a time for cross talk. I took the boy in my arms and gave Peter my coat. We went out to the sledge and drove to the manor.

Next morning the boy was well and happy, but not Blind Peter, for we had to take him to hospital with pneumonia. As often as they could his two fellow kings went to see him, sat silent and stricken, praying beside the old man who lay in a high fever.

Once this crisis was over I was able to speak to Blind Peter. It sounded so simple the way he told it. Peter had been sitting alone in the room, the boy had gone off, and Peter thought that he was with his mother. Then Peter again and again heard his name being called most insistently from outside: "Peter, Peter, the child!"

He jumped up, listened again; again the same insistent call and this time he seemed to hear, "Bring a rope with you."

He put on his coat, seized a washing line, for he knew where everything was in his house, and he rushed outside. He sensed clearly someone standing there telling him to come. As he went along (and of course he could walk just as well in the dark) he felt the footsteps beside him, and trusted in his companion who was leading him. Gradually he noticed that they were going to a part of the estate where he had not been for a long time, but he felt the footsteps beside him were a sure guide. Then suddenly he heard a faint voice calling: "Mr Peter, Mr Peter!" It was the child's voice. He realized that the boy was in the Black Pool. Peter went to the edge, threw the rope several times in vain until finally the boy was able to catch it, and then he slowly pulled him out.

You must not really tell a boy about a most beautiful nixie whom you can see at full moon, and then forbid him to go and see her. Marek had gone to the pool, had fallen through the ice, had been able to hang on to a bush by the bank, but was not strong enough to pull himself out. Now the blind man stood there in the frost with the soaking boy and could not carry him home. Again he heard the voice beside him saying, "Come to the hut."

Then he knew what to do. He had his pipe and lighter in his pocket. In the hut he made a fire, undressed the boy, and wrapped him in his coat, just as we had found him. For a long time "He" had sat beside them. They had talked much, and he had told him that much was now right once more.

Oh, how stupid we are sometimes, I had to ask Peter again: "Who was he?" But Peter was somewhat transformed, no longer so masterful and mocking as usual, but rather serene and serious. A little bit reproachfully he replied, "But my dear Inspector, He of course."

Peter did not die then. He lived on for a time with the boy and the young woman in his hut. Then the storm of war from the East came and scattered us all. But sometimes when I wonder about all the insoluble confusion of the world, who can help us, who can change it all, then I hear his clear bright old man's voice saying, "My dear Inspector, He of course."

The Star-Rider

Jakob Streit

Dark storm clouds covered the night-sky. Fierce squalls whipped the rain in gusts against the ground. It was Advent time. From time to time when the clouds were torn apart in shreds a faint gleam of light showed up for a moment the ghostly outline of the nearby hills and the black mountains in the distance. Along a narrow track that led winding across the lonely moor between Crossmolina and Bangor Erris in County Mayo a rider, overtaken by the night, was fighting his way against the storm, rain and darkness, trying to keep to the track that often was lost amid black bogs which could easily swallow up rider and horse. As he wandered around looking for the track and trying to avoid the bogs he felt that his strength was almost spent, so now he let the reins hang loose and trusted the horse to avoid the dangerous places and find its way back to the track. The icy rain and sleet beat into his face and his hands were stiff with cold. It was nearing midnight. If he had not lost his way he would have arrived in Bangor Erris hours ago.

In his exhaustion the thought crossed his mind: if I die in these bogs no one would ever find my body. I should disappear from the face of the earth — a sunken rider on his horse buried like a hero of olden times. A strange grim indifference had taken hold of him while the horse continued to snort and struggle on. Suddenly as a curtain of the clouds parted slightly he thought he saw a little side-track leading up a hill. Looking upwards he glimpsed a shimmer of light which could only have come from some human dwelling-place. The horse sensed a shelter for without being guided it followed the side-track. As they came nearer to the light the rider heard amid the roaring of the storm the sound of a dog barking. Then he made out a little thatched cottage. The light was coming from the window.

"Thank heaven!" uttered the rider. "Where there is light, there are people, warmth and dry lodging."

The dog did not appear to be a watch-dog in this lonely place. When the rider halted his horse and dismounted, the dog sniffed happily round his boots.

A little wooden gate had been blown open by the storm. The rider entered while the horse made for a haystack that had been set up in the yard. In the gloom of the night the dark door stood out against the whitewashed walls of the cottage. The rider went up to the door and knocked. For a moment he thought he heard hushed voices. The wooden door creaked as it opened and in the light that came from inside stood the dark figure of a crofter blocking the doorway. The rider asked: "Let me in and give me shelter for the night. I have lost my way to Bangor Erris in the storm."

To the astonishment of the rider the crofter did not move from the spot. With his head bent forward a little he looked the stranger up and down, noting his rich clothing. For a while only the patter of the rain could be heard. Then the figure stepped back in the doorway, half shut the door and said in a suppressed voice: "Sir, it is not possible. My cramped cottage is full up. I cannot just take in a noble gentleman like yourself into my poor dwelling. If you ride down into the glen and there turn left along the track you will reach the inn in Belderg in a couple of hours. Safe journey."

Thereupon the door was shut and the rider heard the bolt being drawn, and he was left standing in the cold and darkness. His hand hung limply by his side and he suddenly felt the warm muzzle of the dog, who had obviously taken him as a friend because his master had spoken to him. With the disappointment he was overcome with exhaustion. Assuredly if he were to ride on now his strength would desert him. He would never survive the night, and he began to feel indignant.

He thought: "How could this crofter refuse hospitality to someone who had lost his way in such weather. He should know of the dangers of the bogs in such a stormy night. No, I shall not let myself be driven away!" Angrily he felt for the weapon which he bore under his riding-cloak. "No, I must speak to him again even though I were to make my bed in the ashes; these walls shall save my life."

He turned his riding crop round and struck the oaken boards with the knob. Inside a woman's cry was heard. The door was suddenly pulled open. Once again the dark figure stood in the doorway. An angry voice spoke to the disturber.

"I tell you it is impossible. I have my reasons for not allowing anyone into my house on this particular night."

The stranger answered him with stern dignity: "Would you load your conscience with the death of a man in this night? Give me the smallest corner on the floor of your cottage and I shall be satisfied. I ask for this in the name of the Holy Virgin and Saint Bride. Let me in."

There was something in the way the stranger asked that quelled the crofter's anger. His arms which he had held thrust in the doorway now slid to his side. He struggled with himself. The words came out haltingly.

"You have asked in the name of the Virgin. Now listen. My wife is lying in the pains of her first childbirth. A neighbour is with her. We have only the one room and the one bed. Soon her time is on her. Well enter then in the Virgin's name. Behind the house is a shed for my two cows. I shall put your horse there."

Thereupon the crofter allowed the stranger to enter the warm glimmering room and showed him a little low bench near the hearth. The rider could make out in the dim light the bed in the farthest corner and a woman dressed in black bending over it. He thought he could hear a suppressed groan, but he turned away towards the peat fire, sat down upon the bench and warmed his hands. In the warm air he felt how cold and damp his clothes were.

When the crofter returned and nodded to him, the stranger whispered: "I'll go and get some dry clothes from my saddlebag."

But the crofter seized a milk jug by the fire, and said: "First drink some warm milk. That will do you good."

So the rider who was frozen through sat down again and drank thirstily from the jug. He felt new life flooding into him. He lent against the wall and tried not to hear the whispering and groaning in the background. As feeling returned to his limbs he noticed that his boots were full of water. He stood up quietly, in order to get the change of dry clothing which he had brought with him. He stepped out into the open. Outside a strong wind had torn the clouds apart. The storm and rain were over. The rider went into the shed at the back of the house. and found his horse bedded on the dry floor. He unfastened the leather saddle-bag and changed his clothes as best he could leaning against the side of his horse. As he was going back into the house and his hand was already on the door knob, he turned and looked again at the sky where stars had become visible and a weak half moon was about to set behind the hills.

Suddenly the rider thought: under what star will this crofter's child come into the world? For he had occupied himself all his life with the study of the stars. As he observed the sky which was clearing and noted how certain stars stood to the moon he was startled. From the inside of the house he heard a cry.

He opened the door a little and called urgently: "Crofter come out to me. I have something important to tell you."

In astonishment the man put his head out and answered: "Come in, we can talk quietly together."

"Your wife cried out. Is the child born yet?"

"No she is having a hard time, but it will soon be born. The pains are hard on her."

The stranger seized the crofter by the coat and led him out, so that the door fell shut behind them, and then he exclaimed: "Crofter if you care about the destiny of your new-born child try to hold back the birth. Let the midwife try all she can so that the child is not born for another hour."

The crofter tore himself away from the stranger's grasp and stepped back: "What is the matter with you, sir? Have you lost your senses? My wife has been suffering long enough, and you want us not to help her? Are we to make her agony even longer?"

The rider realized that he had asked too much of this simple man. How could he explain to him what he knew from the stars?

He murmured: "The stars of this birth are malignant, and the moon shines misfortune. Poor child!"

At that moment a fresh cry of pain sounded from the house. The crofter rushed in. For a moment the rider stared at the stars and whispered to himself: "If only the moon were *under* the horizon."

When he went back into the room all was quiet. With a hasty glance he thought he saw how the crofter's hand gently stroked the mother's forehead. He went back to his bench by the fire. Someone had laid two warm potatoes in a dish for him. Hardly ever before in his life had a nocturnal meal tasted so good as these half-burnt potatoes. Gently he laid himself against the wall and stretched out his legs. He wanted to remain awake so as not to miss the moment of birth and then observe the stars again. But the strenuous efforts of the icy ride and now the pleasant warmth and the crackling of the oak logs which the crofter had laid upon the fire wove the cloak of sleep around him. His head which had been leaning against the wall now drooped down upon his shoulder. He began to slumber. Once he started from his sleep as he heard the shrill cry of a baby. Half in sleep he murmured the words, "It is born." Two or three times his head jerked as if he would get up, but immediately he fell back into a deep sleep.

The morning light began to creep through the little window and help the oil lamp to light up the inside of the cottage, and the horseman woke up. His limbs sprawling half on the bench and half on the ground seemed to be out of joint. A child crying all the time brought him completely to himself. He drew his legs back and looked round. The crofter who was sitting on his wife's bed had seen the stranger's movements. He came to him and said happily: "A healthy little boy, sir."

Without congratulating him the stranger asked abruptly: "Had the moon set?"

"Sir, you worried me last night. Yes I went out right away when the baby was born. Only one half of the moon was above the mountain. You had not been long asleep. But the main thing is that mother and child are well."

The stranger turned his face to one side. Shadows lay upon his eyes, and a deep furrow appeared on his forehead. The crofter noticed how he had turned pale. Suddenly the gentleman stood up, went out and returned after a while with his saddle-bag. From this he took out a small leather bag. When he opened it the crofter caught a glimpse of bottles and sealing-wax. The mother had taken the baby to her breast, but her eyes were fixed enquiringly on the stranger, and the woman in black stared at what he was doing as if she suspected some evil magic.

Now the stranger took a piece of paper from his little notebook and began to write minutely upon it. When he had finished he asked the crofter for a nut. By chance the neighbour had brought some. The rider now opened one of the nuts with his pen-knife laying out the two halves. He ate the kernel and cleaned out the shells with his knife. Then he folded the piece of paper together and put it into one of the shells. He took a red linen tape such as is used for seals, knotted the two ends and laid them in the other half shell. From a little bottle he took some glue and stuck the two halves together. He then laid the nut to dry by the fire. At last he spoke: "You are wondering what I am doing. I shall leave this nut behind for your son. Keep it safely! When he is seven years old and he loses his first milk tooth, you must tell him to always wear this nut round his neck. He is not to go into the water with it nor is he ever to open it until his twenty-first birthday. Then he is to open it and read what is written in it. It will be a great comfort for him."

The little one, whom his mother called Liam had fallen asleep peacefully after drinking his mother's milk. The crofter looked earnestly into the horseman's eyes and said: "You entered in the name of the Holy Virgin. Assuredly words of blessing lie in the nutshell. I shall do exactly as you say, sir, for I see that your heart is concerned with the fate of our child. I feel that a good angel has sent you to us through the storm. We give you our thanks. Now drink some milk and eat some porridge for you have a long journey ahead of you."

The rider was constrained to accept the kindly invitation. He would have preferred to ride off straight away so as not to be drawn into conversation, but he did not wish to hurt the feelings of his happy host. He could see that the joy of being a father was greater than the shadow lying over the future which he had cast over them. Silently he ate his porridge and drank his milk.

The crofter who had already fed and watered the stranger's horse insisted on coming out with him and holding his horse for him to mount. The wind had died down completely. The dark clouds had retreated to a distant mountain. The low-lying December sun spread its reddish sheen over the landscape. The rider trotted down the path leading to the track across the moor. The dangerous bogs reflected the fiery glow of the clouds. Some seagulls flew up in fright. When the rider looked back he could see the little white cottage, a bluish smoke curling up from the chimney, a picture of peace and happiness. He stopped his horse and looked around him admiring the countryside, but inwardly he carried the pain of foreknowledge which clouded the joy of the scene. Soon he was galloping on his way to Bangor Erris.

Months went by. With all the demands of his business his experience of the night of storm paled and gradually sank into oblivion, just as so much in our lives sink down and are forgotten.

Years went by. Little Liam was growing bigger. There were now more children in the family. When his father was building an extension to the house for the children, Liam the eldest brought stone after stone for the building. He helped with the thatching of the roof, and he was particularly happy when the house was newly whitewashed in spring for Easter. Liam eagerly helped to paint over the grey winter patches with gleaming white lime-wash. While he was still little he had once asked his father: "Can't people be whitewashed. Then I wouldn't have to wash any more!"

One day when he was six years old his father said to him: "Liam, next Saturday we'll get up early. You can help me to bring the pig to market to sell him. With the money I'll be able to pay the rent to the landlord."

Liam did not understand what his father meant. It was the first time that he had been to a town and saw with his own eyes that there were other houses in the world. And for the first time he saw a church with a bell in the tower.

In the market square there were lots of people, and animals were tethered there. Liam watched all the activity of the market with great interest and marvelled when his father gave the pig away to another man and received some round hard disks which you could not even eat. Then they went to a house which his father called the estate office, and he gave some of the round pieces away. After that they went to another house full of lovely things. They were all on shelves or stacked on the floor. Father exchanged the round pieces for some oil and candles. At last on the way home Liam was so tired that he could not keep up with his father and the latter had to carry him on his shoulders for the last part of the way.

After this visit to the market Liam often thought that there were many things in the world which he did not know about. His father once took him to a hill where they could see the sails of great ships upon the sea and he told him about many other things and Liam felt he would like to go out and see the world when he grew up.

One evening the little family were sitting round the roughly fashioned table eating their meal of potatoes. Each child also received a thin hard piece of bread. When Liam bit hard upon his piece he suddenly jerked, felt in his mouth and held out between his forefinger and thumb his first tooth which he had lost. His eyes filled with tears.

"Now my mouth is all broken" he wailed.

His mother comforted him with the words: "You will get a much bigger and better tooth, and to make it come properly and to make you big and strong your father will give you something."

Liam looked surprised as his father stood up and took out a loose stone from the chimney-piece. He felt in the hole and brought out as if by magic a round nut with a red ribbon. When his father put the stone back in Liam saw a little cross scratched on it which he had not noticed before.

"Here Liam," said his father solemnly, "I'm going to hang this nut round your neck. You must wear it all the time by day and by night.

Mind that you never let it get broken, and keep it away from water. It will bring you luck."

Liam was very impressed. His father was so solemn when he laid the red ribbon round his neck. Yes, certainly he would be very careful that nothing should ever happen to the nut.

Some time later his father said to him: "Now you are old enough for your mother to teach you some letters so that you can read and write. Would you like that?"

"Are those the squiggly little things in mother's prayer-book? Yes I like them because there are lovely pictures beside them"

Seven years later Liam had grown into a clever, strong lad who was able to help his father with all kinds of work. The two of them together thatched the cottage. Liam's father was proud watching his eldest son drive the plough firmly. Together they had built a byre for the cows. There were now three cows and two pigs in it and some twenty sheep grazed upon the hill-land. Liam slept above the room under the thatch where he and his father had made a floor of some wooden planks. Every evening when he went to his bed of straw he took the nut between his hands as his mother had taught him and said his prayers. Then he often played carefully with the nut for a while and felt its little indentations. Sometimes he twisted the ribbon so that it came tight round his neck. Latterly he had often wondered where the nut came from. When his father once took the nut off Liam's neck to see whether the glue were still holding Liam asked suddenly: "Father may I never open the nut?"

With strangely serious eyes his father answered: "Oh yes, in seven years on your twenty-first birthday you may open it."

"Father, who gave it to us?"

"The Star-Rider."

Liam realized that his father did not wish to say any more because the latter stood up and went out of the house. Liam however hung the mysterious nut round his neck again.

In the late summer a wandering teacher came to the crofter's family. Such teachers used to go round the country. This one was a discharged soldier. He taught Liam and his brothers and sisters not only arithmetic, reading and writing, but he also sang songs with them and told them many stories and legends of ancient times. Whenever they were alone Liam would keep asking him about the world and about its people. When the wandering teacher went away again Liam had grown much

more mature and serious. His desire to go out and see the world grew stronger in him.

It was a warm autumn evening. Liam was nearly nineteen. After his hard work in the fields he climbed up to a little lough in the hills where he and his brothers and sister often bathed. He would always take off his neckband and lay it with the nut on a particular stone. This time he went up alone. He took off his shirt and trousers and left them in the heather and walked towards the water. The dark peaty bottom of the lough made a clear mirror for the surface of the water was flat calm. Liam could see his own reflection. "Is that me?" The white sunlit body shone clearly in the reflection. Slowly he opened his arms and moved them in various gestures watching with amusement the antics of the mirrored water-boy who imitated what he was doing. White little clouds were playing round his red-blonde hair. Liam knelt down. He wanted to look closely at his face and look into his own eyes. The nutshell hanging from his neck touched the smooth surface of the water. The nut caused little ripples and his face in the water was distorted so that he had to laugh. He gave a sudden jump and plunged into the distorted picture of himself and swam with powerful strokes in the warm peaty water. He had forgotten to lay his nut aside. After a short bathe he lay down in the heather and shut his eyes. Bees were buzzing and there was a scent of honey. A slight tickling on his knee made him open his eyes. A butterfly was dancing around, alighted, and remained motionless while it held its wings to the sun. Liam kept quite still. Then the colourful visitor flew up and fluttered over to the nutshell right in front of Liam's eyes. The butterfly's wings had black borders and had blood-red markings. The young lad gently reached his finger towards the butterfly trying to entice it on to his hand, but it fluttered away flying round his head and disappeared.

Liam took hold of the nutshell and turned it on the ribbon as he had often done. Perhaps he squeezed it more tightly than usual or perhaps the glue had melted a little in the water. Suddenly he held the two halves in his hand. A little ball of paper rolled out on to his chest. He had not meant to open the nut. Should he put the two halves together again and let the glue dry in the sun? He hesitated and looked round the little lough set among the heather. All was as peaceful as before.

"On your twenty-first birthday you may open it and read it," he heard in his mind his father's solemn voice. He took hold of the nutshell again. The blood rushed to his head. He could feel his pulse beating strongly in his neck and temple.

"I could not help it that the nutshell opened. Perhaps it is God's will that it opened. Perhaps I ought to know today what the secret of the nutshell is."

With trembling fingers he began to unfold the paper which bore clear letters. He rose on his knees. Once more he cast a quick glance around him. Then he began to read. He turned pale. Horror stamped itself upon his face. His eyes opened wide. The paper slid from his trembling fingers and fluttered like a moth to the ground. A cry escaped from his breast. He threw himself forwards and dug his fingers into the heather as if to seek support from the earth, and then his body was racked with sobs.

Half strangled he gasped: "No! No!" And he plunged his head into the heather.

He stood up as he felt a cold shudder pass over his body. A cloud had covered the sun. The cool evening breeze set little ripples criss-crossing the lough. Once more he bent over the yellowed paper and read again the terrible words:

You were born under stars of doom. Know that on your twenty-first birthday you will be hung for a crime of which you are innocent. These lines are to be your comfort in the night before your death. Your innocence is known to one man and to God. C.B.

Liam whispered tonelessly: "The Star-Rider."

Then he picked up the two halves that lay in the heather. He crumpled the paper up in a ball and laid it with the knotted end of the ribbon into the nutshell and pressed the two halves together. Then he knelt for a while. He thought of praying, but he could not find any words. Tears streamed down his cheeks. Only one part of the Paternoster came to his lips: "Thy will be done!"

The wind had grown stronger. Liam's skin grew cooler. Slowly his hands relaxed. The nutshell held together and hung on his neck as before. After he had dressed he gripped the nutshell under his shirt so that his warm hand might harden the glue. No, he could not yet go back home. So he began to wander aimlessly over the heather. The setting sun gilded the land and the hills. Liam had never experienced until then how the beauty of the shining world can bring pain to the heart and somehow he felt glad when it began to grow dark. He wandered on without thinking where he was going. Suddenly he stood again by the lough which now was black as pitch, a gulf of oblivion. He stepped right to the edge which began to crumble beneath his feet.

"Oh if only I could be extinguished like the lough in the darkness, or if only I could sink into the depths."

Then he noticed two bright points in the dark mirror. Stars? Yes up above the two stars were shining in the sky and bit by bit others appeared. Then Liam spoke like a child to the stars: "Stars, what have I done for you to punish me so?"

Suddenly he knew that his parents should know nothing of what he had learnt that day.

"I will go and die far away from home."

It was far into the night when Liam reached home. His mother was still up. She had grown worried because he had not returned. He said that he had fallen asleep by the lough. His mother said anxiously: "The evening turned cold. You will have caught a cold. Here take my warm blanket. Wrap yourself up well. Sleep well."

Liam did not gainsay her. He could not reject his mother's kindness. After she had fed him with warm milk he went up quickly to his bed under the roof. With his right hand he held on to the death-shell and then he listened to the beating of his heart with its strong song of life.

During the next weeks his mother noticed that he had changed. He had grown so serious and silent, hardly laughing and joking with his brothers and sister. But his father praised how well the lad worked. Yes he would get on in the world anywhere.

It was the evening of Liam's nineteenth birthday. His brothers and sister were already asleep. Father, mother and the eldest sat by the fire carding wool. Suddenly Liam asked: "Father you once told me something about the Star-Rider who gave me my nutshell when he stayed here the night when I was born. What did he look like? Was he a good man?"

"Yes, it is now a long time ago and I can tell you about it now."

Then Liam's father told him all that had happened on that night of the storm.

"And here on the bench where you are sitting the gentleman passed the night. Was he good? When he was sitting by the fire he opened his eyes from sleep. They were dark and sparkling. They were stern but good eyes. I believe that he was able to love people much. He wished to help us too. His voice and his heart were moved when he gave me the nutshell. When he had ridden away I found a gold piece under the milk jug by the hearth which he had left there. For that money we could buy three sheep, and today they are twenty. A wise gentleman, a good gentleman. But I did not know what to make of his talk about the stars, but whatever it was he meant it very seriously."

Next night up in his loft on his straw bed Liam did not go to sleep for a long time. He tossed from side to side so that the rafters creaked. When he fell asleep at last he groaned aloud in his sleep and gabbled quick unintelligible words. His father who was woken by this climbed up the ladder to him and laid his hand upon him saying: "What's the matter? Are you ill? You are so restless in your sleep. You'll wake your brothers and sister."

"I'm all right father, I've just had a bad dream, that's all."

"Liam, think of our calf which has just been born, then you will get better dreams."

When father had gone down again Liam knew that he must leave home and go away. "My younger brothers are working well. The shame that I shall be publicly hung shall not be cast over my good parents. I shall go soon." After this decision a great calm came over him. The next day he would speak to his parents about it.

As he was going up to the higher-lying field with his father early in the morning he plucked up courage: "Today we are gathering in the last potatoes, then right through the long winter there is no work which my brothers can't do. So Father let me go out into the world to look for work and earn my living. Once I have got some money together I can pay the rent to the landlord for you."

His father stood still, surprised, looked his son up and down and thought over his answer.

"Liam, I don't want you to go away. Your mother is so fond of you. But you are right. One day it has got to be, and this year's harvest was rather poor. In the world you will get on well, only wait till after Christmas which is not so far off, and talk it over with your mother."

This he did on the same evening. Liam's decision did not seem to surprise his mother although her voice was sorrowful as she said: "I was expecting it, Liam. I know that this thought has given you restless nights. Only promise me that you will come again."

"Yes Mother, if it is God's will, I shall come back."

During the next period Liam doubled his help. He renewed the roof of the byre, he brought osiers from the stream and made a wattle pen for the sheep. He threshed corn with his father. He carved toys for his brothers and for his little sister a little doll with white woolly hair. Christmas Eve was clear and cold when the family went over the dip in the hills to the next glen for the midnight mass. Liam carried his little sister well wrapped up in a potato sack which he had slung over his shoulder. She was playing with him, pulling his ear to the right or left to make him go the way she wanted. Father and mother each held one of the brothers by the hand. Patrick, the second oldest, walked ahead with a long stick and a lantern as guide. Liam felt how he was going to miss them all.

"They must never find out about my shame and misfortune when I am dying on the gallows. I shall go far, far away and take another name. In this way the bad news will never reach them."

When they reached the gap between the hills they had a short rest and could see other lights in the glen making their way to the church. They reached the church as the bells were ringing and knelt down in the pews with the rest of the congregation. Incense, candle-light, singing and the sound of the bell, and on the little side-altar the crib figures. Liam did not pray for himself: his fate was fixed, but he prayed for his family that the stars would be kind to them.

A week later at New Year Liam left home with a stick across his shoulder. Tied to it was a bundle of clothes and some food. He followed the same track that had brought the Star-Rider to his home nineteen years before. Several times he turned round to wave to his family until he rounded a hill and his homestead disappeared. In this way Liam left the North of County Mayo and walked eastward until he came to County Sligo. As a wandering labourer he put his hand to all kinds of work. One time he helped to cut peat for three weeks at a farm. Now he had found temporary work with a blacksmith. One day a landowner dismounted at the smithy as his horse had cast a shoe on the way.

As the smith was shoeing the magnificent horse Liam held its head while the nobleman sat on a bench watching the work. He noticed how Liam calmed the horse by stroking its neck and mane and how the horse unlike its habit quietly held out his hoof.

A good lad, thought the lord, and he asked the smith: "Is that a new apprentice you've got?"

"No," the smith replied, "my apprentice has gone to see his family for a couple of weeks and I have taken on this lad in the meantime."

When the lord had paid the smith and Liam was holding the stirrup and bridle for him, the nobleman asked suddenly: "What are you going to do when the apprentice comes back?"

"My lord, I shall seek other work."

"Come to me. My gardener is growing old and he could use your strong arms. The smith will tell you where to find me. Good-bye."

With that the lord trotted off.

The smith was surprised and said to Liam: "You're lucky. That was Lord Stanford. He's a rich Englishman but not too proud to talk to a smith and an Irish country lad."

So after leaving the smith Liam came and took service with Lord Stanford who owned much land in those parts. In the castle gardens the spring planting had now begun. When Liam was brought before the old gardener he noticed some gardener lads who were working carelessly. The head gardener told him to help them get the flower-beds in front of the castle ready for planting. Liam noticed that as soon as the head gardener was out of sight the lads began to play around, throwing stones at each other and sitting on the wall. Soon he was the only one working. Of course they teased him, but he replied: "I work as I am used to working at home."

Gradually the head gardener noticed that the newcomer carried out all the tasks allotted to him quickly and reliably. Soon Liam was given more difficult jobs, and he learned how to graft the trees and roses. Liam began to enjoy his new job more and more and did his best to please his master. The following year he was appointed under gardener and the other lads who had been there much longer were put under him. Of course they envied him and they tried more than once to bring him into disrepute with the head gardener. Once they said he had not told them to water the sprouting seeds which had dried up. Another time fire broke out in the garden-shed and they said it was Liam's carelessness. But the head gardener saw through the lad's tricks and never accused Liam unjustly.

In this way Liam's second summer on Lord Stanford's country seat went by, and even the lads seemed to have got used to Liam having been set above them, for Liam though hardworking was friendly. By now he had saved up more money than his father needed for the annual rent. So he thought that towards the end of the summer before his doom caught up with him he would keep his promise to his mother and go home once more. He also longed to see his family and to bring them presents with his well-earned money. How he yearned to walk through his quiet native glen with the gushing streams and to take one last bathe in the little lough amid the blooming heather. He was absolutely convinced that the prophecy which he carried with him would be fulfilled although he could not imagine what kind of crime would be ascribed to him. There was not much more time to be lost for the month of September was coming to a close. So once the fruit had been picked he asked for a fortnight's leave to visit his family. The head groom with whom Liam was on a good footing and who sometimes took him with him when he went out riding was ready to lend him a horse so that the journey would be less arduous for him. Liam had already got gifts for his parents and for his brothers and sister and had packed them in an old saddle-bag which the head groom had also lent him.

Before Liam rode off — his horse stood saddled in the courtyard — he went to look for the head gardener in the gardens to take leave of him. Then one of the gardener lads, the laziest of them, crept up to his horse, opened unobserved the flaps of the saddle-bag. He thrust his arm deep into the bag, fastened the flap again quickly and disappeared.

"Today I'll get as far as the inn in Dromore," called Liam to the head groom as he rode away, "and tomorrow I'll reach Ballina."

Liam was not thinking now of his nutshell, nor of the doom which was hanging over him. His soul was filled with the pure joy of returning home.

The day after Liam's departure Lord Stanford's wife discovered that a valuable gold brooch with jewels was missing from her jewelry box, so she summoned the hall porter and questioned him whether he had seen anyone about the place. Now this servant was hand in glove with the malicious gardener's lad.

At first he shrugged his shoulders but then remarked: "O my lady, I just remember that yesterday the gardener lad, Liam, before he rode away was suddenly standing here in the passage. When he saw me he hurried furtively away down the staircase. Shortly after that I heard his horse trotting away."

All this was told to the Lord, and he ordered his young nephew who was staying with him to ride after the supposed thief with two mounted retainers and bring him back captive. They dashed off on the swiftest horses.

On the second evening of his journey, at a late hour as Liam was going up to his room in the inn in Ballina he heard the sound of horses hooves outside. Soon after there was a knock on his door. The innkeeper stood there with a lantern and behind him in the half darkness were three men. Before Liam was aware all three thrust themselves into his bedroom, and he was astonished to see the well-known faces.

The young nobleman spoke sharply to him: "Out with the gold brooch which you have stolen from Lady Stanford."

Liam turned pale, and could not help stepping back and said in his surprise rather hesitantly: "A golden brooch? I don't know anything about it. Here is my saddle-bag."

The nobleman ordered the bag to be emptied, and the whole contents was poured out on to the floor, all the things which Liam had carefully packed for his family. On top of the heap gleamed the gold brooch. All then happened as foreordained. Liam was bound and brought into the stable where two armed retainers stood guard over him. The nobleman took his room. Liam lay on the hard stone floor chained to a ring in the stable and could not sleep. Yes, that was how it had to come about, and no one would believe him that he knew nothing about the golden brooch. Next morning he was tied on to his horse and taken to the prison in the town of Sligo. Everything was taken from him except the nutshell of misfortune that hung round his neck under his shirt.

After two weeks he was brought before the interrogating judge. Liam tried to maintain his innocence but the facts spoke against him. He knew that the penalty for a theft of that nature was death. That was the law in those days. He had an inkling of how the brooch had got into his saddle-bag, but the judge paid no heed to that especially as the evidence of the hall porter was quite definite.

The public trial was set for the third day before Liam's twenty-first birthday. The judge of the assizes from Dublin was to come and pronounce the death sentence. Liam waited in painful resignation for the day. It was good that his parents would never hear anything of it. He did not struggle against his fate, but he was grieved that he had not been able to see his mother, father, brothers and sister again, nor indeed his beloved glen, and this was his sorrow in his narrow cell.

The day of the assizes had come. Curious people came from all parts. Some of the castle servants including the hall porter and the gardener's lads were there. One of the maids said, "That's what comes of making a favourite of some unknown vagabond too quickly and setting him above the others. He can't even say who his parents are and he does not know where he was born, the knave."

When Liam was brought into the court, the judge had just sentenced another prisoner to death. As he went by Liam saw the eyes of the condemned horse-thief wide open with fear, and he found it strange that he could not feel any fear of his own approaching death. He was shown to a bench at the side of the court. After reading through his papers, the judge, in his white wig and black gown, looked long and hard at the accused. Liam held his gaze without flinching. The men who had found the brooch in Liam's saddle-bag were then called as witnesses. When the judge asked Liam what explanation he had to offer about how the brooch came into his saddle-bag, Liam did not answer. Then the old gardener was called who came to witness for the defence. He testified to Liam's honesty and reliability. Once more the judge called upon Liam to answer. The gardener's good words gave Liam courage. He stood up and stepped before the judge. In his presence he was aware of a warm and human gaze born of compassion. The eyes of the judge also gave him courage. It seemed that an inner voice was saying: "Tell him your secret."

Now the judge spoke: "Accused, all the evidence is against you. What is your last word before I pronounce the sentence."

"My lord, I know your sentence. In three days on my twenty-first birthday I shall be brought to the gallows."

The judge leant back surprised: "Can you read a man's thoughts? In truth in three days the hangman is coming from Dublin to this town. This is known only to me. He will carry out two sentences of death, one of which is yours. Accused, how do you know all this?"

In the court it had grown so quiet that you could hear the buzzing of a fly. Suddenly Liam drew out the ribbon of his nutshell, placed the crumpled piece of paper on the table in front of the judge and smoothed it out so that all could see and then he showed it to the judge. He now had lost all his embarrassment and now he spoke in a clear voice that all could hear.

"This paper was written by a man who knew the stars. He had found shelter in our house on the night when I was born. He gave this nut to my father, and after I was seven years old I had to wear it always round my neck. Two years ago when I was bathing the nutshell came apart and I read that on my twenty-first birthday I should be hanged, but be innocent. This is in three days."

The judge had taken the paper in his two hands. As he read he turned pale, for he recognized his own handwriting, signed with his own initials.

A breathless silence reigned in the court. Slowly the judge lowered the yellowed paper and bent his head while he was sunk in memories, pictures of his extremity in that night of storm, the lonely house, the crofter and the stars.

Now he looked deep into Liam's eyes and asked slowly and tonelessly: "Do you or does your father know who wrote this paper?"

"No my lord, my father called him the Star-Rider, and sometimes the Storm-Rider, because a terrible storm had driven him to our house in that night."

The judge raised his head and spoke out loudly so that everyone could hear: "Accused, I will tell you who wrote this paper. It was I myself."

Through the court there was an intake of breath, whispers, suppressed words of astonishment, compassion.

The judge then turned to those on the bench and to the clerks of the court: "Those were troubled days twenty years ago. Soldiers were plundering throughout the land. Warfare had broken out between two leading clans. I had an urgent message to take to the North from Dublin to prevent the North from siding with the wrong side. I had also to visit a castle on Belmullet belonging to my relations the Binghams. On that stormy night I found shelter on the way in that house where the accused was born."

The judge paused for a moment, for before all the people how was he going to reveal the secret that he was concerned with astrology. He spoke quietly so that only those near him could hear what he was saying.

"The influence of the stars on human destiny was something which my ancestors studied and knew about and I have inherited their knowledge. On the night when you were born, the stars of destiny stood in a particularly bad relation to the moon, and I knew that this would lead to a fatal catastrophe in your life in three times seven years. I could see too that this had to do with possessions or money, the theft or damage of which would lead to the gallows. Any delay in your birth would have improved the constellation, but this could not be brought about. I was overcome with exhaustion, and so I wrote this note in the early morning, in order to give you comfort when the doom should come over you. Now I see that you were born outside the power of death. A good fortune has made me your judge."

Liam's blood began to race and hammer. He felt dizzy thinking: "I shall be set free, I shall live, live."

The judge suddenly stood up, cast his eyes over the assembled crowd and called out: "I announce the judgment. There can be no appeal against it in law. The accused is innocent. He is to be freed. Another must be found, who has impugned him with this horrible deed."

Then the judge notice an agitated hustle and bustle at the back of the court. A man was trying to force his way to the door to escape. The judge called out the order: "No one is to leave the court. That man who was trying to escape, come here to the table!"

It was the hall porter whom the guard at the door was now thrusting forward to the table. Before the clear eyes of the judge the man could not deny the charge. He confessed his part in the plot with the gardener's lad who had spurred him on to the deed. Then he pointed to the gardener's lad who was hiding behind a pillar. The two were brought into Liam's cell and later they were sentenced to penal servitude in the West Indies.

When the judge had brought the trial to an end Liam fell at his feet and let his tears fall freely. The judge lifted him up, embraced the sorely tried one and said: "Give my greetings to your father and mother. Thank him who holds sway over the stars. He has brought a good turning to the fatal star."

The news travelled like the wind to Lord Stanford's castle. When the old head gardener and Liam entered the courtyard side by side Lord and Lady Stanford and all the household stepped forth to welcome the freed prisoner.

It was no wonder that Liam not only became head gardener but Lord Stanford promoted him to be manager of his great estates.

Before this happened Liam was allowed to make the journey to his parents and his brothers and sisters and to see his homeland. So it came about that he was able to celebrate his birthday in the quiet glen in the whitewashed cottage. The story of his destiny was never forgotten in the whole of Connaught where it is told to the present day.

The Birth of John the Baptist

From the Gospel of Luke

It so happened that during the reign of Herod, King of Judea, there was a certain priest belonging to the group of Abajah whose name was Zacharias. His wife was descended from Aaron, and she was called Elizabeth. They were both upright people in the sight of God, not failing to keep all the commandments and regulations of the Lord, but they had no children because Elizabeth was barren and they were both advanced in age.

Then it happened that he was acting as priest before God in his order of service, and according to the custom of priesthood it fell to him by lot to enter the shrine of the Lord and burn incense, while all the many people were praying outside at the hour of the censing. And an angel of the Lord appeared to him, standing on the right side of the altar of incense. When he saw this Zacharias was disturbed, and fear fell upon him.

But the angel said to him, "Do not be afraid, Zacharias, because your request has been heard. Your wife Elizabeth will bear you a son, and you shall give him the name John. You will have joy and great happiness, and many will rejoice as he will be great in the sight of the Lord. He shall not drink any wine or strong drink, and he will be filled with the Holy Spirit even from his mother's womb, and will turn many of the sons of Israel to the Lord their God. He will go forth in his sight in the spirit and power of Elijah to turn the father's hearts to the children, and the rebellious to an understanding of what is right, preparing for the Lord a people who are ready for him."

Zacharias said to the angel, "How shall I become aware of this, as I myself am an old man, and my wife is advanced in age?"

The angel answered him, "I am Gabriel, who stand in the presence of God. I was sent out to speak to you and to bring you this good news. But see, now you will be silenced and not have the power to speak until this happens, because you did not believe my words which will be fulfilled in their season."

The people were expecting Zacharias and they were astonished that he delayed in the shrine. When he came out he had not the power to speak, and they became aware that he had seen a vision in the shrine as he signed to them and remained dumb. And when his term of service came to an end he went back to his home.

After this his wife Elizabeth conceived and hid herself for five months, saying, "This is what the Lord has done for me when he looked upon me, to take away my disgrace among the people."

When Elizabeth's time was fulfilled, she bore a son. Then her neighbours and her family on hearing that the Lord had shown her great mercy rejoiced with her. Then on the eighth day they came to circumcise the child and would have given him the name Zacharias after his father, but his mother said, "No, he must be called John."

And they said to her, "No one in your family has been given this name."

They made signs to the father as to what name he wished him to have. He asked for a writing tablet, and wrote, "His name is John." And they were all astonished.

Instantly his mouth was opened, and when his tongue was set free he spoke in praise of God. Fear came upon all the neighbourhood, and these things were discussed in the hill country of Judea. All those who heard of them kept them in their hearts, and said, "What will become of this child?" as indeed the hand of the Lord was with him.

His father Zacharias was filled with the Holy Spirit and he prophesied, saying, "Blessing on the Lord God of Israel, because he has come to his people and he has obtained their release, raising for us a powerful saviour from the house of his servant David, as he told us through the mouth of his holy prophets of old."

The child grew and became strong in spirit.

The Annunciation to Mary

From the Gospel of Luke

Now in the sixth month the angel Gabriel was sent out from God to a town in Galilee, which was called Nazareth, to a virgin promised in marriage to a man whose name was Joseph, belonging to the house of David, and the virgin's name was Mary. When he came to her, he said, "Rejoice, you have been shown favour! The Lord is with you."

She was much troubled by what he said, and considered what sort of greeting this could be. And the angel said to her, "Do not be afraid, Mary, because you have found favour with God. And see, you will conceive and bear a son to whom you should give the name Jesus.

"He will be great and will be called the Son of the Most High, and the Lord God will give him the throne of his father David. And he will reign over the house of Jacob throughout the ages, and his Kingdom will have no end."

Mary said to the angel, "How will this come about, as I have no knowledge of man?"

The angel answered her, "The Holy Spirit will come upon you, and the power of the Highest will overshadow you. Therefore the child who will be born will be called holy, son of God. And see, your cousin Elizabeth has also conceived a son in her old age, and this is her sixth month although she was considered barren, because nothing which he says will be impossible for God."

Mary replied, "See here the servant of the Lord. Let it happen to me as you have said."

And the angel went away from her.

At the Birth of the Child

The Birth of Jesus in Bethlehem

From the Gospel of Luke

Now it happened in those days that a decree went out from Caesar Augustus, that all those living in the land should be registered. This first registration was made when Quirinius governed Syria, and all the people went to be registered, every one to his own city. Therefore Joseph also went up out of Galilee from the town of Nazareth to Judea to the city of David which is called Bethlehem, because he belonged to the house and family of David, to be registered with Mary, his promised bride, who was with child.

Now it so happened that while they were there the number of her days was completed, and she gave birth to her first-born son. She wrapped him in linen bands and laid him in a manger, because there was no room for them in the inn.

In that region there were shepherds who remained out in the fields guarding their flock during the night. And an angel of the Lord came upon them, and the glory of the Lord shone around them, and they were shaken with fear. The angel said to them, "Do not be afraid. See how I bring you news of great joy which will come to all the people. Today in the city of David a saviour has been born to you who is Christ the Lord. And this will be a sign for you: You will find a new-born babe wrapped in linen bands and lying in a manger."

All of a sudden a great heavenly host was there with the angel giving praise to God and saying, "Glory to God in the heights, and peace on the earth among men of good will."

When the angels had gone away from them into heaven the shepherds said to one another, "Let us go to Bethlehem and see what has taken place there which the Lord has revealed to us."

They came with all speed, and found Mary and Joseph with the new-born babe who was lying in the manger. When they had seen it they spread the news of what had been said to them concerning this child.

And all who heard it were astonished at what the shepherds told them. But Mary stored up all these things, dwelling on them in her heart.

And the shepherds returned, giving glory and praise to God, as all that they had heard and seen was just as they had been told.

The Shepherd Boy's Flute

Dan Lindholm

In the night when the Saviour was born a poor shepherd's boy went up on to the hills not far from Bethlehem to look for one of his sheep. That was why he was not among those shepherds of whom we hear in the Gospel.

This boy served a strict master — who knows — perhaps one of the innkeepers of Bethlehem. If ever he came home without all his flock together he was beaten. So he scarcely noticed the wonderful things happening around him. He did not notice how the wind had dropped, he did not hear that the birds were beginning to sing, he did not see that all the stars suddenly were shining twice as brightly. His way led uphill, he looked behind every bush until at last he stood at the top of the hill. From there he could see far and wide over the fields right to the town of Bethlehem.

As he was standing up there it happened that the heavens opened and the night became as bright as day. There appeared a great host of angels, and a song of praise sounded over the earth. Hardly anyone right up into our own times has understood how great the marvel was that happened in that night. So the poor young shepherd can be forgiven for not understanding the tidings at once. He was thinking of his sheep that had got lost and he wanted to go on looking for it. Suddenly an angel stood in front of him and spoke to him: "Do not worry about your little sheep. At this moment a greater shepherd is born. Run quickly to Bethlehem where the Christ-Child, the Redeemer of the world, is lying in the manger."

"I may not stand before the Redeemer of the world without bringing him a gift," said the boy.

"Here, take this flute and play a tune to the child," said the angel, who gave him a flute and vanished immediately. The flute had seven notes, and when the boy put it to his lips, it played all by itself. Grateful and happy the boy ran down the hill. But when he wanted to jump over a stream, he tripped and fell flat among the stones. The flute fell out of his hand and he could not help saying a word that shepherds use. It was not a nice word. When he recovered the flute one note was missing.

There were still six notes left whole. The boy had no time to cry about it. The path was better now, so he ran on as fast as he could. Suddenly he stopped. Right in front of him sat a huge wolf, the devourer of lambs himself, with his fangs bared. The boy grew angry.

"Be off with you," he cried, and without thinking he hurled the flute after the fleeing wolf. When he found it again it would only play five notes.

He had now arrived on the plain where the flocks were. All the animals were resting, and a deep stillness was over all. One sheep only was running about bleating. The boy wanted to bring it into the flock, ran after it, and when it escaped him he threw what he had in his hand at the sheep's legs. It was the flute which now had lost another note.

But where were the other shepherds? The boy did not know that they were already kneeling in the stable in front of the child. But he thought that they were probably in the inn with a tankard of ale while he as the youngest was left to keep watch. In a bad temper he kicked a jar of water that stood by the fire. It seemed that an unseen power had knocked the flute out of his hand, and when he picked it up again it had only three notes.

He now ran on towards Bethlehem. All went well until he tried to go through the city gates. Suddenly he was surrounded by a gang of street urchins who wanted to get the flute off him. But he did not want to part with it and so it came to blows and punches. He did manage to hold on to the flute, but in the struggle one more note was lost.

At last he stood in front of the stable. High above the roof the wondrous star was shining, and in the manger lay the Redeemer of the world.

But the flute had only one single note when he went in, for as he had been passing the door of the house the landlord's fierce dog had set on him. He did not know how to defend himself except with the flute in his hand.

There he stood by the door, not daring to go in to the child. He was deeply ashamed that so little was left of his gift.

He did not know that the way of every human being to the Redeemer of the world is like that.

But Mary beckoned him to enter. He came forward quietly and played his last and only note. It was strangely beautiful. The child listened, everyone in the stable listened, Mary and Joseph, ox and ass. The Christ-Child stretched forth his divine hand and touched the flute, and in that same moment it was made whole again, and sounded full and gloriously, as it had sounded from heaven itself.

Jonas, the Shepherd in the Stable

Georg Dreissig

Jonas, the shepherd, lay tightly wrapped in his blanket in the straw and slept. The summer was long since past and the meadows had been grazed clean. Already in the autumn when the storms were raging over the stubble-fields he had driven his sheep together and sought refuge with them with the innkeeper who had a narrow cave behind his inn, the Crown. There he kept his cow and he let them all squeeze in there together: Jonas, the cow and the sheep. There was no room for anything else, but the shepherd did not mind one bit lying tightly packed side by side with his beloved sheep. The cow was easy-going, dreaming perhaps of the coming spring when she would have the whole cave to herself again, but meantime enjoying the warmth from her woolly companions.

Now and again the icy winter wind blew keenly through the broad chinks in the wooden wall that closed the entrance to the cave, but the wind soon lost its cold power in this poor place that housed both man and beast.

Suddenly the shepherd shot up out of his sleep, rubbed his eyes and looked round in astonishment, inspecting every detail of the place which he knew so well as if it had become quite strange to him in sleep: the uneven walls of rock, which enclosed the cave on three sides and formed the roof, and which were black from the fires which had burnt there; the wall of unplaned wood in which the door hung on its rickety hinges, and though there was no window the chinks in the wall were so wide that you could see through them to what was going on in the courtyard. He felt the straw which sparsely covered the naked earth, and tapped the crib which held the hay for the cow and the sheep to make sure that it was still there.

"Yes, yes," he muttered at last, "It is our stall, only our stall," and he shook his head over and over again unbelievingly. Where had Jonas thought he was?

The shepherd laid his hand thoughtfully on the head of one of the ewes and began to tell about his dream. Some people think it is foolish to talk to animals, because they do not understand a word. But Jonas knew better, and of course his sheep also knew better. They turned their heads calmly to him and listened to the sound of the deep warm voice which gave them the feeling of security and protection.

"Just imagine," Jonas recounted, "I was in a palace, in a golden palace. There was one room so wonderful that I have never seen anything like it: the walls were of purest gold, the ceiling like the sky full of stars, the carpet like a garden blooming with roses and lilies. At the same time the loveliest music was being played by the finest musicians. In the middle of the room stood a four-poster bed with its canopy, and on it the softest pillow. And just imagine, I slept in this feather-bed as softly and comfortably as on angels' wings. Suddenly there was a loud shout: 'The King is coming. Make way!' A servant came running and told me — no, he asked me to move out of the palace to make room for the King. 'O Jonas,' he said, 'you'll do that for the King, won't you?' Then I sat up, but when my foot touched the ground I awoke. And now the palace has gone and I am back here again with you."

The sheep looked at the shepherd steadily with their dark eyes. Had they understood? Were they able to imagine the beautiful room in the golden palace? Once again Jonas passed his powerful hand across his eyes. But the dream could not be wiped away. It remained, and that was meant to be, because an angel of God had made the shepherd dream so for a good reason. Outside the wind was blowing its icy melody. Jonas drew his blanket more tightly round his shoulder. No, this cave was certainly no palace. But it was nice and warm here among the thick coated sheep.

"We are lucky," Jonas averred, "We are lucky that we can be here together. Winter is a harsh host. We are better to keep out of his way."

Then he peeped curiously through the chinks in the wooden wall, for he heard voices in the courtyard; the voice of the innkepper somewhat blustering but not unfriendly, and the tired voice of an old man. Jonas saw neither of them, for the sun had already set, the world was grey, and nothing could be distinguished. Suddenly, however, he saw a light approaching, and there was the innkeeper knocking at the squint-set door and calling softly but insistently: "Jonas, Jonas, are you awake?"

"Yes I am," answered the shepherd, and opened the door. The cold air coming in made him shudder.

"O Jonas, my good friend," the innkeeper addressed him, "just imagine, some more people have come. They can't find any lodging because all the houses are full. They are so tired and so weak, I simply can't send them away. Jonas, for this one night take your sheep out again into the fields. They have a warm coat and won't freeze. Make room for the good people."

The shepherd did not feel the cold winter air any more. He had been listening to the innkeeper in astonishment. His dream stood there shining again before him.

"Good host," he asked piously at last, "Is it the king who is seeking lodging?"

The innkeeper looked at him in surprise, and shook his head incredulously, saying: "What topsy-turvy things you say sometimes, Jonas. The king in my stall! No, no, they're just poor people, an old man and a young woman who's expecting a baby."

That was exactly how the servant had asked in the dream, the shepherd remembered, but all he said to the innkeeper was, "I'll do it."

Then he turned to his sheep and called: "Come my dears, we have to get out. Our palace is needed for poor people."

Not at all hurriedly but willingly enough the sheep followed his call. Jonas seized his long shepherd's crook and marched out in front of his flock. He looked keenly at the strangers as they passed him. No indeed, the innkeeper was right, that was not a king asking to be let in. Jonas saw an old man with his beard fluttering in the wind and with sunken cheeks red with the cold. And there on a skinny little donkey sat a young woman in a blue hooded cloak, whose sad and tired eyes looked out from a pale face. No indeed, it was simply poor people in dire need of shelter.

"Come on my dears, into the fields," Jonas called to his sheep and trod even more resolutely through the snow. He was not going to be done in by the cold.

Out in front of the city gates camp fires were burning, one, two, three, and there were other shepherds who had had to clear out from better places than Jonas for the countless people who were looking for lodging. They were warming themselves by the fire, and were making merry with many nice tit-bits to eat which some of them had brought with them. Jonas was heartily welcomed and what with the songs and talking he soon forgot all about his dream, the stall and the poor people.

It was late before the men snuggled down cosily amongst their sheep. Soon they were wrapped in deep sleep, and so they did not notice the deep peaceful stillness that suddenly filled all the surroundings. Only the sheep raised their heads and looked steadfastly and unswervingly up to the sky where the stars were shining in brightest radiance. What were they looking at then?

At first there was nothing there but that wonderful starlit peace. But suddenly the sky seemed to be torn asunder, and golden light flooded into the world, light before which all darkness must retreat. At the same time the air was filled with the sweetest refrain. The shepherds awoke and stared dreamily into the brightness. They heard the tidings of the birth of the divine child on earth and the anthem of the angelic choirs sounded mightily in their hearts: "Let God be revealed in the Heights, and Peace upon Earth to Men of Good Will."

The shepherds leaped up feeling neither coldness nor tiredness. They wanted to see the child that was the cause of all this jubilation. The heavenly music led them to the town and to the stall. Do you think that Jonas recognized the stall again, the cave with the black walls and the wooden wall in front? Oh no, it all looked so different, for everything was transformed by the birth of the divine child. The walls of the cave were no longer black but of shining gold, and the roof was domed like the starry heavens, while the floor was a carpet of roses and lilies. There in the middle sat a queen with a dress adorned with stars beside a golden cradle, and in the cradle on a golden pillow lay a little baby that looked so lovely and happy that the shepherds' hearts grew sore from their great joy.

For a long, long time they knelt at the crib. First they were quite still, then they prayed, then they sang their shepherds' songs, and they gave the heavenly child what they had brought with them. When the men finally arose and took their leave, Jonas could not help himself, he just had to take the baby's little hand into his huge fist and kiss it. Then he heard quite clearly how the child said: "Thank you, dear Jonas, for making room for me."

The shepherd looked up in confusion. Had he heard the words or had he dreamt them? He could not say, and no wonder. When the heavens descend to the earth and we are allowed to see them with our eyes, I do believe we should not know whether we are awake or are dreaming.

In the end Jonas did get an inkling of where the golden palace stood which he had first seen in his dream and then with his own eyes in that holy night. For after a few days when the innkeeper told him that the cave was vacant again, and he came back with his sheep into the shelter of the stall, the walls were just as black and the wooden wall just as unplaned as ever. But in the crib, yes, in the crib, there lay a golden pillow. The shepherd rubbed his eyes, quite puzzled. A golden pillow? Oh no, no pillow, but the hay was shining golden, as golden as if the heavenly child had lain there himself.

Jonas never spoke about it, and no one else ever saw the gold, only he and perhaps the sheep; but they kept the secret as well as their shepherd. Sometimes however when Jonas was lying in the straw tightly wrapped in his blanket sleeping, he saw the child again and heard him saying: "Thank you, dear Jonas, for making room for me."

The Well of the Star

Elizabeth Goudge

On the road to Bethlehem there is a well called the Well of the Star. The legend goes that the three Wise Men, on their journey to the Manger, lost sight of the star that was guiding them. Pausing to water their camels at the well they found it again reflected in the water.

I

David sat cross-legged by himself in a corner of the room, separated from the other children, clasping his curly toes in his lean brown hands, and wished he were a rich man, grown-up and strong, with bags full of gold and thousands of camels and tens of thousands of sheep. But he was not rich, he was only a diminutive ragged shepherd boy who possessed nothing in the world except the shepherd's pipe slung round his neck, his little pipe upon which he played to himself or the sheep all day long and that was as dear to him as life itself.

At the moment he was very miserable. Sighing, he lifted his hands and placed them on his stomach, pushing it inwards, and noting the deflation with considerable concern. How soon would he be dead of hunger? How soon would they all be dead of hunger, and safely at rest in Abraham's bosom? It was a very nice place, he had no doubt, and suitable to grandparents and people of that type, who were tired by a long life and quite ready to be gathered to their fathers, but hardly the place for a little boy who had lived for only a few short years in this world, who had seen only a few springs painting the bare hills purple and scarlet with the anemone flowers, only a few high summer suns wheeling majestically through the burning heavens.

If only it were summer now, instead of a cold night in midwinter! If only mother would light a fire for them to warm themselves by, a bright fire that would paint the walls of the dark little one-roomed house orange and rose-colour, and chase away the frightening shadows. But there was no light in the room except the flickering, dying flame that came from a little lamp, fast burning up the last of their oil, set on the earth floor close to his mother, where she sat crouched beside her sick husband, swaying herself ceaselessly from side to side, abandoned to her grief and oblivious of the wails of four little cold and hungry children, younger than David, who lay all together on their matting bed.

If only he were a rich man, thought David, then it would not matter that storms had destroyed the barley, that their vines had failed, or that their father, the carpenter of this tiny village on a hill top, could no longer ply his trade. Nothing would matter if he were a rich man and could buy food and wine and oil and healing salves; they would be happy then, with food in their stomachs, their father well, and comforting light in this horrible darkness of midwinter.

How could he be a rich man?

Suddenly there came to David's mind the thought of the wishing well far down below on the road to Bethlehem. It was a well of clear sparkling water and it was said that those who stood by it at midnight, and prayed to the Lord God Jehovah from a pure heart, were given their heart's desire. The difficulty, of course, was to *be* pure in heart. They said that if you were, and your prayer had been accepted, you saw your heart's desire mirrored in the water of the well; the face of someone you loved, maybe, or the gold that would save your home from ruin, or even, so it was whispered, the face of God himself. ... But no one of David's acquaintance had ever seen anything, though they had wished and prayed time and again.

Nevertheless he jumped up and crept noiselessly through the shadows to the door. He had no idea whether his heart was pure or no but he would give it the benefit of the doubt and go down to the well. He pulled open the door and slipped out into the great cold silent night.

And instantly he was terribly afraid. All around him the bare hills lay beneath the starlight in an awful waiting, attentive loneliness, and far down below the terraces of olive-trees were drowned in pitch-black shadow. But the sky was streaming with light, so jewelled with myriads of blazing stars that it seemed the weight of them would make the sky fall down and crush the waiting earth to atoms. The loneliness, the darkness, the cold and that great sky above, turned David's heart to water and made his knees shake under him. He had never been out by himself so late at night before and he had not got the courage, hungry and cold as he was, to go down over the lonely hills and through the darkness of the olive-trees to the white road below where they said that robbers lurked, wild sheep-stealers and murderers who would cut your throat as soon as look at you just for the fun of it.

Then he bethought him that just over the brow of a nearby hill a flock of sheep were folded, and their shepherds with them. His own cousin Eli, who was teaching David to be a shepherd, would be with them, and Eli would surely be willing to leave the sheep to the other shepherds for a short time and go with David to the well. ... At least David would ask him to.

He set off running, a little flitting shadow beneath the stars, and he ran hard because he was afraid. ... For surely, he thought, there was something very strange about this night. ... The earth lay so still, waiting for something, and overhead that great sky was palpitating and ablaze with truimph. Several times, as he ran, he could have sworn he heard truimphant voices crying, "Glory to God! Glory to God!" as though the hills themselves were singing, and a rushing sound as though great wings were beating over his head. Yet when he stopped to listen there was nothing; only the frail echo of a shepherd's pipe and a whisper of wind over the hills.

He was glad when he saw in front of him the rocky hillock behind which the sheep were folded. "Eli'" he cried, giving a hop, skip and a jump, "are you there? Jacob? Tobias? It's David."

But there was no answering call from the friendly shepherds, though there was a soft bleating from the sheep, only that strange stillness with its undercurrent of triumphant music that was heard and yet not heard. With a beating heart he bounded round the corner and came out in the little hollow in the hills that was the sheep fold, his eyes straining through the darkness to make out the figures of his friends.

But they were not there; no one was there except a tall, cloaked stranger who sat upon a rock among the sheep leaning on a shepherd's crook. ... And the sheep, who knew their own shepherds and would fly in fear from a stranger whose voice they did not know, were gathered closely about him in confidence and love. ... David halted in blank astonishment.

"Good evening to you," said the stranger pleasantly. "It's a fine night."

David advanced with caution, rubbing his nose in perplexity. Who was this stranger? The sheep seemed to know him, and he seemed to know David, yet David knew no man with so straight a back and so grand a head or such a deep, ringing, beautiful voice. This was a very great man, without doubt; a soldier, perhaps, but no shepherd.

"Good evening," said David politely, edging a little closer. "'Tis a fine evening, but cold about the legs."

"It is? Then come under my cloak," said the stranger, lifting it so that it suddenly seemed to spread about him like great wings, and David, all his fear suddenly evaporated, scuttled forward and found himself gathered in against the stranger's side, under the stranger's coak, warm and protected and sublimely happy.

"But where are the others?" he asked. "Eli and Jacob and Tobias?"

"They've gone to Bethlehem," said the stranger. "They've gone to a birthday party."

"A birthday party, and didn't take me?" ejaculated David in powerful indignation. "The nasty, selfish brutes!"

"They were in rather a hurry," explained the stranger. "It was all rather unexpected."

"Then I suppose they had no presents to take?" asked David. "They'll feel awkward, turning up with no presents. ... Serve them right for not taking me."

"They took what they could," said the stranger. "A shepherd's crook, a cloak and a loaf of bread."

David snorted with contempt, and then snorted again in indignation. "They shouldn't have gone," he said, and indeed it was a terrible crime for shepherds to leave their sheep, with those robbers prowling about in the shadows below and only too ready to pounce upon them.

"They were quite right to go," said the stranger. "And I have taken their place."

"But you're only one man," objected David, "and it takes several to tackle robbers."

"I think I'm equal to any number of robbers," smiled the stranger. He was making a statement, not boasting, and David thrilled to the quiet confidence of his voice, and thrilled, too, to feel the strength of the arm that was round him and of the knee against which he leant.

"Have you done a lot of fighting, great lord?" he whispered in awe.

"Quite a lot," said the stranger.

"Who did you fight?" breathed David. "Barbarians?"

"The devil and his angels," said the stranger nonchalantly.

David was momentarily deprived of the power of speech, but pressing closer he gazed upwards at the face of this man for whom neither robbers nor devils seemed to hold any terrors, and once he began to look he could not take his eyes away, for never before had he seen a face like this man's, a face at once delicate and strong, full of power yet quick with tenderness, bright as the sky in early morning yet shadowed with mystery. ... It seemed an eternity before David could find his voice.

"Who are you, great lord?" he whispered at last. "You're no shepherd."

"I'm a soldier," said the stranger. "And my name is Michael. ... What's your name?"

"David," murmured the little boy, and suddenly he shut his eyes because he was dazzled by the face above him. ... If this was a soldier, he was a very king among soldiers.

"Tell me where you are going, David," said the stranger.

Now that they had told each other their names David felt that they were lifelong friends, and it was not hard to tell his story. He told it all; his father's illness, his mother's tears, the children's hunger and the cold home where there was no fire and the oil was nearly finished; his longing to be a rich man that he might help them all, and the wishing well that gave their heart's desire to the pure in heart.

"But I hadn't meant to go down to the road alone, you see," he finished. "I thought Eli would have gone with me, and now Eli has gone to that birthday party."

"Then you'll have to go alone," said Michael.

"I suppose the sheep wouldn't be all right by themselves?" hinted David gently.

"They certainly would not," said Michael firmly.

"I'm not afraid, of course," boasted David, and shrank a little closer against that strong knee.

"Of course not," concurred Michael heartily. "I've noticed that Davids are always plucky. Look at King David fighting the lion and the bear when he was only a shepherd boy like you."

"But the Lord God Jehovah guided and protected him," said David.

"And the Lord God will protect you," said Michael.

"I don't *feel* as though he was protecting me," objected David.

"You haven't started out yet," said Michael, and laughed. "How can he protect you when there's nothing to protect you from? Or guide you when you don't take to the road? Go on now. Hurry up." And with a gentle but inexorable movement he withdrew his knee from beneath David's clinging hands, and lifted his cloak from David's shoulders so that it slid back with a soft rustling upward movement, as though great wings were folded against the sky. ... And the winter wind blew cold and chill about the little boy who stood ragged and barefoot in the blackness of the night.

"Goodbye," said Michael's deep voice; but it seemed to be drifting away as though Michael too were withdrawing himself. "Play your pipe to yourself if you are afraid, for music is the voice of man's trust in God's protection, even as the gift of courage is God's voice answering."

David took a few steps forward and again terror gripped him. Again he saw the bare lonely hills, and the shadows down below where the robbers lurked. He glanced back over his shoulder, ready to bolt back to the shelter of Michael's strong arm and the warmth of his cloak. ... But he could no longer see Michael very clearly, he could only see a dark shape that might have been a man but that might have been only a shadow. ... But yet the moment he glanced back he knew that Michael was watching him, Michael the soldier who was afraid neither of robbers nor of the devil and his angels, and with a heart suddenly turned valiant he turned and scuttled off down the hill towards the valley.

II

Nevertheless he had the most uncomfortable journey. Going down the hill he cut his feet on the sharp stones, and fell down twice and barked his knees, and going through the olive grove below he saw robbers hiding behind every tree. There were times when he was so frightened that his knees doubled up beneath him and he came out in a clammy perspiration, but there were other times when he remembered Michael's advice and stopped a minute to play a few sweet notes on his precious pipe, and then he was suddenly brave again and rushed through the terrifying shadows whooping as though he were that other David going for the lion and the bear. ... But all the same it was a most uncomfortable journey and he was overwhelmingly thankful when with a final jump he landed in the road and saw the water of the well gleaming only a few feet away from him.

He leant against the stone parapet and looked at it gravely. ... Water ... In this land that in the summer months was parched with drought and scorched with heat, water was the most precious thing in the world, the source of all growth and all purification, the cure of sickness, the preserver of life itself. It was no wonder that men came to water to pray for their heart's desire, to water the comforter and lord of all life. "Comfort ye, comfort ye, my people." It seemed to him that he heard voices singing in the wind among the olive-trees, as though the trees themselves were singing, voices that sang not to the ear but to the soul. "He shall feed his flock like a shepherd: he shall gather the lambs with his arm, and carry them in his bosom. Wonderful! Counsellor! The mighty God! The everlasting Father! The Prince of Peace!" Surely, he thought, if the Lord God Jehovah cared so for the little lambs he would care also for David's sick father and weeping mother and the little hungry children, and covering his face with his brown fingers he prayed to the Lord God that he might have gold to buy food and wine and oil for that stricken house up above him on the hill. And so hard did he pray that he forgot everything but his own longing, forgot his fears and the cold wind that nipped him through his rags, saw nothing but the darkness of his closed eyes and heard nothing but his own desparate whispering.

Then, sighing a little like a child awakening from sleep, he opened his eyes and peeped anxiously through his fingers at the water in the well. Would he have his heart's desire? Had he prayed from a pure heart? Was that something glittering in the well? He dropped his hands from his face and leaned closer, the blood pounding so in his ears that it sounded like drums beating. Yes, it was gold! Circles of gold lying upon the surface of the water, as though the stars had dropped down from heaven. With a cry of joy he leaned nearer, his face right over the water, as though he would have touched with his lips those visionary gold pieces that promised him his heart's desire. ... And then, in an instant of time, his cry of joy changed to a cry of terror, for framed in those twinkling golden points of light he saw the reflection of a man's face, a bearded, swarthy face with gleaming teeth and eyes, the face of a foreigner.

So the Lord God had not protected him. So the robbers had got him. He stared at the water for a long minute, stark with terror, and then swung round with a choking cry, both his thin hands at his throat to protect it from the robber's knife.

"Do not cry out, little son. I will not hurt you". The man stretched out a hand and gave David's shoulder a reassuring little shake. "I but looked over your shoulder to see what you stared at so intently."

The voice, deep-toned, kindly, strangely attractive with its foreign inflexion, chased away all David's fears. ... This was no robber. ... His breath came more evenly and he wiped the sweat of his terror off his forehead with his tattered sleeve while he looked up with bulging eyes at the splendid stranger standing in front of him.

He was tall, though not so tall as that other splendid stranger keeping the sheep up on the hill, and he wore a purple robe girdled at the waist with gold and a green turban to which were stitched gold ornaments that shook and trembled round his proud hawk-nosed face. David had one pang of agonized disappointment as he realized that it was only the reflection of these gold ornaments he had seen in the water, and not God's answer to his prayer, and then amazement swept all other thoughts from his mind.

For the star-lit road to the well that a short while ago had been empty was now full. While David prayed, his ears closed to all sounds, a glittering cavalcade had come up out of the night. There were black men carrying torches, richly caparisoned camels, and two more splendid grave-faced men even more richly dressed than his friend. The torchlight gleamed on gold and scarlet, emerald green and rich night blue, and the scent of spices came fragrant on the wind. This cavalcade might have belonged to Solomon, thought David, to Solomon in all his glory. ... Surely these men were kings.

But the camels were thirstly and the first king drew David gently away from the well that they might drink. Yet he kept his hand upon his shoulder and looked down upon him with kindly liking.

"And for what were you looking so intently, little son?" he asked.

"For my heart's desire, great lord," whispered David, nervously pleating his ragged little tunic with fingers that still shook from the fright he had had.

"So?" asked the stranger. "Is it a wishing well?"

"They say," said David, "that if you pray to God for your heart's desire from a pure heart, and if God has granted your prayer, you will see a vision of it in the water."

"And you saw yours?"

David shook his head. "You came, great lord," he explained. "I saw you."

One of the other kings, an old white-bearded man in a sea-green robe, was listening smiling to their talk. "We three have lost a star, little son," he said to David. "Should we find it again in your well?"

David thought it must be a joke, for what could three great lords want with a star? But when he looked up into the fine old eyes gazing down into his he saw trouble and bewilderment in them.

"If you heart is pure, great lord."

A shadow passed over the old man's face and he turned back to the third king, a young man with a boy's smooth skin and eyes that were bright and gay.

"Gaspar," he said. "You are young and pure of heart; you look."

Gaspar laughed, his white teeth flasing in his brown face. "Only an old wives' tale," he mocked. "We've lost the star twenty times in the blaze of the night sky and twenty times we have found it again. Why should we look for it now in a well?"

"Yet pray," said the old man sternly. "Pray and look."

Obediently Gaspar stepped up to the well, his scarlet robe swirling about him and the curved sword that he wore slapping against the side, bowed his head in prayer, then bent over the well.

"I can see only a part of the sky," he murmured, "and each star is like another in glory — no — yes." He paused and suddenly gave a shout of triumph. "I have found it, Melchior! It shines in the centre of the well, like the hub of a wheel or the boss of a shield."

He straightened himself and flung back his head, his arms stretched up towards the sky. "There! There!" he cried, and David and the elder kings, gazing, saw a great star blazing over their heads, a star that was mightier and more glorious than the sister stars that shone around it like cavaliers round the throne. . . . And as they gazed it suddenly moved, streaking through the sky like a comet.

"Look! Look!" cried David. "A shooting star!" And he danced out into the middle of the road to follow its flight. "Look! It is shining over Bethlehem!"

The three kings stood behind him, gazing where he pointed, and saw at the end of the road, faintly visible in the starlight, slender cypress trees rising above the huddled roofs of a little white town upon a hill, and above them the blazing star.

Gaspar, young and excited, suddenly swung round and began shouting to the servants to bring up the camels, but the two older kings still stood and gazed.

"Praise be to the Lord God," said the old king tremulously, and he bowed his head and crossed his hands upon his breast.

"Bethlehem," said the king who was David's friend. "The end of our journey."

His voice was infinitely weary, and for the first time it occured to David that these great lords had come from a long way off. Their beautiful clothes were travel-stained and their faces drawn with fatigue. They must, he decided suddenly, be lunatics; no same men, he thought, would come from so far away to visit an unimportant little place like Bethlehem; nor be in such a taking because they had lost sight of a star. Nevertheless he liked them and had no wish to lose their company.

"*I'll* take you to Bethlehem," he announced, and flung back his head and straddled his legs as though it would be a matter of great difficulty and danger to guide them the short way along the straight road to a town that was visible to the naked eye.

"And so you shall," laughed his friend. "And you shall ride my camel in front of me and be the leader of the caravan."

David jigged excitedly from one foot to the other. He had never ridden a camel, for only well-to-do men had camels. He could not contain himself and let out a shrill squeak of joy as a richly caparisoned beast was led up and made to kneel before them; a squeak that ended rather abruptly when the camel turned its head and gave him a slow disdainful look, lifting its upper lip and showing its teeth in a contempt so profound that David blushed hotly to the roots of his hair, and did not recover himself until he was seated on the golden saddle cloth before his friend, safe in the grip of his arm, rocking up towards the stars as the camel got upon its feet.

III

It was one of the most wonderful moments of that wonderful night when David found himself swaying along towards the cypresses of Bethlehem, the leader of a caravan. Because he was so happy he put his pipe to his lips and began to play the gay little tune that shepherds have played among the hills since the dawn of the world, and so infectious was it that the men coming behind began to hum it as they swung along under the stars.

"It is right to sing upon a journey, great lord", said David, when a pause fell, "for music is the voice of man's trust in God's protection, even as the gift of courage is God's voice answering."

"That is a wise child you have got there, Balthasar," said old Melchior, who was riding just behind them.

"I didn't make that up for myself," David answered truthfully. "A man up in the hills told it to me. A man who came to mind the sheep so that Eli and the other shepherds could go with their presents to a birthday party in Bethlehem."

"Does all the world carry gifts to Bethlehem tonight?" questioned Balthasar softly. "Wise men from the desert with their mysteries, shepherds from the hills with their simplicities, and a little boy with the gift of music."

"Do you mean that we are all going to the same place?" asked David eagerly. "Are *you* going to the birthday party too? And am I going with you? Me too?"

"A King has been born," said Balthasar. "We go to worship him."

A king? The world seemed full of kings tonight, and kings doing the most unsuitable things, too, keeping sheep on the hills and journeying along the highway travel-stained and weary. On this wonderful topsy-turvy night nothing surprised him, not even the news that the birthday party was a king's; but desolation seized him as he realized that he wouldn't be able to go to it himself. ... For how could he go inside a grand palace when his clothes were torn and his feet were bare and dirty? They wouldn't let him in. They'd set the dogs on him. ... Disappointment surged over him in sickening waves. He gritted his teeth to keep himself from crying, but even with all his effort two fat tears escaped and ploughed two clean but scalding furrows through the grime on his face.

They were at Bethlehem before he realized it, for he had been keeping his head bent for fear Balthasar should see his two tears. Looking up suddenly he saw the white walls of the little town close in front of him, the cypress trees like swords against the sky and that star shining just ahead of them, so bright that it seemed like a great lamp let down out of heaven by a string. The gate of the town was standing wide open and they clattered through it without hindrance, which surprised David until he remembered that just at this time Bethlehem would be full of people who had come in from the country to be taxed. They would not be afraid of robbers tonight, when the walls held so many good strong countrymen with knives in their girdles and a quick way with their fists. The visitors were still up and about, too, for as they climbed the main street of the little hill town David could see lines of light shining under doors and hear laughter and voices behind them. ... And a good thing too, he thought, for at any other time the arrival of this strange cavalcade in the dead of night might have caused a disturbance. ... The Lord God, he thought, had arranged things very conveniently for them.

"Which way are we going?" he whispered excitedly to his king.

"We follow the star," said Balthasar.

David looked up and saw that the star must have been up to its shooting tricks again, for it had now moved over to their right, and obediently they too swerved to their right and made their way up a narrow lane where houses had been built over caves in the limestone rock. Each house was the home of poor people, who kept their animals in the cave below and lived themselves in the one room above reached by its flight of stone steps.

"The king can't be *here!*" said David disgustedly, as the cavalcade, moving now in single file, picked its way over the heaps of refuse in the lane. "Only poor people live *here*."

"Look!" said Balthasar, and looking David saw that the star was hanging so low over a little house at the end of the lane that a bright beam of light caressed its roof.

"The star is making a mistake," said David firmly, "if it thinks a king could be born in a place like that."

But no one was taking any notice of him. A great awe seemed to have descended upon the three kings, and a thankfulness too deep for speech. In silence the cavalcade halted outside the house at the end of the lane, and in silence the servants gathered round to bring the camels to their knees and help their masters to the ground. David, picked up and set upon his feet by a sturdy Nubian whose black face gleamed in the torch-light like ebony, stood aside and watched, something of the awe that gripped the others communicating itself to him, so that the scene he saw stamped itself upon his memory for ever. ... The torchlight and starlight lighting up the rich colours of the kings' garments and illumining their dark, intent faces as though they were lit by an inner light; the stir among the servants as three of them came forward carrying three golden caskets, fragrant with spices and so richly jewelled that the light seemed to fall upon them in points of fire, and gave them reverently into their masters' hands. ... The birthday presents, thought David, the riches that Balthasar had spoken of, and he looked hastily up at the poor little house built above the stable, incredulous that such wealth could enter a door so humble.

But the door at the top of the stone steps was shut fast and no line of light showed beneath it, or shone out in welcome from the window. The only light there was showed through the ill-fitting door that closed in the opening to the cave below, and it was towards this that Melchior turned, knocking softly on the rotten wood and standing with bent head to listen for the answer.

"But that's the *stable!*" whispered David. "He couldn't be there!"

But no one answered him for the door opened and the three kings, their heads lowered and their long dark fingers curved about their gifts, passed into the light beyond, the door closing softly behind them, shutting David outside in the night with the strange black servants and the supercilious camels.

But his curiosity was too strong for him to feel afraid. There was a hole quite low in the door and kneeling down he pressed his dirty little face against the wood and squinted eargerly through it.

Of course there was no king there; he had said there wouldn't be and there wasn't; looking beyond the kings he saw there was nothing there but the stable and the animals and a few people, poor people like himself. The animals, a little donkey with his ribs sticking through his skin and an old ox whose shoulders bore the marks of the yoke they had carried through many hard years, were fastened to iron rings in the wall of the cave, but both of them had turned their sleepy heads towards the rough stone manger filled with hay, and towards a grey-bearded man who held a lighted lantern over the manger and a woman with a tired white face, muffled in a blue cloak, who lay on the floor leaning back against the wall. . . . But though she was so tired she was smiling at the men who were kneeling together on the hard floor, and she had the loveliest and most welcoming smile that David had ever seen.

And then he saw that the men she was smiling at were Eli, Jacob and Tobias, kneeling with heads bent and hands clasped in the attitude of worship. And before them on the hard floor, just in front of the manger, they had laid their gifts; Eli's shepherd's crook that had been his father's, Jacob's cloak lined with the lamb's wool that he set such store by, and Tobias's little loaf of bread that he always ate all by himself in the middle of the night when he was guarding sheep, never giving a crumb to any one else no matter how hard they begged. And beside these humble men knelt the kings in their glory, and beside the simple gifts were the three rich fragrant caskets, just as though there were no barrier between rich people and poor people, and no difference in value between wood and bread and gold and jewels.

But what could be in that manger that they were all so intent upon it? David had another peep through his hole and saw to his astonishment that there was a baby in it, a tiny new-born baby wrapped in swaddling clothes. Normally David took no interest at all in babies but at the sight of this one he was smitten with such awe that he shut his eyes and ducked his head, just as though he had been blinded by the sight of a king with eyes like flame sitting upon a rainbow-encircled throne.

So this was the King, this tiny baby lying in a rough stone manger in a stable. ... It struck David that of all the extraordinary places where he had encountered kings this night this was the most extraordinary of all. ... And then he gave a joyous exclamation. On the journey here he had cried because he had thought a barefoot dirty little boy would not be able to go to a king's birthday party, but surely even he could go to a birthday party in a stable. He leapt to his feet, dusted his knees, pulled down his rags, laid his hands on the latch of the door and crept noiselessly in.

And then, standing by himself in the shadow by the door, he bethought him that he had no present to give. He had no possessions in the world at all, except his beloved shepherd's pipe, and it was out of the question that he should give that for he loved it as his own life. Noiselessly as a mouse he turned to go out again but suddenly the mother in the blue cloak, who must have known all the time that he was there, raised her face and smiled at him, a radiant smile full of promise, and at the same time the man with the grey beard lowered the lantern a little that it seemed as though the whole manger were enveloped with light, with that baby at the heart of the light like the sun itself.

And suddenly David could not stay by himself in the shadows, any more than he could stay in a dark stuffy house when the sun was shining. No sacrifice was too great, not even the sacrifice of the little shepherd's pipe that was dear as lift itself, if he could be in that light. He ran forward, pushing rudely between Balthasar and Tobias, and laid his shepherd's pipe joyously down before the manger, between Balthasar's jewelled casket and Tobias's humble loaf of bread. ... He was too little to realize, as he knelt down and covered his face with his hands, that the birthday gifts lying there in a row were symbolic of all that a man could need for his life on earth; a cloak for shelter, a loaf of bread for food, a shepherd's crook for work and a musical instrument to bring courage in the doing of it; and those other gifts of gold and jewels and spices that symbolized rich qualities of kingliness and priestliness and wisdom that were beyond human understanding. "Wise men from the desert with their mysteries," Balthasar had said. "Shepherds from the hills with their simplicities, and a little boy with the gift of music." ... But David, peeping through his fingers at the Baby in the manger, did not think at all, he only felt, and what his spirit experienced was exactly what his body felt when he danced about on the hills in the first hot sunshine of the year; warmth was poured into him, health and strength and life itself. He took his hands away from his face and gazed and gazed at that baby, his whole being poured out in adoration.

IV

And then it was all over and he found himself outside Bethlehem, trailing along in the dust behind Eli, Jacob and Tobias, footsore and weary and as cross as two sticks.

"Where's my camel?" he asked petulantly. "When I went to Bethlehem I was the leader of a caravan, and I had three great lords with me, and servants and torches."

"Well, you haven't got them now," said Eli. "The great lords are still at Bethlehem. ... When Jacob and Tobias and I saw you there in the stable we made haste to take you home to your mother, young truant that you are."

"I don't want mother," grumbled David. "I want my camel."

Eli glanced back over his shoulder at the disagreeable little urchin dawdling at his heels. Was this the same child who had knelt in the stable rapt in adoration? How quick can be the fall from ecstacy! "You keep your mouth shut, little son," he adjured him, "and quicken your heels; for I must get back to those sheep."

"Baa!" said David nastily, and purposely lagged behind.

So determinedly did he lag that by the time he had reached the well he found himself alone again. The well! The sight of it brought home to him his desperate plight. From his night's adventure he had gained nothing. Up there on the hill was the little house that held his sick father, his weeping mother and his hungry little brothers and sisters, and he must go home to them no richer than he went. ... Poorer, in fact, for now he had lost his shepherd's pipe, thrown away his greatest treasure in what seemed to him now a moment of madness. ... Now he had nothing, nothing in all the world.

He flung himself down in the grass beside the well and he cried as though his heart were breaking. The utter deadness of the hour before dawn weighed on him like a pall and the cold of it numbed him from head to foot. He felt himself sinking lower and lower, dropping down to the bottom of some black sea of misery, and it was not until he reached the bottom that comfort came to him.

His sobs ceased and he was conscious again of the feel of the earth beneath the grass where he lay, hard and cold yet bearing him up with a strength that was reassuring. He thought of the terraces of olive-trees above him and of the great bare hills beyond, and then he thought of the voices he had heard singing in the wind up in the hills, and singing down below among the trees, and then suddenly he thought he heard voices in the grass, tiny voices that were like the voices of all growing things, corn and flowers and grasses. "They that sow in tears, shall reap in joy," they whispered. "He that goeth forth and weepeth, bearing precious seed, shall doubtless come again rejoicing, bringing his sheaves with him."

He got up, his courage restored, and stumbled over to the well, faintly silvered now with the first hint of dawn. He did not pray to be a rich man, he did not look in it for his heart's desire, he simply went to it to wash himself, for he did not intend to appear before his mother with dirty tear stains all over his face. ... If he could not arrive back home with bags full of gold and thousands of camels and tens of thousands of sheep he would at least arrive with a clean and cheerful face to comfort them.

Like all small boys David was a noisy washer and it must have been the sound of his splashing that prevented him hearing the feet of a trotting camel upon the road; nor could the surface of the well, much agitated by his ablutions, show him at first the reflection of the man standing behind him, it had to smooth itself out before he could see the swarthy face framed in the twinkling golden ornaments. When he did see it he blinked incredulously for a moment and then swung round with a cry of joy.

"So you thought I had forgotten you, did you, little son?" smiled Balthasar. "I would not forget so excellent a leader of a caravan. When you left the stable I followed after you as quickly as I could. See what I have for you."

He gave a bag to David and the little boy, opening it, saw by the first light of the dawn the shine of golden pieces. ... Lots of golden pieces, enought to buy medicines and healing salves for his father and food and warmth for all of them for a long time to come. ... He had no words to tell of his gratitude but the face that he tilted up to Balthasar, with eyes and mouth as round in wonder as coins themselves, was in itself a paean of praise.

Balthasar laughed and patted his shoulder. "When I saw you give your shepherd's pipe to the little king," he said. "I vowed that you should not go home empty-handed. ... I think it was the little king himself who put the thought into my head. ... Now I must go back to my country, and you to your home, but we will not forget each other. Fare you well, little son."

As he went up through the shadows of the olive-trees David was no longer frightened of robbers, for he was far too happy. The trees were singing again, he thought, as the dawn wind rustled them. "Comfort ye, comfort ye, my people," they sang. And when he got out beyond the trees, and saw the great bare stretches of the hills flushed rose and lilac in the dawn, it seemed as though the hills themselves were shouting "Glory to God!"

The Shepherds

The oldest legend from Spain

Ruth Sawyer

You who keep Christmas, who keep the holy-tide, have you ever thought why a childs needs must be born in the world to save it? Here is a Christmas story about God, meaning Good. It begins far back when the world was first created.

In the beginning God had two favourite archangels: one was called Lucifer, meaning Light, and one called Michael, meaning Strength. They led the heavenly hosts; they stood, one on the right hand and one on the left hand of God's throne. They were his chosen messengers.

Now the Archangel Michael served God with his whole heart and angelic soul. There was no task too great for him to perform, no thousand years of service too long. But the Archangel Lucifer chafed at serving any power higher than his own. As one thousand years swept after another thousand years — each as a day — he became bitter in his service and jealous of God.

The appointed time came for God to create the Universe. He made the sun, the moon, the stars. He made earth and water, and separated them. He made trees and flowers and grass to grow; he made creatures to walk the earth and eat thereof; and he made birds for the air and fish for the waters. And when all else was created, he made a man and called him Adam, and a woman and called her Eve. It took him six heavenly days to create this Universe; and at the end he was tired and rested.

While the Creation was coming to pass and God was occupied most enormously, Lucifer went stealthily about Heaven. He spoke with this angel and with that, whispering, whispering. He spoke with the cherubim and seraphim — to all and everyone who would give him an attending ear. And what he whispered was this: "Why should God rule supreme? Why should he be the only one to create and to say what shall be created? We are powerful. We are worthy to rule. What say you?"

He whispered throughout the six days of Creation; and when God rested Lucifer led a host of rebellious angels against God; they drew their flaming swords and laid siege to God's throne. But the Archangel Michael drew his flaming sword; he led God's true angels to defend Heaven. The army of Lucifer was put to rout and his captains were taken prisoner and led before God's throne. And God said: "I cannot take life from you, for you are celestial beings. But you shall no longer be known as the hosts of light; you shall be the hosts of darkness. You, Lucifer, shall bear the name of Satan. You and those who have rebelled must seek a kingdom elsewhere. But I command you this — leave this Earth, which I have but freshly made, alone. Molest not my handiwork." So spoke God.

So Lucifer was banished with his minions; and henceforth he was known as Satan. He established a kingdom under the Earth and called it Hell. But because God had commanded him to leave Earth untouched, he straightway coveted Earth for his own. He sent his spirits abroad to tempt and make evil those born upon Earth. So it came to pass that the people of Earth knew at last the power of evil as well as of good; they felt the long reach of darkness even while they lifted their eyes to the Face of Light.

And now the years became millions. Earth became peopled in its four corners; and God looked down upon it and sorrowed. He called Archangel Michael to him and spoke: "It has come to pass that Satan's power upon Earth is great. No longer can my angels prevail. A kingdom of destruction, of greed, of hate, and of false-witnessing has been set up among my people on the Earth I have created. Their hearts have grown dark with evil; their eyes no longer see the light. I must send to Earth my own spirit that evil may be conquered. He shall be one conceived of Heaven and born of Earth, none less than my own beloved Son." So spoke God.

Earth had been divided into countries, some great and powerful, some small and weak. And the strong reached out even with their armies and took the weak. Now such a one, taken, was called Judea. Within its rolling hills, its olive groves, its high pastures and twisting rivers, men had built a little city called Bethlehem — King David's city. And to this city the conquering Romans had ordered all of the tribe of Jesse to come and render tribute unto Caesar.

Beyond the city, on the high pastures, many shepherds herded their sheep. And it came to pass that God chose Bethlehem to be the place of birth for his Son; and the time to be the taxing time of the year. He chose to reveal the coming to the shepherds, they being men of simple faith and pure hearts. And God sent forth a star to show them the way, and commanded angels to sing to them of the glad tidings.

The night had grown late. High in the pastures the shepherds had built fires to keep themselves warm, to frighten off stray wolves or robbers. All slept but Esteban, the boy. He alone saw the angel, heard the tidings; and straightway he woke the sleeping ones: "Lo, an angel has but now come among us, singing. Wake — wake, all of you! I think this night must have great meaning for us."

Now at this time Satan stood at the gateway of Hell. Of late he had been troubled in mind, a sense of impending doom moved him. And as he gazed abroad upon the Earth he saw the angel appear. Then did his troubled mind grow fearful. He summonded his hosts of Hell, commanding them to make ready: "Tonight I think again we defy God's power over the Universe. We fight, I think, for Earth, to make it ours. I go to it now. Come when I smite the ground."

Swift as his thought Satan reached the Earth. He came as a wanderer, upon his head a wide sombrero, about his shoulders and falling to the ground a cloak, in his hand a staff. Across the Earth he travelled even as the lightning crosses the sky. He was here — he was beyond. And so he came to the high pastures of Judea and stood at one of the fires about which the shepherds watched. Again the angel came, shouting God's tidings: "Fear not! For unto you is born this day in the city of David a Messiah!"

Satan covered his face and spoke: "What means that message?"
The shepherds cowered. "We know not."
"What is that Saviour — that Messiah yonder apparition shouts of?"
"We know not."
Satan dropped his cloak that they might see the fire that damns and burns shining even in his eyes: "I command you to know!"
It was Benito, the oldest shepherd, who asked: "In the name of God, who are you?"
And Satan answered: "In my own name I am a wanderer. Once I had taken from me a mighty kingdom. I am here to restore it unto myself."
Could this be the Saviour of whom the angels sang? The shepherds drew close — close. They looked. And to each came terror. Here truly was darkness, not light; here was nameless evil, not good. Here was one

104

who had denied the name of God. Together they shouted: "Begone!" They drew brands from the fire and crossed them, making fiery crosses to burn between themselves and Satan.

While they had been talking among themselves Esteban, the boy, had gone far off seeking stray lambs. Now Satan sought him out. "You heard the angel sing. Where is this City of David?"

"I know not."

"Who is this Messiah?"

"You speak of Matías?" The boy was stupid with fear. "You mean my mother's brother, a shepherd, wise and faithful? But he is ill. I tend his sheep."

"Idiot! Dolt! Fool!" The voice of Satan rose like a whirlwind. "In your great stupidness you sin against me, and that is more terrible than sinning against God. For this you die!"

The boy tried to open his mouth to shriek for mercy. Before words could come, before Satan's hand could smite him, there came between them, out of the vast spaces of the Universe, one who thrust a flaming sword between the Devil and the boy; while through the vast dome of Heaven rang a voice: "Thou shalt not take the innocent!"

It was the voice of the Archangel Michael. He stood now, all in shining armour, beside Esteban, he sword shielding him. And again he spoke: "How dare you break God's command!"

"I dare do more than that." Satan spoke with mockery. "God's Earth is no longer his but mine. My minions rule it. But tonight I shall fight you for it. I shall take it from you by right of sword and mightier hosts."

He stamped the ground. It split asunder, and from its very bowels came forth rank after rank of devils, waving their double-bladed swords forged in Hell's own fires. Then Michael thrust his sword aloft and behold a mighty stairway, even like Jacob's ladder, was built between Earth and Heaven. Down its shining way came rank on rank of the heavenly hosts. Across the sky rang the shout of "Combat!"

Then such a battle was fought between the armies of darkness and the armies of light as had not been waged since the beginning of all things. And Michael's sword pinioned Satan to the ground so that he could not rise; and Michael's hosts put Satan's to rout, so that the Earth's crust broke with them and they were swallowed in belching flames. And when the Earth was rid of them, Michael spoke to Satan: "You have asked of many this night who is the Saviour — the Messiah. I will answer you, defeated. He is God's Son, and Man's. He is Peace.

He is Love. He is one against whom your evil cannot prevail. For next to God he is supreme."

The face of Archangel Michael shone with the light of conquering Heaven, all goodness, all strength. And Satan, crawling to his feet, looked upon it and hated it. "I am conquered now. But wait another thousand years, two thousand!"

Meanwhile the boy Esteban watched. And with the crawling of Satan back to Hell, Michael commanded Esteban to lead the shepherds to Bethlehem that they might look upon the face of their Saviour, and worship him.

And as the boy joined the shepherds about their fires, there came the angel again, the third time; and with it was a multitude of the heavenly host, praising God and singing hallelujahs! While over all shone a star of a magnitude never seen by them before in all the heavens.

But of the many watching their flocks that night only a few heeded. These wrapped their cloaks about them and followed the boy Esteban. As they walked he pointed out the roadsides, guarded by rank on rank of angels in shining armour. But none saw them save the boy.

Yet a great joy welled up in each heart, so that every shepherd needs must raise his voice in song. Benito, the oldest, gave them words for the beginning:

> Yonder star
>> in the skies
> marks the manger
>> where He lies.

Then Andrés caught the air and gave them the second verse to sing:

> Joy and laughter,
>> song and mirth
> herald in
>> our Saviour's birth.

Miguel lifted his voice in a great swelling tumult of thanksgiving:

> Now good will
>> unto all men.
> Shout it, brothers,
>> shout again!

Carlos caught from him the song and threw it back to the others with gladness:

> Peace then be
>> among us all:

upon great nations
and on small!

It was Esteban who gave the words for the last, singing them down the end of the road, leading them to the stable opening:

Let each shepherd
raise his voice
till the whole world
shall rejoice;
till in one voice
all shall sing —
Glory to our
Saviour-King!

The star overhead lighted the way into the stable. Within they found a young woman, very fair, and on the straw beside her a small, new-born child. Benito spoke the questions that were in the minds of all: "What is thy name, woman?"

"They call me Mary."

"And his — the child's?"

"He is called Jesus."

Benito knelt. "*Nene Jesús* - Baby Jesus, the angels have sent us to worship thee. We bring what poor gifts are ours. Here is a young cockerel for thee." Benito laid it on the straw beside the child, then rose and called: "Andrés, it is thy turn."

Andrés knelt. "I, Andrés, bring thee a lamb." He put it with the cockerel, rose, and said: "Miguel, give thine."

Miguel knelt. "I bring thee a basket of figs, little one. Carlos, thy turn."

Carlos knelt and held out shepherd-pipes. "I have made them. Thou shalt play on them when thou art grown. Juan, what hast thou?"

Juan knelt. "Here is some cheese — good goats' cheese."

In turn they knelt, each shepherd, until all but Esteban, the boy, had given his gift. "Alas, *Nene Jesús,* I have little for thee. But here are the ribbons from my cap. Thou likest them, yes? And now I make a prayer: 'Bless all shepherds. Give us to teach others the love for all gentle and small things that is in our hearts. Give us to see thy star always on this, the night of thy birth. And keep our eyes lifted eternally to the far hills.'"

And having made the prayer, and all having given their gifts, the shepherds departed into the night, singing.

The Legend of the First
Christmas Tree

Elizabeth Goudge

There were trees in and about Bethlehem in those days. There were oleander, almond and quince trees in the gardens, vines and olives on the terraced hillsides, oak-trees, mulberries, figs and citrons. They did not grow thickly, there were no forests or tangled copses, they never hid the rocky hillsides, the far glimpse of the mountains or the great stretch of the sky, the strength of these things could always be seen through their leaves and branches, but they flung a veil of beauty over the harshness of the land and their bounty made to the people who lived there all the difference between death and life.

The gaunt old fir-tree up above them all on the hill where the sheep were folded watched them as spring passed to summer and summer to autumn. He rejoiced in the pink and white fruit blossom flung like spray against the blue sky, in the tender green of the new young mulberry leaves and the shimmering silver of the olives. He waved his arms in satisfaction when he saw the citrons hanging among their leaves like small golden suns, the rich clusters of the grapes, the mulberries and figs that would give food and drink to his people. For he always thought of the people of this country as *his* people, simply because he loved them. He had stood there high on the hillside, looking down on them all, for longer than anyone could remember. He knew all about them, for the people of Bethlehem loved to climb the hill and sit and talk to each other beneath his branches, and he would listen and remember all that they said. And when they were sad they would come and sit alone at his feet and he would hear their broken murmurs. And he would hear the shepherds talking, too, when they were taking care of the sheep. In this way he would learn not only about the personal joys and sorrows of his people but about all that happened to them as a nation. He would hear old men talking of the past history of Israel, and sometimes on Sabbath days he would hear the scholars among them repeating to each other the hallowed words of the Prophets and speaking in low soft voices of the Redeemer, he that should come, the Wonderful, the Councillor, the Prince of Peace. And sometimes he would hear one of the shepherd boys singing aloud the songs of the shepherd boy David, and that he liked the best of all, because in the loveliness of the words and the sweetness of the music he found great comfort for his grief.

For he suffered great grief because of his uselessness to the people he loved. Those other trees gave so much but he had neither fruit nor blossom, nothing but his fir-cones, which he sometimes dropped hopefully on the heads of his people, knowing them good to burn; but they seldom bothered to pick them up. He had not even beauty to delight his people for he was an ugly old tree, fantastically twisted by all the winter storms he had endured through all the years. He was no good to anyone, as far as he could see; except perhaps to the sheep who liked to rub themselves against him when they itched ... And perhaps very occasionally to those who sat by themselves among his twisted roots and to whom he murmured softly, opening to them the treasure of the wisdom of the trees.

But did they listen to it? They would sit very still, leaning back against his trunk with their eyes half shut against the sun, or leaning forward with their elbows on their knees and their chins in their hands, staring at the far blue distance, and he would tell them many things. But if they heard they gave no sign. Yet he persevered, never quite despairing, cradling them among his roots as he talked as a mother cradles her babe in her arms. All trees are wise, possessing a wisdom of a much higher order than man can attain to in this world, but fir-trees are wiser than all the others, and this fir-tree especially possessed a knowledge of good and evil that had come to him not only from his own lifetime of looking, listening and remembering, but from the wisdom of all his ancestors, stretching back and back to the first fir-tree of all, a very wise tree that had grown in the first garden of all, the one that the Lord God planted eastward of Eden and made so very fair.

That first fir-tree was not in the least like his descendants. He was the most beautiful tree in the garden. In spring his blossoms were lovelier than those of the almond, his leaves were pure silver like the olive, but larger, and shaped like hands placed palm to palm in prayer, and his fruit was of a brighter gold than that of the citron. It must have been of the wisdom and beauty of that first fir-tree that King Solomon was thinking when he said that a word fitly spoken is like apples of gold in

109

pictures of silver. But the Lord God had forbidden the man and woman who lived in the garden to eat those golden apples, for they were not yet ready for the wisdom of them. The fir-tree knew that and whenever they came near him he did his best to hide his golden apples under his silver leaves, lest those frail mortal creatures should be tempted by them. And he talked to them too, whispering softly and silverly when they sat at his feet cradled in his comfortable roots, explaining to them that being human beings and not gods they could not know evil unless they practised it, and so they must refrain from that knowledge and be content to know only good. Love God, he told them, be humble, obedient and contented children and all will be well with you. But they paid no attention to the fir-tree. They wanted to be arrogant gods, ordering other people about, instead of loving children humbly doing what they were told. And so they ate of the fruit of the tree.

It was not in the least the fir-tree's fault but he felt that it was. He was so grief-stricken that his heart broke within him and the sap dried up in his body. His golden fruit withered to hard brown cones and his silver leaves rolled up into tiny dry spears. He died of grief there in the garden, his cones tumbling to the ground ... But there were seeds in the cones and the birds and the winds carried them away from the garden and his children took root and grew up all over the world.

But they never again were beautiful as their ancestor had been in the first days. They grew upon bare hillsides, torn by winds and lightnings, wailing and lamenting for the sin of the world, bearing no life, neither flowers nor leaves nor fruit. But they retained their deep and heavenly wisdom and whenever they could they would gather men and women and children about them and tell them the things that they knew. These descendants of Adam and Eve paid no more attention than Adam and Eve had done, but they did come to have a special love for fir-trees, and in almost every country in the world there grew up an idea that if you had a fir-tree near your dwelling you were lucky ... They were such comforting trees. They never blew down in a storm or changed with the seasons. In them was no variableness or shadow of turning.

Everyone at Bethlehem felt like that about the fir-tree upon the hill. He did not know it. He was quite unaware that when things went wrong with them they came and curled themselves up among his roots, even as they were unaware that it was because he had chosen to share their sorrow and pain that they found him so satisfying, a sort of shadow of what they longed for.

A God who was eternal, unchangeable, and yet who at the same time shared all things with them, that was the paradox that they wanted, whether they knew it or not. And this was what the fir-tree wanted for them, longing for it with increasing passion and desperation as the years went by. He saw that it was the one thing that would save them. The love and obedience they had withheld in the garden they would perhaps give to a God like that. If this God could himself be obedient and loving, then, when they strove to be like him (for always it seemed that these ridiculous human creatures had to emulate God), they would not destroy themselves, as they had done in the garden, but save their souls alive. If this could only happen, thought the fir-tree, he believed that he would be so happy that his stiff needles would unfurl into silver leaves again and his hard brown cones turn into golden fruit. "The desert shall rejoice and blossom as the rose," he had heard them say, when they sat at his feet and talked of the coming of the Redeemer of Israel. Something like that, he was sure, would happen to him.

And it did. It was midwinter, with the sky swept bare of clouds and ablaze with those angelic stars which men believe sing as they sweep upon their way. But as yet they were too far away to be heard. The world was in profoundest quietness and night in the midst of her swift course. The shepherds were heavy-eyed that night and the fir-tree was awake, guarding the sheep for them. He did this very often, awaking them with a low warning murmur if any danger threatened. But nothing threatened tonight; indeed it seemed to the fir-tree that just for tonight the earth was swept as clear of evil as the sky of clouds, so that a deep serenity possessed him, from his topmost spike of needles down to his deepest root. A mighty love possessed him too, both for the stars blazing like great angels in the sky above him and for the weary men and beasts sleeping beneath his branches. He had a feeling that he would have liked to link the two together in love, to stretch up his arms to the sky and pull down the stars upon the earth.

"Glory to God in the highest and on earth peace." Who was singing? The fir-tree looked down at his feet, where little Reuben the shepherd boy, who so delighted him by singing the songs of David to the music of his pipe, was curled up like a dormouse among his roots ... But Reuben was fast asleep ... Besides, this was not one voice singing, it was many voices, and they were singing at a vast distance. Yet the music was drawing nearer, rising and dying away, then rising again more power- fully, like the ebb and flow of a great wind. But nothing stirred upon the earth and no wind that ever blew could sound those notes of breathtaking beauty, a beauty that shook the fir-tree from top to bottom yet left him with his serenity even deeper than before. "Arise, shine, for thy light is come, and the glory of the Lord is risen upon thee." It was the stars themselves that were singing, and they were coming down to earth. The fir-tree gave a great shout of triumph and held up his arms to them, and then the singing was sweeping over him in great waves of glorious sound and he was drenched and drowned in light, so blinded and deafened by glory that in his body all his senses died and for a little while it seemed that he ceased to be.

When he came to himself it was still and quiet again, the stars were once more back in the sky and the shepherds had gone. But he knew where they had gone, for during the time when he had seemed to cease to be he had been told good tidings of great joy ... Yes, they'd gone, and gone quickly, taking their gifts with them ... Yes, they'd gone — all except one — all except young Reuben — what ailed the child?

The fir-tree looked down at Reuben and Reuben looked up at the fir-tree, wide-eyed with delight, his cheeks scarlet and his mouth wide open, jigging on his toes and letting out a long shrill whistle of ecstasy as a small boy will when he is beside himself with pleasure at some astounding sight. The fir-tree could see the excited small boy as clearly as though a thousand candles were burning, and for a moment or two he was at a loss to know where the light was coming from. Then he saw that it was coming from himself. The stars, when they went back to their appointed places, had not withdrawn their gift of light. Every withered needle on him had become a leaf of silver and every hard dry cone a golden fruit. He stood there robed in light, glorious and beautiful as a young god in the dawning of the world.

"Take me!" he cried to Reuben. "Take me!" Would the child understand? They never did understand when he spoke to them. But Reuben did; he was young enough. He reached up and broke off the glowing branch that the fir-tree held out to him and raced off with it down the hill to Bethlehem. He ran so fast that he was not far behind the other shepherds, and when they had presented their gifts he knelt down and presented his. He stuck it upright in a pitcher beside the manger, all bright and glowing, and when the Baby saw it he laughed ... It was the first Christmas tree.

The next morning the fir-tree looked as usual, but he did not feel as usual, for all his grief had gone ... It had happened. The Lord God had visited and redeemed his people...He cried aloud in delight and stretched up his branches to the clear blue sky. "A hallowed day hath dawned upon us," he cried. "Come, ye nations, and worship the Lord; for on this day a great light hath descended upon the earth."

And besides his overwhelming joy in this great light he had his own private reason for happiness. He saw the future of the fir-trees, his children and descendants. They might stand hard and dry and gaunt upon their hillsides through the spring and summer and autumn, when other trees were giving their blossom and leaves and fruit, but when the December birthday of the Son of God came round once more, and other trees were stripped and bare, it was they who would keep watch beside the manger, robed in silver and gold, bringing joy to the hearts of little children and peace and good-will to men.

A Candle for Saint Bridget

A modern folk-tale

Ruth Sawyer

Here is a personal Christmas story. Yet it is pure folk-tale. It pulses with
the faith and the feeling of simple people; it has the background that is
indigenous to all folk-telling. It begins many years ago in Ireland; and
the words of old Michael Barron come back to me as I write: "Aye, it
takes more than a handful of years for a good tale to ripen."

I went to Ireland to follow the trail of folk and fairy lore, to search out
the best living storytellers from Malin Head to County Cork. That is how
I came to find Michael Barron in his cabin on the moors in Donegal. The
cabin was perched alone at the borderland where the moors stop and
the jagged, sea-hewn cliffs of the Ulster coast begin. East, west, north,
and south there wasn't another sign of life except the sea gulls and
mews, circling and screaming the lee long day.

Michael was among the last of the seanachies; by far the odlest, I had
been told, and the most knowledgeable. I found him on a day in
midsummer, sitting outside the cabin sunning himself. He was pulling at
any empty cuddy pipe for solace. He had not had tobacco to fill it since
spring. He seemed centuries old — a human being over whom time had
command no longer. His flesh had shrunken from his frame, and over it
the skin was as brown and wrinkled as one of our butternuts. His eyes
were of that pale opaque blue of extreme age; they held the childish
look of perpetual inquiry. His lips were shirred around the stem of his
pipe; from under his vagabond hat showed a thatch of colourless hair. I
never saw Michael without his hat and his pipe, indoors or out.

His greeting was characteristic of those who still speak Gaelic: "God
and Mary welcome ye. 'Tis a brave day." Then he took out his pipe,
sucked at the air a momet, and asked: "Might ye be the Wee One?"

Having settled the fact of my identity he called in a high, quavering voice: "John — Delia — both of ye come out and bring the childher. Here's the Wee One, the Yankee lass we've been expecting the lee long time."

John and Delia came — his grandchildren: and the "childher" who flocked outside with them were Michael's great-grandchildren. It took no keen scrutiny to disclose the poverty that hung on them. A brood of half a dozen, aerach-shinned children, barely nourished; a sickly, stooping man with a cough, the beaten look in his eyes; a woman gaunt as poverty, flat-breasted, as bleached as the corn in November, wearing a rag of a dress and no shoes; and last of all Michael himself, an old man living beyond his time and usefulness, taking a share of the scant food that might have gone into the stomachs of the children. All these housed in a two-room cabin bare of everything but the bones of necessity. Such were Michael Barrow and his kindred; yet I would travel the length and the breadth of Ireland today to find Michael Barron again.

The meal-chest was empty; the last pinch of tea had gone into the pot for breakfast, the last potatoes had been cooked that morning. This I learned afterwards. With that hospitality that acknowledges no defeat, Delia hung a fresh kettle over the hearth and set the pan warming against a baking of griddle bread. John and the oldest boy tramped to a cabin in the hollow a mile distant to ask the loan of tea and meal, and borrow a white egg from one of the hens, so that the stranger under their roof might not be sent away hungry.

That the lapse of time and the thin subterfuge might not be discovered, Michael Barron folded his hands with dignity and asked would I like to be hearing a tale, and would I like best to be hearing a *loidhe* about the Wandering of Oisin or a tale of the Blessed Saint Bridget?

I chose both. Whereupon, with a chuckle of delight, Michael whispered to Delia, who knelt at his side blowing the turf: "She has the right sense for listening to tales, and the heart, too. She might have Irish blood in her."

First he chanted the *loidhe* of Oisin. As I listened to those running minor cadences, rising, falling, in rhythmic perfection, I knew I was listening to a great traditional story-teller, one whose forebears had been bards at the court of the High King. His Gaelic was the purest I had ever heard, and afterwards Delia told me that a certain professor at Oxford had spent five successive summers there, brought a tent and camped out on the headlands above the sea, that he might be taught by the best Gaelic scholar in Ireland. "Aye, 'tis the truth," agreed Michael. "And what's more, Quiggan's grown to be a fair-to-middling scholar himself, the now."

We had the tale of Saint Bridget, then. The legend has been made immortal by Fiona Macleod in his* stories of Iona. But I heard it first from Michael Barron that day. Before he had finished John had returned from his borrowings and Delia had the griddle bread mixed and baking. The brown, sweet smell of it filled the cabin as Michael's last words came like a lilting chrous: "So 'twas the Blessed Saint Bridget who came back to Iona, gone in her own thinking while a throstle sang; and yet in Time's reckoning it made a year and day. 'Twas herself told the Druids of that first Christmas and fetched the message of peace on earth. And she had the proof of what she was telling in the shawl she wore about her shoulders and in which she had cradled the wee Lord. For every thread in it was turned to gold, and the pattern of the weaving made the creatures in the byre at Bethlehem — ox and ass and lamb."

There was gooseberry jam to eat with the griddle bread, and tea long-steeped, black and bitter as sloe. The family made merry, as if the meal-chest were not empty and the food on the table borrowed. I had two half-crowns with me and slipped them into the fist of the "wee-est one" fast asleep in her cradle. On the way back I remember I made a special prayer to Saint Bridget that Delia would find the money before the baby woke and swallowed it. When I reached the little town on the hill's end I sent back the fillings for Michael's pipe by Mickey the postboy.

After that I came often to the cabin. Always Michael was ready with a new tale, or could be coaxed into telling again a favourite. Poverty no longer stalked the cabin; instead wonder came, and laughter, and we walked together the highway of good fellowship, whereon all walk who have known the sharing of good tales. Often at day's ending Michael would chuckle with delight and say: "Now ye have something to put in your head and fetch home with ye." And once he spoke plaintively: "If ye could write them down, the now, there'd be plenty of lads and lasses across the water thinking long for Ireland and the old tales. They'd be homesick, just, to be hearing them."

Next to telling stories Michael Barron liked to be telling about his grandchild Cassie, sister to Delia. She had gone to America, married a good man there, had two bonny children, and, like as not, would be bringing them back to Donegal a summer soon. Michael showed with

* Fiona Macleod was the pseudonym of William Sharpe.

pride Cassie's picture — a cheap, glazed photograph. But its lack of all art could not hide Cassie's Irish beauty, or the health and charm of the children. "Aye, they be's doing grand," was Michael Barron's comment.

I sailed late in October. The last person I went to see was Michael. He was watching for me from outside the cabin, even though the day was bitterly cold. Delia had wrapped him in an old quilt and a homespun shawl so that only his hat and pipe showed. I had not breasted the hill, however, before he saw me coming and was on his feet, waving me a welcome: "Sure, wasn't I telling Delia, just, ye'd be back for one more visit, to drink a last cup of tea and hear a last tale. Wasn't I telling Delia that!" He was like a child transported with delight, a child who can throw care and the morrow to the four winds and live in the contentment of today.

We gathered about the turf, our eyes red with the smoke from it, our hearts free as birds. Mickey the postboy dropped in bringing currants to bake in the griddle bread, and a pat of butter to spread thickly on it. We had not one story but many, and sat far into candle-time. And the last tale of all was the one about Saint Bridget. Delia sat with her foot on the cradle keeping the "wee-est one" hushed, while Michael took us over the hills again to Bethlehem. He brought us to the byre with its rude stalls; he showed us the crib with the hay filling it and the Babe asleep on it. He showed us Bridget gathering the Wee Lord to her breast, and he made us hear the first cradle-song croned for him. A few times, from far off, I have glimpsed Bethlehem; but never before nor since have I ever entered there.

Michael's last words still ring down the years: "Ye'll mind to find my Cassie — no matter whatever else ye fail to do. Tell her ye've seen Delia and the childher, and they be's doing grand. Tell her ye've seen her grandda, and he be's braver than anyone. Tell her that; and God and Mary go with ye."

When I sailed from Londonderry, Mickey the postboy sailed steerage. He was coming to America to find his fortune as many an Irish lad before him had done. I saw him on board several times, and just before landing I marked his eyes, already full of homesickness. He clung to me feverishly. "I might be coming soon to see ye. Maybe ye'd be a bit lonesome yourself for an Irish face."

I agreed that it was more than probable. But Mickey did not come. I made one attempt to find Cassie. At the address that Michael had given me, the janitor told me she had moved away more than a year before. He referred me to possible neighbours who might know where she had gone, and to the corner grocer. After one or two more inquiries I gave up.

And this brings us to Christmas Eve of that year. I was very tired. The bed was strewn with packages, ribbon, seals, and there were half a dozen more packages to tie. Two gold pieces, one for our old Negro laundress, one for Ole Jensen, our janitor, lay on the corner of the bureau. I was wondering how to wrap them up when the telephone rang. The hallboy below reported a person to see me who would give no name but appeared "kinda hurried and nervous." A moment later Mickey the postboy stood on the threshold.

He was blue with cold; he twirled his cap uncomfortably. I asked him in but he shook his head. The gander had his tongue, as the Irish say. So I spoke: "Merry Christmas, Mickey. Like New York?"

He fumbled for his words: "Tisn't so good a Christmas — not for Michael Barron's Cassie. Ye mind Cassie?" His face was troubled; there was a gentle accusation in it, too, as if I should have found out Cassie for myself and not left it wholly to him.

"I looked for her." It was a lame excuse. "What is it, Mickey?"

"She be's in trouble, aye heavy trouble. Ye'll go with me to her the night." It was a command. I turned at the door to get my things when his voice halted me: "If ye've got some silver — a bit of money would come in mortal handy."

It was a bitter night. Mickey and I took the old elevated for the Battery. On the train he told me something of his search for Cassie. It had been fruitless until that day. He had gone into the Little Church of Saint Anthony early, to pray, and caught the half-glimpse of a face under a shawl that looked like Cassie. She had slipped out ahead of him but he followed, trailed her to a tenement, saw her go in. Then he waited, saw her come out again, hesitated this time, and lost her. He went back to the tenement and talked with her neighbour across the hall. Michael's own telling of what he heard was brief enough: "Her man's dead — dead a year. The long illness has eaten up their savings. She is after working now in a factory making skirts, paying the neighbour a shilling a day to look after the childher. But she can't earn enough to keep the wolf from the door. Back rent to pay and naught left for food or fixings. That's how it is. Fighting the wolf off and the wolf getting in at last."

We walked half a dozen blocks and turned into a smear of a street. The tenement sagged and smelled even in that clear, frosty air. A foul and dingy flare of gas lighted the hallways below. There were four flights to climb and Michael stumbled ahead, reached the top, and was knocking at a door before I had reached the end of the last flight.

The door opened. There stood Cassie in her black dress, a black shawl tight around her, her face gone white, a candle-end in her hand. I can still see the room behind her, ill lit as it was, and the red rings about her eyes from long crying. Mickey need not have told, nor the neighbour, of the sorrow and trouble that had come to Cassie; it was all written plainly in her face for the whole world to read. She looked out blankly into the dark hall at the two of us there. And then we saw her face lighten; there was a sharp expectancy in her voice: "Could it be someone from home — someone from the old country?" she asked.

She took a quick step, holding the candle closer to us. The flame barely grazed Mickey's nose. She gave her breath a sudden intake, her words came in an awed whisper: "Holy God, if it isn't Wullie O'Neills Mickey!" She leaned against the doorjamb to steady herself, while her voice took on strength: "Lar — lad — where did ye drop from this bitter night?"

Mickey pulled her into the room and I followed. His words ran together like huddling sheep. He explained himself; he explained me. He spoke messages from all in Donegal. And last of all he spoke of Michael Barron. "Your grandda's doing brave. She'll tell ye," and his thumb waggled at me. "She'll tell ye how the lee long summer she's been a-listening to Michael Barron's telling of tales, as brave a seanachie as ever he was. She'll tell ye that the tales are as thick on his tongue as ripe gooseberries on their bush." And he turned to me with impatience. "Aye, speak up — tell Cassie the words her heart's a-hungering to hear."

And then a Barron of County Donegal spoke: "Ye'll be after stopping a having first a sup o'tea." Cassie's hand, the one that did not hold the candle, closed over mine and drew me to the table. "Bless ye for coming, the both of ye; bless ye for coming this night."

The room we had entered was the kitchen. Cassie lifted an empty kettle off a cold stove and went out again. She crossed the hall; we heard her knocking at a neighbour's door. Mickey and I avoided each other's eyes. Irish hospitality held here in a New York tenement even as it held beyond on the moorland overlooking the sea; and again a grandchild of Michael Barron had gone out to borrow food that the stranger within the door might be fed.

Neither Mickey nor I spoke. Our eyes searched every corner of the room for the poverty written there. No heat of any sort in the small flat. No gas. A deal table, two wooden-bottom chairs, a highchair, a few dishes in the corner cupboard. No sign of food anywhere. Across the room was stretched a line and on it hung a few garments, pitifully revealing: two thin little cotton shirts, two small pairs of black cotton stockings, well darned, a faded pink print dress, a well-washed pair of tiny blue cotton pants and the blue jumper that went with it.

Mickey spoke first, there was amazement in his voice: "I never went into a cabin in Ireland so bare. And not so much as a crumb left in the cupboard! Ye can see for yourself that the stove's as cold as a gander's nose. Aye, 'tis all true as the neighbour-woman said."

"There's a grocery store open at the corner." I took out "the bit of silver" Mickey had reminded me to bring and shoved it across the table to him. He put it in his pocket as Cassie returned. She brought in a steaming kettle; the other hand held a tray with sliced bread, a cup holding dry tea, a half-filled jar of jam, and a small end of butter. "The good tea. I'll have ye warm in a minute."

She steeped the tea. She spread the bread with butter and jam, and served us and then herself and worked to put a bit of merriment in all she did. "Now tell me — tell me all! Does Grandda look himself — does he still step out brave as any buchail across the moor? Is Delia as clever at making griddle bread? I mind the way it would taste with currants in it!"

And so I told of the summer, poured into her heart that for which she had hungered so long. She drank her tea but she ate no bread. Was she saving it for the morrow? Was she hoping to make a Christmas feast for the children out of it? Mickey pushed back his cup first and stood up. "Cassie, are ye minding that Saint Stephen's Day is coming, when the Wran Boys will be coming round in Ireland? And it's bad luck at every door that doesn't be opening to them, on every house that has nothing to offer them. Come on, lass, we'll be going out to see what can we find for the Wran Boys."

It was Mickey's way of saying celebration was at hand. The Wran Boys for Ireland are what the waits are in England; they go from door to door chanting their Song of the Wran and demanding hospitality. Cassie went without protest. I listened to their feet stumbling down the

dark stairs. It was rare good fortune that Cassie lived in a neighbourhood where immediate necessity was the watchword and where shop-
doors stood open to serve the eleventh-hour customer. I had said
nothing to Mickey about toys for the children; but I counted on his
training as postboy to meet all emergencies. Thinking of the children, I
opened the second door leading out of the kitchen and found them.

It was a small, dimly lighted bedroom, cold as Greenland. The light
came from one half-burned candle; but I paid it no attention then. The
two children were in one crib, curled up like kittens to keep warm. The
empty cot beside the crib was stripped of all covers; everything had
been put over the children, tucked snugly in to keep out the cold. I
looked and wondered what Cassie had expected to do that night — no
fire to sit by, no bed with covering to it.

Two piles of nondescript little garments were folded neatly on two
small chairs. Two stubbed-out pairs of small shoes stood, to to toe,
beside the chairs. And then I turned my attention to the candle; I
wanted to see better the faces of the sleeping children. I started to pick it
up and stopped, for the candle wasn't just a candle. It was a small,
flickering shaft of prayer — a petition burning through the bitter night to
the All-Seeing Eyes, the All-Hearing Ears. I stooped to look closer at the
plaster figure before which it stood. It was Saint Bridget.

Hard as I looked at Cassie's children, I could see no marking of
misery on their faces. By some miracle of motherhood she had kept
them strong, happy. Their cheeks were rounded, pink as thorn-bloom.
Their lips curved to half-smiles. There were no hollows under their eyes.
I knew if those fast-shuttered lids should lift I would see deep Irish eyes,
blue as cornflowers. They were bonny children, as Michael Barron had
said.

I took the candle back to Saint Bridget. I took one shoe of each pair
and in them I put the gold pieces meant for Ole Jensen and our Negro
laundress. Cheques would do very well for them. I put the shoes, toe to
toe, on the chest beside Saint Bridget. The gift was hers — not mine.

Cassie, Mickey, and the grocery boy made gayer entrance than
Mickey and I had made. They were laden to the ears: coal, kindling,
food, bundles. While Mickey laid and kindled the fire, Cassie and I put
boxes and paper bags neatly in the cupboard. She sorted the bundles,
leaving some to open on the table. And all the while we worked Cassie's
lips sang little words of thanksgiving: "The good meal. The good butter
and bread. The meat. The good milk. Food for today. Food for

tomorrow. Aye, feel the good fire. The stove will be full and roaring this many a day!"

It was a miracle what that stove did for all of us and the room. Our tongues loosened. Security came in, unseen, and took her place at the table. The little garments on the line looked less pitiful. Cassie set the kettle again — for more tea. "We'll toast the bread, brown." Mickey found a jar of gooseberry jam on a top shelf and climbed a ladder to get it. "We'll be having that." She laughed liltingly this time, as if joy, long banished, had come back.

Cassie opened the bundles on the table slowly, as if removal of twine and paper was a sacrament. Each thing she held up for us to see. "The good wool! I'll be knitting sweaters for them to wear under their thin coats. Feel the good flannel. There is enough for two dresses for Maggie and two little suits for Tim. Stockings — six pairs of them. Mittens! Warm woollen caps to pull over their wee ears. The last time I had them out they cried with the frost in them."

Her arms dropped across the table; her eyes took in the wealth they guarded. I opened the toys, Mickey the candy and a few ornaments for a tiny tree. While we trimmed it Cassie set the table afresh. We sat long, planning a better future for Cassie and the children. Under the glow of promise and the warming cheer of the fire Cassie's face lost much of its load of care and grew unbelievably young and fair again. She was all for tossing our cups and reading the fortune in the tea leaves when the bells of the Little Church of Saint Anthony rang out for the midnight Mass. We stood and bowed our heads as the Christmas Day rang in. Cassie tiptoed to the bedroom door and opened it, and beckoned us to the threshold. She pointed to the crib and then to the candle guttering in its holder.

"Ye mind the tale? Like as not Grandda told ye. I was telling the childher it again the night and Maggie said: 'If we light a candle to Saint Bridget, will she find her way to us as she did to the wee Lord?' " Cassie flung a hand across her eyes. Tears were running fast now that trouble was lifted. "Faith, the candle's done for. It's lighted her way — straight."

I can see Cassie's face still, as she stood at the head of the stairs, lighting us down. We were almost at the bottom when her farewell came: "When ye write home to Grandda, tell him we're doing brave. God and Mary go with ye!"

The Christmas Night

The Wee Christmas Cabin of Carn-na-ween

They tell it still in Ireland

Ruth Sawyer

A hundred years ago and more, on a stretch of road that runs from the town of Donegal to Killybegs and the sea, a drove of tinkers went their way of mending pots and thieving lambs. Having a child too many for the caravan they left it, new-born, upon a cabin doorsill in Carn-na-ween.

The cabin belonged to Bridget and Conal Hegarty. Now these two had little wish for another child, having childher aplenty of their own; but they could not leave the wee thing to die at their door, nor had they a mind to throw it into the turf-pit. So Bridget suckled it with her own wean; she divided the cradle between them. And in time she came to love it as her own and fought its battles when the neighbours would have cursed it for a tinker's child.

I am forgetting to tell you that the child was a girl and Bridget named her Oona. She grew into the prettiest, the gentlest-mannered lass in all the county. Bridget did her best to get the lads to court her, forever pointing out how clever she was with her needle, how sweet her voice when she lilted an air, the sure way she had of making bannock, broth, or jam.

But the lads would have none of her. Marry a tinker's child? Never! Their feet might be itching to take her to a cross-road's dance, their arms hungering to be holding her, but they kept the width of a cabin or the road always between her and them. Aye, there was never a chance came to Oona to marry and have childher of her own, or a cabin she could call hers.

All of Bridget's and Conal's lasses married; but Oona stayed on to mind the house for them, to care for them through their sicknesses, to help them gently into their graves. I think from the beginning Oona had a dream — a dream that, having cared lovingly for the old, someone would be leaving her at long last a cabin for her own keeping. Bridget, before she died, broke the dream at its beginning. "The cabin goes to Michael," she said. "He and his young wife will not be wanting ye, I'm thinking. Go to the chest and take your share of the linen. Who knows but some man, losing his wife, will be glad to take ye for his second. I'd not have ye going empty-handed to him."

Oona held fast to the dream; she let neither years nor heart-aches shatter it. There was always a cabin waiting to welcome her as soon as another had finished with her. From the time when Oona left the Hegarty cabin, a bonny lass still, with strength to her body and laughter in her eyes, to the time when she was put out of the MacManuses', old and with little work left in her, the tale runs thin as gossamer. But if you are knowing Ireland and the people of Donegal it is not hard to follow the tinker's child through that running of years.

From cabin to cabin, wherever trouble or need abided, there went Oona. In a cabin where the mother was young, ailing, with her first-born, there you would find Oona caring for the child as it had been her own. In a cabin where the childher had grown and gone dandering off to Belfast, Dublin, or America and left the old ones behind, there she tended them as she would have tended her own had she ever known them. In a cabin where a man had lost his wife and was ill-fitted to mind the house and the weans alone — aye, here she was the happiest. She would be after taking over the brood as a mother would, gentling the hurt that death had left behind, and for herself building afresh the dream.

But her birth betrayed her at every turn of the road. No man trusted her to be his first or second wife. Not one of the many she served and loved guessed of the hunger that grew with the years for a cabin she could call hers. All blessed her name while she lived; and for the hundred years since she has been gone from Carn-na-ween the tales about her have been kept green with loving memory. Those she served saw that she never went empty-handed away. So to Bridget Hegarty's linen was added a griddle, pans, kettles, crocks, creels, and dishes.

Each thing she chose from the cabin she was leaving was something needed to make the home she dreamed of gay and hold comfort. As the years went by, the bundle of her possessions grew, even as she dwindled. Men, women, and childher who passed her on the road at such times as she might be changing cabins would stop to blather with her. Pointing to the size of her bundle they would say: "'Tis twice your size, the now. Ye'll have to be asking for oxen and a cart to fetch it away from the next cabin." And they would laugh. Or they would say: "Ye might be asking the Marquis to build ye a castle next his own. Ye'll be needing a fair-sized place to keep all ye've been gathering these many years."

Always she would blather back at them. For all her dream was dimming she was never one to get down-daunted. "Ye can never be telling," she would say, "I may yet be having a wee cabin of my own some day. I'm not saying how and I'm not saying when." And she would nod her head in a wise, knowledgeable way, as if she could look down the nose of the future and see what was there.

She was in the cabin of the MacManuses' when the great famine came. The corn in the fields blighted; the potatoes rotted in the ground. There was neither food for man nor fodder for beast. Babies starved at their mothers' breasts, strong men grew weak as childher, dragging themselves into the fields to gnaw at the blistered grass and die under a cruel, drouthing sun. Everywhere could be heard the crying of childher and the keening for the dead. At the beginning neighbour shared with neighbour until death stalked them. Then it was every cabin for itself, and many a man sat all night, fowling-piece across his knee, to keep guard over a last cow in the byre or the last measure of meal in the bin.

So old had Oona grown by famine-time that the neighbours had lost all count of her years. She moved slowly on unsteady feet. Her eyes were dulled; her speech was seldom coming now. But for all that she was worth the sheltering and the scanty food she ate. She milked, she churned, she helped the oldest lad carry the creel to the bog, she helped at the cutting of the turf. So long as there was food enough for them the MacManuses kept her and blessed the Virgin for another pair of hands to work.

But famine can put stones in the place of human hearts, and hunger can make tongues bitter. As the winter drew in, Oona for all her dullness saw the childher watching every morsel of food she put to her lips. She heard the mother's tongue sharpen as she counted out the spoonfuls of stir-about that went into the bowls. Harvest had come and gone, and there was no harvest. The cold, cruel winds of December rattled at their doors and windows. Of one thing only was there enough: there was always turf in the bog to cut, to dry, to keep the hearth warm.

The childher in the cabin cried from cock-crow till candletime. Oona wished her ears had been as dulled as her eyes. But for all that she closed her heart to the crying, telling herself she had earned what little food she took, and the good heat for her old body. But a night came when she could stand the crying no longer, when the spoon scraped the bottom of the meal-bin, when the last of the praties had been eaten, their skins with them.

Saying never a word she got up at last from the creepie where she had been thawing her bones and started to put together again her things into her bundle. The MacManuses watched her, and never a word said they. The corners of the great cloth were tied at last. Over her bent shoulders Oona laid her shawl. The cabin was quiet the now, the childher having cried themselves asleep with hunger. Oona dragged her bundle to the door; as she lifted the latch she spoke:

"Ye can fend for yourselves. Ye'll not want me the now."

"Aye, 'tis God's truth." It was the wife who said it.

Timothy MacManus reached for her hand: "Hush, are ye not remembering what night it is?"

"Aye, 'tis Christmas Eve. What matter? There be's not sense enough left in the old one's mind to know it. And in times such as these there is naught to put one night ahead of another."

"'Twill be a curse on us, the same, if we let her go."

"'Twill be a curse on her if she stays."

"God and Mary stay with ye, this night," Oona called, going out the door.

"God and Mary go with ye," the two mumbled back at her.

Outside Oona lifted the bundle to her back. How she had strength for this I cannot be telling you. It often comes, a strange and great strength, to those who have borne much and have need to bear more. Oona took the road leading to Killybegs and the sea. A light snow was falling and the wind had dropped to a low whispering. As she went down the village street she stopped to glimpse each cabin and the lighted room within. Hardly a cabin but she had lived in; hardly a face but she had read long and deeply over many years. Her lips made a blessing and a farewell for every door she passed.

All cabins were left behind as the road grew steeper. She climbed with a prayer on her lips — what prayer I do not know, but it lightened the load she carried on her back and in her heart, it smoothed the roughness of her going. She came at last to the bogland. It stretched on and on beyond the reach of eye, even in the daylight. In the dark she sensed only a levelling off, where feet could rest. She stumbled from the road and found shelter under a blackthorn which grew on the fringe of the bog.

"I like it here," she said as she eased the bundle from her back. "Always, I have liked it here. Many's the time I have said: some day I will take the whole of it and climb the hill and sit under this very thorn, the way I'll be feeling the wind from the sea and watching the sun set on it, and the stars lighting it; and, mayhap, hearing the sound of fairy pipes. I never came; I never had the day whole."

She said it in a kind of wonder. She was safe here from the reach of neighbours. It was in her heart that she could never again bear to have man or woman offer her food needed for young mouths. Too many times she had folded tired hands; too many times she had shut weary eyes, not to know what a gentle companioning death could give the old at the end. "'Tis a friend, he is, that I have known long. 'Tis as a friend he will be coming, calling softly, wishfully: 'Come, Oona!'"

After that her head grew light. She lost all count of time; she lost all track of space. She felt no cold, no tiredness. She could gather years into her mind as cards into the hand, shuffle them about and draw out the ones she liked best. She remembered suddenly that one of the reasons for wanting to climb the hill was to find the fairy rath that lay somewhere along the bog. Conall of a Thousand Songs had slept a Midsummer Night with his head to this rath and had wakened in the morning with it filled full of fairy music — music of enchantment. Wully Donoghue had crossed the rath late one May Eve and caught the fairy host riding abroad. Many a time, herself, she had put a piggin of milk with a bowl of stirabout on the back steps of those cabins she had lived in, remembering how well the Gentle People liked milk and stirabout. Aye, the Gentle People, the Good People! She hoped famine had not touched them. It would be a sorry thing to have the fairy folk starved off the earth.

She slept a little, woke, and slept again. Above the sleeping her mind moved on a slow current. Snow had covered her, warm. This was Christmas Eve, the time of the year when no one should go hungry, no one cold. It would be a white Christmas on the morrow, and the people of Donegal had a saying that when a white Christmas came the Gentle People left their raths and trooped abroad to see the wonder of it. Aye, that was a good saying. They would make good company for a lonely old woman.

Her legs were cramping under her. She strove to move them, and as she did so she had a strange feeling that she had knocked something over. Her old eyes peered into the darkness, her hand groped for whatever it was she had upset. To her amazement when she held her hand under her eyes there was a fairy man, not a hand high. His wee face was puckered with worry. "Don't ye be afeard, wee man," she clucked to him. "I didn't know ye were after being where ye were. Was there anything at all ye were wanting?"

"Aye, we were wanting ye."

"Me!"

"None else. Look!"

And then she saw the ground about her covered with hundreds upon hundreds of Gentle People, their faces no bigger round than buttons, all raised to hers, all laughing.

"What might ye be laughing at?" she asked. "Tell me, for it be's a lee long time since I had laughter on my own lips."

"We are laughing at ye, tinker's child. Living a lifetime in other folks' cabins, serving and nursing and mothering and loving, and never a cabin or kin ye could call your own."

"Aye," she sighed, "aye, 'tis the truth."

"'Tis no longer the truth. Bide where ye be, Oona Hegarty, and sleep the while."

She did as she was bidden but sleep was as thin as the snow which covered her, breaking through in this place and that, so that she might see through it what was going on about her. Hither and yon the Good People were hurrying. They brought stones, they brought turf. They laid a roof-tree and thatched it. They built a chimney and put in windows. They hung a door at the front and a door at the back. As they worked they sang, and the song they made drifted into Oona's sleep and stayed with her:

> 'Tis a snug Christmas cabin we're building the night,
>   That we're building the night.
> The stones make the walls and the turf chinks it tight,
>   Aye, the turf chinks it tight.
> There'll be thatch for the roof to keep wind out and rain,
>   To keep wind out and rain.
> And a fire on the hearth to burn out all pain,
>   Aye, burn out all pain.

The meal in the chest will stand up to your chin,
　　Well up to your chin;
There'll be Christmas without, and Christmas within,
　　Always Christmas within.
There'll be plenty of currants, and sugar, and tea,
　　Aye, plenty of tea;
With the chintz at the windows as gay as can be,
　　All as gay as can be.

There was more to the song. It went on and on, and Oona could not tell where the song ended and the dream began, so closely woven were the two together. She felt of a sudden a small, tweaking hand on her skirt and heard a shrill voice piping: "Wake up — wake up, Oona Hegarty!"

"'Tis awake I am, entirely," said Oona, sitting up and rubbing her eyes. "Awake and dreaming at the same time, just."

"We'll be after fetching in your bundle, then; and all things shall find their rightful places at last."

Ten hundred fairy men lifted the bundle and bore it inside, with Oona following. She drew her breath through puckered lips; she let it out again in sighs of wonderment. "Is everything to your liking, ma'am?" inquired the fairy man she had knocked over.

She made the answer as she looked about her: "The bed's where it should be. The chintz now — I had a mind to have it green, with a touch of the sun and a touch of the flaming turf in it. The dresser is convenient high. Wait till I have my bundle undone and the treasures of a lifetime put away."

The Gentle People scuttled about helping her, putting the linen in the fine oak chest, the dishes on the dresser. The kettle was hung above the hearth, the creepie put beside it. The rug spread along the bedside and the griddle left standing by the fire, ready. All things in their right places, as the tinker's child had dreamed them.

"Is it all to your liking?" shouted the Gentle People together.

"Aye, 'tis that and more. Crocks and creels where they do belong. The fine, strong spoon to be hanging there, ready to stir the griddle-bread. The knife with the sharp edge to it, to be cutting it." She turned and looked down at the floor, at the hundreds of wee men crowding her feet: "I'm not asking why ye have done this thing for me this night. But I ask one thing more. On every white Christmas let you be bringing folk to my door — old ones not needed longer by others, children crying for their mother — a lad or a lass for whom life has gone amiss. Fetch them that I may warm them by the hearth and comfort them."

"We will do that, tinker's child; we will do that!" The voices of the Gentle People drifted away from her like a wind dying over the bog: it was there — it was gone. A great sleep took Oona Hegarty so that her eyes could stay open no longer. She put herself down on the out-shot bed. She pulled the warm blanket over her and drew the chintz curtains.

The next night — Christmas — hunger drove Maggie, the middle child of the MacManuses', out of their cabin. She went like a wee wild thing, knowing only the hunger-pain she bore and the need of staying it. Blindly she climbed the hill to the bogland. Weak and stumbling she was, whimpering like a poor, hurt creature. She stumbled off the road, she stumbled over the sudden rise on the bog which nearly laid her flat. Rubbing her eyes she looked up at a wee cabin standing where no cabin had ever been. Through the windows came a welcoming light. In wonderment she lifted the latch and went in.

"Come in, Maggie, I've been looking for ye, the lee long day." It was Oona's voice that spoke to her; aye, but what a changed Oona! She knelt by the hearth turning the griddle-bread, her eyes as blue as fairy-thimbles, her hair the colour of ripened corn. There were praties boiling in the kettle, tea making on the hearth. Enough to eat and to spare. But that was not what filled the child's eyes with wonder. It was Oona herself, grown young, with the look of a young bride on her. "Take the creepie." Her voice had the low, soft calling of a throstle to its young. "Ye'll be after eating your fill, Maggie, and not knowing hunger again for many a day."

And it's the truth I am telling. Maggie went back and told; but although half of Carn-na-ween hunted the cabin throughout the year none found it. Not until a white Christmas again came round. Then old Seumus MacIntyre the cobbler died, leaving his widow Molly poor and none to keep her. They were coming to fetch her to the workhouse that Christmas Eve when she took the road climbing to Killybegs and the sea, and was never seen again.

And so the tales run. There are enough to be filling a book, but why should I go on with them? You can be after telling them to yourselves. This I know: given a white Christmas this year the wee fairy cabin of Carn-na-ween will be having its latch lifted through the night by the lone and the lost and the heart-broken. Aye, Oona Hegarty, the tinker's child, will be keeping the griddle hot, the kettle full, and her arms wide to the childher of half the world this night — if it be's a white Christmas.

Schnitzle, Schnotzle, and Schnootzle

From the Austrian Tirol

Ruth Sawyer

The Tirol straddles the Alps and reaches one hand into Italy and another into Austria. There are more mountains in the Tirol than you can count and every Alp has its story.

Long ago, some say on the Brenner-Alp, some say on the Mitterwald-Alp, there lived the king of all the goblins of the Tirol, and his name was Laurin. King Laurin. His kingdom was under the earth, and all the gold and silver of the mountains he owned. He had a daughter, very young and very lovely, not at all like her father, who had a bulbous nose, big ears, and a squat figure, and looked as old as the mountains. She loved flowers and was sad that none grew inside her father's kingdom.

"I want a garden of roses — red roses, pink roses, blush roses, flame roses, shell roses, roses like the sunrise and the sunset." This she said one day to her father. And the king laughed and said she should have just such a garden. They would roof it with crystal, so that the sun would pour into the depths of the kingdom and make the roses grow lovely and fragrant. The garden was planted and every rare and exquisite rose bloomed in it. And so much colour they spread upwards on the mountains around that the snow caught it and the mortals living in the valley pointed at it with wonder. "What is it makes our Alps so rosy, so glowing?" they asked. And they spoke of it ever after as the alpen-glow.

I have told you this that you might know what kind of goblin King Laurin was. He was merry, and he liked to play pranks and have fun. He liked to go abroad into the valleys where the mortals lived, or pop into a herdsman's hut half-way up the mountain. There were men who said they had seen him — that small squat figure with a bulbous nose and big ears — gambolling with the goats on a summer day. And now I begin my story. It is an old one that Tirolese mothers like to tell their children.

Long ago there lived in one of the valleys a very poor cobbler indeed. His wife had died and left him with three children, little boys, all of them — Fritzl, Franzl, and Hansl. They lived in a hut so small there was only one room in it, and in that was the cobbler's bench, a hearth for cooking, a big bed full of straw, and on the wall racks for a few dishes, and, of course, there was a table with a settle and some stools. They needed few dishes or pans, for there was never much to cook or eat. Sometimes the cobbler would mend the Sunday shoes of a farmer, and then there was good goats' milk to drink. Sometimes he would mend the holiday shoes of the baker, and then there was the good long crusty loaf of bread to eat. And sometimes he mended the shoes of the butcher, and then there was the good stew, cooked with meat in the pot, and noodles, leeks and herbs. When the cobbler gathered the little boys around the table and they had said their grace, he would laugh and clap his hands and sometimes even dance. "Ha-ha!" he would shout. "Today we have the good ... what? Ah-h ... today we eat ... Schnitzle, Schnotzle, and Schnootzle!"

With that he would swing the kettle off the hook and fill every bowl brimming full, and Fritzl, Franzl, and Hansl would eat until they had enough. Ach, those were the good days — the days of having Schnitzle, Schnotzle, and Schnootzle. Of course, the cobbler was making up nonsense and nothing else, but the stew tasted so much better because of the nonsense.

Now a year came, with every month following his brother on leaden feet. The little boys and the cobbler heard the month of March tramp out and April tramp in. They heard June tramp out and July tramp in. And every month marched heavier than his brother. And that was because war was among them again. War, with workers taking up their guns and leaving mothers and children to care for themselves as best they could; and there was scant to pay even a poor cobbler for mending shoes. The whole village shuffled to church with the soles flapping and the heels lopsided, and the eyelets and buttons and straps quite gone.

Summer — that was not so bad. But winter came and covered up the good earth, and gone were the roots, the berries, the sorrel, and the corn. The tramp of November going out and December coming in was very loud indeed. The little boys were quite sure that the two months shook the hut as they passed each other on the mountainside.

As Christmas grew near, the little boys began to wonder if there would be any feast for them, if there would be the good father dancing about the room and laughing "Ha-ha," and singing "Ho-ho," and saying: "Now, this being Christmas Day we have the good ... what?" And this time the little boys knew that they would never wait for their father to say it; they would shout themselves: "We know — it is the good Schnitzle, Schnotzle, and Schnootzle!" Ach, how very long it was since their father had mended shoes for the butcher! Surely — surely — there would be need soon again, with Christmas so near.

At last came the Eve of Christmas. The little boys climbed along the beginnings of the Brenner-Alp, looking for faggots. The trees had shed so little that year; every branch was green and grew fast to its tree, so few twigs had snapped, so little was there of dead, dried brush to fill their arms.

Their father came in when they had a small fire started, blowing his whiskers free of icicles, slapping his arms about his big body, trying to put warmth back into it. "Na-na, nobody will have a shoe mended today. I have asked everyone. Still there is good news. The soldiers are marching into the village. The inn is full. They will have boots that need mending, those soldiers. You will see." He pinched a cheek of each little boy; he winked at them and nodded his head. "You shall see — tonight I will come home with ... what?"

"Schnitzle, Schnotzle, and Schnootzle," they shouted together, those three.

So happy they were they forgot there was nothing to eat for supper — not a crust, not a slice of cold porridge-pudding, not the smallest sup of goats' milk. "Will the soldiers have money to pay you?" asked Fritzl, the oldest.

"Not the soldiers, perhaps, but the captains. There might even be a general. I will mend the boots of the soldiers for nothing, for after all what day is coming tomorrow! They fight for us, those soldiers; we mend for them, ja? But a general — he will have plenty of money."

The boys stood about while their father put all his tools, all his pieces of leather into a rucksack; while he wound and wound and wound the woollen scarf about his neck, while he pulled the cap far down on his head. "It will be a night to freeze the ears off you," he said. "Now bolt the door after me, keep the fire burning with a little at a time; and climb into the straw-bed and pull the quilt over you. And let no one in!"

He was gone. They bolted the door; they put a little on the fire; the climbed into the big bed, putting Hansl, they smallest, in the middle. They pulled up the quilt, such a thin quilt to keep out so much cold! Straight and still and close together they lay, looking up at the little spot of light the fire made on the ceiling, watching their breath go upwards in icy spurts. With the going of the sun the wind rose. First it whispered: it whispered of good fires in big chimneys; it whispered of the pines on the mountainsides; it whispered of snow loosening and sliding over the glaciers. Then it began to blow: it blew hard, it blew quarrelsome, it blew cold and colder. And at last it roared. It roared its wintry breath through the cracks in the walls and under the door. And Fritzl, Franzl, and Hansl drew closer together and shivered.

"Whee ... ooh ... bang, bang! Whee ... ooh ... bang, bang!"

"Is it the wind or someone knocking?" asked Franzl.

"It is the wind," said Fritzl.

"Whee ... ooh ... knock, knock!"

"Is it the wind or someone knocking?" asked Hansl.

"It is the wind *and* someone knocking!" said Fritzl.

He rolled out of the bed and went to the window. It looked out directly on the path to the door. "Remember what our father said: do not open it," said Franzl.

But Fritzl looked and looked. Close to the hut, beaten against it by the wind, stood a little man no bigger than Hansl. He was pounding on the door. Now they could hear him calling: "Let me in! I tell you, let me in!"

"Oh, don't, don't!" cried Hansl.

"I must," said Fritzl. "He looks very cold. The wind is tearing at him as a wolf tears at a young lamb"; and with that he drew the bolt and into the hut skipped the oddest little man they had ever seen. He had a great peaked cap tied onto his head with deer–thongs. He had a round red face out of which stuck a bulbous nose, like a fat plum on a pudding. He had big ears. And his teeth were chattering so hard they made the stools to dance. He shook his fist at the three little boys. "Ach, kept me waiting. Wanted to keep all the good food, all the good fire to yourselves? Na-na, that is no kind of hospitality."

He looked over at the little bit of a fire on the hearth, making hardly any heat in the hut. He looked at the empty table, not a bowl set or a spoon beside it. He took up the big pot, peered into it, turned it upside down to make sure nothing was clinging to the bottom, set it down with a bang. "So — you have already eaten it all. Greedy boys. But if you have saved no feast for me, you can at least warm me." With that he climbed into the big straw-bed with Franzl and Hansl, with his cap still tied under his chin. Fritzl tried to explain that they had not been greedy, that there had never been any food, not for days, to speak of. But he

was too frightened of the little man, of his eyes as sharp and blue as ice, of his mouth so grumbling.

"Roll over, roll over," the little man was shouting at the two in the bed. "Can't you see I have no room? Roll over and give me my half of the quilt."

Fritzl saw that he was pushing his brothers out of the bed. "Na-na," he said, trying to make peace with their guest. "They are little, those two. There is room for all if we but lie quiet." And he started to climb into the bed himself, pulling gently at the quilt that there might be a corner for him.

But the little man bounced and rolled about shouting: "Give me room, give me more quilt. Can't you see I'm cold? I call this poor hospitality to bring a stranger inside your door, give him nothing to eat, and then grudge him bed and covering to keep him warm." He dug his elbow into the side of skinny little Hansl.

"Ouch!" cried the boy.

Fritzl began to feel angry. "Sir," he said, "sir, I pray you to be gentle with my little brother. And I am sorry there has been nothing to give you. But our father, the cobbler, has gone to mend shoes for the soldiers. When he returns we look for food. Truly, this is a night to feast and to share. So if you will but lie still until he comes I can promise you ..."

The little man rolled over and stuck his elbow into Fritzl's ribs. "Promise — promise. Na-na, what good is a promise? Come get out of bed and give me your place." He drew up his knees, put his feet in the middle of Fritzl's back and pushed with a great strength. The next moment the boy was spinning across the room. "There you go," roared the little man after him. "If you must keep warm turn cartwheels, turn them fast."

For a moment Fritzl stood sullenly by the small speck of fire. He felt bruised and very angry. He looked over at the bed. Sure enough, the greedy little man had rolled himself up in the quilt leaving only a short corner of it for the two younger boys. He had taken more than half of the straw for himself, and was even then pushing and digging at Hansl. He saw Franzl raise himself up and take the place of his littlest brother, that he should get the digs.

Brrr ... it was cold! Before he knew it Fritzl was doing as he had been told, turning cartwheels around the room. He had rounded the table and was coming toward the bed when — plop! Plop — plop — plop! Things were falling out of his pockets every time his feet swung high over his head. Plop — plop — plop! The two younger boys were sitting up in bed. It was their cries of astonishment which brought Fritzl's feet back to the floor again, to stay. In a circle about the room, he had left behind him a golden trail of oranges. Such oranges — big as two fists! And sprinkled everywhere between were comfits wrapped in gold and silver paper. Fritzl stood and gaped at them.

"Here, you, get out and keep warm yourself!" shouted the little man as he dug Franzl in the ribs. "Cartwheels for you, boy!" And the next minute Franzl was whirling in cartwheels about the room. Plop — plop — plop — things were dropping out of his pockets: Christmas buns, Christmas cakes covered with icing, with plums, with anise and caraway seeds.

The little man was digging Hansl now in the ribs. "Lazy boy, greedy boy. Think you can have the bed to yourself now? Na-na, I'll have it! Out you go!" And he put his feet against the littlest boy's back and pushed him onto the floor. "Cartwheels ... " he began; but Fritzl, forgetting his amazement at what was happening, shouted: "But, sir, he is too little. He cannot turn ... "

"Hold him up in the corner, then. You keep warmer when your heels are higher than your head. Step lively there. Take a leg, each of you, and be quick about it."

So angry did the little man seem, so fiery and determined, that Fritzl and Franzl hurried their little brother over to the chimney corner, stood him on his head and each held a leg. Donner and Blitzen! What happened then! Whack — whack — whickety-whack! Whack — whack — whickety-whack! Pelting the floor like hail against the roof came silver and gold pieces, all pouring out of Hansl's pockets.

Fritzl began to shout, Franzl began to dance. Hansl began to shout: "Let me down, let me down!" When they did the three little boys danced around the pile, taking hands, singing "Tra-la-la," and "Fiddle-de-dee," and "Ting-a-ling-a-ling," until their breath was gone and they could dance no longer. They looked over at the bed and Fritzl was opening his mouth to say: "Now, if you please, sir, we can offer you some Christmas cheer ... " But the bed was empty, the quilt lay in a heap on the floor. The little man had gone.

139

The three little boys were gathering up the things on the floor — putting oranges into the big wooden bowl, buns and cakes on to the two platters, silver and gold pieces into this dish and that. And right in the midst of it in came their father, stamping, puffing in through the door. He had brought bread, he had brought milk, he had brought meat for the good stew — and noodles.

Such a wonder, such a clapping of hands, such a singing as they worked to get ready the Christmas feast! Fritzl began the story about their Christmas guest; Franzl told it mid-through; but little Hansl finished, making his brothers stand him in the corner again on his head to show just how it was that all the silver and gold had tumbled out of his pockets.

"Na-na," said the cobbler, "we are the lucky ones. I did not know it was true; always I thought it was a tale the grandfathers told the children. The saying goes that King Laurin comes every year at the Christmas to one hut — one family — to play his tricks and share his treasure horde."

"He was a very ugly little man," said Hansl. "He dug us in our ribs and took all the bed for himself."

"That was the king — that is the way he plays at being fierce. Say: *'Komm, Herr Jesus, und sei unser Gast,'* then draw up the stools. Ah-h ... what have we to eat?"

The little boys shouted the answer all together: "Schnitzle — Schnotzle — and Schnootzle!"

Stefan Vasilivich, the Highwayman

Jeanna Oterdahl

The north wind blew over the plain sweeping before it clouds of fine snow, the flakes driven as razor-sharp nails through the air. At times the snow was piled up in drifts with sharp edges and again these were blown away so that the short frozen grass became visible. The banks of the frozen river that meandered through the plain had become one with the land round about.

No one would have guessed that a river was there if it had not been for the withered rushes, bent by the wind and susurrating a lament for the hardship of life and the fleeting dream of summer.

Between gusts the wind bore the faint sound of church bells with it. The nuns of the cloister of St Michael had the festival bell ringing, because it was Christmas Eve, and the bell sounded light and joyful as if it knew that it was bringing in a glad high day.

Along the snow-covered road that followed the course of the stream a solitary wayfarer was walking with difficulty, his back bent as he fought against the keen wind; and every time the sound of the bells reached his ear he laughed malevolently and quickened his pace.

"You've done a lot in your time, Stefan Vasilivich, but this time I think you're going to surpass yourself," he said aloud and laughed again. "Up till now you've been content if you could frighten the life out of the peasants and make the highways unsafe. You've earned yourself an infamous name, that is sure and certain. Even the tiniest child knows that the worst encounter anyone could have in this region is to cross the path of Stefan Vasilivich. You can hit on the best things and you have the quietest step and the most cunning brain of all your peers. The peasants hate you like the plague because you have robbed them of so many calves, because you have set so many farms on fire, and because you have broken into so many money chests. But that is not enough: such things will be forgotten after the course of years. Tonight Stefan

Vasilivich is going to perform a highwayman's deed which will make him as famous as a hero or a saint."

The wind drove a shower of razor-sharp hailstones into his face, but that was nothing to him. With his hat pressed down over his brow and his savage face, he went on with difficulty but without pausing. Already he could see the lights of the nunnery of St. Michael shining through the darkness and the snowstorm.

"When I was still a child," thought Stefan Vasilivich, "I had the same obdurate character that I have now. I knew nothing so senseless as compassion and weakness.

" 'Mind out,' said my father once, 'In the end someone will come who can tame you!'

"Just imagine, Father! I have been beaten more than anyone else, I have suffered hunger and cold, and there is no prison that can hold me. I should like to meet that person who can tame me."

And Stefan Vasilivich laughed again with that malevolent self-satisfied laugh, which was borne away by the wind over the expanse of snow. As he drew nearer to the nunnery, he walked more slowly and his little cunning eyes gleamed.

Vespers were over and the nuns were going in pairs from the chapel to the refectory. Right behind and all alone walked the youngest of the sisters. She was small and finely built, and had a pair of great brown starry eyes hidden under her wimple. Her eyes were still reflecting the sheen of the candles in the chapel and her lips were moving gently as if she were still singing.

Sister Ecatarina was just fifteen years old; she was the pet and the little singing bird of the nunnery and everyone loved her, and because she was still such a child they forgave her when she sometimes forgot some of her many duties. Now Sister Ecaterina was so sunk in her own thoughts that she was walking more slowly and forgot that she ought to be following the others.

Now she stopped in the snow right in the middle of the cloister courtyard. Her heart was so full of joy because of the Child that was born on earth in this night, that she did not even notice the keen cold or the snow which lay thick upon her thin clothing and blew into her face.

Sister Ecaterina had folded her hands and was praying that God might give her the chance of serving the Christ-Child. As she stood there deep in prayer, without noticing that the others had long since entered the warm dining-hall, she was suddenly disturbed by a faint knocking at the cloister-gate.

She forgot that it was not her task to open the door to strangers, and she hastened to the gate. Her heart beat with hopeful expectation for she thought that perhaps God had heard her prayer already, and that this very evening was going to put her love for the Christ-Child to the test.

As Sister Ecaterina ran over the snow-covered courtyard she wondered who might be standing outside, perhaps a child or a very old man, because the knocking came with pauses and sounded unsteady and weak. Without further thought and without considering for whom she might be opening the door, she slid back the heavy bar and beckoned to the man waiting outside to come in.

If the little nun with the great starry eyes had known that the man who stood before her was Stefan Vasilivich, the murderer and robber, of whom she had so often heard with fear and horror, she would surely have fallen down in the snow with terror, not daring to move let alone to speak. But how could Sister Ecaterina guess that the old man with silken silvery beard and the broad-brimmed hat adorned with shells was anyone else than the exhausted pilgrim which he appeared to be? When he asked in God's name and in the name of St Michael for a roof over his head and a morsel of bread, she only felt joy that God had heard her prayer so soon. With her face shining with joy she led the old man into the dining hall, where the nuns were all seated in their places round the long table.

"Sister," said the abbess, who was sitting at the head of the table with blind Sister Elizabeth. "Have you forgotten that it is your turn to share round the bread? Have you also forgotten that it is not your duty to open the door to strangers? Sister, sister, when will you be like the others at last?"

But little Sister Ecaterina, who was a prince's daughter, and the sister of a prince, knelt on the stone floor and prayed so humbly for forgiveness, that the abbess had not the heart to punish her.

After the sisters had sung the hymn of thanksgiving, Sister Ecaterina shared round the fresh gloriously smelling Christmas bread, and for the pilgrim with the long silvery beard she chose the largest and whitest piece of bread.

Stefan Vasilivich laughed silently at the psalm and the simple meal, and his evil heart rejoiced in anticipation. For he knew that the nunnery was rich in icons adorned with gold and pearls, and possessed holy vessels inlaid with jewels of many colours, even though the nuns lived in great poverty and abstinence.

When supper was over and the hymn had been sung, Sister Ecaterina asked permission to wash the feet of the pilgrim, and the abbess was glad at her eagerness to serve God.

But Stefan Vasilivich could hardly contain his joy at the fact that he had played his part so well, and he peered cautiously from one nun to another and imagined their terror when his time would come.

"If you are truly as pious as I believe you are, reverend father," said the little prince's daughter, as she knelt upon the hard stone floor and undid the laces of Stefan Vasilivich's boots, "then the water will be even purer and more transparent after I have washed your feet than it is now," and her childlike spirit rejoiced over her words.

And behold, after Sister Ecaterina had spent some time washing the pilgrim's feet with great care as if she had been performing an important task, the water really was purer, as pure as if it had been taken from a spring, and the little nun cried aloud with joy.

But in Stefan Vasilivich's wicked heart, which only harboured evil feelings, there arose a great amazement. What powers were at work here? He found that the moment had come to tear off the white beard and to throw aside the pilgrim's hat, but he could not stand up. He remained sitting paralysed, staring into the fresh clear water which had made his feet whiter than snow, and yet had retained its own purity.

Sister Ecaterina had approached the abbess and knelt at her chair. "Pious Mother," she said, her voice trembling with joy, "our guest is truly a very holy man. Allow me to wash the eyes of our poor blind sister with the water with which I have washed the pilgrim's feet. Perhaps God will perform a miracle through the pilgrim's piety."

The abbess gave her permission and Sister Ecaterina, radiant with hope, filled a bowl with the water and went up to the blind nun. Sister Elizabeth had not seen daylight for thirty years and shook her head sadly. She had prayed so much that she might receive back her sight and now she had peacefully accepted her complete darkness, and no longer rebelled against it.

"Dear child," she said, "it is God's will that I should live in darkness until I shall finally enter into eternal light, where even the blind can see."

"Sister Elizabeth," begged the little nun, "do let me but try."

And the blind nun smiled, for neither could she oppose Sister Ecaterina.

And behold, as the first drops of the water flowed over the smitten eyes the veil was removed that had closed them for thirty years.

The longer the little nun washed the clearer everything became for Sister Elizabeth until finally she stood up and looked around her with folded hands and with clear-sighted radiant eyes. And all the sisters who were in the dining hall began to sing a hymn of praise, while Ecaterina, the prince's daughter, threw herself again upon her knees before the pilgrim and kissed his feet with tears.

Then the stranger sprang up and cried out loud as a man in uttermost anguish of soul.

"Who art thou, O God?" he cried tearing off the silken beard and casting away his pilgrim's cloak. "Who art thou, Almighty, who hast conquered me? Ye nuns, know that I am Stefan Vasilivich, the robber and murderer. I have never believed, neither in God nor in the Devil. I have filled towns and villages with terror. No blows have been able to quell me, no prison walls have been able to hold me. Know, sisters that this evening I came to rob and murder."

Again he cried as if he were in the greatest pain.

"Who art thou, Almighty," he cried, "Sticks and blows have only hardened me, Neither the wheel nor the rack have been able to bend me. But this evening thou hast beaten me with the scourge of mildness, as thou hast wrought a miracle through the faith of this child. Glory be to thy holy name in eternity!"

When Stefan Vasilivich had spoken these words he fell on his knees. All the sisters began to sing a hymn of praise to God and Sister Ecaterina's voice sounded high above the other voices.

Fiddler, Play Fast, Play Faster

A *danse macabre* from the Isle of Man

Ruth Sawyer

It is a strange island and an enchanted one — our Isle of Man. It took many a thousand years and more before mankind discovered it, it being well-known that the spirits of water, of earth, of air and fire did put on it an enchantment, hiding it with a blue flame of mist, so that it could not be seen by mortal eye. The mist was made out of the heat of a great fire and the salt vapour of the sea and it covered the island like a bank of clouds. Then one day the fire was let out, the sea grew quiet, and lo, the island stood out in all its height of mountains and ruggedness of coast, its green of fens and rushing of waterfalls. Sailors passing saw it. And from that day forth men came to it and much of its enchantment was lost.

But not all. Let you know that at all seasons of the year there are spirits abroad on the Isle, working their charms and making their mischief. And there is on the coast, overhanging the sea, a great cavern reaching below the earth, out of which the Devil comes when it pleases him, to walk where he will upon the Isle. A wise Manxman does not go far without a scrap of iron or a lump of salt in his pocket; and if it is night, likely, he will have stuck in his cap a sprig of rowan and a sprig of wormwood, feather from a seagull's wing and skin from a conger eel. For these keep away evil spirits; and who upon the Isle would meet with evil, or who would give himself foolishing into its power?

So it is that in the south upon the ramparts of Castle Rushen the cannon are mounted on stone crosses above the ramparts; and when a south Manxman knocks at his neighbour's door he does not cry out: "Are you within?" But rather he asks: "Are there any sinners inside?" For evil is a fearsome thing, and who would have traffic with it?

I am long at beginning my tale, but some there may be who know little of our Isle and a storyteller cannot always bring his listeners by the straightest road to the story he has to tell. This one is of the south, where the mists hang the heaviest, where the huts are built of turf and thatched with broom, where the cattle are small and the goats many, and where a farmer will tell you he has had his heard brought to fold by the fenodyree — a goblin that is half goat, half boy. But that is another tale.

Let me begin with an old Manx saying — it tunes the story well: "When a poor man helps another, God in his Heaven laughs with delight." This shows you that the men of Man are kind to one another, and God is not far from them even when the Devil walks abroad.

Count a hundred years, and as many more as you like, and you will come to the time of my story. Beyond Castletown in the sheading of Kirk Christ Rushen lived, then, a lump of a lad named Billy Nell Kewley. He could draw as sweet music from the fiddle as any fiddler of Man. When the Christmas-time began, he was first abroad with his fiddle. Up the glens and over the fens, fiddling for this neighbour and that as the night ran out, calling the hour and crying the weather, that those snug on their beds of chaff would know before the day broke what kind of day it would be making. Before Yule he started his fiddling, playing half out of the night and half into the day, playing this and playing that, carrying with him, carefully in his cap, the sprig of rowan and the sprig of wormwood, with the iron and salt in the pocket of his brown woollen breeches. And there you have Billy Nell Kewley on the Eve of Saint Fingan.

Now over Castletown on a high building of cliff rises Castle Rushen. Beyond stands the oldest monastery on the Isle, in ruin these hundreds of years, Rushen Abbey, with its hundred treens of land. It was through the Forest of Rushen Billy Nell was coming on Saint Thomas's eve, down the Glen to the Quiggan hut, playing the tune "Andisop" and whistling a running of notes to go with it. He broke the whistle, ready to call the hour: "Two of the morning," and the weather: "Cold — with a mist over all," when he heard the running of feet behind him in the dark.

Quick as a falcon he reached for the sprig in his cap. It was gone; the pushing through the green boughs of the forest had torn it. He quickened his own feet. Could it be a buggan after him — an ugly, evil one, a fiend of Man who cursed mortals and bore malice against them, who would bring a body to perdition and then laugh at him? Billy Nell's feet went fast — went faster.

But his ear, dropping behind him, picked up the sound of other feet; they were going fast — and faster. Could it be the fenodyree — the hairy one? That would be not so terrible. The fenodyree played pranks, but he, having once loved a human maid, did not bring evil to humans. And he lived, if the ancient ones could be believed, in Glen Rushen.

And then a voice spoke out of the blackness: "Stop, I command!"

What power lay in that voice! It brought the feet of Billy Nell to a stop — for all he wanted them to go on, expected them to keep running. Afterwards he was remembering the salt and iron in his pocket he might have thrown between himself and what followed so closely after him out of the mist. But he did nothing but stop — stop and say to himself: "Billy Nell Kewley, could it be the Noid ny Hanmey who commands — the Enemy of the Soul?" And he stood stock still in the darkness too frightened to shiver, for it was the Devil himself he was thinking of.

He who spoke appeared, carrying with him a kind of reddish light that came from everywhere and nowhere, a light the colour of fever, or heat lightning, or of the very pit of Hell. But when Billy Nell looked he saw as fine a gentleman as ever had come to Man — fine and tall, grave and stern, well clothed in knee breeches and silver buckles and lace and such finery. He spoke with grace and grimness: "Billy Nell Kewley of Castletown, I have heard you are a monstrous good fiddler. No one better, so they say."

"I play fair, sir," said Billy Nell modestly.

"I would have you play for me. Look!" He dipped into a pocket of his breeches and drawing out a hand so white, so tapering, it might have been a lady's, he showed Billy Nell gold pieces. And in the reddish light that came from everywhere and nowhere Billy saw the strange marking on them. "You shall have as many of these as you can carry away with you if you will fiddle for me and my company three nights from tonight," said the fine one.

"And where shall I fiddle?" asked Billy Nell Kewley.

"I will send a messenger for you, Billy Nell; half-way up the Glen he will meet you. This side of midnight he will meet you."

"I will come," said the fiddler, for he had never heard of so much gold — to be his for a night's fiddling. And being not half so fearful he began to shiver. At that moment a cock crew far away, a bough brushed his eyes, the mist hung about him like a cloak, and he was alone. Then he ran, ran to Quiggan's hut, calling the hour: "Three of the clock," crying the weather: "Cold, with a heavy mist."

The next day he counted, did Billy Nell Kewley, counted the days up to three and found that the night he was to fiddle for all the gold he could carry with him was Christmas Eve. A kind of terror took hold of him. What manner of spirit was the Enemy of the Soul? Could he be anything he chose to be — a devil in Hell or a fine gentleman on Earth? He ran about asking everyone, and everyone gave him a different answer. He went to the monks of the Abbey and found them working in their gardens, their black cowls thrown back from their faces, their bare feet treading the brown earth.

The Abbot came, and dour enough he looked. "Shall I go, your reverence? Shall I fiddle for one I know not? Is it good gold he is giving me?" asked Billy Nell.

"I cannot answer any one of those questions," said the Abbot. "That night alone can give the answers: Is the gold good or cursed? Is the man noble or is he the Devil? But go. Carry salt, carry iron and bollan bane. Play a dance and watch. Play another — and watch. Then play a Christmas hymn and see!"

This side of midnight, Christmas Eve, Billy Nell Kewley climbed the Glen, his fiddle wrapped in a lamb's fleece to keep out the wet. Mist, now blue, now red, hung over the blackness, so thick he had to feel his way along the track with his feet, stumbling.

He passed where Castle Rushen should have stood. He passed on, was caught up and carried as by the mist and in it. He felt his feet leave the track, he felt them gain it again. And then the mist rolled back like clouds after a storm and before him he saw such a splendid sight as no lump of a lad had ever beheld before. A castle, with courtyard and corridors, with piazzas and high roofings, spread before him all a-glowing with light. Windows wide and doorways wide, and streaming with the light came laughter. And there was his host more splendid than all, with velvet and satin, silver and jewels. About him moved what Billy Nell took to be highborn lords and ladies, come from overseas no doubt, for never had he seen their like on Man.

In the middle of the great hall he stood, unwrapping his fiddle, sweetening the strings, rosining the bow, limbering his fingers. The laughter died. His host shouted:

"Fiddler, play fast — play faster!"

In all his life and never again did Billy Nell play as he played that night. The music of his fiddle made the music of a hundred fiddles. About him whirled the dancers like crazy rainbows: blue and orange, purple and yellow, green and red all mixed together until his head swam with the colour. And yet the sound of the dancers' feet was the sound of the grass growing or the corn ripening or the holly reddening — which is to say no sound at all. Only there was the sound of his playing, and above that the sound of his host shouting, always shouting:

"Fiddler, play fast — play faster!"

Ever faster — ever faster! It was as with a mighty wind Billy Nell played now, drawing the wild, mad music from his fiddle. He played tunes he had never heard before, tunes which cried and shrieked and howled and sighed and sobbed and cried out in pain.

"Play fast — play faster!"

He saw one standing by the door — a monk in a black cowl, barefooted, a monk who looked at him with deep, sad eyes and held two fingers of his hand to his lips as if to hush the music.

Then, and not till then, did Billy Nell Kewley remember what the Abbot had told him. But the monk — how came he here? And then he remembered that, too. A tale so old it had grown ragged with the telling, so that only a scrap here and there was left: how long ago, on the blessed Christmas Eve, a monk had slept through the Midnight Mass to the Virgin and to the new-born Child, and how, at complin on Christmas Day, he was missing and never seen again. The ancient ones said that the Devil had taken him away, that Enemy of All Souls, had stolen his soul because he had slept over Mass.

Terror left Billy Nell. He swept his bow so fast over the strings of his fiddle that his eyes could not follow it.

"Fiddler, play fast — play faster!"

"Master, I play faster and faster!" He moved his own body to the mad music, moved it across the hall to the door where stood the monk. He crashed out the last notes; on the floor at the feet of the monk, he dropped iron, salt, and bollan bane. Then out of the silence he drew the notes of a Christmas carol — softly, sweetly it rose on the air:

> *Adeste fideles, laeti triumphantes,*
> *Venite, venite in Bethlehem:*
> *Natum videte, Regem angelorum:*
> *Venite adoremus, venite adoremus,*
> *Venite adoremus — Dominum.*

Racked were the ears of Billy Nell at the sounds which surged above the music, groans and wailing, the agony of souls damned. Racked were his eyes with the sights he saw: the servants turned to fleshless skeletons, the lords and ladies to howling demons. And the monk with the black cowl and bare feet sifted down to the grass beneath the vanishing castle — a heap of grey dust. But in the dust shone one small spark of holy light — a monk's soul, freed. And Billy Nell took it in his hand and tossed it high in the wind as one tosses a falcon to the sky for free passage. And he watched it go its skimming way until the sky gathered it in.

Billy Nell Kewley played his way down the Glen, stopping to call the hour: "Three of this blessed Christmas Morning," stopping to cry the weather: "The sky is clear ... the Christ is born."

Moss-Maggie

Peter Rosegger

Year in, year out, there stood by the grey clay plastered wall of the stove in our living-room an oaken footstool. It was always smooth and clean, for, like the other furniture, it was rubbed every Saturday with fine river sand and a wisp of straw. In spring, summer, and autumn-time this stool stood empty and lonely in its corner, save when of an evening my grandmother pulled it a little forward to kneel on it and say her evening prayer. On Saturdays, too, while my father said the prayers for the end of the week, grandmother knelt upon the stool.

But when during the long evenings in late autumn the farm-hands were cutting small household torches from the resinous logs, and the maids, along with my mother and grandmother, spinning wool and flax, and all during Advent time, when old fairy tales were told and hymns were sung — then I always sat on the stool by the stove.

From out my corner I listened to the stories and songs, and if they became creepy and my little soul began to be moved with terror, I shoved the stool nearer to my mother and covertly held on by her dress; and could not possibly understand how the others still dared to laugh at me, or at the terrible stories. At last when bedtime came, and my mother pulled my little box-bed out for me, I simply could not go to bed alone, and my grandmother must lie beside me until the frightful visions had faded and I fell asleep.

But with us the long Advent nights were always short. Soon after two o'clock, the house began to grow restless. In the attics above one could hear the farm-lads dressing and moving about, and in the kitchen the maids broke up kindling wood and poked the fire. Then they all went out to the threshing floor to thresh.

My mother was also up and about, and had kindled a light in the living-room; soon after that my father rose, and they both put on somewhat better clothes than they wore on working-days and yet not

their Sunday best. Then mother said a few words to grandmother, who still lay a-bed, and when I, wakened by the stir, made some sort of remark, she only answered, "You lie nice and quiet and go to sleep again!"

Then my parents lighted a lantern, extinguished the light in the room, and left the house. I heard the outer door close, and saw the gleam of light go glimmering past the window, and I heard the crunching of footsteps in the snow and the rattling of the house-dog's chain. Then, save for the regular throb of the threshers at work, all was once more quiet and I fell asleep again.

My father and mother were going to the morning service at the parish church, nearly three hours away. I followed them in my dream. I could hear the church bell, and the sound of the organ and the Advent song, "Hail Mary, thou bright morning star!" I saw, too, the lights open the high altar; and the little angels that stood above it spread out their golden wings and flew about the church, and the one with the trumpet, standing over the pulpit, passed out over the heath and into the forests and blew throughout the whole world that the coming of the Saviour was near at hand.

When I awoke the sun had long been shining into the windows; outside the snow glittered and shimmered, and indoors my mother went about again in workaday clothes and did her household tasks. Grandmother's bed, next mine, was already made, and she herself now came in from the kitchen and helped me to put on my breeches, and washed my face with cold water, that stung me so that I was ready to laugh and cry at the same moment. That over I knelt on my stool and prayed with grandmother the morning prayer:

> In God's name let us arise
> Towards God to go,
> Towards God to take our way,
> To the Heavenly Father to pray,
> That he lend to us
> Dear little angels three:
> The first to guide us,
> The second to feed us,
> The third to shelter and protect us
> That nothing mischance us in body or soul.

After these devotions I received my morning soup, and then came grandmother with a tub full of turnips which we were to peel together. I sat close beside it on my stool. But in the matter of peeling turnips I could never quite satisfy grandmother: I constantly cut the rind too thick, or here and there even left it whole upon the turnip. When, moreover, I cut my finger and instantly began to cry, my grandmother said, very crossly, "You're a regular nuisance, it would be a good thing to pitch you right out into the snow!" All the while she was binding up my wound with unspeakable love and care.

So passed the Advent season, and grandmother and I talked more and more often about Christmas Eve and of the Christ Child who would so soon be coming among men.

The nearer we came to the festival the greater the stir in the house. The men turned the cattle out of the stall and put fresh straw there and set the mangers and barriers in good order; the cowman rubbed the oxen till they looked quite smooth; the stockman mixed more hay than usual in the straw and prepared a great heap of it in the hayloft. The milkmaid did the same. Threshing had already ceased some days ago, because, according to our belief, the noise would have profaned the approaching Holy Day.

Through all the house there was washing and scrubbing; even into the living-room itself came the maids with their water-pails and straw wisps and brooms. I always looked forward to the cleaning, because I loved the turning topsy-turvy of everything, and because the glazed pictures in the corner where the table was, the brown clock from the Black Forest with its metal bell, and the various things which, at other times, I saw only at a distance high above me, were taken down and brought nearer to me, and I could observe them all much more closely and from all sides. To be sure, I was not allowed to handle such things, because I was still too clumsy and careless for that and might easily damage them. But there were moments in that eager scrubbing and rubbing when people did not notice me.

In one such moment I climbed from the stool to the bench, and from the bench to the table, which was pushed out of its place and on which lay the Black Forest clock. I made for the clock, whose weights hung over the edge of the table, looked through an open side-door into the very dusty brass works, tapped several times on the little cogs of the winding-wheel, and at last even laid my finger on the wheel itself to see if it would go; but it didn't. Eventually I gently pushed a small stick of wood, and as I did so the works began to rattle frightfully. Some of the wheels went slowly, others quicker, and the winding-wheel flew round so fast that one could hardly see it at all. I was indescribably frightened, and rolled from the table over bench and stool down on to the wet, dirty floor; then my mother gripped me by my little coat — and there, sure enough, was the birch-rod! The whirring inside the clock would not leave off, and finally my mother laid hold of me with both hands, carried me into the entrance, pushed me through the door and out into the snow, and shut the door behind me. There I stood like one undone; I could hear my mother — whom I must have offended badly — still scolding within doors, and the laughing and scrubbing of the maids, and through it all the whirring of the clock.

When I had stood there sobbing for a while and still nobody came to call me back into the house, I set off for the path that was trodden in the snow, and I went through the home meadow and across the open land towards the forest. I did not know whither I would go, I only conceived that a great wrong had been done me and that I could never go home again.

But I had not reached the forest when I heard a shrill whistle behind me. That was the whistle my grandmother made when she put two fingers in her mouth, pointed her tongue, and blew. "Where are you going, you stupid child?" she cried. "Take care; if you run about in the forest like that, Moss-Maggie will catch you! Look out!"

At this word I instantly turned round, for I feared Moss-Maggie unspeakably. But I did not go home yet. I hung about in the farmyard, where my father and two of our men had just killed a pig. Watching them I forgot what had happened to myself, and when my father set about skinning it in the outhouse I stood by holding the ends of the skin, which with his big knife he gradually detached from the carcase. When later on the intestines had been taken out and my mother was pouring water into the basin, she said to me, "Run away or you'll get splashed."

From the way in which she spoke I could tell that my mother was once more reconciled with me and all was right again; and when I went into the dwelling-room to warm myself a bit, everything was back in its own place. Floor and walls were still moist, but scrubbed clean, and the Black Forest clock was once more hanging on the wall and ticking. And it ticked much louder and clearer than before through the freshly ordered room.

At last the washing and scrubbing and polishing came to an end, the house grew peacefuller, almost silent, and the Sacred Vigil was upon us. On Christmas Eve we used not to have our dinner in the living-room, but in the kitchen, where we made the large pastry-board our table, and sat round it and ate the simple fasting fare silently, but with uplifted hearts.

The table in the dwelling-room was covered with a snow-white cloth, and beside it stood my stool, upon which, when the twilight fell, my grandmother knelt and prayed silently.

The maids went quietly about the house and got their holiday clothes ready, and mother put pieces of meat in a big pot and poured water on them and set it on the open fire. I stole softly about the room on tiptoe and heard only the jolly crackling of the kitchen fire. I gazed at my Sunday breeches and coat and the little black felt hat which were ready hanging on a nail in the wall, and then I looked through the window out at the oncoming dusk. If no rough weather set in I was to be allowed to go with the head farm-servant, Sepp, to the midnight Mass. And the weather was quiet, and moreover, according to my father, it was not going to be very cold, because the mist lay upon the hills.

Just before the "censing," in which, following ancient custom, house and farm were blessed with holy water and incense, my father and my mother fell out a little. Maggie the Moss-gatherer had been there to wish us all a blessed Christmastide, and my mother had presented her with a piece of meat for the feast-day. My father was somewhat vexed at this; in other ways, he was a good friend to the poor, and not seldom gave them more than we could well spare; but in his opinion one ought not to give Moss-Maggie any alms whatever.

The Moss-gatherer was a woman not belonging to our neighbourhood, who went wandering around in the forests without permission, collecting moss and roots, making fires and sleeping in the half-ruined huts of charcoal-burners. Besides that, she went begging to the farmhouses, offering moss for sale, and if she did but poor business there she wept and railed at her life. Children at whom she looked were sore terrified, and many even became ill; and she could make cows give red milk. Whoever showed her kindness, she would follow for several minutes, saying, "May God reward you a thousand and a thousandfold right up into heaven!" But to anyone who mocked, or in any other way whatsoever offended her, she said, "I pray you down into the nethermost hell!"

Moss-Maggie often came to us, and she loved to sit before the house on the grass, or on the stile over the hedge, in spite of the loud barking and chain-clanking of our house-dog, who showed singular violence towards this woman. She would remain there until my mother took her out a cup of milk or a bit of bread. My mother was glad when Moss-Maggie thereupon gave her a thousandfold-right-up-to-heaven-may-God-reward-you; but my father considered the wish of this person worthless, whether as curse or blessing.

Some years earlier, when they were building the schoolhouse in the village, this woman had come to the place with her husband and helped at the work, until one day the man was killed at stone-blasting. Since then she had worked no more, nor did she go away; but she just idled about, nobody knowing what she did nor what she wanted. She could never again be persuaded to do any work — she seemed to be crazed.

The magistrate had several times sent Moss-Maggie out of the district, but she always returned. "She wouldn't always be coming back," said my father, "if she got nothing by begging in the neighbourhood. As it is she'll just stay about here, and when she's old and ill, we shall have to nurse her as well: it's a cross that we ourselves have tied round our necks."

My mother said nothing in reply to such words, but when Moss-Maggie came she still gave the usual alms, and today in honour of the great feast a little more.

Hence then arose the little dispute between my father and mother, which however was at once silenced when two farm-hands bearing the incense and holy water entered the house. After the censing my father placed a lighted candle on the table; today pine-splinters might only be burned in the kitchen. Supper was once again eaten in the living-room. During supper the head farm-servant told us all manner of wonderful stories.

When we had finished my mother sang a shepherd's song. Rapturously as I listened to these songs at other times, today I could think of nothing but the church-going and longed above everything to get at once into my Sunday clothes. They assured me there would be time enough for that later on; but at last my grandmother yielded to my urgent appeal and dressed me. The cowman dressed himself very carefully in his festal finery, because he was not going home after the midnight mass, but would stay in the village till morning. About nine o'clock the other farm-servants and the maids were also ready, and they kindled a torch at the candle flame. I held on to Sepp, the head servant; and my parents and grandmother, who stayed at home to take care of the house, sprinkled me with holy water that I might neither fall nor freeze to death. Then we started off.

It was very dark, and the torch, borne before us by the cowman, threw its red light in a great disk on the snow, and the hedge, the stone-heaps and the trees past which we went. This red illumination, which was broken too by the great shadows of our bodies, seemed very awful to me, and I clung fearfully to Sepp, until he remarked, "Look here, leave me my coat; what should I do if you tore it off my back?"

For a time the path was very narrow, so that we had to go one behind the other, and I was only thankful that I was not the last, for I imagined that he for certain must be exposed to endless dangers from ghosts.

There was a cutting wind and the glowing splinters of the torch flew far afield, and even when they fell on the hard snow-crust they still glowed for a while.

So far we had gone across open ground and down through thickets and forest; now we came to a brook which I knew well — it flowed through the meadow where we made hay in summer. Then the brook had been noisy enough; to-day one could only hear it murmur and gurgle, for it was frozen over. We passed along by a mill where I was badly scared because some sparks flew on to the roof; but there was snow lying upon it and the sparks were quenched. When we had gone some way along the valley, we left the brook and the way led upwards through a dark wood where the snow lay very shallow but had no such firm surface as out in the open.

At last we came to a wide road, where we could walk side by side, and now and again we heard sleigh-bells. The torch had already burned right down to the cowman's hand, and he kindled another that he had with him. On the road were visible several other lights — great red torches that came flaring towards us as if they were swimming in the black air, behind which first one and then several more faces of the churchgoers gradually emerged, who now joined company with us. And we saw lights on other hills and heights, that were still so far off we could not be sure whether they were still or moving.

So we went on. The snow crunched under our feet, and wherever the wind had carried it away, there the black patch of bare ground was so hard that our shoes rang upon it. The people talked and laughed a great deal, but this seemed not a bit right to me in the holy night of Christmas. I could only think all the while about the church and what it must be like when there is music and High Mass in the dead of night.

When we had been going for a long time along the road and past isolated trees and houses, then again over fields and through a wood, I suddenly heard a faint ringing in the tree-tops. When I wanted to listen, I couldn't hear it; but soon after I heard it again, and clearer than the first time. It was the sound of the little bell in the church steeple. The lights which we saw on the hills and in the valley became more and more frequent, and we could now see that they were all hastening churchwards.

The little calm stars of the lanterns floated towards us, and the road was growing livelier all the time. The small bell was relieved by a greater, and this one went on ringing until we had almost reached the church. So it was true, what grandmother had said: at midnight the bells begin to ring, and they ring until the very last dweller in the farthest valleys has come to church.

The church stands on a hill covered with birches and firs, and round it lies the little God's-acre encircled by a low wall. The few houses of the village are down in the valley.

When the people came close to the church, they extinguished their torches by sticking them head downwards in the snow. Only one was fixed between two stones in the churchyard wall, and left burning.

And now from the steeple in slow, rhythmical swing, rang out the great bell. A clear light shone through the high, narrow windows. I longed to go into the church; but Sepp said there was still plenty of time, and stayed where he was, laughing and talking with other young fellows and filling himself a pipe.

At last all the bells pealed out together; the organ began to play inside the church, and then we all went in. There it looked quite different from what it did on Sundays. The candles burning on the altar were clear, white, beaming stars, and the gilded tabernacle reflected them most gloriously. The lamp of the sanctuary light was red. The upper part of the church was so dark that one could not see the beautiful painting of the nave. Mysterious shapes of men were seated in the chairs, or standing beside them; the women were much wrapped up in shawls and were coughing. Many had candles burning in front of them, and they sang out of their books when the *Te Deum* rang out from the chancel.

Sepp led me between two rows of chairs towards a side altar, where several people were standing. There he lifted me up on to a stool before a glass case, which, lighted by two candles, was placed between two branches of fir trees, and which I had never seen before when I went to church with my parents. When Sepp had set me on the stool, he said softly in my ear. "There, now you can have a look at the crib."

Then he left me standing, and I gazed in through the glass. Thereupon came a friendly little woman and whispered, "Look here, child, if you want to see that, somebody ought to explain it to you."

And she told me who the little figures were. I looked at them. Save for the Mother Mary, who had a blue wrapped garment round her head which fell down to her very feet, all the figures represented mere human beings: the men were dressed just like our farm-servants or the elder peasants. Even St Joseph wore green stockings and short chamois-leather breeches.

When the *Te Deum* was over, Sepp came back, lifted me from the stool, and we sat down on a bench. The sacristan went round lighting all the candles that were in the church, and every man, including Sepp, pulled a little candle out of his pouch, lighted it, and fastened it on to the desk in front of him. Now it was so bright in the church that one could see the paintings on the roof clearly enough. Up in the choir they were tuning fiddles and trumpets and drums, and, just as the little bell on the door of the sacristy rang, and the priest in his glittering vestments, accompanied by acolytes and tall lantern-bearers, passed over the crimson carpet to the altar, the organ burst forth in all its strength, joined by a blast of trumpets and roll of drums.

The incense smoke was rising, and shrouding the shining high altar in a veil. Thus the High Mass began, and thus it shone and sounded and rang in the middle of the night. Throughout the Offertory all the instruments were silent, only two clear voices sang a lovely shepherd-song; and during the Benedictus a clarionet and two horns slow and softly crooned the cradle-song. During the Gospel and the Elevation we heard the cuckoo and nightingale in the choir, just as in the midst of the sunny spring-time.

Deep down in my soul I understood it, the wonder and splendour of Christmas. But I did not exclaim with delight; I remained grave and silent, I felt the solemn glory of it all. But while the music was playing I could not help thinking about father and mother and grandmother at home. They are kneeling by the table now in the light of the single candle, and praying; or they are even asleep, and the room is all dark — only the clock ticking — while a deep peace lies upon the forest-clad mountains, and the Eve of Christmas is spread abroad over all the earth.

The little candles in the seats were burning themselves out, one after another, as the service neared its close at last; and the sacristan went round again and extinguished the lights on the walls and altars and before the pictures with the little tin cap. Those on the high altar were still burning when a joyous march music sounded from the choir and the folk went crowding out of the incense-laden church.

When we came outside, in spite of the thick mist which had descended from the hills, it was no longer quite so dark as before midnight. The moon must have risen; no more torches were lighted. It struck one o'clock, but the schoolmaster was already ringing the prayer bell for Christmas morning.

I glanced once more at the church windows. All the festal shine was quenched, I saw only the dull red glimmer of the sanctuary lamp.

And now, when I wanted to renew my hold on Sepp's coat, he was no longer there: I found myself among strangers, who talked together for a little, and then immediately set out for their several homes. My guide must be already on ahead. I hurried after him, running quickly past several people, hoping soon to overtake him. I ran as hard as my little feet were able, going through a dark wood and across fields over which such a keen wind was blowing, that warm as I otherwise was I scarcely felt my nose and ears at all. I passed houses and clumps of trees; the people who were still on the road a short time before had dropped off little by little; I was all alone, and still I hadn't overtaken Sepp. I thought he might just as well be still behind me, but I determined to hurry straight home.

Here and there I saw black spots on the road, the charcoal that folk had shaken down from their torches on their way to church. I made up my mind not to look at the bushes and little trees which stood beside the way and loomed eerily out of the mist, for they scared me. I was specially frightened whenever a path cut straight across the road, because that was a crossroad, where on Christmas Eve the Evil One loves to stand, and has chinking treasure with him with which he entices the hapless children of men to himself. It is true the cowman had said he did not believe it, but such things must be or people would not talk so much about them. I was very agitated; I turned my eyes in all directions, lest a ghost should be somewhere making for me. Then I determined to think no more of such nonsense; but the harder I made up my mind, the more I thought about it.

And now I had reached the path which should take me down through the forest and into the valley. I turned aside and ran along under the long-branched trees. Their tops rustled loudly, and now and again a great lump of snow fell down beside me. Sometimes it was so dark that I did not see the trunks until I ran up against them; and then I lost the path. This I did not mind very much, for the snow was shallow and the ground nice and level. But gradually it began to grow steep and steeper, and there were a lot of brambles and heather under the snow. The tree-stems were no longer spaced so regularly, but were scattered about, many leaning all awry, many with torn-up roots resting against others, and many, in a wild confusion of up-reaching branches, lying prone upon the ground.

I did not remember seeing all this on our outward journey. Some-times I could hardly get on at all, but had to wriggle in and out through the bushes and branches. Often the snow-crust gave way under me, and then the stiff heather reached right up to my chest. I realized I had lost the right path, but told myself that when I was once in the valley and beside the brook I should follow that along and so was bound to come at last to the mill and our own meadows.

Lumps of snow fell into the pockets of my coat, snow clung to my little breeches and stockings, and the water ran down into my shoes. At first all that clambering over fallen trees and creeping through under-growth had tired me, but now the weariness had vanished; I didn't heed the snow, and I didn't heed the heather, nor the boughs that so often scratched me roughly about the face, but I just hurried on. I was constantly falling, but as quickly picking myself up again. Then, too, all fear of ghosts was gone; I thought of nothing but the valley and our house. I had no notion how long I had been astray in the wilderness, but felt strong and nimble, terror spurring me on.

Suddenly I found myself standing on the brink of a precipice. Down in the abyss a grey fog lay, with here and there a tree-top rising out of it. The forest was sparser about me, it was bright overhead and the half-moon stood in the sky. Before me, and away beyond that, there was nothing but strange cone-shaped, forest-clad mountains.

Down there in the depths must be the valley and the mill. It seemed to me as if I heard the murmur of the brook; but it was only the soughing of the wind in the forest on the farther side.

I went to right and to left, searching for a footpath that might take me down, and I found a place where I thought I should be able to lower myself by the help of the loose rocks which lay about, and of the juniper bushes. In this I succeeded for a little, but only just in time I clutched hold of a root — I had nearly pitched over a perpendicular cliff. After that I could go no farther, but sank in sheer exhaustion to the ground. In the depths below lay the fog with the black tree-tops. Save for the soughing of the wind in the forest, I heard nothing. I did not know where I was. If only a deer would come I would ask my way of it; quite probably it would be able to direct me, for everyone knows that on Christmas Eve the beasts can talk like men.

I got up to climb back again, but only loosened the rocks and made no progress. Hands and feet were aching. I stood still and called for Sepp as loud as ever I could. Lingering and faint, my voice fell back from the forests and cliffs. Then again I heard nothing but the soughing of the wind.

The frost was cutting right into my limbs. "Sepp! Sepp!" I shouted once more with all my might.

Again nothing but the long-drawn-out echo. Then a fearful anguish took possession of me. I called quickly, one after another, my parents, my grandmother, all the farmhands and maids of our household by name. It was all in vain.

I began to cry miserably.

There I stood trembling, my body throwing a long shadow aslant down the naked rock. I went to and fro along the ledge to warm myself a little, and I prayed aloud the the holy Christ Child to save me.

The moon stood high in the dark heavens.

I could no longer cry or pray, I could scarcely move any more. I crouched down shivering on a stone and said to myself. "I shall go to sleep now; it's all only a dream, and when I wake up I shall either be at home or in heaven."

Then on a sudden I heard a rustling in the juniper bushes above me, and soon after I felt that something was touching me and lifting me up. I wanted to scream, but I couldn't — my voice was frozen within me. Fear and anguish kept my eyes fast shut. Hands and feet, too, were as if lamed. I could not move them. Then I felt warm, and it seemed to me as if all the mountain rocked with me.

When I came to myself and awoke it was still night; but I was standing at the door of my home and the house-dog was barking furiously. Somebody had let me slip down on the hard-trodden snow, and had then knocked loudly on the door and hurried away. I had recognized this somebody; it was the Moss-wife.

The door opened, and grandmother threw herself upon me with the words, "Jesus Christ, here he is!"

She carried me into the warm living-room, but from thence quickly back again into the entrance. There she set me on the bread-trough, and hastened outside and blew her most piercing whistle.

She was quite alone. When Sepp had come back from church and not found me at home, and when, too, the others came and I was with none of them, they had all gone down into the forest and through the valley and up the other side to the high road, and in all directions. Even my mother had gone with them, and everywhere, all the time, had called out my name.

So soon as my grandmother believed it could no longer harm me, she carried me back into the warm room, and when she drew off my shoes and stockings they were quite frozen together and almost frozen to my feet. Thereupon she again hurried out of doors, whistled again, brought some snow in a pail, and set me barefoot down in it. Standing thus I felt such a violent pain in my toes that I groaned; but grandmother said, "That's all right; if it hurts, your feet aren't frozen."

Soon after that the red morning light shone in through the window, and one by one all the farm-hands came home. At length my father, and quite last of all — when the red disk of the sun was rising over the Wechselalpe, and after grandmother had whistled countless times — came my mother. She came to my little bed, where they had tucked me up, my father sitting beside me. She was quite hoarse.

She said I ought to go to sleep now, and she covered the window with a cloth so that the sun should not shine in my face. But my father seemed to think I ought not go to sleep yet: he wanted to know how I had got away from the servant without his noticing it, and where I had been wandering. I at once related how I had lost the path, and how I got into the wilderness; and when I had told them about the moon and the black forests, and about the soughing of the wind and the rocky precipice, my father said under his breath to my mother, "Wife, let us give God praise and thanks that he is here — he has been on the Troll's rock!"

At these words my mother gave me a kiss on the cheek, a thing she did but seldom, and then she put her apron before her face and went away.

"Well, you young scaramouch, and how did you get home after all?" asked my father. I said I didn't know; that after a prolonged sleeping and rocking, I found myself at our door, and that Moss-Maggie had stood beside me. My father asked me yet again about this circumstance, but I told him I hadn't got anything else to say about it.

My father then said he must be off to High Mass in the church, because today was Christmas Day; and he bade me go to sleep.

I must have slept many hours after that, for when I awoke it was twilight outside, and in the dwelling-room it was nearly dark. My grandmother sat nodding beside my bed, and from the kitchen I heard the crackling of the fire on the hearth.

Later, when the servants were all sitting at the evening meal, Moss-Maggie was with them at table. During the morning service she had been out in the churchyard, cowering on her husband's grave; and after

High Mass my father went and found her there and brought her with him to our house.

They could get nothing out of her about the event of the night, save that she had been searching for the Christ Child in the forest. Then she came over to my bed and looked at me, and I was scared at her eyes.

In the back part of our house was a room in which there were only old, useless things and a lot of cobwebs. This room my father gave Moss-Maggie for a dwelling, and put a stove and a bed and a table in it for her.

And she stayed with us. She would still very often go rambling about in the forest, and bring home moss, and then return and sit for hours upon her husband's grave; from which she could never more tear herself away to return to her own district — where, indeed, she would have been just as lonely and homeless as everywhere else. Of her circumstances we could learn nothing more definite: we could only conjecture that the woman had once been happy and certainly in her right mind; and that grief for the loss of her mate had robbed her of reason.

We all loved her, for she lived peacefully and contentedly with all and caused nobody the least trouble. The house-dog alone, it seemed, would never trust her, he barked and tore furiously at the chain whenever she came across the home meadow. But the creature was meaning something quite different than we thought, all the time; for once when the chain broke he rushed to the woman, leapt whining into her bosom and licked her cheeks.

At last in the late autumn, when Moss-Maggie was almost always in the graveyard, there came a time when, instead of barking cheerily, the dog howled by the hour together, so that my grandmother, herself very worn and weary by then, said, "You mark my words; there'll soon be somebody dying in our neighbourhood now, when the dog howls like that! God comfort the poor soul!"

And a little while after that Moss-Maggie fell ill, and when winter came she died.

In her last moments she held both my father and mother by the hand and uttered the words, "May God requite you a thousand and a thousandfold, right up into heaven itself!"

The Candle

Willem Brandt

Ah no, this is not really a Christmas story. It is not really a story either, it is an account, a plain account of something that happened somewhere. But it is not present-day news which is what most reporting is about. This thing happened more than thirty years ago, but what does that matter? After all the Christmas story, the real Christmas story, was not actually a story as such, and it is now old news too, just short of two thousand years old. What then are thirty years here or there?

Furthermore, there is even a remarkable similarity, even though you might find it a bit far-fetched. The old Christmas story took place in a stall. The one that happened thirty years ago was also in a stall. Well, not a proper stall, but it looked like one. It was a dark gloomy shed. Inside it was always half-light or darkness, but outside the light shone bright and glorious by day, and even at night it was still light outside, for the shed was in a tropical region under a glowing burning sun, as well as under a wonderful starry sky, and the moon seemed much bigger than here. People lived in the shed. "Lived" is expressing it rather strongly. They were housed in it, because a little further off the sun or the moonlight sparkled from the barbed wire where it had not rusted in the course of the years. For by now it had lasted years; or was it perhaps centuries? We could not tell any more. We were too tired and too sick and too weak to think about it, to count up the hours and the days. We had done that in the beginning, but that was long since past. We were much more concerned with eternity than with the day or the hour. Because so many were dying, beside us, opposite us, from hunger, dysentery and other tropical diseases; or simply because they did not want to live any more, their last spark of hope had been extinguished.

We did try a bit to keep going in that Japanese concentration camp. We did not really know any more why. For a long time we no longer believed that the war would end and that we would be liberated. We just went on living out of force of habit, numbed and deadened, and with one great desire that now and again leapt at your throat like a wild beast: and that was to eat, eat no matter what. But there was nothing to eat, we were being systematically starved. Once in a while someone would catch a snake or a rat. But just forget it, no one who has survived it wants to talk about it.

There was one man in that camp who still possessed something edible. A candle. A plain wax candle. Of course he had not brought it originally or kept it just to eat it up. A normal person does not eat candle-fat, although they say that the Cossacks used to be very fond of it. In any case it is fat, and that you must not underestimate, when all you see around you are starved bodies and you know yourself to be one of them.

When the torture of hunger became beyond bearing he would take out the candle which he kept well hidden in a little dented tin box and he would nibble at it, but he did not eat it. He regarded the candle as a last resort. As soon as everyone should go mad with hunger (and that would not be long now) he was going to eat the candle up. I hope you don't find that insane or gruesome. I, who was his friend, found it quite normal at the time. Besides, he had promised me a bit of the candle. It became my life's task, my constant care, to watch out that he should not eat the candle all by himself after all. I kept watch and spied on him and his tin box day and night. Perhaps I remained alive because I had such an important task to carry out.

Now, all of a sudden, we discovered that it was Christmas. Quite by chance someone found out after some lengthy calculations made from little nicks and notches cut in a plank. He told it to everyone and added in a rather flat and expressionless tone of voice, "Next year, we'll be home for Christmas."

We nodded or made no comment at all. We had heard that now for several years. But there were a few who held fast to the idea. After all you never knew.

Then someone spoke, perhaps not with any particular intention, but perhaps on purpose after all — I never really found out: "At Christmas the candles are burning and the bells are ringing."

That was a strange thing to say. It sounded as a faint hardly audible sound from a great distance, from long ago, something completely unreal.

Now I must say that the remark simply went past most of us, it just did not have anything to do with us, it spoke about something quite outside our existence, but it had the strangest and most unexpected consequences. When it had grown late in the evening and everyone had more or less lain down on the boards with his own thoughts or actually quite without thoughts, my friend became restless. He groped for his box and brought the candle out. I could see it very well in the gloom, that white candle. "He'll eat it up," I thought, "Will he remember me?" and I looked at him through my eyelashes. He set the candle on his plank-bed and I saw him disappear outside to where a little fire was smouldering. He came back with a burning stick. Like a ghost that little flame wandered about through the hut till he got back to his place again. Then the strange thing happened: he took the burning stick, that flame, and he lit the candle.

The candle stood on his bed and was burning.

I do not know how everyone noticed it right away, but it was not long before one shadow after the other drifted over, half naked fellows, whose ribs you could count, with hollow cheeks and burning hungered eyes.

In the silence they made a ring round the burning candle.

Bit by bit they came forward, those naked men, and the minister and the priest. You could not see that they were minister or priest, they were just pieces of starved skeleton, but we happened to know they were.

The priest said in a croaking voice: "It is Christmas. The Light shines in the darkness."

Then the minister said: "And the darkness overcame it not."

That, if I remember rightly, comes from St John's Gospel. You can find it in the Bible, but that night, round that candle, it was no written word of long ago. It was the living reality, a message for that moment and for us, for each one of us.

Because the Light did shine in the darkness. And the darkness did not overwhelm it. We could not then reason it out, but it was what we felt, gathered silently round that candle light.

There was something extraordinary about it. The candle was whiter and more slender than I ever saw one later in the world of people. And the flame. It was a candle flame that reached to the sky and in the flame we saw things that were not of this world. I cannot describe it. None of us who are still alive can. It was a mystery. A mystery between Christ and ourselves. For we knew then quite certainly that it was him, that he was living among us and for us. We sang in silence, we prayed without a word, and then I heard the bells beginning to ring and a choir of angels intoning their songs. Yes, I know that for a fact, and I have a good hundred witnesses, of whom the greater part can no longer speak, they are no longer here. Nevertheless they know. Out there, deep in the swamps and the jungle, sublime angelic voices sang Christmas carols to us, and we heard the chimes of a thousand bells. It was a mystery where it came from. The candle burned taller and taller and more and more elongated, till it reached the highest point of the high dark shed and then right through it, right up to the stars, and everything became incandescent with light. So much light nobody ever saw again. And we felt ourselves uplifted and free and knew hunger no more. The candle had not just fed my friend and me; no, the candle had fed us all and made us stronger.

There was no end to the light.

And when someone said softly: "Next Christmas we'll be home," then we believed it implicitly this time. For the light proclaimed it to us, it was written in the candle flame in fiery letters; you can believe me or not, but I saw it myself.

The candle burned all night. There is no candle in the world that can burn so long and so high.

When it was morning there were a few who sang. That had never happened in any year before. The candle had saved the lives of many of us, for now we knew that it was worthwhile going on, wherever it might lead, but that somewhere in the end a home was waiting for us all. That's how it was.

Some went home before Christmas of the following year. They are back in life now in Holland. But they find the candles on our trees are small, much too small. They have seen a greater light, one that is always burning.

Most of the others had also gone home before it was Christmas again; I myself helped to lay them in the earth behind our camp, a dry spot between the swamps. But when they died their eyes were not as dull as before. That was the light from the strange candle. The light that the darkness had not overcome.

Semyon

Edzard Schaper

Semyon dwelt quite far from the vast forests on the bare open marshes together with his family. Once, long ago, he had been a forester and the forests had stood here, where now the bog-water came welling up at every step. But in those times the river, that flowed near his house, had not been the frontier between two countries; then it had flowed still and slowly through the widespread forests; still and slowly, as it now flowed through the swamps. But whether it dwindled during the height of summer or cut deeply into its banks on the left and the right in the springtime spate, its slowly streaming and bubbly centre had become a frontier a few years ago. However great the amount of water was, it remained the border to Red Russia. The frontier was the middle of the ice in wintertime. It had been too late for Semyon to feel at home elsewhere when the river was chosen to form the frontier, when the forests on either side, these forests he had tended so long, were felled. Then the boggy ground began to turn into open marshes and Semyon had started to cut the miserable peat in the low lying flats near the river. Everything far and wide had soon fallen to the axe, but his little house had not been taken down. It stood alone on the bare place and did not flourish like the aftergrowth of alder-thickets, but rather sank deeper and deeper and began to rot like old tree-stumps while it gained a few new strange neighbours.

On its own side small blockhouses were raised a few miles apart for the soldiers, who as frontier-guards were to patrol along the river by day and by night; and on the far side, in the Red Russian land, small towers had grown out of the desolation, complete with searchlights on the roofs, with telephones and signal lamps and a constant guard at the machine guns.

No storm, sweeping over the bare marshes, had succeeded in sweeping Semyon's hut away, no flood had washed it away, no driving ice-masses had born it from its foundations. But a few times it had barely escaped a penstroke of the Ministry of War that would have whisked it many miles inland. The lonely house by the river was not much liked, shelter for spies was not wanted, and only Semyon's reputation — as far as a reputation could exist in such a lonesome district — had kept him from being forced to another abode; but he had been steadfast against the temptations from the other shore and was God-fearing and pious. Thus one trusted that he would do nothing to harm his own country nor would he join those who denied God.

Semyon had lost his wife a couple of years earlier and lived alone with four children in the marshes, working hard from morn till night. In summer and still long after the coming of the frost he cut peat, and in winter he would haul it, like a shaggy, panting horse, on a broad sledge to the distant villages, when he was not busy with the two elder children, Marfa and Kyrill, gathering cranberries from under the snow with which he would trade and earn a little. He also caught fish in the river for the frontier guards.

Now Christmas had come to the lonely marshes, too, and in the dusk of Christmas Eve, Semyon was coming home from such a journey to the villages. The sweat dripped from under his fur cap and he groaned as he pulled his broad sledge, to which a little fir tree and a tightly tied bundle were fastened, through the newly fallen snow. At his approach his children came pelting and tumbling along inquisitively snuffling at the bundle like so many puppies. He drove them away with kindly scolding. They could not guess what the bundle contained, but Semyon allowed them to loosen the fir tree and to drag it into the hut, where it was soon standing as in the forest; for snow even lay in the hut, whither it had been blown through gaps and cracks by the hissing wind. It lay right up to the stove, and it was as cold there as if the hut had lost its walls.

Semyon, already on the threshold, with the bundle under his arm, sniffed the air and looked at the stove with amazement. He took off his mittens and even touched the tiles, then he looked at his children: Marfa, the twelve-year-old, Kyrill, two years younger, and at last Polya and Natasha the little ones, snuggling into Marfa's smock, all with blue faces and noses white from frost though a faint blush of joy was now hovering on their cheeks.

"Why is the stove cold, Marfa?" Semyon asked morosely.

Marfa stood dejected and silent, the little ones hid themselves behind the fir tree which was hardly to be seen anymore in the encroaching dusk; Semyon went to the icon in the corner to cross himself, but he found that even the eternal light under the image of the miracle-worker had gone out.

"Give me the matches, Marfa!" he said, wanting quickly to light a fire, and thinking the girl had been neglectful; but now Marfa confessed that she had no matches left. Semyon searched his pockets for his own but could not find any. He comforted himself and the children.

"There must be some somewhere!" And they all began to search: above the stove where they used to sleep, behind the stove, in all their clothes and boxes. But no, nothing anywhere with which to light a fire. Semyon put his head into the stove and poked around in the ashes to see whether there was not a tiny spark of fire left, but no, the stove was cold. Then it occurred to him that he used to have an old tinder-box with flint and steel, but he could not remember where to find it. Nevertheless, he began to search and all the children with him, only meanwhile it had become almost dark. He almost tore up all the floorboards to see if the tinder-box might be found under them.

At last he noticed that he began to freeze, and he put on his fur coat again and let the children dress in their warmest clothes. Now he had to consider what to do. Celebrate Christmas — light the tree — oh yes, but no light can burn if it is not lit! They all wanted to eat; oh yes, but bread and cold water are not a festive meal! They would freeze to death if the stove could not be lit. And the children had been looking forward to the shining tree with joy beyond measure! It was the first time in their lives that they should have seen one, they had not known it before, as in their district it was not the habit to have one. And now here was the first one, and no match, no spark in the hearth to light the candles.

Semyon sat on the seat by the stove and held his head in his hands. For warmth's sake he put on his mittens again and by and by the children climbed down from the stove and crept closely up to him.

"How is it that we have no matches?" Semyon asked. "Why does God send us such a misfortune on this day?"

The children were silent; Semyon had not directed the question to them.

"How can this be?" he pondered half audibly and he thought on the evil one, but as he felt remorse that he had even thought of him in this night he crossed himself and wanted to look at the icon ... it remained hidden by the dark and by Marfa's pale face close at his shoulder.

"Father ..." said little Polya, only wanting to be remembered as children do who reach little higher than their father's knee.

"Marfa, how is it? Where have our matches got to?" Semyon asked now, as awakening from a dream of hunger and weariness. None of the children answered, they only clung the closer to him. Feeling guilty! It suddenly struck Semyon, and what with hunger and cold and depression, he even grew a little angry. "Now tell me where they are!" he urged the girl severely, but immediately he felt sorry and put his heavy hand in the mitten on her head, around which she had tied a scarf. Marfa's eyes filled with tears, and haltingly she confessed, looking past her father to the window through which a pale reflection from the snow fell. Semyon fell almost asleep hearing the thin soft voice and he never once interrupted her ...

Three days ago, Father had gone to the villages and it had been warm in the hut until yesterday morning. But yesterday, before she had lit a new fire in the stove, one of the frontier guards had come and asked for a match to light his pipe and by mistake he had taken the whole box along. Only long after the man had left had she realized that this box had been the only one in the house. And since then it had been cold, as the stove had burned out entirely through the strong wind which had been blowing the previous night. The whole day long they had kept watch at the window to see if someone should pass, but nobody, nobody had come. And they had not dared to go out and to wait for the soldiers on patrol to ask them for matches, as they remembered their father's bidding never to go far from the hut for the danger of wolves. Nor had they seen any man from the house ... Oh yes, once a soldier on the other side of the river, but they could not have called him to come over. Then they had comforted themselves that father would come back soon, and that he certainly would have matches on him.

"Yes, yes, yes ... " Semyon murmured to himself. He did not want to scold; it was nobody's fault. As his children had been cold since yesterday morning and had had no warm food since the day before yesterday; yes — yes ... He did not stir, and kept silent, and when he had sat quietly for a long time he took his hands from his face and, reaching out to right and left he took the whole small group into his arms, hearing the beating of their hearts and the breathing of their bodies which wafted tenderly towards him from their faces.

"Do you know what?" he asked all of a sudden, smiling secretly into his beard. "Do you know what Father will do now? He is going to look for a soldier — even if he has to go to the next blockhouse — and he will fetch a light. And when he comes back again, we will light the candles on the tree and kindle the fire in the stove and we will celebrate Christmas as other people do at this hour!"

"Yes, father ... " the children around him were sighing, happily though, as if they could hardly grasp it all, and after Semyon had once again reminded them not to leave the house and to look out for him, even if it would take a little longer, he went on his way. But already at the threshold he turned back, thinking, "What if I meet someone who can give me only one match? Then my going would have been all in vain!" So he put a candle-stump into his pocket; this he would be able to light and then he could carry the flame home. The night was quite still, and he and his friends had practised keeping a candle alight on many a candle-light procession while still boys. No wind was going to blow out his candle so easily!

It remained quiet in the hut when Semyon closed the door behind him and listened to the house behind him and to the night. Now and then the darkness of the night flickered — only noticeable in the reflections in the sky while the origin of the light remained distant and hidden. The riverbank here lay still. The river was covered with ice, the snow stretched endlessly and the sky shed light over the just and the unrighteous and sent its gifts disregarding frontiers that had been set up by men. While the soldiers had marked the middle of the river with bundles of brushwood, the newly fallen snow had covered the little bundles and wiped out all frontiers. Stillness was in the house behind Semyon. He had told the children to stay above the stove till he returned. Up there, under the ceiling it would still be warmest, and Marfa could tell them a fairy tale to make the time pass quicker or sleep come sooner. Stillness stretched out before him, far and wide. The sky seemed strangely alight as if the moon were hidden in thick clouds. Only the fine snow crystals dancing in the air made him feel dazed and bewildered. They glittered and scintillated in all the colours of the rainbow and continuously conjured lights before his eyes where there were none at all.

Semyon decided which direction he would take and trudged off — not just lightfooted! He thought: those soldiers, they are well off! Like ghosts they slither about on their snowshoes, in their white cloaks and hoods seemingly one with the white moor, just like snow hares, so that you can hardly see them. Only their rifles, those oblique crossbeams over their shoulders made you aware of them. The house had long vanished behind Semyon, when he thought to himself that there was little sense in just trudging on and on. He would have to look around, maybe he would catch sight of a soldier even before reaching the blockhouse. But when he stood still, listening into the icy stillness and trying to pierce the glimmering darkness he felt how dead-tired he was. And he became even more tired from staring into the darkness, sore tired by each shimmering snow-crystal dancing like a shooting star before his eyes.

Nothing was to be seen, nothing ... and he trudged on. Sometimes he did no longer even watch in which direction he was going. Just as the cold drinks up the water more and more, until the brook is frozen down to its bed, so this icy stillness robbed him of all purpose to decide which way to take and to reckon where he might find a soldier the soonest.

Now and then he stopped and breathing deeply wiped the sweat from his forehead, and he looked up to the sky, which was neither dark nor light. "Ah!" he thought, "this is as if you were looking through a frosted window into a festival hall. You know that it is bright and gay in there and yet you cannot see a thing. Would not the angels be flying and singing up on high also this night? And he, like all men on the far earth could not see it, but only divined it from the strange shimmer in the clouds ... "

When he stopped the next time he stared with a heavily beating heart around himself, for all that was distant seemed near and all that was close just as distant. Snow far and wide, from which here and there a small stunted tree rose, all seemed so forlorn. It was still alive, yes, but it was not live where the eye beheld it. Quite similarly he himself had forgotten the hut and did not even know it. He, too, was still alive, but not as he usually lived.

It may have been hunger, the weariness in his limbs, his sagging knees that reminded him of the lovely bundle of nourishing food that lay at home and before Semyon quite realized what he did, he had pulled the candle stump out of his pocket and bitten off an end of the soft, fragrant church wax. But the icy, dark quiet of the night had frozen his reason almost to the ground and there was only a thinnest trickle left in the very depths of his self, some hazy assumptions about his direction, and these, too, trickled away or transformed into the glassy stillness of strange dreams, into a stillness like the one into which the murmuring waters of a winter brook dies away. He sat down in the snow to rest a little and, as it were to forewarn himself, he held the candlestump in his right hand. He did want to fetch a light! He thought still and closed his eyes as the snow seemed to burn itself into them — and then he wanted to carry peat into the room, to light the stove and to cook a sweet pap of groats. Quite secretly he would light the fire while the children slept. Oh, warm, so warm it would waft up to them! And silently, candle by candle he would light the tree. One little light, a second light ... a third ... "Father?" the question would sound from the stove, and look, Polya there yawning and stretching herself. "Father what is it?" they all would ask, and he would stand by the tree with all its burning lights laugh up at them and then go up to them, just as the warmth from the stones ... Below the tree stood and shone and shone like the dear Saviour himself. But that was not enough! "Here, take it, Marfa, the Lord has given it!" He would say, and did not Marfa there hold a pair of new stockings in her hands, Polya a scarf, Kyrill new boots and Natasha on top of it all, a doll? "The Lord has given it, you blessed children, the Lord in this night when he came into the world. The Lord has given the light too, the Lord is the light, the flame for our cold darkness. And look, from him the fire burns in the stove, the candles burn on the tree, burns our heart ... With us is God!" Thus he would speak, he would say the festival prayer of the holy church, and for the wolves they would throw a bone out of the door, for the unredeemed creatures, for they, too, waited for their redeemer, just as mankind. "Blessed night, blessed night!"

Semyon squatted in the snow, the candle stump in his cold hand. It seemed as if he were looking at it, but his eyes had long been closed. And now, when he had thought all this, the icy stillness had frozen up the last trickle of all thinking life within him. As a light reflects itself in an ice crystal in many glowing colours so dreams reflected in him what happened around him. Not far ahead a searchlight flared up and its beam glided over the wasteland, sometimes lingering, sometimes abruptly jerking sideways, closer and closer to the crouching man until it rested fully, and blindingly on him, closing upon him like a gigantic hand that will not release what it once has gripped, and then, just as suddenly withdrew, extinguished in the deepest darkness. Semyon's eyelids trembled while the beam fell on them. For some seconds it seemed as if he were blinking but then his eyes closed again. The light went out, but it had penetrated into him, like a lonely ray into a deep dungeon and there it continued to shine with celestial radiance ...

"What, what ..." he dreamed, "what is it? The snow is burning? Is it all fire? I want to kindle my light, my light ... " Ah no, ah no, it was delusion. It was dark, pitch dark. But after a while someone came out of the dark towards him, a tall figure surrounded by fire. Calmly he walked over the highest snowdrifts as over waves ... "This is the Lord, it is the Saviour!" thought Semyon, "He is coming, he is coming, he is coming. It is his night, the holy night ... " He wanted to throw himself at his feet as soon as he would see him, Semyon, and humbly he would beg him for fire. But would he see him ... ? Semyon arose and tried to lift his stiffened arms up to heaven, before he pitched forward without a sound.

Yes, he saw him, the Son of God; but Semyon could not look at him, because it was as if the snow were afire, so purely the fire flamed around him, of such clear radiance was his heavenly body and from his face the eyes shone out like the stars in winter. Light and sublime he walked towards the lying man ... now he even stood before him ...

Semyon pressed his face into the snow. "Semyon, Kyrill's son, were you seeking me?" The question rang from above, and now — Semyon heard it — now the angels were singing as they had sung once at Bethlehem, above the shepherds.

"Yes, Lord. You know that I sought Thee!" Semyon breathed into the snow, and a wondrous warmth kissed his lips.

"Semyon, Kyrill's son, did you seek me truly?" the question sounded again and rang all the world.

Semyon pressed himself still deeper into the snow. "Lord, Lord," he whispered at last, "I did seek thee, though today I went out to find light for my hut, for the candles on the tree: fire for the stove, warmth for my children, they are freezing ... "

And all at once he found new courage. He lifted his head and held out his hand with the candle-stump. "Lord!" he spoke quietly into the great radiance. "Give thou the fire to me, thou benefactor of men! May I not hold my candle to thy flaming mantle? Even the least thing is alight in Thee!"

"Take of my light," the Saviour spoke kindly, "take of my light, my servant, take it from me, in peace. Feed the flame with it so that it may shine and give warmth."

"Yes, Lord ..." Semyon sighed and dipped his hand with the candle into the great flame. So warm he felt, so wonderously warm! Tears of joy trickled down into his beard. "They will be happy, my own ones, Lord" he stammered.

"Take, Semyon, take as much as you need of my light. It will not become less!" the voice sounded from above.

Before Semyon's eyes now the candle burned quietly in the night while beyond its sweet glow, the greater radiance around the Saviour began to pale and mount towards the sky. Now he had the fire! Semyon stared happily into the golden flame and sheltered it carefully in the hollow of his hand. But was it not now time to go home? Else the wax would be used up before he could light the fire in the stove with it! Oh how happy the children would be! Yes, now he had to get up however stiff he had become. Only, careful with the candle!

Semyon was still crouching forward in the snow when he was struck in the side by the boot of a Russian soldier who had been sent out from the nearby watch tower to investigate what it was they had detected earlier in their beam.

Once more life began to stir in the benumbed man. Groaning, Semyon got up and mumbling something the soldier did not understand, and pressing his hands together as if he were holding something between them, he tried to hasten away.

"Halt!" the soldier shouted, but Semyon did not hear it. Stumbling and staggering he half ran over the snow without heeding any direction, for his legs were hardly able to carry him.

"Halt! Or ... " yelled the soldier, raising his rifle, following the stumbling man.

"Now it's time to get a move on, make haste," Semyon was dreaming. "Oh, how the children will be waiting!" Then it was as if his legs were pulled away from under his body. If only his light would not go out! Already, it began to flicker before his eyes, that light, and at times he lost it from sight like a distant, tiny star in the sky ... He had to light the stove, to cook the meal, to give the boots to Kyrill at last, the stockings to Marfa ...

Then a blazing fire ran over his back and he saw how his light went out. But beyond it — beyond it there appeared again the greater radiance around the form of the Redeemer! Small as it was the flame of the candle had kept hidden this from him. The Lord! Honour and Praise! Unnoticed he had walked before him ...

Semyon's knees gave way. He felt as if he were hurled into the night, into the sky that began right before his eyes; and between the stars, which seemed to sparkle like fiery rain down towards the depths, there burned the pure flame around the Saviour of all the world ...

"Lord, Lord!" Semyon groaned and he stretched out the hand with the extinguished candle, "it has gone out! Lord have mercy and light it once more for me!" In Semyon's ears there sounded the rushing of all the winds of heaven around God the Father's throne. As he lay in the snow, before him there stood the Son, to whom this night on earth belonged, and he looked at Semyon till his senses faded. "Give the light to me!" the Saviour said softly and Semyon's hand groped towards him through the snow. "Give it!" the Saviour said still more softly, "I shall light it again for you, but not here, here it will burn no more."

"Thanks, thou benefactor!" Semyon groaned for the last time and he wept in immeasurable happiness before the great glory and slowly, like a wave running out of force on the shore, his arm stretched out giving back the candle stump and with it the last spark of life. That was before the soldier had come up to him and turned over his body to stare down at his face, which now was turned up towards heaven ...

The frontier, this wound, that had grown together and been closed by the ice, broke open this night and bled as though it could never heal and close entirely. In those men sitting at their searchlights and machine guns on the towers on yonder river bank, there must have lived a tremendous fear that the Saviour of the earth might secretly enter their apostate realm during this, his own night. Hardly had the news of the death of the frontiersman spread along the banks of the river, when the hands of searchlights from all towers began to feel over the wastelands yard by yard. And when the frontier guards in the blockhouses on the other side of the river within sight of the uneasy watchtowers began to light their Christmas trees in the open air and to sing, the machine gun posts started to snarl with a furious fusillade against the devout singing as if to hinder any word or sound of the joyful message from crossing the river, though Semyon had met the Saviour there.

Towards midnight, quiet fell again over the frontier and its secret war, and except for an odd rifle-shot it became still. Only the beams of light from the towers untiringly kept searching, as it were to catch Christ. But he had found shelter in many a heart, without those guards knowing it, and many a candle was secretly lit at his light.

Semyon's children had already climbed down from the stove by this time. Marfa had been the first, Kyrill had followed her and at last the youngest ones joined them wanting father, food, and the tree lit. Marfa comforted them as best as she could and pressed them against herself in the cold. They stood all at the west window looking out incessantly. Hour after hour passed and father did not return. At times it seemed to Marfa as if she had to wake up under the gaze of her brother, who having become weary of staring out into the night, and seeking advice, did not take his eyes from her. Then Marfa tried to smile, that he should not lose heart and she said sighing — just as if the waiting was only a little nuisance — "Ah, why does he not come!"

The smile remained on her face as if frozen there, and Kyrill, her brother, shrugged his shoulders, dug his chin deeper into his collar and began again to look out. Marfa sighed, tired of waiting and standing and looked out, too. If she only could sleep! she thought, and envied Polya and Natasha, who were breathing quietly against her breast in the shelter of the warm shawl. Then the machine guns began to fire, and Marfa and Kyrill started back. They were used to shots being fired by day and by night, but firing had never been as heavy as now. They trembled and breathed quickly like birds, turning scared towards the wall, for in this cold night it sounded as if the salvoes were being fired just behind their house. The hammering of the machine-guns shredded and tore the stillness and the searchlights dipped into the dark at the same time. They rayed out in bundles, stood still in sheaves, shimmering quite unreal above the snow; and like stars that had been hidden hitherto, the scintillating crystals in the air began to glow, to glimmer and glitter before their window.

Awakened by the gunfire Polya and Natasha crept out from under the shawl and were sleepily staring out, their cheeks pressed against Marfa's breast, their hands clinging to hers.

"Has father not come back?" one of the little ones asked, but Marfa did not hear it among the cracking of the shots; she did not want to hear it, so that she would not have to answer. It was as if a sower was standing high above the hut, strewing light into the darkness, with the beams of the searchlights flickering across the sky. They chased each other, as if corn had been thrown and was now falling to earth drawing shimmering traces along its way earthwards. And the whole marsh outside the window was shimmering in the colours of the rainbow; the snowdust was glinting green, red, golden seeds trickling down from an inexhaustible store. The shots came in such swift succession, that it seemed as if what had been glittering high above a moment before, fell rocketting towards the depths. It was a fearsome sowing at which the children sought comfort from each other. With scared, staring eyes they looked at the uproar. Still and quiet as the night had been, it was now a tempest bleeding, lighting, torn and wounded. Once, in summer a hailstorm had caught them while they were picking berries on the moor; then, too, they had cowered down, filled with fear, unspeakable fear as now. All common sense had been beaten out of them by the hailstones as now in this Christmas night by the fiery cast of seed.

"Father!" Polya called out aloud suddenly.

"Where? Where?" they shouted in confusion, all bending forward still more. "Where, Polya, where can you see him?"

The eyes of the little girl were wide open. "There, there ... " she raised her finger and pointed out of the window. "There, there ... " her little mouth stammered again and again, "Oh, he is waving, he is coming, he has brought somebody with him ... !"

The shooting had suddenly ceased, only in the distance a lone machine gun kept up its hammering. The children had been closely huddling together until then, but at Polya's call they had sprung apart and were now spread over the whole length of the window.

"There, there ... " Polya stammered, still filled with happiness, and though it had become so silent all at once, the silence seemed to roar in their ears. Bright and radiant like a flowering garden, the snowfield lay before them and like a rain of blossom the snowflakes drifted slowly down. In the middle of it — "there, there" Polja stammered and pointed with her finger — yes, in the middle of it, so it appeared to them all, father was standing; tall, cheerful, radiant with light. And next to him — Polya was quite right — next to him stood somebody he had brought along, someone else on whom all the searchlights seemed to fall, for he was quite surrounded by light. And just as you can only divine the charcoal as a dark centre within the white glow of a brightly burning birch log, so you could only guess at the figure of the stranger within the light and the radiance. You might have thought that a whirlwind had raised a snowpillar there, as you can see in the marshes now and then ...

What they did now happened as if in a dream: they seemed to be looking at what they themselves were doing, and yet they acted spontaneously — all out of a strange common will, a common beholding, almost as if of one body, so entirely united seemed their senses.

Marfa ran to the door and stepped onto the threshold. Father Semyon's bidding not to leave the house even if it should take a little longer, was forgotten for, for ... their father himself was calling them! Marfa was hardly outside before her brother and sisters were with her

and they all saw one and the same. In the midst of the brightened night stood their father and the stranger, and father seemed amazingly tall, as if he were hovering above the snow, and he was young and radiant as only on Saturdays when he came from the bathhouse. And it was as if father no longer wanted to come right up to the hut for he smiled at them and beckoned that they should come. Marfa, Kyrill, Polya and Natasha all were chattering at once about all they saw, some more sensibly, the others but stammering, but they all saw one and the same.

"Come!" said Marfa sighing, and took Polya by the hand. "Kyrill, you take Natasha, the snow lies deep!" she told her brother. "Let us go to father!"

And thus it happened that into the stillness, restless with the flickering lights, the children began to walk. Each of the elder ones led one of the small ones by the hand. But soon they all stood still like sleepwalkers, and when Kyrill saw that Marfa lifted up Polya, this little bundle of clothes and rags he did the same with Natasha and he carried her on his arm. And so they went to their father, four children in the middle of the vast night, under the four winds, between the high sky and the deep snow, through the labyrinth of light beams which were crossing and penetrating each other and stood or lay like bundles or sheaves. Yet it was not difficult to find the way; easy to keep to it. They were dead tired and their eyes closed time and again; but even through the smallest gap they could see that their father, together with the stranger, walked before them. He did not wait for them, and that was sad. But every time one of them, either Kyrill or Marfa stumbled to their knees — every time father would stop and wait until the fallen one had regained his footing: and every time he looked round and smiled and gave them courage for the hard way. It became easier the further they went, and if one of them fell, it happened as in a dream when falling is as soft as floating, so painless, so quiet. What was around them they did not know. They walked along as through a deep, dark gorge. The walls on the right and the walls on the left, all were swallowed up by darkness, only the light above the gap they saw, only father before them, and step by step they followed his footmarks, their sisters on their arms.

"Father!" Marfa sighed happily, and Kyrill dared take some carelessly long steps before he fell. But even now, lying in the snow and trying to shelter the little sister on his arm from the cold, he did not let his eyes stray from what was happening. Father Semyon, who had waited patiently for a long time, came walking back. Lightly, as if the snow were as smooth as a threshing floor, he came towards his children, while his companion remained in the distance. The children felt him coming nearer and nearer, they felt rather than saw his approach: they closed their eyes and yet saw him. Father appeared strange to them as he came, as strange as in former times when he had come home from church, from Holy Communion, and still in a mood of devotion had come into the house to kneel for a while before the icon. Now it seemed as if he were but coming for a visit only to leave again soon; but where he walked there it was bright and it was warm all around him like under the sun. Kyrill, still lying in the snow felt his approach as if summer was coming and as if he were lying with closed eyes by the brook on the moor under the hot sun. Father was so clear, his face as bright as if of ice and snow and his voice came kindly, like a soft murmur towards them. A pillar of light hovered closer; a ray of sunlight wandered on, but it had spoken so that it rang in their ears; all their names seemed to have been called.

What should they do? Marfa and Kyrill felt how it was becoming dark and as cold as before and they opened their eyes. It was as if they had slept for a long time. The sisters in their arms had woken up and were trying to wriggle their heads out of their wrappings, and when they succeeded they called for father. Marfa and Kyrill had got up quickly.

"Yes, yes, father ... " they said comfortingly to the little ones and trudged on.

"There, there ... " Polya stammered as if still dreaming of all that had happend in the hut.

Father with his shining companion was again close ahead of them, but the more the children in their growing longing tried to catch up with them, the more distinct became the radiant travellers. The great light around them scattered into thousands of little golden stars and between these stars appeared the green forest. Ah! they must have travelled far if they had reached the forest! Surprised, they stoood and thought back. How far was it now back home? Far, very far! And to father? Marfa and Kyrill strained their eyes, but that was not necessary! In a great united radiance their father and his companion stood quite close to them and the stars among which they had vanished before, shimmered all around them. They had both turned round towards the children, as if now they would always be awaiting them and go together with them. The stranger was hidden from them in his great radiance but they could see clearly enough that in his hand he held a candle-stump like the one father had taken with him, and his arm was round their father as if he were his dearest friend. And he, seeing his children so close, seemed sad, yet he smiled and waved his hand to them, and then looking round a last time he waved while he vanished gently before their eyes with his companion among the green fir trees and the stars.

The children had stopped when they had come so close to their father, but now they tramped on. They did not take their eyes from the place where he had disappeared. They did not want to miss the door that had to be there and whose hidden entrance they wanted to find. How good it was that suddenly the snow seemed less deep, that the earth seemed swept smooth, for now they could walk much faster and more safely and they could hope to catch up with those who had vanished.

The frontier guards, in the district to the west of the hut in the marshes, relate that in the Holy Night, while they were standing around their Christmas tree in front of the blockhouse, two children had all at once stepped into their circle, a boy and a girl, carrying their two younger sisters in their arms. Silently, without them noticing it — not being just very watchful — they had suddenly stood before the lit Christmas tree, their eyes half closed like sleepwalkers. And behind them, close to the house, a pack of wolves had been lying that must have followed them to this place. Without seeing anyone standing around it, the boy and the girl had walked straight towards the tree. Only when they were quite close and when the astonished exclamations had woken them out of the dream into which this tree must have shone, did they awake to reality. How difficult, it was, accompanied by so much trembling and tears — this the soldiers would remember all their lives. Not only were the four half-starved and frozen and falling over with fatigue and weakness, they had also tumbled into reality like a sleepwalker into a gaping abyss. As long as their eyes were able to see the Christmas tree they stared into the light of its candles as if they had come from another world.

Of all that the children stammeringly told — of father, how he had gone out to fetch a light, of his radiant companion, and of how both had vanished among the green fir trees, perhaps this very Christmas tree — the soldiers could understand nothing. They only saw that four half-starved and frozen children had come to them, and they fed them and warmed them as if they were their own.

The following day, however, they had to realize that something miraculous had led these four to them. Not one of them would have survived in their hut until morning, for that night such frost set in as if every breathing thing between heaven and earth should be frozen to death. But when at last the news of Semyon's death reached them, and first the one and then the other remembered the incoherent tales of the children, they became aware that in that night Christ must have been in the lonely marshes to guide those to whom the kingdom of heaven belongs.

Christmas in all the World

Rösli of Stechelberg

Jakob Streit

The Family of Allmen

More than a hundred years ago, when there was no telephone connecting the high-lying villages with the low-lying ones and the towns, the first December snow had fallen in the Lauterbrunnental. Behind the valley on the Stechelberg, Father Allmen trudged along the snow-covered path up to his cabin. His lean frame was bent beneath a heavy bale of hay, and he was thinking: "Good that I've brought it out of the barn in the valley. If it goes on snowing I wouldn't be able to carry such a load up the hill path tomorrow. Now our two goats will have enough fodder till Christmas."

As he climbed the hill children's voices sounded down to him from the cabin: "Father, Father, you've got a gigantic bale of hay, nearly as big as our little house!" Soon he was surrounded by the children helping to carry the hay with their little arms.

"Come in out of the snow!" their mother now called through the open doorway, "Your house-shoes will get quite wet! Fritz has his wooden shoes on, he can help Father to unload."

Fritz, the oldest, opened the door of the hay-loft for his father. Rösli brushed the snow off her little sisters' shoes with fir-twigs. These house-shoes consisted of rags roughly stitched together, and looked more like a mouse's nest than shoes.

"Come, supper's ready," Mother called from the kitchen. "Rösli, lay the table."

It was soon laid: nine spoons, and a knife for father. When they were all seated round the pot of soup, Mother said grace, and everyone put his spoon into the bowl, for this was the ancient custom in the mountains. How could the Allmens have afforded eight soup bowls? Now Father cut a slice of bread for each child. Mother cut a piece of cheese for Father's slice; for every day he had to do heavy work in the woods.

Father happened to look out of the little kitchen window into the dusky evening and his eyes came to rest on a dark patch on the edge of the wood nearby: a chamois, nibbling at something. It had already appeared there several times towards evening, and Father Allmen always had the same idea: "If I were to shoot the animal, wife and children could eat meat once again and would not have to eat only porridge or watery soup every day."

The children also now looked out of the kitchen window.

"Is it the father-chamois or the mother-chamois?" asked Rösli.

"The father-chamois likes to go alone through the wood and fields," Father Allmen explained. After these words he went quickly into the living room. Mother followed him. There he lifted down his dusty military rifle from the wardrobe, and from a cupboard he took out a little tin box. Mother, shocked, laid her hand on his shoulder and said: "Hans, you're not going to ..."

"Yes I am, let me be! For a long time now I've felt it a shame that our children never get any meat, and do you think that I enjoy eating my cheese by myself every day? If we had chamois meat a few times we should all have the strength to stand the winter well."

But the mother demurred: "But you know Hans, it's against the law and poaching is heavily punished. Let the beast live."

But Allmen replied: "You've said that before. I see no sin in it when we have hungry children, and God lets some meat run about in front of the window."

While they were thus arguing the chamois disappeared again among the fir-trees. Mother breathed a sigh of relief, but Father Allmen left the house by the back door rather disgruntled. He took the gun and cartridges up into the hay-loft. It was growing dark quickly and the mother was putting the little ones to bed. The youngest, only a few weeks old, was already asleep in the basket in the bedroom. After a time Father came back into the room and started carving some wood with his knife, making a cradle. But his thoughts kept going back to his gun and the chamois.

In the dusk of the following evening, when already the oil lamp was burning, a loud shot rang out behind the house. It re-echoed among the escarpments and its echoes only slowly died away. Mother Allmen, who was sewing a patch, was startled and pricked her finger with the needle.

When the children wanted to rush out she spoke sharply to stop them: "No one's to go out!"

"Mother what was that shot? Did Father shoot? Has he killed the father-chamois?" The children's voices sounded together. With their foreheads pressed against the window panes they looked out towards the edge of the wood, where Allmen was just lifting something dark on to his shoulder, and who then made his way laboriously along the side of the hill through the deep snow towards the house. No one said a word, and even Mother, with her pricked finger pressed between her lips, stared fascinated out of the window.

But in the little village the shot had been heard. Gertsch Peter, their nearest neighbour, who lived alone in a cabin lower down the hill, had noticed clearly where the shot had come from. He had been sawing wood in front of his house. Now he quickly put down the saw and crept up the hill towards the Allmens' cabin. Once up there he kept hidden behind some hazel bushes. He could just make out how Allmen disappeared with the shot chamois into the cellar. Gertsch Peter had always been a dour neighbour, and he envied Allmen his hard-working wife and his jolly crowd of children, even envying their laughing and hilarity, that often resounded from the hill in summertime. And now this Allmen had taken the liberty of going poaching in the days before Holy Christmas! That would have to be reported! With this in mind Gertsch Peter marched down the hill, changed from his working smock into something better, lit his pipe and headed for the village inn.

Next day, towards noon the *Landjäger*, the canton's game-warden from Lauterbrunnen, appeared. When he knocked at Allmen's kitchen door Mother opened. She turned pale with fright when the *Landjäger* asked brusquely for Allmen. With difficulty Mother managed to say: "Fritzi, go and call Father. He's in the shed."

Then she sank down on a chair in the kitchen. Her legs were trembling. But Fritzi said to the stranger: "I'll just go and call Father, he's in the shed sharpening knives."

The other children crowded to the door and gazed shyly at the dark bearded man with the wide blue cape. Only little Werni asked: "Are you Saint Nicholas? Are you bringing us something?"

The *Landjäger* took no notice of the question but turned towards the shed into which Fritz had disappeared. With a black look Allmen now came out into the open, shut the bolt of the shed door and asked: "What's up?"

In the meantime Mother had pulled herself together and taken all the children back into the living-room. Full of anxiety she heard the *Landjäger* opening the cellar door. Then she could no longer abide staying in the room. She rushed down the stairs, stood in front of the cellar with her husband, laid her hand on his shoulder as if to say: "I stand by you, and bear the consequences with you!"

The *Landjäger* came out soon again, and said, "This chamois belongs to the State, Allmen. I am sorry for you, but I must do my duty. Take a sledge and bring the animal with me to Lauterbrunnen. Then we must go further. The law-court is in Interlaken."

These words came like hammer-blows one after the other on Mother Allmen's heart. If only Hans doesn't suddenly do something rash, she thought trembling. She caught at his clenched fist for a moment and said, "Do go Hans. Take the little sledge. Don't forget your cap."

A little while later Mother and children gazed after Father as he went away out of the valley with the chamois in a bundle on his sledge. The man in the blue cape marched behind him. Mother explained: "See, Father has to take the chamois a long way, right as far as Interlaken, because they need it there."

Rösli asked: "Do they need Father in Interlaken too?"

"Yes, for a time."

Rösli cried bitterly: "But Mother it's soon Christmas, and we need Father at home with us, and he has still to finish the cradle for my doll."

Then Rösli saw that tears were running down her mother's cheeks. She clasped her vehemently and began to sob loudly. The others began to cry too and to wail: "Father's gone away! The man in blue has taken Father away! He's got to come back again!" The little low room was filled with lamenting. They all clutched at Mother, holding her apron, her arms and legs. Even the baby in the basket was crying. Mother freed herself gently from the tangle and comforted them: "Don't cry. Father has to go and help the man in blue for a time. They need him in Interlaken. He'll come back again to us."

Ten days had gone by. No word of Father came to Stechelberg. Fritzi fed and milked the goats. In the little house of the Allmens it had grown very quiet. Happy play and laughter could no longer be heard. Mother did not sing any more. It was as if someone dear had died in the house. Rösli and the little ones often stood for hours at the window and gazed down the valley, especially towards evening when it began to grow dark. It was already nearing the twentieth of December.

Christmas was almost upon them. It was Rösli who had taken it most to heart that her Father had gone away. She did not ask her mother about him any more, since she noticed how sad it made her, and all Mother could say was: "They still need him for another few days."

At night Rösli slept restlessly and often woke up. Then it occurred to her that Father could forget out there in the world that here in the valley it would soon be Christmas. Who knows, perhaps they had no idea out there, where there were only big houses and hotels, and no mountain firs, what a real Christmas was like; where a fir-tree shines in the room; where Father tells stories and reads from the Bible; where you may sing lovely carols with Mother, and pluck something nice from the tree once in the year, because in Bethlehem on that night the angels appeared to the shepherds and showed them the way to the manger.

Then Rösli slipped quietly out of her straw sack from under the blankets and crept to the window. Outside the stars were shining. As she looked right to the end of the valley it seemed to her that far far away a faint light was shining. Perhaps Father was coming home in the middle of the night with a lantern. She stood by the window for a time and her eyes bored into the distance, but the light did not come any nearer and suddenly went out. The cold forced her to go back to bed, but in her mind the decision was forming: "I must go and bring Father home again! I must tell him that it's Christmas here. The man with the blue cape must give him back to me. Without Father we can't have any Christmas."

The Flight

The next morning after Fritzi had milked the goats and the family had eaten their breakfast of milk and bread, Rösli said to her mother: "I'll take the broom and go and sweep this morning's fall of snow off the path."

So she slipped into her wooden shoes, pulled her bonnet over her ears and put on her gloves. She began to sweep back and forth down the path away from the house. Once she got round the hazel bushes she threw the broom into them.

For one moment she hesitated; should she ask mother? Then she felt fear in her heart: "No, Mother would never allow me to go to Lauterbrunnen, let alone as far as Interlaken which must be much further away." Rösli's heart was beating right up into her throat: "I must

195

get Father! Mother will surely be glad and sing again when I bring him home."

Suddenly she ran down the hill like a startled deer and reached the snow-covered road that led out of the valley. Not once did she dare look round, for fear someone would wave to her to come back. The little girl, flying along, pulled her bonnet even tighter over her ears, so that she would not hear anyone calling. But no one beckoned and no one called her back. Her flight had not been noticed.

The road on this winter morning was empty of people and completely untrodden and so it was heavy trudging for little legs with their heavy wooden shoes. Snow-flakes were still falling softly. When Rösli finally dared to look back after half an hour she could see no trace of her little village or of her house. A curtain of snow-flakes hid what lay behind her. Suddenly, just before she came to Lauterbrunnen, she heard the little bells of a horse sleigh coming towards her. The fright went right into her limbs when she thought she could be taken on the sleigh and brought back to Stechelberg. Quickly she crept behind a snow-covered bush a little way off the road. The sledge went on and the sound of the bells grew faint. As Rösli went on she looked up at the mighty wall of rock where in summer the Staubbach cascaded down, and she saw towers of glistening ice built on to the face of the cliff. Oh, the ice-palace of the winter dwarfs, thought the child, and stopped for a moment to admire the hundreds of pinnacles and pillars. If her heart had not been so set on finding Father she would have loved to climb up to the ice-palace. The nearer she came to the village of Lauterbrunnen the more fearful she became. What if someone should stop her and send her back home? As she hurried by the village bakery, the doors opened and a woman from Stechelberg came out and called in surprise: "Hey, Rösli, where are you going? Did you come all alone to the village?"

"I'm going to get Father," she called back hastily, and ran on.

Once she was past the last houses the road led downhill to the bottom of the valley. Because some wooden sledges had passed over it slippery ice had formed, and Rösli was now sliding along on her wooden shoes downhill and was delighted at going so fast. The snow flakes were now falling larger and wetter. She stopped once to get her breath and leaned against a wall beside the road. There she felt how her clothes had soaked through, especially on her shoulders and back, and the cold seeped through the cloth. She never had had a coat. So she would have to speed along again and get warm! About midday the road suddenly entered a forest. Oh how a hot plate of Mother's soup would have done her good now! She stopped by a fir-tree and wiped the snow off its roots with her wet gloves and sat down for a moment. But hardly had she sat still before her teeth started chattering with cold so that she started off again in a fresh hurry.

"Did Father have a warm room in Interlaken? Was there any warm gruel there? Perhaps he even had a stove with a ledge where you could dry clothes."

Rösli's steps grew slower and her shoes heavier. Only once when a wooden sledge came towards her did she speed up. The forester turned his head to look at her and wondered why this little frozen creature was wandering all by herself in winter. At times the forest was more open, revealing a small snow-covered patch of pasture-land. Then she noticed a short way off the road a little barn with a byre. There are sure to be animals in there, she thought, and I could get some warmth. She made her way to it, and softly drew open the bolt. Inside the byre there lay two cows and a calf. A pleasant warmth met her. Quietly she closed the byre door behind her and felt her way to the calf who was lying on a plentiful bed of straw. The cows did not let themselves be disturbed in their chewing of the cud, and Rösli knelt down by the little calf very carefully so that it would not get up. She tickled it behind the ears, spoke to it, and laid her arm gently on its back. How lovely and warm it was in there! Here she could rest for a while. She covered herself with some armfuls of straw as there was plenty at hand. The little girl was so exhausted after her long walk, that she soon fell asleep with her back nestling against the calf.

Suddenly Rösli woke up when something wiped across her face. Where was she? Who had caressed her? It was the little calf licking her cheeks. "To Father, to Father," the inner voice insisted. After clearing herself of the straw and stroking the calf she slipped through the byre-door and out into the damp cold again. Praise be it was still bright afternoon. The short sleep had revived her strength, and now she bravely continued on the road to Interlaken.

In Interlaken

It must have been getting towards four o'clock when Rösli found out that she was in Interlaken. Yes, there were the big houses too; but nearly all had their shutters closed. Did the people sleep also by day? Was even Father asleep now? She would have to ask. She stopped a woman carrying a heavy basket.

"Please can you tell me where my Father is?" she asked

"Hm, who's your Father, and who are you?"

"I am Rösli Allmen. I've come for my Father; we need him."

"I don't know where your Father is; ask further in the town."

And the woman staggered on with her basket.

Rösli thought it was strange that no one here knew where her Father was staying. Inside the town she spoke to an older man, for Mother had once said that when one grew older one grew wiser.

"Please can you tell me where I can find my Father? He's helping the man with the blue cape."

"Dear child, where do you come from?" the old man asked so kindly, that Rösli became quite trusting.

"I am Rösli Allmen from Stechelberg and I've come to Interlaken because I've got to get my Father. We've got to have him back for Christmas."

The old man shook his head perplexed and asked: "Well what kind of work is your Father doing here in Interlaken?"

"He's helping the *Landjäger* with the blue cape; he brought the chamois he shot here for him on a sledge."

The old man was not much the wiser, but because the girl had said something about a *Landjäger* he pointed out a big house beside the church and said, "Go over to that big house, a *Landjäger* lives there. Perhaps he can tell you where your Father is."

Although she was now bone weary and miserable, her joy shone from her eyes.

"A thousand thanks, dear dear man," she cried, and hurried over to the big house by the church. But the nearer she got to it the slower her steps became. The house seemed so grand. It was surely a palace. It had little towers and such remarkably big windows and doors and many chimneys on its roof. Did a king live there? When Mother told stories of palaces there was always a king and a princess living in them. Did her father now live in such a magnificent place! Which door should she knock at? There were so many. Hesitantly she went up to one of the doors, lifted the iron knocker and let it fall. Oh what a fright, how loudly it rang out through the big house! Footsteps could be heard and a maid opened the door.

"Does my Father live here? We need him back for Christmas!"

"Who are you and where do you come from?"

"I am Rösli Allmen from Stechelberg and I've come to Interlaken today to collect our Father from the *Landjäger*. Isn't he here?"

Rösli's eyes filled with tears, and her small body trembled with exhaustion and cold.

"Come in," said the maid gently and led her by the hand into the house. "Oh dear how wet and cold you are! Come quickly to the warm fire in the kitchen."

After setting the girl on a kitchen chair by the fire the maid went to get her mistress, who was the magistrate's wife and bore the title of Frau Präsident, for it was at the magistrate's door that Rösli had knocked. Rösli now repeated her errand to this lady and did not conceal the affair with the *Landjäger* in the blue cape and the chamois.

Then it began to dawn on the people of the mansion who Rösli's Father was, and the Frau Präsident said: "Yes, yes, I think your Father is staying with us, but he's in the house at the back. But before you can go to him you must have something hot to eat and put on some dry clothes; you're wet through and through!"

So some soup was heated up, and bread and cheese cut. Rösli got a warm woollen cloth laid over her back and she thankfully stilled her hunger. Meantime Frau Präsident rummaged in a wardrobe and looked out some children's clothes belonging to her own daughter who had long since grown-up. Soon Rösli was being properly dried on the warm ledge above the stove and dressed like a princess. She hardly knew what was happening to her. Why, she even got stockings and hand-made leather shoes. A cosy warmth flowed into her limbs so that she forgot all her tiredness. The door of the room opened and the magistrate, the Herr Präsident himself, came in. He had already heard from his wife of the strange visit.

"So, my little one," he greeted her kindly, "You came all the way from Stechelberg on foot to get your Father?"

"Yes, may I go to him now, so that I can tell him he must come home because it's soon Christmas."

"We'll have him brought here," answered the Herr Präsident.

He wrote a few words on a slip of paper and sent the maid out to the house at the back with it. Turning to Rösli he said: "Just you stay on the stove until all your toes are nice and warm."

Frau Präsident now climbed up and sat down beside Rösli, undid her wet plaits, and spread her blond hair out to dry on a cloth which she laid round her shoulders. It was a good twenty years since she had dressed her own little girl in this blue dress and sat beside her on the stove. Now Rösli told about her home, about her mother, about her seven brothers and sisters, about the gruel every day, about their two goats in the stall, about the doll's cradle that Father had almost finished and how hard it was for them to bear that Father was in Interlaken and not at home where Mother often wept.

Rösli stopped her chatter, for in the passage firm footsteps were sounding. The door opened. In came the maid, Father, and with him a stranger. The blue angel flew down from the stove to Father's breast and cried: "Now I've found you again! Father, dear, dear Father. Why don't you come home? Have you forgotten that it's soon to be Christmas? You wanted to finish making my doll's cradle. You'll come now, won't you?"

What was the matter with Father? For quite a while he could not speak a word and just held his little one in his arms. In the end he whispered huskily: "Rösli, Rösli, what's all this?"

"We need you, Father, and that's why I've come."

"And did Mother let you go, or didn't you tell her?"

"O Father, I did find it hard to run away like that without telling, but Mother would never have let me go, and then perhaps we should have lost you altogether. You're not angry with me are you?"

Father's eyes filled with tears. He clasped the little one closer in his arms and said softly: "No, no, you wouldn't have lost me. I am coming back to you."

Now the Herr Präsident went into the hall with the gaoler to discuss the extraordinary situation. Frau Präsident told Allmen to sit up on the stove with Rösli. When Herr Präsident came back in after a while he said to Rösli: "Actually we needed your father for another ten days; but because Christmas Eve comes before that he can go home for Christmas. I promise you that, and then you can keep him for ever; we won't need him ever again. I'm sure your mother is worrying a lot about you, so in a little while a *Landjäger* with a horse and sledge will drive you home to Stechelberg. Tell them at home, Father is coming home for Christmas in four days time, or let's say in three days so that he can finish your doll's cradle in time. Till then he's staying here."

Rösli nodded and said, "I had better put my own clothes on again for the journey home."

"No," said Frau Präsident. "What you have on I'll give you for Christmas."

Rösli then looked down reverently at her blue dress and said: "Then I won't lie in the byre in this dress."

"What do you mean, a byre," asked Frau Präsident in surprise.

"This afternoon I was so tired I went into a byre to warm myself with the little calf, and that was nearly as nice as here with you in the palace. The little calf licked me awake, otherwise I might have been sleeping there still."

Then everyone laughed heartily, even Father. Meantime the gaoler had gone off to arrange the horse and sledge. Frau Präsident went into the kitchen with the maid to pack all kinds of eatables in a basket, and looked out a little cloak to keep Rösli warm on the cold journey. No more time was lost and a quarter of an hour later Rösli was sitting in the sledge well wrapped up, and beside her sat the driver in a blue cape. He had young merry eyes and no beard. Then the sleigh-bells tinkled, hands waved and the blue princess drove off home.

The Homeward Journey

The moon shone brightly over the valley of Lauterbrunnen when the sledge was passing the ice-palace of Staubbach. The moonlight was reflected in the ice-towers, but Rösli saw nothing of the glittering of the night. She lay sleeping, leaning against the blue coachman, who had put his arm protectively round the princess wrapped in rugs, so that she should not fall off the sledge. With his other hand he held the reins loosely and let the horse trot along freely as it liked.

When they arrived in Stechelberg nearly everybody in the houses had gone to bed. At the first house the *Landjäger* stopped. Rösli was sound asleep. But he knocked at a window where there was a faint glimmer of light. He enquired where the girl's family lived. Below the hill, away over there where old Gertsch lived a light was still burning. The coachman drove off in that direction. Gertsch Peter had heard the approaching bells and was already standing outside with a lantern, when the sledge stopped in front of his house. He realized at once who was being brought there. He came up and shone the lantern into Rösli's face, "Thank heavens, Rösli is back again."

He helped the *Landjäger* to lead his horse into his stable and to spread a warm blanket over his steaming back.

Then he led the way with his lantern, so that the *Landjäger* could better carry the sleeping girl up the hill. Gertsch took the basket which the *Landjäger* had given him. When the light swung against Allmen's little house the front door burst open and several excited voices cried: "Have you got Rösli? Are you bringing her back?"

"Yes," called the old man with the lantern, "we're bringing her home."

Only when her mother, sobbing, took her in her arms did Rösli wake up. She looked round in surprise for a moment and then comforted her mother with the words: "Mother, don't cry! Father's coming! Only three more nights and then he'll be back again."

All the children rejoiced. But old Gertsch had a queer feeling. The blood rushed to his face. He wished he could sink into the ground. But as he could not do that he held on to the balustrade of the steps with one hand so that he could hold the lantern steadier with the other, shining it on to the stately-clad child emerging from the brown rug. The *Landjäger* held out to Mother the basket which Peter had placed on one of the steps and said: "The Frau Präsident sends you this. Please empty it so that I can take the basket back to her."

When the *Landjäger* was going back down with Peter Gertsch, the latter invited him in for a warm drink before his return journey and placed bread and mountain cheese in front of him. In this way Peter found out all about Rösli's strange journey, and that the people in the mansion in Interlaken could show feeling for a poor family with lots of children, but they still had to maintain the law. Peter did not tell that it was he who had reported Allmen and was to blame that the children had had to do without their father.

Father comes home

On the forenoon of the twenty-third of December, in Allmen's cabin on the hill, all the time you could see children's heads with their noses pressed against the window panes of the living-room. Their eyes were keeping watch on the end of the valley. Especially Rösli could not be dragged away. Already she had dressed and undressed her wooden doll several times, and in between she had always looked out of the window. Mother had allowed her to put on the blue dress from the mansion in Interlaken in order to welcome Father home. Outside, deep snow was lying. Fritz, the oldest, had been allowed to take the shovel and clear the path down to the village. He was eagerly shovelling the snow out left and right so that Father might be able to walk up better. At the steeper places he cut steps with the shovel. When he got near Gertsch Peter's house which was by the path, Gertsch came out and went up to the boy. He handed him a handful of dried pieces of pear and said, "Take and eat, they'll make you strong."

Fritz held the unexpected gift in his wet hand, quite flummoxed. Never before had Gertsch Peter ever given him anything.

"You must eat them up. Don't stand there gaping!" the old man declared.

Then he enquired whether Father would soon be coming home, whether they had had any news from Interlaken. Fritz enjoyed the cuttings and while he was chewing away he explained: "Yes, Father's coming home today, that's why I'm shovelling."

After the midday rest the call resounded: "Father's coming, Father's coming."

Everyone ran to the window. He was already round the corner by the hazel-bushes. But what was that! He was bent under a big heavy sack. He was pulling the sledge behind him and on it there was another sack tied, and what was that green sticking up on top? A Christmas tree! Now there was a tumult in Allmen's cabin. Doors flew open, cries of joy resounded, and twelve hands helped Father to lift the sack from his back. Mother stood in the doorway with the baby in her arms and smiled. Father could not take another step forward, because all the children were hanging on to his arms, back and legs. But little Sämi called: "Open it, open it." All together they hauled the sack into the room. And they untied the other one and brought it into the room too. Meanwhile Father had taken the littlest one from Mother and sat down on the ledge of the warm stove with him. Fritz came with scissor to let the contents out of the sack.

Then Father called laughing: "Stop. Mother and I will look after that. Frau Präsident has taken far too much trouble carefully packing everything for us to throw it all out to the hens. Only the big rucksack, that you can plunder!"

Immediately the bulging sack was surrounded and Fritz loosened the cord. How the fiery red apples rolled out on to the floor. Very soon all the cries of jubilation were silenced as all reverently enjoyed the rare and wonderful food. Father put the little one on to Rösli's lap, and went and reached down into the other sack. He brought out something wrapped up, "That's from the Präsident himself."

The smell of smoked ham spread through the room, and the children did not know what it was.

"You'll find out at supper time," said Father, winking at Mother. While Father and Mother slowly unpacked the sacks, delighted sounds were heard in the room that had heard so many sighs for so many days. In one of the sacks there were clothes, cloth, shoes, stockings and shirts of all sizes, and in the other, things to eat, bread and sausage, sugar, flour and even Christmas tree candles. Mother could not believe it and kept saying: "Oh we're so rich, oh we're so rich!"

Father explained: "Frau Präsident told all her acquaintances about Rösli's visit to the mansion, and so she received from everybody all these wonderful things for us."

"Yes, yes," said Rösli. "They're good people, the Interlaken folk. But Father, you won't forget my doll, will you?"

"Oh yes, your little cradle, That was to be my first job when I got home, for it was you dear Rösli who has given us all these lovely things."

"No," Rösli protested: "It was the Holy Christ, at this time he makes people's hearts good."

A little while later Father was heard working in the shed, and in the room Mother was practising carols with the children for Christmas Eve.

The Fir Tree

Hans Christian Andersen

Out in the wood was a fir tree, such a pretty little fir tree. It had a good place to grow in and all the air and sunshine it wanted, while all around it were numbers of bigger comrades, both firs and pines. But the little fir tree was in such a passionate hurry to grow. It paid no heed to the warmth of the sun or the sweetness of the air, and it took no notice of the village children who went chattering along when they were out after strawberries or raspberries; sometimes they came there with a whole jugful or had got strawberries threaded on a straw, and then they sat down by the little tree and said, "Oh, what a dear little tree!" That was not at all the kind of thing the tree wanted to hear.

The next year it had shot up a good deal, and the year after that its girth had grown even bigger; for, with a fir tree, you can always tell how old it is by the number of rings it has.

"Oh, if only I were a tall tree like the others," sighed the little fir. "Then I'd be able to spread out my branches all round me and see out over the wide world with my top. The birds would come and nest in my branches and, whenever it was windy, I'd be able to nod just as grandly as the others."

It took no pleasure in the sunshine or the birds or the pink clouds that, morning and evening, went sailing overhead.

When winter came and the snow lay sparkling white all around, then a hare would often come bounding along and jump right over the little tree — oh, how annoying that was! ... But two winters passed and by the third winter the tree had grown so tall that the hare had to run round it. Yes, grow, grow, become tall and old — that was much the finest thing in the world, thought the tree.

In the autumn the woodcutters always came and felled some of the tallest trees. That used to happen every year; and the young fir, which was now quite a sizeable tree, trembled at the sight, for the splendid great trees would crack and crash to the ground; their branches were lopped off, and they looked all naked and spindly — they were hardly recognizable — and then they were loaded on to waggons and carted away by horses out of the wood.

Where were they off to? What was in store for them?

In the spring, when the swallow and the stork arrived, the tree asked them, "Do you know where they've gone — where they've been taken to? Have you seen anything of them?"

The swallows knew nothing, but the stork looked thoughtful and replied with a nod, "Yes, I believe I know. I came across a lot of new ships, as I flew here from Egypt; they had splendid masts — I daresay it was them — I could smell the fir, and they asked to be remembered to you. Oh, how straight they stand!"

"How I do wish that *I* were big enough to fly across the sea! And, as a matter of fact, what sort of a thing is this sea? What does it look like?"

"That would take far too long to explain," said the stork and went his way.

"Rejoice in your youth," said the sunbeams; "rejoice in your lusty growth, and in the young life that is in you." And the wind kissed the tree, and the dew wept tears over it, but this meant nothing to the fir tree.

As Christmas drew near, quite young trees were cut down, trees that often were nothing like so big or so old as our fir tree, which knew no peace and was always longing to get away. These young trees — and they were just the very handsomest ones — always kept their branches; they were laid on waggons and carted away by horses out of the wood.

"Where are they off to?" asked the fir tree. "They are no bigger than I am; there was even one that was much smaller. Why did they all keep their branches? Where are they going?"

"We know, we know!" twittered the sparrows. "We've been peeping in at the windows down in the town; we know where they're going. All the glory and splendour you can imagine awaits them. We looked in through the window-panes and saw how the trees were planted in the middle of a cosy room and decorated with the loveliest things: gilded apples, honey cakes, toys and hundreds of candles."

"And then?" asked the fir tree, quivering in every branch. "And then? What happens then?"

"Well, we didn't see any more. But it was magnificent."

"I wonder if it will be my fate to go that dazzling road," cried the tree in delight. "It's even better than crossing the ocean. How I'm longing for

Christmas! I'm now just as tall and spreading as the others who were taken away last year. Oh, if only I were already on the waggon — if only I were in the cosy room amidst all that glory and splendour! And then? Yes, there must be something still better, still more beautiful in store for me — or why should they decorate me like that? — Something much greater, and much more splendid. But what? Oh, the labouring and longing I go through! I don't know myself what's the matter with me."

"Rejoice in me," said the air and the sunlight; "rejoice in your lusty youth out here in the open."

But the fir tree did nothing of the kind. It went on growing and growing; there it was, winter and summer, always green — dark green. People who saw it remarked, "That's a pretty tree"; and at Christmas time it was the first to be felled. The axe cut deep through pit and marrow, and the tree fell to the earth with a sigh, faint with pain, with no more thoughts of any happiness; it was so sad at parting from its home, from the place where it had grown up. For it knew that never again would it see those dear old friends, the little bushes and flowers that grew around — yes, and perhaps not even the birds. There was nothing pleasant about such a parting.

The tree didn't come to itself till it was being unloaded in the yard with the other trees and it heard a man say, "That one's a beauty — that's the one we'll have."

Now came two lackeys in full fig and carried the fir tree into a splendid great room. There were portraits all round on the walls, and by the big tile fireplace stood huge Chinese vases with lions on their lids. There were rocking-chairs, silk-covered sofas, large tables piled with picture-books and toys worth hundreds of pounds — at least, so said the children. And the fir tree was propped up in a great firkin barrel filled with sand, though no one could see it was a barrel because it was draped round with green baize and was standing on a gay-coloured carpet. How the tree trembled! Whatever was going to happen? Servants and young ladies alike were soon busy decorating it. On the branches they hung the little nets that had been cut out of coloured paper, each net being filled with sweets; gilded apples and walnuts hung down as if they were growing there, and over a hundred red, blue and white candles were fastened to the branches. Dolls that looked just like living people — such as the tree had never seen before — hovered among the greenery, while right up at the very top they had put a great star of gold tinsel; it was magnificent — you never saw anything like it.

"Tonight," they all said, "tonight it's going to sparkle — you see!"

"Oh, if only tonight were here!" thought the tree. "If only the candles were already lighted! What happens then, I wonder? Do trees come from the wood to look at me? Will the sparrows fly to the window-panes? Shall I take root here and keep my decorations winter and summer?"

Well, well, — a nice lot the fir tree knew! But it had got barkache from sheer longing, and barkache is just as bad for a tree as headache is for the rest of us.

At last the candles were lighted — what a blaze, what magnificence! It made the tree tremble in every branch, until one of the candles set fire to the greenery — didn't that smart!

"Oh dear!" cried the young ladies and quickly put out the fire. It was so afraid of losing any of its finery, and it felt quite dazed by all that magnificence ... Then suddenly both folding doors flew open, and a flock of children came tearing in, as if they were going to upset the whole tree. The older people followed soberly behind; the little ones stood quite silent — but only for a moment — then they made the air ring with their shouts of delight. They danced round the tree, and one present after another was pulled off it.

"Whatever are they doing?" thought the tree. "What's going to happen?" The candles burned right down to their branches and, as they did so, they were put out, and the children were allowed to plunder the tree. They rushed in at it, till it creaked in every branch; if it hadn't been fastened to the ceiling by the top and the gold star, it would have tumbled right over.

The children danced round with their splendid toys, and nobody looked at the tree except the old nurse, who went peering among the branches — though this was only to see if there wasn't some fig or apple that had been overlooked.

"A story — tell us a story!" cried the children, dragging a little fat man over towards the tree. He sat down right under it, "for then we are in the greenwood," he said, "and it will be so good for the tree to listen with you. But I'll only tell one story. Would you like the one about *Hickory-Dickory* or the one about *Humpty-Dumpty, who fell down-stairs and yet came to the throne and married the Princess?*"

"*Hickory-Dickory,*" cried some; "*Humpty-Dumpty,*" cried others. There was such yelling and shouting; only the fir tree was quite silent and thought, "Shan't I be in it as well? Isn't there anything for me to do?" But of course, it *had* been in it — done just what it had to do.

The little fat man told them the story of *Humpty-Dumpty, who fell downstairs and yet came to the throne and married the Princess.* And the children clapped their hands and called out, "Tell us another story! One more!" They wanted to have *Hickory-Dickory* as well, but they only got the one about *Humpty-Dumpty.* The fir tree stood there in silent thought: never had the birds out in the wood told a story like that. "Humpty-Dumpty fell downstairs and yet married the Princess — well, well, that's how they go on in the great world!" thought the fir tree, and felt it must all be true, because the story-teller was such a nice man. "Well, who knows? Maybe I too shall fall downstairs and marry a Princess." And it looked forward to being decked out again next day with candles and toys, tinsel and fruit.

"I shan't tremble tomorrow," it thought. "I mean to enjoy my magnificence to the full. Tomorrow I shall again hear the story about Humpty-Dumpty and perhaps the one about Hickory-Dickory as well." And the tree stood the whole night in silent thought.

The next morning in came manservant and maid.

"Now all the doings will begin again," thought the tree. Instead, they hauled it out of the room, up the stairs and into the attic, where they stowed it away in a dark corner out of the daylight. "What's the meaning of this?" wondered the tree. "What is there for me to do here? What am I to listen to?" And it leaned up against the wall and stood there thinking and thinking ... It had plenty of time for that, because days and nights went by. No one came up there and when at last somebody did come it was to put some big boxes away in the corner; the tree was completely hidden — you might have thought it was utterly forgotten.

"It's winter by now outside," thought the tree. "The ground will be hard and covered with snow, people wouldn't be able to plant me; so I expect I shall have to shelter here till the spring. How considerate! How kind people are! ... If only it weren't so dark and so terribly lonely in here! Not even a little hare ... It was so jolly out in the wood, when the snow was lying and the hare went bounding past; yes, even when it jumped right over me, though I didn't like it at the time. Up here it's too lonely for words."

"Pee-pee!" squeaked a little mouse just then, creeping out on the floor; and another one followed it. They sniffed at the fir tree and slipped in and out of its branches. "It's horribly cold," said the little mice, "though this is actually a splendid place to be in, don't you think, old fir tree?"

"I'm not a bit old," answered the fir tree. "There are lots of people who are much older than I am."

"Where do you hail from?" asked the mice. "And what do you know?" (They were being dreadfully inquisitive). "Do tell us about the loveliest place on earth. Have you ever been there? Have you been in the larder, where there are cheeses on the shelves and hams hanging from the ceiling — where you can dance on tallow candles and you go in thin and come out fat?"

"No. I don't know the larder," said the tree, "but I know the wood, where the sun shines and the birds sing"; and then it told all about the days when it was young. The little mice had never heard anything like it before, and they listened closely and said, "Why, what a lot you've seen! How happy you must have been!"

"I?" said the fir tree and pondered over what it had just been saying, "Yes, they were really very pleasant times." But then it went on to tell them about Christmas Eve, when it had been tricked out with cakes and candles.

"Ooh!" said the little mice, "you *have* been a happy old fir tree."

"I'm not a bit old," repeated the tree; "I've only this winter come from the wood. I'm just in my prime; my growth is only being checked for a while."

"What lovely stories you tell!" said the little mice; and they came back the following night with four more little mice who wanted to hear the tree tell stories, and the more it told the better it remembered everything itself, thinking, "Those were really rather jolly times. But they may come again, they may come again. Humpty-Dumpty fell downstairs and yet won the Princess; perhaps I too may win a Princess." And then the fir tree suddenly remembered such a sweet little birch tree growing out in the wood; that, for the fir tree, would be a real beautiful Princess.

"Who is Humpty-Dumpty?" asked the little mice. Then the fir tree told them the whole fairy tale; it could remember every word; and the little mice were ready to jump up to the top of the tree for sheer enjoyment. The night after, many more mice turned up and, on the Sunday, even two rats. But these declared that the tale was not at all amusing, which disappointed the little mice because now they didn't think so much of it either.

"Is that the only story you know?" asked the rats.

"Only that one," replied the tree. "I heard it on the happiest evening of my life, but I never realized then how happy I was."

"It's a fearfully dull story. Don't you know any about pork and tallow candles? One about the larder?"

"No," said the tree.

"Well, then, thank you for nothing" answered the rats and went home again.

In the end, the little mice kept away as well, and the tree said with a sigh, "It really was rather nice with them sitting round me, those eager little mice, listening to what I told them. Now that's over too ... though I shall remember to enjoy myself, when I'm taken out once more."

But when would that happen? Well, it happened one morning when people came up and rummaged about the attic. The boxes were being moved, and the tree was dragged out. They certainly dumped it rather hard on to the floor, but one of the men at once pulled it along towards the stairs where there was daylight.

"Life's beginning again for me!" thought the tree. It could feel the fresh air, the first sunbeams — and now it was out in the courtyard. Everything happened so quickly that the tree quite forgot to look at itself, there was so much to see all around. The yard gave on to a garden where everything was in bloom. The roses smelt so sweet and fresh as they hung over the little trellis, the lime trees were blossoming, and the swallows flew around saying, "Kvirra-virra-veet, my husband's arrived!" But it wasn't the fir tree they were thinking of.

"This is the life for me!" it cried out joyfully, spreading out its branches. Alas! They were all withered and yellow, and the tree lay in a corner among weeds and nettles. The gold-paper star was still in its place at the top and glittered away in the bright sunshine.

Playing in the courtyard itself were a few of the merry children who at Christmas time had danced round the tree and were so pleased with it. One of the smallest ran up and tore off the gold star.

"Look what I've found still there on the nasty old Christmas tree!" he said, trampling on the branches so that they cracked under his boots.

And the tree looked at the fresh beauty of the flowers in the garden, and then at itself, and it wished it had stayed in that dark corner up in the attic. It thought of the fresh days of its youth in the wood, of that merry Christmas Eve, and of the little mice who had listened with such delight to the story of Humpty-Dumpty.

"All over!" said the poor tree, "if only I had been happy while I could! All over!"

And the man came and chopped up the tree into small pieces, till there was quite a heap. It made a fine blaze under the big copper; and the tree groaned so loudly that every groan was like a little shot going off. This made the children who were playing run in and sit down before the fire; and as they looked into it they shouted "bang!" — but at every pop (which was a deep groan) the tree thought of a summer's day in the wood, or of a winter's night out there when the stars were shining; it thought of Christmas Eve and of *Humpty-Dumpty,* the only fairy tale it had ever heard and was able to tell ... And by this time the tree was burnt right up.

The boys were playing in the yard, and the smallest of them had on his chest the gold star which had crowned the tree on its happiest evening. That was all over now, and it was all over with the tree, and so it is with the story. That's what happens at last to every story — all over, all over!

A Christmas Story from the Mountains

C.E. Pothast-Gimberg

Impatiently Sep fiddled with the little wooden figure that he had been busy carving. Finally he put it aside, discouraged. "It won't come right. I don't know how his face should be and I can't get hands right ever."

His father looked up thoughtfully from the porridge which he was stirring with a big wooden spoon.

As long as Sep could remember, and he was now fourteen years old, it was Father who had always cooked their food, swept the floor and mended his clothes. Sep's mother had been dead a long time now. And now he lived with his father in the little wooden house set in the steep slope of the mountain.

In the summertime together they herded the village cows and goats. At six o'clock in the morning Sep would blow his great cow horn in the narrow village street. Then everywhere the byre and pen doors were opened and the animals joined the growing herd.

Joyfully they went off together to the mountain meadow high above their house, where the alpine roses blossomed profusely among the rocks and the gentian made dark blue cushions amid the juicy alpine grass.

Then the cowbells and the little bells of the goats rang out and tinkled so clearly, and Sep and his father yodelled a two-part song that echoed far into the mountains.

But Sep liked the winter even better, with its endless white expanses where his snow-shoes left a single lonely track. He enjoyed the wind cutting across his cheeks till they were gloriously warm and he had to take off his thick wind-jacket because the sun baked him with its fierce rays. Then in the evenings it was so good to be at home. There the tall stone stove was burning in the corner of the room and they would sit on the bench round it. Together they carved wooden spoons and little animals which they tried to sell to the winter-sports guests in the hotels.

Sometimes the roof creaked beneath the weight of the thick layer of snow lying on it, and then he and Father would have to act quickly to clear the weight away. It was getting on for Christmas. All round their house were the mountains as far as you could see under a white sparkling dress. Sometimes the snow was blown into such heaps that they needed a few hours to clear the door and the windows.

But inside the stove roared and the wind blew in gusts through the chimney so that the flames sometimes shot up high. Binny, the goat, stuck her head over the partition that divided her corner from the room, and the whole place smelled deliciously of fresh goat's milk porridge.

But this time Sep could not enjoy all this cosiness.

A few days previously he had said to his father: "I'm going to carve the Holy Family: Joseph, Mary and the Child. The shepherds will be there too and the ox and the ass."

Then he had started straight away with the animals. They were already finished: a little donkey with his head bent down and a faithful ox, gazing out benevolently.

"But the people, Father, their hands and their faces, I'm stuck with them."

"You mustn't rush it, my boy," was all he said. "A human face is something more than two cheeks with eyes in them and a nose between."

There, Father was saying exactly what Sep himself was thinking: he could easily make such a doll's face, but that was not what he wanted to do at all.

He looked at his father's old head bent full of care over the pot. All at once he saw how robust and strong Father's face was in fact, with its short grey hair and the weather-beaten colour of someone who is constantly out of doors. He saw the clear blue eyes that were accustomed to looking into the far distance after straying cows or goats. And the wide wrinkles on his forehead, that spoke of a life of many great and small cares.

"What a fool I am!" he thought suddenly. "There I have right in front of me what I am looking for!" He could hardly wait to finish his porridge. His hands were itching to begin. And while Father calmly went on working at the sprigs of edelweiss in the handle of a ladle, the boy's sharp knife slid quickly and now surely through the wood.

The father now and again stole a glance at his son's work. Sep could do more than he could, that was certain. Sep could do what he had always wanted to do, he could make a human form.

214

"Finished," said the son at last, and he placed a wooden figure on the table in front of him. His eyes even now were travelling from his father's face to that of his carving. It was not his father, but it was a bit like him, when he was faithfully herding his flocks.

Father took the short pipe out of his mouth, pointed with it to the carving and only said: "That's a shepherd."

Then Sep knew that his work was good.

He carved three more and all three were different; one was leaning on his staff, one was kneeling and the third was standing bent down.

Now he had to start on an angel and then on Joseph and Mary. The Child he wished to leave to the end.

The whole of the following day he tried to get the features of an angel before his eyes. In the evening when he and his father were again sitting by the big stove he suddenly picked up his carving.

But he had hardly started before he jumped up. "Father I hear the church bells, I think."

They both ran to the door, and right enough the alarm bells were ringing darkly through the night. Already lights were showing from all directions, hurrying along the side of the mountain, the rescue team.

Kurt, one of the best guides in the village, went skiing past them laden with rope and an ice-axe, and called to them: "A climber, fallen on the North Wall!"

Instinctively father and son turned their heads in the direction of the mountain. The older man immediately got himself ready, and Sep knew what his work at home was to be: to have hot water and a warm drink ready, because their house was the first house on the way from the North Wall.

He watched his father go, who was racing along over the snow to join the others.

The tolling of the bell sounded mournful and gloomy in the dark night.

Meanwhile Sep had snow melting in the great kettles on the hot stove. Then he milked Binny, who was already sticking her head anxiously over the partition.

Through the little window Sep could see a long line of lanterns moving upwards. How he would have liked to go with them, but Father considered that he was still too young. Sep leaned against the doorpost and heard in the distance sometimes a cow horn sounding monotonously. From all parts of the mountain the signal was answered. That is how the men kept in touch with each other.

Finally, late in the evening, a guide came rushing through the snow and stopped with a swerve in front of the door.

"Found," he announced briefly. "Unconscious and a broken leg."

Not long afterwards came a stretcher. The rescuers brought their burden silently into the little room. One or two of them took off their clothes and began to do everything to revive the injured man. That succeeded fairly soon, but then the procession was to go on down to the village where a doctor would have to set the leg.

The young man's face lay there so wan and still on the floor. A faint smile played about his lips; a lock of hair fell curling under his cap and rested lightly on his high white forehead.

"Oh," thought Sep, and it was as if he saw a light: "That's how my angel should look."

And when the men had gone on down to the village with the young climber and father had gone to his straw-sack, Sep's knife slid feverishly through the soft wood. In the dim light he formed a calm face with regular features and with eyes that saw more than the things of this world.

Christmas was approaching. The hotels in the village were full of winter guests who came to ski or to toboggan. Every evening Sep's neighbour, Lise, went to the kitchen of one of the biggest hotels to help with the washing up. She was poor and mother of six young children. Her husband did not earn very much in the winter with his carving.

That morning Lise had called Father to her youngest child, a little toddler of two, who was seriously ill. Sep's father knew many healing herbs which he gathered in the summer on the Alpine meadows.

He came home from the sickbed with an anxious face.

"Very ill," he said, and both of them thought then of Lise having to leave the house for the whole evening. Around the time when she usually left, Sep fastened on his snow-shoes and nodded to his father,

"I'll go down and help with the washing up instead of Lise." On the way he caught up with her.

"Go back home, neighbour. I'll do it for you this evening."

No more was said, but the woman laid a hand on his shoulder, then she went back swiftly; but Sep had caught a glimpse of her face that looked careworn and grateful, and of her smooth hair parted in the middle. He felt the light touch of her hand on his shoulder which had given him for a moment an unknown feeling of being cared for.

And with his hands still wrinkled from the washing up water, that evening he carved a simple pure woman's face with a warm caring

expression in her fine features, and with hair that was parted in the middle and which fell away on both sides under a large white cap; the Mary of his Christmas crib. She sat on a stool and had a broad motherly lap. There the Christ-Child would come to lie. But how was he to make a holy figure of that? And tomorrow evening it was Christmas Eve, and the Child must be there then!

Joseph he had already finished: an old man with a long beard and strong lined hands reaching out towards the Child.

On the morning before Christmas he placed his figures on a shelf by the wall. Father took one of them up now and again to examine it and then he nodded encouragingly. That morning Sep carved a little naked child, but his face he left unworked.

The little figure fitted so well on Mary's lap. One hand was raised: the other rested in a fold of her robe. Joseph was looking at them both and the shepherds stood reverently round them. The angel was hovering above the group held by a string tied to the ceiling. In the afternoon father and son tidied up the little dwelling. Sep cut a beautiful fir branch with a few long cones and nailed it behind his Christmas stall. He put a

217

few candles in among it. He also stuck a few candles on the rough wooden table. On the stove a large currant dough for sweet bread was set to rise.

Once more Sep took his Child Jesus in his hand. "It won't come right, Father," he said discouraged. "There must be a Christ-Child for Christmas Night."

"Perhaps this evening after church," the old man comforted him.

They went together to the village where the houses were all lit up in festival and there was a scent of fir branches and baking coming towards them from every open door. The people were going merrily to church and from all sides sounded a hearty "Grüss Gott!"

The little church with its delicate green weathered spire was adorned with Christmas tree branches, and in among them white candles were burning. The organ was playing an old church hymn and the minister told the beautiful Christmas story: "Joseph and Mary were bending tenderly over the little crib in which the little baby Jesus had been laid. The donkey was wiping his soft lips along the child's hand and the ox was staring in dreamy adoration over the edge. And the shepherds who had been called by the angels to visit the child stood for a moment hesitating by the door of the little stable where the Child, poor and almost naked, was lying.

" 'Will he be our king?' they asked each other, a little bit disappointed and unbelieving.

"But at the same moment Jesus looked up at them. From the poor crib with the motionless reverent figures round it there streamed forth such a heavenly peace that the shepherds came nearer. Then the Child received them with his shining gaze and they were so filled with great joy and new faith, that they fell on their knees and worshipped the King of the World with their whole hearts."

Sep listened full of devotion and while he sat here in the building with the white walls and saw how the light of the candles shone on the exalted faces of the people, he thought now that he could carve the features of the Christ-Child.

After the service Father remained standing in the churchyard to talk. But Sep hurried home: he was burning to finish his Christ-Child. It was hard walking against the cold wind up the mountain. His lantern gave out only a sparse light. But finally he reached the last turn before their house.

But what did he hear? He listened more attentively. Was it the whine of a child? The wind blew the sound away for a moment. But then the sound came again much clearer. It was the cry of an animal in danger!

He looked round him in dismay. Then he realized, with horror that it must be Binny their goat! As quickly as he could, he climbed on up, and around the corner—

A reddish glow came towards him and an oppressive smell of smoke came to his nostrils. Their house!

Sep screamed with fright: "Father! Father! Our Binny!"

But Father was still far below and the goat was bleating in her deadly danger.

How could he get to her? The wailing of the animal sounded wildly above the crackling of the fire. In dismay Sep looked round him. Father would be here in a minute, but then it would be too late for the animal. And he ... did he not dare? Suddenly Sep ran through the smoke to Binny's pen. He did not feel the fire that scorched his hair and licked round his hands, but he wrenched the tether free from the goat that was stamping wildly round and round. Then he seized its head and dragged it out through the doorway where the doorposts were already burning.

And there, God be thanked, there was Father to catch him. The goat pressed itself between them. Wonder upon wonder, she was hardly scathed.

Now Sep felt his hands: the skin was blackened and the nails were curled up here and there.

Father rubbed them in a handful of snow; that cooled them a little. Sep bit on his lips so as not to cry with pain. But he mastered himself for his father's sake, who could not take his eyes off the ruins of his little possession. Fortunately Binny at least was saved.

Nothing else could be saved: the wooden house was too easy a prey, and Sep needed help. They could not stay any longer in the cold.

Neither of them spoke a word, as they went slowly down to Lise's hut. There Sep's hands were bandaged and Binny got a place beside their neighbour's goat.

After a while Father, the neighbour and Sep went back up again. Disconsolately they stared at the heap of ashes that had once been their house.

"And my Christmas stable," said Sep softly with tears in his eyes.

But Father bent down and picked up a bit of burnt wood: it was part of Mary's lap where a half burnt baby's body lay.

Surprised Sep stretched out his bandaged hands to it. Much moved, the three people bent down to look at the Child's face that was wonderfully lit by the last flickering remains of beams and joists. The dying flames cast a heavenly expression on that child's face and ensouled it with a glory that Sep's knife could not have made more beautiful.

Now there lay a scorched wooden doll in Father's hands, who seemed to look at them for a moment full of love and brought into their grief-stricken hearts something of the peace of Christmas.

The men bent their heads. They stood there alone on the white slope of the mountain. Above them a sparkling starlit sky arched itself over the mighty mountains and over the heap of ashes of their humble possession.

The same wind which had probably blown the fatal fire out of the stove now brought the sound of the Christmas bells from the village, while the child lay there still and radiant looking at them.

In the end the neighbour said calmly: "You were good to that animal, Sep. Now it is as if Christ would say to you: 'Truly, as you have done it to one of the least of these my brethren, you have done it to me'."

Suddenly Sep felt himself completely comforted and he knew too that his work on the Christmas stall had not been in vain.

What he had been able to make by looking attentively round him he kept in his heart, and what went beyond his powers seemed to be given to him by a miracle.

That Christmas Eve they sat together round Lise's hospitable stove and sang the old carols.

"We'll get through the winter together," said Lise warmly, and while she looked with veneration at the little wooden figure that stood on her table, she added devoutly, "After all Christ is with us."

The First Christmas Tree

Jakob Streit

Near the town with the great church there lived long ago a poor basket-maker with his family. As it was now winter, and the farmers had finished harvesting all the fruit, his trade was going badly. No one wanted to buy his baskets. The basket-maker's children were still little. Franz, the oldest, was getting on for nine. It was nearly Christmas when the basket-maker's wife in great poverty gave birth to a baby. They took one of the unsold baskets, laid some straw in it and put the new-born baby on the straw. Father cut an old cloth to size and covered the baby with it. Franz saw the little child for the first time on Christmas Eve. He thought: "If only I had a little money to buy my little brother a white napkin like the one I saw last year at Christmas in the great church; for the Child in the manger was wrapped in it."

And as he saw his mother lying pale in bed the thought came to him: "Mother should get a big bottle of milk from me. She should drink it all herself. Milk makes rosy cheeks."

Now little Franz could think of nothing other than how he could get hold of a napkin and a big bottle of milk. He had heard that in many houses in the town people would buy branches of fir, holly, mistletoe and suchlike evergreen for the Holy Nights. At that time the Christmas tree was unknown. Franz thought it over: "The nearby woods belong to the lord of the castle. I may not cut down any trees there. The holly is buried in deep snow, and mistletoe is difficult to find in the snow-covered trees."

Sadly Franz went up to the basket of his little newly born brother and looked into his sleeping face. His old grandmother had once told him that the heathens used to believe that before a little child was born into the world his soul slept out in the fields under the great druid stone. He had often stood listening beside the ancient stone surrounded by bushes and rocks. Suddenly Franz had an idea: "There are some little fir-trees there where I could get one. The heath belongs to no one."

Soon Franz was trudging through the knee-deep snow out to the druid stone. As he got nearer to it black ravens flew up and away, croaking loudly as they disappeared over the fields. He forced his way through the bushes and thorn hedges to the stone, and sure enough he found two little fir-trees standing close together. He shook the snow out of their branches. With his hands almost frozen stiff he laboriously worked his rusty knife to saw through their slender stems. Then he loaded the twin trees on to his back and hastened to get back to the town before it grew dark.

That day it seemed to him a long way. The deep snow hindered him, but he strode manfully forward. He was panting freely before he reached the main road. A well-appointed horse-sledge came rushing towards him from the town. He had to step right to the side of the road to get out of the way, but he slid over the edge and down the slope of the embankment. The snow got into his clothes and the little trees were full of snow once more. With difficulty he crawled back up. If only he had brought a rope with him! He worked his way up on all fours, using the bottom end of the tree as a stick. Back up on top, he stood at the edge of the road and pulled out the fir needles which had stuck themselves into the palms of his hands when he had gripped the fir-trees so tightly. Because he had no gloves his fingers were almost frozen stiff. He blew hard into his fists and slapped his arms round his body as he had learnt from his father in order to warm them up again.

As he was standing there and busy scraping the snow and ice-crusts from his clothes or warming his hands again, a farm-sledge slowly approached pulled by an old nag. The sledge was laden with brush-wood. The peasant was sitting on top. He was bringing a load of firewood to sell in the town. The sledge stopped beside Franz, and the driver with a wave of his hand invited him to climb on behind. Franz quickly climbed on, pressed the two little trees between his legs, the tops of the trees showing proudly once more. The peasant never said a word, not even when they drove through the gates of the town. He stopped suddenly, and with his thumb pointing down signed to Franz to get off. He hardly heard the softly spoken word of thanks from the boy, for his fur-cap was pulled down well over his ears.

Franz put both his arms round the trees so that he could put his hands in his coat pockets, and wandered slowly towards the square in front of the great church which he knew well. Every now and again he shyly tried to accost some one: "Do you want to buy some green for Christmas? Would you like to buy a fir-tree?"

Some of the people addressed shook their heads, others avoided him and hurried past. One woman, coming along arm in arm with her husband, pointed questioningly at the boy with the little trees, but the man drew her to one side, remarking: "They're not nice, all grown to one side."

Franz was shocked, and examined his little trees. Yes indeed it was so. As they had grown beside each other and into each other, each one actually only formed one half of a single fir-tree. Less and less often Franz cried his wares: "Do you want to buy some green for Christmas? Would you like to buy a fir-tree?" No one wanted buy one. In this way Franz came to stand in front of a baker's shop near the church. He leant against the wall of the house, tired out. A glorious smell of Christmas baking wafted towards him. How lovely it was to breathe it in! If only his feet were not so cold! It was growing noticeably darker and a few snowflakes were swirling through the air.

Suddenly Franz noticed a faint gleam of light shining through the coloured windows of the church. He thought: "Perhaps the verger could use some fir-twigs for the Child in the manger. He could cut the branches off the trees."

While Franz was thinking about this the verger was busy setting up the Christmas crib in the choir of the church. Out of a great chest he was bringing the wooden figures: angels, shepherds, Mary, Joseph and the Kings. He blew the dust out of their robes, and then he shook out some yellow straw into a little wooden crib. For fifty years now he had been arranging the Holy Family on this evening, and with a friendly murmur he greeted each figure as he lifted it out of the chest, and set it carefully in its place. Almost at the bottom of the chest appeared the figure of the Jesus child. It was still wrapped in the same white linen which he had wrapped it in the year before. As he was shaking it out something fell out and jingled on the floor. It was a coin. In the half-dark the verger groped for it, picked it up without looking at it closely, and put it in his pocket. He muttered: "It must have been put as an offering to the Child in the crib last year and slipped into a fold in the cloth."

When all the figures were standing there in order he strewed some ivy leaves and fir-twigs between the crib figures, so that it looked like a green field. Once more the verger regarded his group with satisfaction and by chance raised his eyes to the glass window that rose above the crib into the choir. It was the window of paradise, and in it were Adam,

Eve and the two trees: the Tree of Life and the Tree of Knowledge. Below, the wicked serpent was winding, seeking entrance. Above, a white dove was shining.

"Indeed the twenty-fourth of December is Adam and Eve's Day," murmured the verger. "I've been setting up the crib under the window of paradise all these years and never noticed how well that goes together. What does the old hymn say: 'As all die through Adam, so all shall live in Christ'? But the white dove? What is the dove doing above the trees? Must ask the vicar."

Thus the old man was speaking to himself as he stepped out of the church. He was surprised to see on the steps a freezing boy, who was holding two little fir-trees under his arms. The verger asked him: "What are you doing with the little trees here on the steps?"

The boy answered shyly: "Will you buy fir twigs for the Child in the crib? You can cut off the branches."

The verger was about to send him away, grumpily telling him that he had enough and better branches, when he saw two shining beseeching eyes. He hesitated and said: "Put them there at the back by the church wall."

He fished in his pocked and gave the boy the coin which he had found.

"What do you need money for?" asked the old man.

The boy replied, "I got a little brother today and want to buy him a napkin as he is lying nearly naked in his basket."

The verger lowered his head for a moment, mumbled something to himself, took the boy by the hand and went back into the church with him. He went to the crib, and carefully lifted the Child out, unwound the white linen, shook out the dust, folded it and laid it on the boy's arm. He covered the Jesus-child with plenty of straw so that only his hands and face could be seen. Little Franz stood there amazed and stared at the cloth on his left arm. Now the old man turned to him again and said: "Go home and take it to your little brother."

After these words he pushed the boy out of the church door into the open. With the coin in one hand and the linen cloth in the other Franz hurried through the streets of the town and out of the gates. In the darkness he could no longer recognize the people whom he met. A few crystal flakes were still falling. In front of the town he passed a farm. The farmer's wife was just carrying a pail of milk from the byre into the kitchen. Franz went up to her, produced his coin and spoke to her:

"Please give me some milk for this money. Mother had a baby early this morning."

In the lantern light the farmer's wife recognized Franz the basket-maker's son and she said: "On Christmas Eve I won't sell any milk to any one who has just had a baby. Take this jug, you can get it filled here every evening as long as it's winter and snow is on the ground. In the spring your father can make me a big basket."

With these words she poured out some milk from her pail into the jug and handed it to the boy.

Franz walked very steadily now so that he would not spill the milk. Then he went into a baker's shop by the roadside. He wanted to buy a large Christmas bun for his mother. The baker took the coin in his hand, turned it over in the light and exclaimed in wonder: "Where did you get this piece of money, boy?"

"The verger gave it to me."

Franz had to tell the baker all about it and show him the white cloth. Finally the baker said: "It's a pure gold piece. For this coin you can come and get a loaf of bread every day till Easter. And here is your Christmas bun."

Franz did not know what was happening to him.

"Every day a loaf till Easter?"

He nearly jumped into the air with the jug of milk. With the napkin, milk and roll he hurried home.

Outside it had stopped snowing. The bright Christmas stars were shining when Franz came to his poor hut. The bells were ringing from all the church-towers in the town. It seemed to him that they were sounding the song which his grandmother had taught him the year before at Christmas: "In dulci jubilo, now sing with hearts aglow."

The two fir-trees remained unnoticed by the wall of the great church until the sexton's two boys spotted them just as it was growing dark. One of them said: "Let's stick them on the snow-mound we built behind the church. They'll look nice there. They can be our mountain forest."

So the boys took the trees and put them in the snow-mound. After that they went home to play indoors in the light and warmth.

Towards midnight the church filled with all the people coming to the Christmas service. The verger lit the candles by the crib so that it was bright in Bethlehem. When the festive singing started he sat down beneath the pulpit by a pillar rather hidden away. He was tired after his long day's work. When the Gospel of the birth of Christ was being proclaimed to the faithful the old man was sleeping peacefully. Nevertheless he dreamed he saw the poor basket-maker's boy bringing the two fir-trees into the church and placing them beside the crib. The verger tried to stop him. The boy then pointed to the child in the crib, and the child rose up, took hold of the two fir-trees and flew up into the paradise window with them. When he placed them beside the two paradise trees red roses blossomed on the fir branches. Now the Jesus-child flew on higher right up to the white dove, plucked a few feathers from her and put them on the green branches. Then they shone like bright lights. And there was wonderful singing and music all around, and the trees of light shone so marvellously that the verger thought he was in heaven with the angels.

When he slowly woke up and came to himself again, the gloria of the choir and organ had long ceased in the church and the people were already leaving. He passed his hand over his eyes and looked across to the paradise window. It was completely dark, and only down below at the Bethlehem group the candles were burning. When the last steps had died away he did his usual rounds, putting out the lights in the church and on the altar.

The clock struck one when the old man took the great church key to his sacristy nearby.

On Christmas morning the verger found the two fir-trees standing upright on the snow mound behind the church. They were standing exactly behind the paradise window of the choir, as if they had fallen down from above and had got stuck in the snow. He stroked their branches and murmured: "You should be lit with bright lights this evening in my room, as you had them on Christmas Eve in paradise."

So he carried the little trees into his house. Secretly he fixed some votive candles on to their branches. No one was to know about his secret until his children and his children's children had gathered together in his room in the evening, when they came to visit him for their Christmas dinner. Suddenly the old father carried the fir-trees in and lit their candles, to the great joy of everyone. Then he began to sing a carol in honour of Christ's birth, and they all joined in. After that a wonderful happy festive stillness came over everyone as they contemplated the bright warm lights on the tree. All at once the old father stood up and said: "See, children, one tree I have lit for the poor shepherds. That is the shepherds' tree. Its light is love and warms human hearts. The other tree belongs to the kings. It is the kings' tree. Its light is shining wisdom. Both of them once stood in paradise, and they have been reawakened to new life for us through the light of Christ."

Everyone was astonished at these words, for it had never been the old father's habit to put into words what he bore in his heart.

From that time on more and more people have lit the new paradise tree in the Christmas tree, and more and more people have rejoiced in the lights that warm our hearts and tell of the peace of heaven upon earth.

The Troll who Wanted to be Human

Jeanna Oterdahl

There was once a little troll. he was very ugly to look at: his skin was
dark, his hair matted, his eyes red-rimmed and he had hairy ears. Like
the other trolls he lived in the depths of the forest, where stunted little
fir-trees stood by little boggy woodland lakes the waters of which
glowered like wicked little eyes, and where rock-falls and storm-laid
trees barred the way to human approach. When storms roared through
the tops of the trees he howled and laughed like the other trolls; he did
damage like they did, and the more harm he could do the better
pleased he seemed to be. Even so he was not quite like the others. Not
quite.

The other trolls hated human beings. Ugh! A human being is the
worst thing there is! The clearer a person's gaze is the less the trolls can
stand him. They abhor all things that belong to the light, because their
power comes from the night and darkness, and where light is victorious
they are defeated.

But this young troll had a strange liking for humans. he did not dare
show it or speak about it. For if any of his kindred should have found
out about it that would have been the end of him. So no one hissed so
angrily as he did when the word "human" was mentioned, and no one
spoke of human beings and their actions as spitefully as he did. In this
respect he was a very promising young troll.

But deep in his little dark troll-heart he cherished the strange wish to
become like a human himself. Humans were straight and tall. Humans
had resonant voices and a springy step. Humans were courageous and
generous. They overcame wild animals and made themselves masters
of woodland and moorland. There were more things about humans that
he did not understand and that could not be expressed in the troll
language. He could not think of anything more to be envied than a
human being.

228

For that reason he crept as much as he dared into the realm of human beings. He climbed among the gigantic mossy stones of the ancient feudal manor where he could not be seen, for he himself looked just like a mossy lump of stone, and with his fiery eyes peered along the path. From the distance his two eyes looked like a couple of grains of shining yellow mica. But if you took pains to look deeper into his eyes you would have seen in them such a violent longing that you would have done everything possible to help the poor little fellow.

But no one ever caught sight of him. The young troll, however, usually managed to see a few charcoal-burners and wood-carters in winter, and now and again an old woman gathering sticks in spring or some children looking for berries in summer, though they never saw him.

Often he would have to remain sitting without seeing any living creature except squirrels or birds or weasels, who lived in the walls.

Sometimes there came up from the village a wonderful sound which made the troll's heart beat in a wild and strange measure. It was the sound of church bells. He did not know if he hated or loved them. It seemed to him that they had the power to kill him. And yet it would be better to end his life in their solemn ringing than to die the ordinary troll's death, which meant gradually solidifying and becoming silent and one with mountain and moor, or merely to sink into the earth and disappear when one grew too old and frail. Two or three times he had slipped into the village when the bells had been ringing for evensong.

It was winter and dark and in the starlight he came creeping along like a little fearful shadow that knows it has come on a forbidden path. When he arrived at the little white-limed church he clambered up to one of the windows out of which a friendly light was shining through the green panes. He had not been able to see very much, because the glass had been frosted up. But he caught a glimpse of one or two faces shining peacefully and festively, and something of the singing and the booming of the organ reached him. What was going on in there he did not know, and there was nobody there who could have explained it to him. But from his ugly little eyes tears dropped down into the snow below and froze into ice-pearls. Lonely and sad he slipped back into the troll-forest and howled in the nightly storm like the others, while the desire to become like a human being hurt in his poor heart.

One autumn evening, as the storm blew in the tops of the trees and wild clouds chased over the forest, he crouched in front of the charcoal-burners' hut inside which Matthes the charcoal-burner sat upon the plank-bed talking with his grandson who had brought him his food from home. Matthes was an old man with a furrowed face and clever eyes beneath his broad brow. The boy sitting opposite him was listening attentively to what he had to say.

"That's how it is," said Matthes the charcoal-burner, cutting himself a thick slice of rye bread. "If anyone is to become anything, he must learn to think of others more than of himself. Anyone who does not bother how it is with others and who does not care for others can never become a proper human being."

"That's the same as what mother says, Grandfather," replied the boy.

"Take it to heart," said the old man while he began to spread butter on the bread, "See, Erik, it is certainly so, the secret of being a human being is to bother about other people. Those who cannot learn that, never become anything but a pack of trolls."

The boy nodded. He did not want to become like a troll, that was certain.

Outside, the young troll grew thoughtful. He could hardly believe it. But was not the old man sitting in there teaching him how to behave in order to become a human being? No one could have done him a greater service!

But it was difficult. That it would not do him much good to bother about his own relations, that he understood. They would not understand that at all and would soon send him packing. No, if he were to help anyone and care for someone it would have to be a human being. But how to effect that he could not imagine. For even though he longed to become like a human being he was more afraid of them than of anything else. In his utter ugliness he would never dare to show himself to a human being.

His head began to work so hard that he thought it would burst. He would do anything if only he knew how to set about it. One day he was crouching as usual among the blocks of stone of the ancient wall, looking out for human beings. It was clear weather; the sky was blue above the tops of the trees, and the sun was playing on the moss. So it was not surprising that on such a day three little bare-footed children came out into the forest to gather cranberries. They had cans to put the berries in, and these they then emptied into baskets which they had left on the moss.

Now if the little troll had been of the ordinary kind of troll he would have had fun tipping over the basket and giving the children an awful fright. But after all he was not like the other trolls, and as he rejoiced at their bright eyes and rosy cheeks it occurred to him that now he should follow the old charcoal-burner's advice. As soon as he was sure that the children could not see him he crept up, tore the bark off a birch tree and made it into a dish. Then he filled it with the loveliest blueberries that he could find. These he tipped into the basket. The oldest of the three children scratched her fingers in her flaxen hair; her eyes grew round with amazement. "Someone has been helping us, and we should like to thank him whoever it was!"

"Thank you, thank you!" cried the other two children. And the young troll, who was now sitting again in his old place between the stones, was happier than he had ever been before. Never before had anyone ever said thank you to him.

From then on people considered it lucky to go up into the forest. Everyone who had any work up there, whether it was charcoal-burning, cutting wood, carting wood or gathering berries, received some kind of help, but always so that they could not find out who had helped them. The forest became famous for miles around, and more people came into it than ever before. And the longer he was at it the faster the young troll learned to help, the more skilful he became and the more he enjoyed doing it.

But inside the forest, there where he had his home, things did not go well for him. It was not that he dared say anything about what he was doing, but they smelled that something was wrong.

"What's the matter with you?" they cried, pinching him. "You're growing horribly tall. You're getting bigger than a troll ought to be, and much more slender, almost like a human being, ugh! You're getting less hairy, you changeling, and your eyes are not running like a proper troll's."

He let them pinch him and push him around. But inwardly he laughed. If it were really true that he was beginning to become human he would happily endure it all.

In this way many summers passed until finally his finest experience came. A girl came into the forest more often than the others. Her light blonde plaits hung down her back; she had two true-hearted eyes, the clearest that he had ever seen. She had much to do. Sometimes she brought food to someone working up there, sometimes she picked flowers, honeysuckle blossoms and dame's violets, and at other times she came for blueberries, cranberries or mushrooms.

As she picked she sang, and the troll thought that he had never heard anything more beautiful. His own voice was rough and hoarse. But her voice had the sound of water falling between thin clear ice in winter. No other human being had he served so eagerly as he did her now. He had learnt to glide along as silently as a snake, and to disappear like a shadow. So he could always be near her, and lead her to where the flowers blossomed most abundantly, and where the berries and mushrooms stood at their thickest. Also he filled her basket before she could think. She realized that a friendly power was helping her, for she never left the forest without saying thank you, and often she laid aside part of her midday meal as a return gift for her invisible friend.

"Whoever you are," she said, "you will be the better of this little bite, and even if you don't want it there are enough birds and other animals who can appreciate it."

Sometimes she thought that she heard a hoarse voice, a vaguely whispered answer, but it might just as well have been a rustling in the bushes or a stone rolling down the mountain. Nevertheless she knew that she had an unseen helper, for more than once she had been exposed to wild animals or other dangers, but nothing had ever happened to her. At the last moment the bear had trotted off in another direction, and the withered fir-tree threatening to crush her in its fall had been hurled aside so that she had been able to step aside unscathed. But despite her assiduous searching she never saw a trace of her rescuer.

Then one day in autumn she came to the forest for the last time that year. Her basket was now filled to the brim with gleaming brown and snow-white mushrooms. The leaves were falling from the trees like pieces of gold, and settled on her head and shoulders. Titmice and finches were twittering around her while she sat on a mossy stone, and the sun played on her white linen blouse and her home-spun skirt.

"Dear helper, whoever you are," she said, "if only you would show yourself to me and tell me how I might thank you best. No one could have helped me better."

The troll trembled with joy, but he did not dare to come forth. How could he have brought himself to frighten her!

"If you do not wish to be seen by human eyes, you could at least speak to me. No one would like to receive so much help without giving some service in return. Ask me for something. I should love to do anything for you that I can."

Then the girl thought she heard a whispering coming from some-where, she did not know where.

"At the next Christmas Mass breathe on the north window of the church until the ice on it melts."

"That is a strange request," thought the girl, but she said, "yes, if that's all you want, that's easily done, but if ever we should meet I should like to have some way of knowing you. Take my little silver cross. It will bring you good fortune and it is the best thing I have to give you."

Then she arose to go away, and the troll watched her go until she disappeared where the forest thinned. Then he glided forward and took the gift that she had laid upon the stone.

It was a poor worn cross of thin silver, nothing of value, and a troll who could easily possess so much gold and precious stones would never have given anything for it. But for the troll who wanted to become a human being it was the greatest treasure. Carefully and lovingly he let his fingers play over it; he held it up in the sun so that it gleamed and he touched it with his lips as humans do with something that they love. Finally he hung it round his neck by its slender blue ribbon and pushed it carefully in below his fur coat.

From that day on his desire to become of human kind doubled. Whenever he could not help people he assisted the animals, large and small, but mostly the very little ones and those who were defenceless. He could not think why, but it seemed to him that the silver cross which he wore on his breast was the sign of what was most human in the world. Sometimes he felt that it was burning him as if to remind him not to flag in his endeavour and hope. But his relations the trolls grew daily more and more ill-disposed towards him.

As he was now it was impossible for him to behave as if he were the same as the others. He could no longer howl like they did, nor could he harm humans and animals and pester them. That was now quite impossible. When he once tried in order to pretend to the others, the silver cross on his breast hurt him like burning fire. The pain was so great that it could not be born. Anything else was better.

"You're no longer a troll!" the others roared at him and attacked him with their sharp claws, "You're getting a clear skin like a human being. Ugh! Your eyes are shining like human eyes. Away with you! You don't belong to us any more!"

And they chased him away with dagger-thrusts and threw stones at him. He had to run for his life in the grim winter night. He knew only too well that he was not yet a human being. But now he was no longer a troll either. As an intermediate inhabitant between the world of the trolls and that of human beings he had to live until he should succeed in becoming a true human being, or until he should become a troll again, but that he did not want: no, no, no.

He froze till he was shivering. That must mean that he was becoming like a human, for as long as he had been a troll he had not felt the cold. Perhaps humans had things difficult in their way too, but he would gladly endure whatever that might entail if only he could belong to the human race.

Freezing and bleeding he wandered about in the forest. Gradually he came nearer and nearer to the village, leaving a bloody trail of footsteps. Finally he could go on no longer and he fell down in the snow.

"Now I am going to die," he thought. "Now I shall sink down into the snow and dissolve into nothingness, before being able to partake of the glory of human life."

For a time he lay there almost sunk in lethargy, when a distant sound of bells reached his ear. He raised his head.

"Those are the church bells," he thought. "They are ringing for the Christmas Mass."

He struggled to his feet and began to walk towards the village although his limbs were stiff with cold and the frost in his wounds was hurting him. In the far distance he could see the church-goers with torches and sledges. The sleigh-bells sounded in the night while the stars sparkled high above. From the silver cross on his breast there emanated a gentle warmth, and he knew that if he could only endure he would be able to look through the church-window and share in the joy of the humans.

In the little low church there stood the girl with the bright hair and she was breathing on the window. The ice had grown in thick sparkling leaves over the little panes. Breathing was not enough, she had to lay her two warm hands and her cheeks against it to melt it.

"What are you doing there, child? Come and sit down in the pew," chided the mother.

"I am letting the Christmas carols shine out for those outside, Mother," replied the girl, and went on with her work.

Now the organ began to play and the carol sounded forth, but the girl still stood there while the ice melted and ran down the pane. All the time she was singing with her clear voice.

"Perhaps," she thought, "he of the woods will find his way here more easily if he hears my voice."

The priest now stood at the altar, and the mother turned again to the girl.

"What are you doing there child? Come and sit down in the pew."

"I am letting Christmas shine out to those who are in darkness, Mother," she said.

And while she listened to the holy word she made the last ice-flower melt into clear water.

The priest had now mounted the pulpit, and the mother grew angry.

"Child, you are shaming us in front of the whole congregation. Come here at once and sit down in the pew."

But the girl did not answer. She saw a face pressed against the pane, a face with two dark eyes full of longing and sadness. One hand lifted the silver cross up to her. She saw and understood.

"Dweller of the woods, dweller of the woods," she whispered, "welcome!"

Up in the pulpit stood the priest with young, shining eyes and preached of the mercy from above. His voice penetrated out through the window, and what the troll there heard made his face shine.

"Shame on you," thought the girl, "standing here in the warm church while another person is out there freezing in the snow on this Christmas night. Whatever he is, troll or heathen, I shall bring him into the church."

"Child, child," scolded the mother, "have you lost your wits?"

But without listening to her the girl hurried away along the aisle and out of the door.

Once again the priest was standing by the altar while the Christmas lights were shining benignly. The door opened and the girl came in again. Her hair was shining like the halo of a saint. By the hand she was leading a stranger whom no one had seen before. He was a slender young man, clothed in furs, with a strong smell of resin and forest. Stiff black hair fell over his pale trembling face, and his eyes were shining with a strange radiance. Many people shuddered and took refuge in the pews as far away as possible, for there was something about him that smacked of wildness and heathendom. But in his right hand he held up a little silver cross which shone forth so strongly that in the end nothing else could be seen.

The girl led the stranger up to the choir, where they both knelt down. But when the stranger saw the priest's face he covered his own with his hands and bent down to the ground trembling.

The priest left the altar steps and the whole congregation rose to their feet to see and to hear.

"Who are you, stranger?" asked the priest.

The stranger bent even lower and did not answer.

The priest stepped close and laid his hand on the dark head.

"Do not be afraid, no harm will come to you," he said, "Who are you?"

The stranger looked up. His face was working as if he wished to answer and could not do so.

But the priest took the hand that was holding the little silver cross, and repeated his question for the third time.

"In the name of the Cross that you are holding in your hand, who are you?"

Then the stranger cried out with a voice full of grief and longing: "I was born a troll, but I wish to become a human being. That is why I have been chased away from my kindred."

The priest however bent down, lifted him up and held him in his arms in front of the whole congregation.

"If that is so, welcome here!" he said. "Welcome to the world of human beings! here you see your kindred. You are like us all, for the longing to become truly human is what joins us all together."

The Last Dream of the Old Oak Tree

Hans Christian Andersen

Up in the wood, at the top of the slope going down to the open shore, stood an old oak tree, such a hoary old oak, just 365 years old — though a long time like that was no more for the tree than so many days would be for us. We are awake in the daytime and sleep at night, and that's when we have our dreams; but the tree is quite different. The tree is awake during three of the seasons, and it isn't till winter that it gets its sleep. Winter is its time for sleeping, winter is its night after the long day that is called spring, summer and autumn.

Many a warm summer's day had a day-fly danced round the top of the tree — lived and hovered and felt happy — and if ever the little creature rested for a moment in quiet contentment on one of the big cool oak-leaves, the tree would remark: "Poor little thing! Just a single day is the whole of your life. How short that is! It's terribly sad."

"Sad!" the day-fly would answer. "What makes you say that? Why, everything's so wonderfully bright and warm and lovely, and I'm so happy."

"But only for one day, and then it's all over and done with."

"Done with!" said the day-fly. "What's done with? Will you be done with, too?"

"No, I shall live for perhaps thousands of your days, and my day is whole seasons long. That's something so long that you simply can't reckon it out."

"No, because I don't understand you. You may have thousands of my days, but I have thousands of moments to be pleased and happy in. Does all this world's loveliness come to an end, when you die?"

"No," said the tree. "I expect it goes on longer — far, far longer — than I can imagine."

"Well, in that case, you and I must have just the same, mustn't we, only we reckon differently."

238

And the day-fly danced and swerved in the air, revelled in the delicate working of its wings and their velvety gauze, revelled in the warm air that was filled with perfume from clover in the fields and from wild roses and elder-blossom and honeysuckle that grew on the hedges, not to mention sweet woodruff, cowslip and pennyroyal. So strong was the scent that it made the day-fly feel quite tipsy. The day was long and beautiful, full of joy and happy impressions; and then, as the sun was setting, the little fly would feel pleasantly tired out with all that gaiety. Its wings could not carry it any longer and, ever so gently, it glided down on to a soft swaying blade of grass, nodded its head in the way that it does and fell happily asleep. That was death.

"Poor little day-fly!" said the oak tree. "What a short life that was!"

And every summer day it happened again: the same dance, the same talk, answers and passing away. It happened, one after another, to whole generations of day-flies, and all of them were just as happy and cheerful. The oak tree stood there awake all through its morning of spring, its noonday of summer and its evening of autumn. Now its time for sleeping — its night — was drawing near; winter would soon have come.

Already the gales were singing: "Good-night, good-night! There goes a leaf, there goes a leaf! We're plucking, we're plucking! Now then, go to sleep. We'll sing you to sleep, we'll ruffle you to sleep, but that does the old branches good, doesn't it? Makes them groan in sheer enjoyment! Sleep well, sleep well! This will be your three-hundred-and-sixty-fifth 'night' — you're only a one-year-old really, — sleep well! The clouds are sprinkling snow; there'll soon be a regular sheet and a cosy blanket for your toes. Sweet sleep and pleasant dream!"

And there was the oak tree, stripped of all its leaves, ready to go to bed the whole long winter through and in it to dream many a dream, always of some adventure just as in human dreams.

It, too, had once been small — yes, with an acorn for its cradle. After our reckoning, it was now over three hundred years old. It was the largest and finest tree in the forest, its top towered above all the other trees and could be sighted far out at sea, a landmark for ships; but it never gave a thought to all the eyes that were on the look-out for it. High up in its green summit the woodpigeons built their nests and the cuckoo kept calling; and in the autumn, when the leaves glowed like slabs of beaten copper, the migrant birds came and rested there before they flew away across the sea. But now winter had come, and the tree stood leafless; it was easy to see how bent and rugged were its outstretched branches. Crows and jackdaws came and settled there in turn and chattered of the hard times ahead and how difficult it was to get food in winter.

It happened to be the holy time of Christmas and it was then that the tree dreamt its loveliest dream. We really must hear that.

The tree had a clear impression that it was a season of festivity and that, round about, it could hear all the church-bells ringing; and, moreover, it was as soft and warm as on a lovely summer's day. The tree spread out its mighty crown, so fresh and green; sunbeams played among the leaves and branches; the air was full of the fragrance of herbs and undergrowth. Gay butterflies were playing "touch last", and the day-flies were dancing as though everything existed merely for them to dance and enjoy themselves. All that the tree had been through and seen around it for years past went trailing by like a regular pageant. It saw old-time knights and their ladies on horseback, with plumes in their hats and hawks at their wrists, riding through the wood. It heard the sound of the huntsman's horn and of hounds in full cry. It saw enemy troops with gleaming weapons and glittering uniforms , with spears and and halberds, pitch their tents and then strike them; there were watch-fires blazing, and song and sleep beneath the spreading branches of the tree. It saw lovers meeting in silent happiness here in the moonlight, cutting the initial letter of their names in the grey-green bark. Zither and aeolian harp had once — so many years ago — been hung in the branches of the oak by gay, wandering prentices; now they were hanging there again and twanging there again so charmingly. The wood-pigeons cooed as if to describe what the tree was feeling, and the cuckoo called out how many summer days it had to live.

Then it seemed as if a fresh current of life went rippling right through it down to the lowest roots and up to the topmost branches out into the very leaves. The tree could feel itself spreading and spreading — feel, too, at its roots that also down in the earth there was life and warmth. It felt itself getting stronger, as it grew taller and taller. The trunk shot up without a pause, more and more it grew, its crown spread more lustily, outward and upward ... and as the tree grew, so grew its vigour, its blissful longing to come higher and higher, right up to the bright warm sun.

Already it had grown high up above the clouds that trailed away below it like dusty troops of migrants of great snowy flocks of swans.

And every one of its leaves could see, as though it had eyes. The stars became visible by day, great shining stars, that winked at one like human eyes, so dear and gentle. They made it think of kind eyes that it had known, children's eyes. lovers' eyes where they met under the tree.

It was a joyful, delicious moments. And yet in the midst of all this joy the tree felt that it longed for all the other forest-trees down there, the bushes and herbs and flowers, to be able to soar with it and to share its gladness and splendour. The mighty oak, in all the glory of its dream, was not completely happy until the others came with it, all of them, big and little; and this feeling quivered through the leaves and branches as deeply and strongly as in a human breast.

The tree-top stirred as if looking for something that it missed. Then, glancing back, it caught the scent of woodruff and, after that, the even stronger scent of violets and honeysuckle. It fancied it could hear the cuckoo answering back.

Yes, through the clouds peeped out the green summit of the wood. Down below it saw the other trees growing and rising up beside it. Bushes and herbs shot high into the air; some tore themselves loose, root and all, and flew more swiftly up. Swiftest of all was the birch. Like a pale streak of lightning its slim trunk went hustling upward, and the branches swayed like green gauze banners. The whole woodland scene, even the brown-plumed reeds, went up with it, and the birds joined in and sang, while there on its blade of grass that fluttered and flowed like a long green silk ribbon sat the grasshopper fiddling on his shinbone with his wing. "Boom!" went the cockchafers, "zoom!" went the bees, the birds all raised their beaks and sang. From every side flowed joyful songs right up to heaven.

"But the small red flower beside the brook, that must come too," said the oak tree; "and the blue bell-flower, and the little daisy" — yes, the oak wanted them all to come.

"Here we are, here we are!" came the echoing answer.

"But last summer's sweet woodruff — and the year before we had glorious lilies-of-the-valley — and the wild apple tree, how lovely it looked! — and all the beauty of the woods for years and years and years — if only it had gone on living till now, then that too could have joined us."

"Here we are, here we are!" came the echoing answer from yet higher up, just as though they had flown on ahead.

"Oh, but it's all too wonderful to be true!" was the happy cry of the old oak. "Why, I've got them all here, big and little — not one has been forgotten. How ever can all this happiness be possible and imaginable?"

"Possible and imaginable in God's heaven," came echoing back. And the tree, while still it grew, felt that it's roots were loosening from the earth.

"This is the best of all," said the tree. "Now there is nothing to keep me back. In light and splendour I can fly up to the Most High, and all those dear ones with me. Big and little, all of them with me."

"All!"

That was the oak tree's dream and, while it was dreaming, a violent gale swept over land and sea that holy Christmas Eve. The sea flung heavy breakers on to the shore; the tree cracked, crashed and was torn up by the roots just as it dreamed that its roots were loosening. Down it fell. Its 365 years were now like a day for the day-fly.

When the sun came out on Christmas morning, the gale had gone down. The church-bells were ringing merrily; and from every chimney, on even the smallest cottage roof, the smoke rose blue as from the altar at a Druid's feast — the incense of gratitude. The sea turned calmer and calmer, and on a large vessel out there, which had weathered the storm in the night, every flag was being hoisted with a fine air of Christmas.

"The tree's gone!" cried the sailors. "The old oak — our landmark — it's come down in last night's gale. Who can find us such another? No one!"

That was the funeral sermon, short but well-meant, that the tree was given, as it lay stretched out upon the carpet of snow beside the beach; and away over it from the ship came the sound of a hymn, a song of Christmas joy and the saving of men's souls through Christ and the life eternal:

> Let hymn on hymn to heav'n succeed.
> Now man has all that man can need,
> Great joy beyond comparing.
> Alleluia! Alleluia!

So ran the ancient hymn, and everyone there in the ship was uplifted in his own way by the hymn and its prayer, just as the old tree was uplifted in its last, its loveliest dream on Christmas Eve.

Frau Holle and the Glassblower

Karl Paetow

The glassblower Heinrich Kunkel climbed up towards the snow-covered woods which cloaked the Hirschberg in hoar frost like a silver fur coat. The master-blower was bitter with life and sad unto death. At other Christmas times he had blown green balls and little bottles, or toys and trinkets, hares, foxes and birds for Christmas in the market town, but this year a cloud of misfortune cast its cold shadow over his smelting oven.

With tired eyes the glassblower climbed slowly towards the edge of the wood. He did not see the furry frost and the flash of crystals on each stalk. He did not hear the silvery tinkle of the Hirschborn fountain breaking through the gleaming skin of ice. Everything indeed was like cold glass, but he had no wish to see the glassy likeness. All he could see was the many hungry mouths round his table and the silent sorrow of his wife. For the Count of Kassel had made a stern law forbidding all glass-makers to cut wood in the forests of his domain, because they were fast dwindling. But how should he heat glass without wood for smelting? For it was from glass alone that his daily bread came. Thus he reviled God and the weight of his need pressed him right down to the ground.

A mighty full-grown beech-tree raised its bare crown in the evening light. From here you could see the valley of Kassel in the gloaming and the castle on the River Fulda where the Count gave out the law. But here you were nearer to the stars than down below in the valley, though a pale grey blanket of cloud hid the lights of the sky. This was the place where the master glassblower was going to make an end to his life that now seemed to have become senseless. He climbed on to a gnarled root and tried the strength of the lower branch. Then he threw the rope over it and with trembling hands he tied the knot of a noose.

"Glass-maker, why is the rope swinging on the tree?" a voice asked. Startled, Kunkel turned round. A tall white figure stepped out of the trunk of the tree.

"Are you going to set your hand to yourself," said the woman, "so that your children can die of hunger?"

"It is because they are dying of hunger," he stammered, "no firewood, no glass, no bread." But the elf-woman took the rope off the branch and laid the noose on the ground.

"Look into the noose," she commanded.

The man obeyed and looked through the coil as through a window. "What do you see?"

"I can see," said the glass-maker, "the whole mountain under me is transparent as if made of poured glass. And I can see deep into the depths where the elements are seething together."

"What do you see above that?"

"I see," said the master-blower, "how all the flowers are resting in the ground of their roots, and all animals and worms are keeping their winter sleep in their holes. The fat badger is lying down there in his lair and is blinking slyly up. Between the animals and the elements in it is swarming with kobolds who are busy at work. They are shovelling and carrying, chipping and cleaning, an industrious lot."

"Those are the souls of the unborn and the dead," said the woman. "They live down there and work on for the living. But what are those people doing now?"

"I see some are setting precious stones in sparkling rings. Others come and build crystal bridges in flowering gardens. Others are making clear vessels and chalices of fine molten glass, the like of which I have never seen. With coloured enamel on the clear walls of glass they are painting the horseman as he is hunting the deer on a green ground. The white hounds are running under the horse's belly and are baying. Everything is shining so happily. Oh, if only I could create such glorious things in my day's work."

"Mark all these things well," said the benign woman. "What they are making down there, very soon you too will soon be blowing and creating. But tell, what else is going on?"

"I see in tremendous depths the fiery roots of a stone tree. It is growing up out of the sea of fire as a dark trunk and it has thrust its crown of blue basalt right into the dome of the mountain. In its shadow crystals of salt and alum have formed in layers."

"And what appears now?"

"Below I see fathoms of black layers in waves, but I do not know what it is, nor what it purports."

"This is a seam," said the woman, "decayed wood from mighty forests which have grown here against your suffering since uncounted days of earth. The dwarfs call it coal and have used it for a long time, for it heats better than wood. Look here!"

With her golden shoes she moved a black stone, which the badger had rolled out of his den.

"Here is such coal, and there lies more. Gather it all up, turn back to your hut and fan up a good fire. Then you must blow glass like those made by the folk beneath the earth. For your last bread is not baked by a long way."

The apparition melted back gently into the tree and merged in the dusk with its bark.

Kunkel gathered up the stones into his apron. He was surprised how lightly they weighed. But they gave more heat to his glass oven than the knotty logs of the Count's wood. Already the glass was melting in the fiery pot. Impatiently the master-blower dipped his blowing tube in and blew a glowing chalice. This he fashioned into a wonderful shape, as he had seen the folk of the underworld doing. Thus the secret of glass-painting had been revealed to him in grace.

In his exhilaration he called his wife and told her breathlessly about the burning stones. But the poor woman could only believe that her husband had lost his wits from sorrow and suffering, for how on earth could he manage to heat with stones?

"Heinrich, remember," she warned, "how the Venetian once came sniffing round here. At that time he promised us mountains of gold. But in the end the gravy was dearer than the meat. You're like the mouse that can only see the cheese and won't see the trap."

"He who can see his goal is already half way there," cried Kunkel full of confidence, opening the oven door and throwing a few stones into the furnace. Immediately the fierce glow cast its light through the room, and the glass in the pot melted glowing hot. In this way his wife saw the wonder, laughed as if she had lost her senses, raised her arms high and danced round the workshop. Then she hung on to her husband's neck and kissed his stubbly face.

"Oh, it must be true," she cried, "for today is New Year's Eve. Frau Holle comes down from the Meissner Mountain and appears among people. And wherever she goes, there's gifts I suppose."

By looking into the noose of death the soul of the artist had been released. Kunkel, the glass-maker, now created a new kind of glass. Crystal clear vessels and tankards bright as picture books came from the workshop in his village. Young maidens desired the glasses and flasks as bridal gifts for their lovers. The Count himself, when the artistic goblets were brought to him, found his pleasure at table increased, and would only drink out of such glasses. All the great noblemen imitated him and ordered their glasses from Kunkel, for the master glass-maker adorned them with mottoes and pictures.

He and his journeymen achieved the masterpieces of the under-world. The fame of his craft reached beyond the boundaries of Hessen, and the creative fire in his shop never went out, for it was fed with Frau Holle's coal which Kunkel's men dug out from the mountains.

Thus his misery came to an end, and the glassblower lived with his family in honourable prosperity and every day there was plenty of good baking and food in his house.

The Miner and his Wife

Karl Paetow

This story is of the time when Frau Holle still came into people's houses. That is not so long ago, and many an old peasant can remember hearing in his ears the sound of her whip which promised so much when she came riding on her gift-coach into the village at Christmas time. And so it was that once she came before the door of a poor miner. There seven children had put their little shoes out of the window hoping for Frau Holle's gifts in the night.

"Oh," sighed the miner's wife who was still sitting spinning industriously, when she heard the crack of the whip and the tinkle of the bells, "oh, if only it is Frau Holle! For seven children and a hard winter gnaws at my heart."

So she stole to the door and pushed aside the heavy bar. But there between the threshold and the path to the door stood the white horse in the snow — and behind a tall white apparition signed to her with a finger and said, "Because you are a sorrowful woman and your children are innocent and in need, take this spindle. But this is my advice: take this spindle, keep your true self, otherwise my gift will vanish."

Happily the miner's wife weighed the golden spindle in her experienced hand. She curtsied and gave thanks, and was still thanking and curtsying when Frau Holle was long since over the mountain. Now she no longer needed to go hungry, for the spindle span the finest thread and its flax never ran out. When the children took down their shoes from the window-ledge the next morning they found plenty of apples and nuts in them.

One piece of good fortune goes with another. At the same time the miner himself was climbing up from the deepest shaft. He had already doused his lamp down below in the tunnel, for in his great poverty he always came out of the shaft without light in order to save wick and oil.

Once he was out the night engulfed him like a chasm and not a star shone.

In the Black Water Valley the darkness flowed like pitch from the cliffs, and even the snow, forming clumps beneath his boots, gave no reflection. But the man knew his way, for he had walked it since he was a boy. But against the raven-black night no knowledge of mile and stile could help. He groped his way as in a strange cavern and often slid dangerously on the steep slope.

"The night is so black, and my light I must lack," he groaned, quite exhausted when he stumbled again over a sharp stone. There in front of him blossomed a little spark of light waving in the darkness like a good star, and the miner could make out a figure by the Bilstein swinging and waving a lantern.

"Hi, my friend," called the miner, "shine and lend me your light. I don't know where I am any more in the darkness."

But the stranger went on swinging his lantern calmly. The miner then recognized the mighty old man with his flowing beard. It could only be the Old Man of the Mountain, lighting him home for Christmas. And there was a sweet odour round that lamp, like honey and rare spices.

The Old Man of The Mountain spoke: "I have no time, I must go further. But I shall lend you a stub of candle. But this is my advice: 'Keep your true self, else the light will go out'."

He fished in his coat pocket and produced a tiny wax candle, lit it, and held it under the frightened miner's nose. The miner wanted to thank the Old Man but started to sneeze violently. When he looked up the apparition had faded away into the gloom. Only the sweet smell of the honey remained round him and the light gave out a lovely golden shine, did not go out and went on burning.

The still flame warmed the poor man's heart, and he thought on his way home: "How care will fall from the goodwife's shoulders when she sees the candle!"

But even then doubt crept into his joy. "She'll go and blabber it to her neighbour and it will get rumoured that I have an everlasting lamp, and what's greatly envied will soon be stolen."

So he disguised the joy of his heart under a grumpy expression and entered the room with his usual sigh.

His wife had already made his evening supper. She put a candle in the decorations of the pyramid because it was Christmas. But she considered within herself, "If he gets an inkling that I have the key to wealth, he'll just go off to the Jug and Bottle. And where there is a brewery there's no bakery."

And so she too kept her good fortune secret.

Now on many a day after the soup there was beef. The woman spun flax as fine as a hair. She sold the fine thread and soft linen and saved up many a penny for her children. But she kept her secret. The miner too saw better days with his everlasting lamp. He found a rich vein of silver, rose in importance and was finally made foreman over the diggers and carriers.

But money without blessing is like summer without rain. Although they were now living in ease and comfort, and the children no longer needed to go begging, the bond of trust between the parents was broken, and each lived without the other in his stubborn way.

The miner came home once again drunk. He looked bad. Crow's feet were growing round his eyes, and sharp grooves round his mouth. The woman looked at him from the side and said, "If you go on swilling that bright golden stuff from the full cow-bells your children will soon be eating orphan's bread."

That made the man angry and he burst out, "If you grudge me a few draughts after a hard day's work, then I don't care a bit what the sparrows are whistling about the dung, you witch."

"What's the gallows bird croaking at now?" cried the woman, brandishing a wooden spoon. "And you must be stealing that ill-gotten money or else you had long since gone a-begging, for you can't keep within moderation."

"And you, you gibberer, you slappergoosh, who has woven those sinful sheets for you, eh?" yelled the miner.

There they stood, facing each other, and hatred shot into their fists. Suddenly the quarrellers were startled by the sound of little bells and the cracking of a whip, and this reminded them of the misused gifts. It was Frau Holle passing by that winter. Lightning struck the house, the light went out, the beams cracked, the plaster fell off the walls and a voice threatened:

> Your fortune goes,
> You're back to your woes.

And as each of them groped for his magic gift in the darkness, the enchanted light and the magic spindle had vanished.

But no misfortune is so great but that it bears in its lap some good fortune. Now there was nothing left for the couple to distrust each other with or to keep secret from each other. The man and his wife had to pull together in order to earn their daily needs. And because the miner also stopped his drinking, their wealth increased in honest fashion without the magic gifts.

When then Frau Holle passed by the following Christmas she looked again into that room. There she saw the same family in the candlelight. Father and mother were just sharing sweet baked things among the children. Then Frau Holle smiled in her stern goodness and said: "Fortune return!"

The Lady's Coach

Karl Paetow

You have now heard how strange things happen during the twelve holy nights. Once there was a peasant who was going up to the high woods with his axe on his shoulder. In the mountains the wild birds were singing as in May. As the man trod forward he listened to the beautiful singing in astonishment and was happy in his mind thinking back on his busy winter day's work which was now over and he was going home to rest, for there his young wife with their first-born little boy was awaiting him. And even though in his poverty all he possessed was "ten acres of wind at the back of his house" as his neighbour had said in mockery, his heart was clear, as clear as the ground under his feet, for the fresh snow crystals were glistening in the silvery moonlight.

As he was entering the wood in this way and thinking of home, he chanced to strike his left foot against a knobbly root hidden under the snow. Then the night wind arose out of a chasm and lifted him up as on wings from his path, billowed out his clothes like a sail, and blew him away in a trance. The man hardly knew where he was, all seemed now so unreal, for the whole wood seemed transformed in this Christmas night. All the trees had a light on them, the big trees big lights, the little trees little lights and all these lights were shining like row upon row of stars. The wood grew thicker and thicker, and the magic shining brighter and brighter, which quite confused the man. It seemed to him that all the trees were growing out of one tremendous root and as if the whole wood was one single mighty tree.

There came a roaring like the steeds of the storm-wind, and all the tree-tops bowed before it, and the waving lights gave way to a coach drawn to the spot by two steaming white horses. Inside the delicate coach sat a white lady spinning a long thread, and her golden spindle danced far below right into the earth. But just as a great wave rises upon

251

the shore and stops so the hooves arrested the thundering progress and the coach stood still.

"You come as if I had called you!" said the spinning-lady, bending down to the peasant. "Take your hand-axe quickly and mend my coach, but be careful that the pins are made of the best heart-wood, for heaven and earth must hold together in a tight hub. And if it breaks the world will fall apart. So hasten and make a good job. On the smallest job hangs the order of the greatest things."

The man took his axe off his shoulder, knelt down and examined the damage. The wedging pin of the left wheel was split and the wheel was in danger of coming off. Then he looked up at the gracious spinning-lady and said: "To help in need, is to help indeed."

Without more ado he felled a little sound tree, dressed it so that chips and shavings flew, and made a strong wedge-pin. Then he drove the wedge before the hub and fixed it in masterly fashion. Finally he mended the shafts and sorted the harness. The horses strained at the golden chain, snorted, and set off at a gallop.

> Put the shavings together
> That's your payment whatever.

He heard the coach-woman still call and then everything, lady and coach, vanished in the dusky light of the enchanted wood. The snowflakes were gathering in the draught of the night wind.

Thoughtfully the man turned up his collar and shouldered his axe. Then he set off homewards taking no more notice of the shavings lying there than he did of the snowflakes. He was only a little disappointed that the lady after such exalted words only wanted to pay him with worthless left-overs. While he was still turning over in his mind the meaning of the encounter his boots gave him trouble and he felt something sharp in his heel, so that in the end he had to sit down on a tree-stump. There he sat and took his boot off and tipped it out. When he put it on again two considerable heaps of shavings were shining in the snow. They glistened in the moonlight like pure gold and weighed like proper minted guilders. Then the carpenter realized it was precious payment and that it had been Frau Holle's coach which he had fixed and quoined.

In a happy frame of mind he entered the cabin and brought his wife and child the great news of Frau Holle's tour and laid the little heap of gold in the housemother's lap. It enabled the simple couple to live comfortably, and whatever from that time on the man undertook flourished and brought blessing. Then he understood the wisdom that heaven and earth depend upon the honest work of man.

At that time there lived in the same village a young wise-ling. He had heard about the carpenter's meeting and what he had missed by not picking up the shavings. But he thought himself nine times as clever, as fools often think, chalked up the particular day on his calendar, and the next year he wandered off with his axe through the same part of the wood. Again Frau Holle drove by with her coach and horses. She leant over the rail of the coach and asked the intruder sharply what his business was. He trembled in all his limbs and he stammered his little piece about an axe and a wedge and the golden reward.

Frau Holle upbraided him with the words, "I've got tools myself, and my axe is at hand. But because you have offered your axe out of greed, you will get your reward through the axe."

No sooner had she spoken but she struck his axe into his shoulder, so that his breast and his backbone met together and back and front were disfigured with a huge hump. Then the horses strained at the harness, and lady and coach faded in the haze of the distance. The lad however returned home shocked, bearing his disfigurement as a sign of his guilt.

When it came round to Christmas again and the misshapen one had honestly pondered on his unwarranted greed and repented of it, the more fortunate carpenter advised him to implore with a pure heart the help of the lady who had upbraided him. So upon the appointed evening he made for the wood again.

Once again Frau Holle drove by, reined in her horses, bent over and asked him his business. The lad showed her his misshapenness, confessed cleanly that he had insulted and angered the noble lady the previous year through his greed and presumption.

Then Frau Holle raised her finger and smiled, "Know that it was not me whom you insulted then, but you yourself. I do remember it. A year ago on this spot I struck my axe into a right cross-grained log. The log remains, but the coarse grain is gone. I shall take the axe out of the log."

Hardly had she spoken but the lad stood up straight and tall again like the trees in Frau Holle's wood. But when he considered his good fortune and wished to speak his thanks, the apparition had vanished. And though no golden shaving fell to his lot he took back home the finest gift, a healthy and strong body as God had once made and intended it.

Alice and her Doves

Anonymous

Alice, the weaver's little daughter, stood in front of the door of her house surrounded by her doves. There were many beautiful doves in the little village of Maussane in the South of France, but Alice's doves were the most beautiful of all. They tripped along turning their heads and puffing up their breasts in the sunshine that washed over them in a golden stream, and their slender mobile necks and folded wings shone in all the colours of the rainbow, purple, rose, blue and grey.

But of all the doves only Blanche and her mate Blanc were pure white, and it was these two that the curé had chosen to be carried in the procession for the adoration of the shepherds at the Christmas festival in honour of the child Jesus.

These doves of Alice were not only beautiful but they were also specially tame, and they would sit on her shoulders and eat out of her hand whenever she called them.

While Alice was standing in the midst of her darlings Monsieur le Docteur came along the narrow street of Maussane and stopped to admire them.

Monsieur le Docteur was a great man who had come from Lyons to spend a week in Maussane. In the village it was told of him that he had already restored the sight of many blind people.

Blind Barbara, sitting against the wall of her house knitting, had sighed patiently when she heard the story. She thought that, if only she had the money for the cost, perhaps this great physician might be able to make her see again. But because she was quite poor she knew that that was impossible and that she must stay blind.

Now although Monsieur le Docteur was a famous man he was nevertheless particularly friendly, and he often chatted amiably with the inhabitants of Maussane. So it happened that he came and stood by Alice and tried whether the doves would also eat out of his hand — and see, they did! First one dove settled on his shoulder, then a second, and even later they pecked the peas out of his hand which he held out to them.

Blanche and Blanc he admired most of all and before he went on he said to Alice: "My child, perhaps you would sell the two white doves to me. I have a little daughter Angélique at home and she has often asked me for a pair of white doves. She would be so happy if I were to bring her these two. I would give you a good sum of money for them."

But Alice quickly shook her head: "No, I'm afraid not Monsieur, I couldn't possibly do that," she answered. "I got the doves from my cousin Gaspard who brought them to me last spring from the mountains of Amergue. And, you see, besides the fact that I love them so much, there is another reason why it cannot be. Monsieur le Curé has chosen them from all the doves of the village to be carried by the shepherds in the procession at the great Christmas festival which we always celebrate here."

When the Doctor realized that it was impossible he made no further attempt to persuade her.

Often Monsieur le Docteur stopped and stood by the wall where blind Barbara sat knitting, and he would chat with her. On the day before his departure he spoke earnestly with her about her eyes.

"It is not at all impossible, Barbara, that you should get back your sight. If you will come to Lyons to my clinic and trust yourself to my care we can see if anything can be done. And it won't need to cost you anything."

Blind Barbara thanked him heartily, but she did not promise anything. She knew only too well that Lyons was quite a distance away, and that she had no means wherewith to pay for the expensive journey, but she did not say anything of that to Monsieur le Docteur. When Alice came to sit with her she confided to her what the good doctor had said and promised.

"What are you telling me!" exclaimed Alice, "Did he say that he might be able to make you see again! Then you must go, Barbara, of course you must go: when you can see once more then you can make beautiful lace again as you did before, and then you won't have to sit all the time knitting, knitting, knitting. If I had enough money for the journey to Lyons, then you would get it at once so that you could go to the great doctor."

Blind Barbara shook her head in negation. "I can't do lace any more," she said calmly. "I can only knit socks for the shepherds. It is not much, but Monsieur le Curé has said that it does not matter how humble our work is. If we always do it with love then Jesus is content with us."

That evening when Alice was looking after her doves as they flew round in circles and flashed in the light of the setting sun, she remembered how much Monsieur le Docteur wanted to take Blanche and Blanc with him for his daughter Angélique. And suddenly it struck her that she had said to blind Barbara that very afternoon that if only she had the money for the journey to Lyons she would have given it willingly to her. But she so loved Blanche and Blanc that at the thought alone of parting with them the tears sprang to her eyes.

But she loved Barbara even more, and if Barbara were to regain her sight then she would not have to sit in darkness any more and be always knitting because she could not do anything else. Perhaps for the doves Monsieur le Docteur would give her the price of the journey to Lyons.

"Must I sell them for Barbara's sake?" she asked herself. "Yes of course. But wait a moment, wait. After all, these doves have to take part in the shepherds' procession. I shall have to go and speak to Monsieur le Curé about it."

Without more ado Alice hastened away in the twilight to the parsonage. The curé listened earnestly to everything Alice told him and remained in thought for some time.

Anxiously Alice raised her eyes to him and said: "But it is for poor blind Barbara, perhaps Jesus will understand that."

Monsieur le Curé bent over and kissed her kindly on her upturned forehead.

"I don't doubt that for a minute, dear child," he answered.

Monsieur le Docteur was going to leave for Lyons early next morning, so Alice realized that she must bring him the doves immediately.

Now that she had Monsieur le Curé's permission, she hastened to the dovecote, where Blanche and Blanc were roosting, cooing in their sleep among the other doves. Alice climbed up and took them carefully out. She stroked their delicate heads while she climbed down the ladder. Then she put the doves in a basket which she had got ready. She shut the basket and ran off to Monsieur le Docteur.

"My dear child," he exclaimed in astonishment when he saw her, "do you mean to say that I can take the doves for Angélique after all? For didn't you say that you could not part with them? And furthermore you told me that these doves were chosen to be borne by the shepherds in the procession of the Christmas festival?"

"That's right, monsieur," answered Alice softly and rather embarrassed, "but if you will give me the cost of the journey to Lyons for my doves you can have them."

"The journey to Lyons?" repeated the astonished doctor, drawing her to him.

"Yes," answered Alice. "I need the money for the journey to Lyons."

The good doctor did not question her any further, took the basket with the doves from her and gave her as much money as the journey to Lyons and back cost.

There was no railway station in Maussane. People wanting to go to Lyons from there had to take the coach drawn by five strong horses driven by Arnulph Manier. Monsieur le Docteur was well on his way to Lyons when Alice knocked at the door of blind Barbara's house next morning.

"Come in," called Barbara from the room.

"Barbara, dear Barbara, you'll be able to see again, you'll be able to see everything again, because here is the money for the journey to Lyons!" cried Alice excitedly, running to her. She put the money into Barbara's hands which were lying open in her lap.

Blind Barbara could not say anything for sheer astonishment, but when she had recovered a bit from the sudden surprise, and heard from Alice how she had come by the money, she said quite decidedly, "You have sold your doves? And that for me? No, no, Alice I can't allow that. You must take that money back immediately to Monsieur le Docteur, and he must give you back your doves."

Barbara would not listen to anything Alice tried to say. Only when Monsieur le Curé had spoken earnestly with her and had used all his persuasive powers did she finally agree. He said, "Don't you understand, Barbara, that when she does this for you Alice is only obeying a good injunction of her heart, and that we should not only give but also be able to receive? Therefore you should not refuse her."

Then Barbara no longer made any objection.

On the day when blind Barbara went off to Lyons, half Maussane was present at the departure of the coach to wish her farewell and good luck. Monsieur le Curé helped her up into her place and gave Arnulph Manier all sorts of directions about where to put her down, and how to find Monsieur le Docteur.

Winter came to Provence. The fields were bare and in the evening the cold mistral bent the tops of the olive trees standing in long grey rows.

Barbara had now been away for three weeks, and the next day was the day of the great Christmas festival which in Provence had always been celebrated in such a special fashion.

Alice waited impatiently for the arrival of the coach because she thought that Barbara would want to be home before the Christmas festival. And she was not mistaken. When Arnulph came careering into the narrow street of Maussane and came to a stop with a tug at the reins, Barbara was the first to step out, but without any help from anyone, for she was no longer "Blind Barbara" — everyone could see that at once. When Barbara stepped out, all her friends from the village came from all directions out of all the little side-streets to welcome her.

The first was Monsieur le Curé. But Barbara embraced Alice first of all, spoke to her from her heart and told her that she had a message from Monsieur le Docteur: "He asks you to look into the sky in the direction of Lyons this evening towards sunset."

At the hour of sunset, so Alice was watching the sky in the direction of Lyons as Monsieur le Docteur had asked her to do. All those present were also watching. Far away, like snowflakes against the rose-tinted hills, two tiny birds became visible flying straight towards Maussane. They were flying quickly.

All eyes were fixed on them expectantly, and when the birds came nearer and were bigger it could be seen that they were doves, doves returning home.

Alice guessed which doves they were, but did not yet dare believe it. She raised her arms and with a voice full of love and longing she cried: "Blanche and Blanc!"

"O Barbara, Barbara, do you really believe that it is them?"

They were not kept in doubt much longer. Cleaving the air with powerful wing-beats as if they could not fly fast enough, the doves swooped down and perched on her outstretched hands, cooing happily.

"Alice's doves, Alice's doves," cried the shepherds of Maussane with joy, while Alice herself clasped the beautiful white doves to her bosom. While she was thus holding the doves she noticed a little roll of paper fastened to a ring around Blanche's leg. With trembling fingers she unfastened it and gave it to Monsieur le Curé who unfolded it and read out aloud so that everyone could hear him:

> *Dear Alice,*
> *My little Angélique and I are sending you back the doves which you gave to help blind Barbara. Because nothing is more worthy*

to be laid at the feet of the Child Jesus than this gift with which you have helped a fellow mortal, we both ask that these doves may be carried on the great Christmas festival in the shepherds' procession.

So after all Alice's white doves were carried through the church on the glorious Christmas Festival of Maussane.

Barbara, now no longer blind, stood upright in the middle of the broad nave of the church and held Alice's hand in her own, while she watched the shepherds going past her with the white lamb and the white doves. Then she bent her head low and thanked the Father in heaven.

The Christmas Rose

Selma Lagerlöf

Robber Mother, who lived in Robbers' Cave in Göinge forest, went down to the village one day on a begging tour. Robber Father, who was an outlawed man, did not dare to leave the forest, but had to content himself with lying in wait for the wayfarers who ventured within its borders. But at that time travellers were not very plentiful in Southern Skåne. If it so happened that the man had had a few weeks of ill luck with his hunt, his wife would take to the road. She took with her five youngsters, and each youngster wore a ragged leathern suit and birch-bark shoes and bore a sack on his back as long as himself. When Robber Mother stepped inside the door of a cabin, no one dared refuse to give her whatever she demanded; for she was not above coming back the following night and setting fire to the house if she had not been well received. Robber Mother and her brood were worse than a pack of wolves, and many a man felt like running a spear through them; but it was never done, because they all knew that the man stayed up in the forest, and he would have known how to wreak vengeance if anything had happened to the children or the old woman.

Now that Robber Mother went from house to house and begged, she came one day to Övid, which at that time was a cloister. She rang the bell of the cloister gate and asked for food. The watchman let down a small wicket in the gate and handed her six round bread cakes — one for herself and one for each of the five children.

While the mother was standing quietly at the gate, her youngsters were running about. And now one of them came and pulled at her skirt, as a signal that he had discovered something which she ought to come and see, and Robber Mother followed him promptly.

The entire cloister was surrounded by a high and strong wall, but the youngster had managed to find a little back gate which stood ajar. When Robber Mother got there, she pushed the gate open and walked

260

inside without asking leave, as it was her custom to do. Övid Cloister was managed at that time by Abott Hans, who knew all about herbs. Just within the cloister wall he had planted a little herb garden, and it was into this that the old women had forced her way.

At first glance Robber Mother was so astonished that she paused at the gate. It was high summertide, and Abbot Hans' garden was so full of flowers that the eyes were fairly dazzled by the blues, reds, and yellows, as one looked into it. But presently an indulgent smile spread over her features, and she started to walk up a narrow path that lay between many flower-beds.

In the garden a lay brother walked about, pulling up weeds. It was he who had left the door in the wall open, that he might throw the weeds and tares on the rubbish heap outside.

When he saw Robber Mother coming in, with all five youngsters in tow, he ran toward her at once and ordered them away. But the beggar woman walked right on as before. She cast her eyes up and down, looking now at the stiff white lilies which spread near the ground, then on the ivy climbing high upon the cloister wall, and took no notice whatever of the lay brother.

He thought she had not understood him, and wanted to take her by the arm and turn her toward the gate. But when the robber woman saw his purpose, she gave him a look that sent him reeling backward. She had been walking with back bent under her beggar's pack, but now she straightened herself to her full height. "I am Robber Mother from Göinge forest; so touch me if you dare!" And it was obvious that she was as certain she would be left in peace as if she had announced that she was the Queen of Denmark.

And yet the lay brother dared to oppose her, although now, when he knew who she was, he spoke reasonably to her, "You must know, Robber Mother, that this is a monks' cloister, and no woman in the land is allowed within these walls. If you do not go away, the monks will be angry with me because I forgot to close the gate, and perhaps they will drive me away from the cloister and the herb garden."

But such prayers were wasted on Robber Mother. She walked straight ahead among the little flower-beds and looked at the hyssop with its magenta blossoms, and at the honeysuckles, which were full of deep orange-colored flower clusters.

Then the lay brother knew of no other remedy than to run into the cloister and call for help.

He returned with two stalwart monks, and Robber Mother saw that now it meant business! With feet firmly planted she stood in the path and began shrieking in strident tones all the awful vengeance she would wreak on the cloister if she couldn't remain in the herb garden as long as she wished. But the monks did not see why they need fear her and thought only of driving her out. Then Robber Mother let out a perfect volley of shrieks, and, throwing herself upon the monks, clawed and bit at them; so did all the youngsters. The men soon learned that she could overpower them, and all they could do was to go back into the cloister for reinforcements.

As they ran through the passage-way which led to the cloister, they met Abbot Hans, who came rushing out to learn what all this noise was about.

Then they had to confess that Robber Mother from Göinge forest had come into the cloister and that they were unable to drive her out and must call for assistance.

But Abbot Hans upbraided them for using force and forbade their calling for help. He sent both monks back to their work, and although he was an old and fragile man, he took with him only the lay brother.

When Abbot Hans came out in the garden, Robber Mother was still wandering among the flower-beds. He regarded her with astonishment. He was certain that Robber Mother had never before seen an herb garden; yet she sauntered leisurely between all the small patches, each of which had been planted with its own species of rare flower, and looked at them as if they were old acquaintances. At some she smiled, at others she shook her head.

Abbot Hans loved his herb garden as much as it was possible for him to love anything earthly and perishable. Wild and terrible as the old woman looked, he couldn't help liking that she had fought with three monks for the privilege of viewing the garden in peace. He came up to her and asked in a mild tone if the garden pleased her.

Robber Mother turned defiantly toward Abbot Hans, for she expected only to be trapped and overpowered. But when she noticed his white hair and bent form, she answered peaceably, "First, when I saw this, I thought I had never seen a prettier garden; but now I see that it can't be compared with one I know of."

Abbot Hans had certainly expected a different answer. When he heard that Robber Mother had seen a garden more beautiful than his, a faint flush spread over his withered cheek. The lay brother, who was standing close by, immediately began to censure the old woman. "This is Abbot Hans," said he, "who with much care and diligence has gathered the flowers from far and near for his herb garden. We all know that there is not a more beautiful garden to be found in all Skåne, and it is not befitting that you, who live in the wild forest all the year around, should find fault with his work."

"I don't wish to make myself the judge of either him or you," said Robber Mother. "I'm only saying that if you could see the garden of which I am thinking you would uproot all the flowers planted here and cast them away like weeds."

But the Abbot's assistant was hardly less proud of the flowers than the Abbot himself, and after hearing her remarks he laughed derisively. "I can understand that you only talk like this to tease us. It must be a pretty garden that you have made for yourself amongst the pines in Göinge forest! I'd be willing to wager my soul's salvation that you have never before been within the walls of an herb garden."

Robber Mother grew crimson with rage to think that her word was doubted, and she cried out: "It may be true that until today I had never been within the walls of an herb garden; but you monks, who are holy men, certainly must know that on every Christmas Eve the great Göinge forest is transformed into a beautiful garden, to commemorate the hour of our Lord's birth. We who live in the forest have seen this happen every year. And in that garden I have seen flowers so lovely that I dared not lift my hand to pluck them."

The lay brother wanted to continue the argument, but Abbot Hans gave him a sign to be silent. For, ever since his childhood, Abbot Hans had heard it said that on every Chritmas Eve the forest was dressed in holiday glory. He had often longed to see it, but he had never had the good fortune. Eagerly he begged and implored Robber Mother that he might come up to the Robbers' Cave on Christmas Eve. If she would only send one of her children to show him the way, he could ride up there alone, and he would never betray them — on the contrary, he would reward them, in so far as it lay in his power.

Robber Mother said no at first, for she was thinking of Robber Father and of the peril which might befall him should she permit Abbot Hans to ride up to their cave. At the same time the desire to prove to the monk that the garden which she knew was more beautiful than his got the better of her, and she gave in.

"But more than one follower you cannot take with you," said she, "and you are not to waylay us or trap us, as sure as you are a holy man."

This Abbot Hans promised, and then Robber Mother went her way. Abbot Hans commanded the lay brother not to reveal to a soul that which had been agreed upon. He feared that the monks, should they learn of his purpose, would not allow a man of his years to go up to the Robbers' Cave.

Nor did he himself intend to reveal his project to a human being. And then it happened that Archbishop Absalon from Lund came to Övid and remained through the night. When Abbot Hans was showing him the herb garden, he got to thinking of Robber Mother's visit, and the lay brother, who was at work in the garden, heard Abbot Hans telling the Bishop about Robber Father, who these many years had lived as an outlaw in the forest, and asking him for a letter of ransom for the man, that he might lead an honest life among respectable folk. "As things are now," said Abbot Hans, "his children are growing up into worse malefactors than himself, and you will soon have a whole gang of robbers to deal with up there in the forest."

But the Archbishop replied that he did not care to let the robber loose among the honest folk in the villages. It would be best for all that he remain in the forest.

Then Abbot Hans grew zealous and told the Bishop all about Göinge forest, which, every year at Yuletide, clothed itself in summer bloom around the Robbers' Cave. "If these bandits are not so bad but that God's glories can be made manifest to them, surely we cannot be too wicked to experience the same blessing."

The Archbishop knew how to answer Abbot Hans. "This much I will promise you, Abbot Hans," he said, smiling, "that any day you send me a blossom from the garden in Göinge forest, I will give you letters of ransom for all the outlaws you may choose to plead for."

The lay brother apprehended that Bishop Absalom believed as little in this story of Robber Mother's as he himself; but Abbot Hans perceived nothing of the sort, but thanked Absalon for his good promise and said that he would surely send him the flower.

Abbot Hans had his way. And the following Christmas Eve he did not sit at home with his monks in Övid Cloister, but was on his way to Göinge forest. One of Robber Mother's wild youngsters ran ahead of him, and close behind him was the lay brother who had talked with Robber Mother in the herb garden.

Abbot Hans had been longing to make this journey, and he was very happy now that it had come to pass. But it was a different matter with the lay brother who accompanied him. Abbot Hans was very dear to him, and he would not willingly have allowed another to attend him and watch over him; but he didn't believe that he should see any Christmas Eve garden. He thought the whole thing a snare which Robber Mother had, with great cunning, laid for Abbot Hans, that he might fall into her husband's clutches.

While Abbot Hans was riding toward the forest, he saw that everywhere they were preparing to celebrate Christmas. In every peasant settlement fires were lighted in the bath-house to warm it for the afternoon bathing. Great hunks of meat and bread were being carried from the larders into the cabins, and from the barns came the men with big sheaves of straw to be strewn over the floors.

As he rode by the little country churches, he observed that each parson, with his sexton, was busily engaged in decorating his church; and when he came to the road which leads to Bösjo Cloister, he observed that all the poor of the parish were coming with armfuls of bread and long candles, which they had received at the cloister gate.

When Abbot Hans saw all these Christmas preparations, his haste increased. He was thinking of the festivities that awaited him, which were greater than any the others would be privileged to enjoy.

But the lay brother whined and fretted when he saw how they were preparing to celebrate Christmas in every humble cottage. He grew more and more anxious, and begged and implored Abbot Hans to turn back and not to throw himself deliberately into the robber's hands.

Abbot Hans went straight ahead, paying no heed to his lamentations. He left the plain behind him and came up into desolate and wild forest regions. Here the road was bad, almost like a stony and burr-strewn path, with neither bridge nor plank to help them over brooklet and rivulet. The farther they rode, the colder it grew, and after a while they came upon snow-covered ground.

It turned out to be a long and hazardous ride through the forest. They climbed steep and slippery side paths, crawled over swamp and marsh, and pushed through windfall and bramble. Just as daylight was waning, the robber boy guided them across a forest meadow, skirted by tall, naked leaf trees and green fir trees. Back of the meadow loomed a mountain wall, and in this wall they saw a door of thick boards. Now Abbot Hans understood that they had arrived, and dismounted. The child opened the heavy door for him, and he looked into a poor mountain grotto, with bare stone walls. Robber Mother was seated before a log fire that burned in the middle of the floor. Alongside the walls were beds of virgin pine and moss, and on one of these beds lay Robber Father asleep.

"Come in, you out there!" shouted Robber Mother without rising, "and fetch the horses in with you, so they won't be destroyed by the night cold."

Abbot Hans walked boldly into the cave, and the lay brother followed. Here were wretchedness and poverty! And nothing was done to celebrate Christmas. Robber Mother had neither brewed nor baked; she had neither washed nor scoured. The youngsters were lying on the floor around a kettle, eating; but no better food was provided for them than a wartery gruel.

Robber Mother spoke in a tone as haughty and dictatorial as any well-to-do peasant woman. "Sit down by the fire and warm yourself, Abbot Hans," said she, "and if you have food with you, eat, for the food which we in the forest prepare you wouldn't care to taste. And if you are tired after the long journey, you can lie down on one of these beds to sleep. You needn't be afraid of oversleeping, for I'm sitting here by the fire keeping watch. I shall awaken you in time to see that which you have come up here to see."

Abbot Hans obeyed Robber Mother and brought forth his food sack; but he was so fatigued after the journey he was hardly able to eat, and as soon as he could stretch himself on the bed, he fell asleep.

The lay brother was also assigned a bed to rest upon, but he didn't dare sleep, as he thought he had better keep his eye on Robber Father to prevent his getting up and capturing Abbott Hans. But gradually fatigue got the better of him, too, and he dropped into a doze.

When he woke up, he saw that Abbot Hans had left his bed and was sitting by the fire talking with Robber Mother. The outlawed robber sat also by the fire. He was a tall, raw-boned man with a dull, sluggish appearance. His back was turned to Abbot Hans, as though he would have it appear that he was not listening to the conversation.

Abbot Hans was telling Robber Mother all about the Christmas preparations he had seen on the journey, reminding her of Christmas feasts and games which she must have known in her youth, when she lived at peace with mankind. "I'm sorry for your children, who can never run on the village street in holiday dress or tumble in the Christmas straw," said he.

At first Robber Mother answered in short, gruff sentences, but by degrees she became more subdued and listened more intently. Suddenly Robber Father turned toward Abbot Hans and shook his clenched fist in his face. "You miserable monk! Did you come here to coax from me my wife and children? Don't you know that I am an outlaw and may not leave the forest?"

Abbot Hans looked him fearlessly in the eyes. "It is my purpose to get a letter of ransom for you from Archbishop Absalon," said he. He had hardly finished speaking when the robber and his wife burst out laughing. They knew well enough the kind of mercy a forest robber could expect from Bishop Absalon!

"Oh, if I get a letter of ransom from Absalon," said Robber Father, "then I'll promise you that never again will I steal so much as a goose."

The lay brother was annoyed with the robber folk for daring to laugh at Abbot Hans, but on his own account he was well pleased. He had seldom seen the Abbot sitting more peaceful and meek with his monks at Övid than he now sat with this wild robber folk.

Suddenly Robber Mother rose. "You sit here and talk, Abbot Hans," she said, "so that we are forgetting to look at the forest. Now I can hear, even in this cave, how the Christmas bells are ringing."

The words were barely uttered when they all sprang up and rushed out. But in the forest it was still dark night and bleak winter. The only thing they marked was a distant clang borne on a light south wind.

"How can this bell ringing ever awaken the dead forest?" thought Abbot Hans. For now, as he stood out in the winter darkness, he thought it far more impossible that a summer garden could spring up here than it had seemed to him before.

When the bells had been ringing a few moments, a sudden illumination penetrated the forest; the next moment it was dark again, and then the light came back. It pushed its way forward between the stark trees, like a shimmering mist. This much it effected: The darkness merged into a faint daybreak. Then Abbot Hans saw that the snow had vanished from the ground, as if someone had removed a carpet, and the earth began to take on a green covering. Then the ferns shot up their fronds, rolled like a bishop's staff. The heather that grew on the stony hills and the bog-myrtle rooted in the ground moss dressed themselves quickly in the bloom. The moss-tufts thickened and raised themselves, and the spring blossoms shot upward their swelling buds, which already had a touch of colour.

Abbot Hans' heart beat fast as he marked the first signs of the forest's awakening. "Old man that I am, shall I behold such a miracle?" thought he, and the tears wanted to spring to his eyes. Again it grew so hazy that he feared the darkness would once more cover the earth; but almost immediately there came a new wave of light. It brought with it the splash of rivulet and the rush of cataract. Then the leaves of the trees burst into bloom, as if a swarm of green butterflies came flying and clustered on the branches. It was not only trees and plants that awoke, but crossbeaks hopped from branch to branch, and the woodpeckers hammered on the limbs until the splinters fairly flew around them. A flock of starlings from up country lighted in a fir top to rest. They were paradise starlings. The tips of each tiny feather shone in brilliant reds, and, as the birds moved, they glittered like so many jewels.

Again, all was dark for an instant, but soon there came a new light wave. A fresh, warm south wind blew and scattered over the forest meadow all the little seeds that had been brought from southern lands by birds and ships and winds, and which could not thrive elsewhere because of this country's cruel cold. These took root and sprang up the instant they touched the ground.

When the next warm wind came along, the blueberries and lignon ripened. Cranes and wild geese shrieked in the air, the bullfinches built nests, and the baby squirrels began playing on the branches of the trees.

Everything came so fast now that Abbot Hans could not stop to reflect on how immeasurably great was the miracle that was taking place. He had time only to use his eyes and ears. The next light wave that came rushing in brought with it the scent of newly ploughed acres, and far off in the distance the milkmaids were heard coaxing the cows — and the tinkle of the sheep's bells. Pine and spruce trees were so thickly clothed with red cones that they shone like crimson mantles. The juniper berries changed colour every second, and forest flowers covered the ground till it was all red, blue, and yellow.

Abbot Hans bent down to the earth and broke off a wild strawberry blossom, and, as he straightened up, the berry ripened in his hand.

The mother fox came out of her lair with a big litter of black-legged young. She went up to Robber Mother and scratched at her skirt, and Robber Mother bent down to her and praised her young. The horned owl, who had just begun his night chase, was astonished at the light and went back to his ravine to perch for the night. The male cuckoo crowed, and his mate stole up to the nests of the little birds with her egg in her mouth.

Robber Mother's youngsters let out perfect shrieks of delight. They stuffed themselves with wild strawberries that hung on the bushes, large as pine cones. One of them played with a litter of young hares; another ran a race with some young crows, which had hopped from their nest before they were really ready; a third caught up an adder from the ground and wound it around his neck and arm.

Robber Father was standing out on a marsh eating raspberries. When he glanced up, a big black bear stood beside him. Robber Father broke off an osier twig and struck the bear on the nose. "Keep to your own ground, you!" he said; "this is my turf." Then the huge bear turned around and lumbered off in another direction.

New waves of warmth and light kept coming, and now they brought with them seeds from the star-flower.

Golden pollen from rye fields fairly flew in the air. Then came butterflies, so big that they looked like flying lilies. The bee-hive in a hollow oak was already so full of honey that it dripped down on the trunk of the tree. Then all the flowers whose seed had been brought from foreign lands began to blossom. The loveliest roses climbed up the mountain wall in a race with the blackberry vines, and from the forest meadow sprang flowers as large as human faces.

Abbot Hans thought of the flower he was to pluck for Bishop Absalon; but each new flower that appeared was more beautiful that the others, and he wanted to choose the most beautiful of all.

Wave upon wave kept coming until the air was so filled with light that it glittered. All the life and beauty and joy of summer smiled on Abbot Hans. He felt that earth could bring no greater happiness than that which welled up about him, and he said to himself, "I do not know what new beauties the next wave that comes can bring with it."

But the light kept streaming in, and now it seemed to Abbot Hans that it carried with it something from an infinite distance. He felt a celestial atmosphere enfolding him, and tremblingly he began to anticipate, now that earth's joys had come, that the glories of heaven were approaching.

Then Abbot Hans marked how all grew still; the birds hushed their songs, the flowers ceased growing, and the young foxes played no more. The glory now nearing was such that the heart wanted to stop beating; the eyes wept without one's knowing it; the soul longed to soar away into the Eternal. From far in the distance faint harp tones were heard, and celestial song, like a soft murmur, reached him.

Abbot Hans clasped his hands and dropped to his knees. His face was radiant with bliss. Never had he dreamed that even in this life it should be granted him to taste the joys of heaven, and to hear angels sing Christmas carols!

But beside Abbot Hans stood the lay brother who had accompanied him. In his mind there were dark thoughts. "This cannot be a true miracle," he thought, "since it is revealed to malefactors. This does not come from God, but has its origin in witchcraft and is sent hither by Satan. It is the Evil One's power that is tempting us and compelling us to see that which has no real existence."

From afar were heard the sound of angel harps and the tones of a miserere. But the lay brother thought it was the evil spirits of hell coming closer. "They would enchant and seduce us," sighed he, "and we shall be sold into perdition."

The angel throng was so near now that Abbot Hans saw their bright forms through the forest branches. The lay brother saw them, too; but back of all this wondrous beauty he saw only some dread evil. For him it was the devil who performed these wonders on the anniversary of our Saviour's birth. It was done simply for the purpose of more effectually deluding poor human beings.

All the while the birds had been circling around the head of Abbot Hans, and they let him take them in his hands. But all the animals were afraid of the lay brother; no bird perched on his shoulder, no snake played at his feet. Then there came a little forest dove. When she marked that the angels were nearing, she plucked up courage and flew down on the lay brother's shoulder and laid her head against his cheek.

Then it appeared to him as if sorcery were come right upon him, to tempt and corrupt him. He struck with his hands at the forest dove and cried in such a loud voice that it rang throughout the forest, "Go thou back to hell, whence thou art come!"

Just then the angels were so near that Abbot Hans felt the feathery touch of their great wings, and he bowed down to earth in reverent greeting.

But when the lay brother's words sounded, their song was hushed and the holy guests turned in flight. At the same time the light and the mild warmth vanished in unspeakable terror for the darkness and cold in a human heart. Darkness sank over the earth, like a coverlet; frost came, all the growths shrivelled up; the animals and birds hastened away; the rushing of streams was hushed; the leaves dropped from the trees, rustling like rain.

Abbot Hans felt how his heart, which had but lately swelled with bliss, was now contracting with insufferable agony. "I can never outlive this," thought he, "that the angels from heaven had been so close to me and were driven away; that they wanted to sing Christmas carols for me and were driven to flight."

Then he remembered the flower he had promised Bishop Absalon, and at the last moment he fumbled among the leaves and moss to try and find a blossom. But he sensed how the ground under his fingers froze and how the white snow came gliding over the ground. Then his heart caused him even greater anguish. He could not rise, but fell prostrate on the ground and lay there.

When the robber folk and the lay brother had groped their way back to the cave, they missed Abbot Hans. They took brands with them and went out to search for him. They found him dead upon the coverlet of snow.

Then the lay brother began weeping and lamenting, for he understood that it was he who had killed Abbot Hans because he had dashed from him the cup of happiness which he had been thirsting to drain to its last drop.

When Abbot Hans had been carried down to Övid, those who took charge of the dead saw that he held his right hand locked tight around something which he must have grasped at the moment of death. When they finally got his hand opened, they found the thing which he held in such an iron grip was a pair of white root bulbs, which he had torn from among the moss and leaves.

When the lay brother who had accompanied Abbot Hans saw the bulbs, he took them and planted them in Abbot Hans' herb garden.

He guarded them the whole year to see if any flower would spring from them. But in vain he waited through the spring, the summer, and the autumn. Finally, when winter had set in and all the leaves and the flowers were dead, he ceased caring for them.

But when Christmas Eve came again, he was so strongly reminded of Abbot Hans that he wandered out into the garden to think of him. And look! As he came to the spot where he had planted the bare root bulbs, he saw that from them had sprung flourishing green stalks, which bore beautiful flowers with silver white leaves.

He called out all the monks at Övid, and when they saw this plant bloomed on Christmas Eve, when all the other growths were as if dead, they understood that this flower had in truth been plucked by Abbot Hans from the Christmas garden in Göinge forest. Then the lay brother asked the monks if he might take a few blossoms to Bishop Absalon.

And when he appeared before Bishop Absalon, he gave him the flowers and said: "Abbot Hans sends you these. They are the flowers he promised to pick for you from the garden in Göinge forest."

When Bishop Absalon beheld the flowers, which had sprung from the earth in darkest winter, and heard the words, he turned as pale as if he had met a ghost. He sat in silence a moment; thereupon he said, "Abbot Hans has faithfully kept his word and I shall also keep mine." And he ordered that a letter of ransom be drawn up for the wild robber who has outlawed and had been forced to live in the forest ever since his youth.

He handed the letter to the lay brother, who departed at once for the Robber's Cave. When he stepped in there on Christmas Day, the robber came toward him with axe uplifted. "I'd like to hack you monks to bits, as many as you are!" said he. "It must be your fault that Göinge forest did not last night dress itself in Christmas bloom."

"That fault is mine alone," said the lay brother, "and I will gladly die for it; but first I must deliver a message from Abbot Hans." And he drew forth the Bishop's letter and told the man that he was free. "Hereafter you and your children shall play in the Christmas straw and celebrate your Christmas among people, just as Abbot Hans wished to have it," said he.

Then Robber Father stood there pale and speechless, but Robber Mother said in his name, "Abbot Hans has indeed kept his word, and Robber Father will keep his."

When the robber and his wife left the cave, the lay brother moved in and lived all alone in the forest, in constant meditation and prayer that his hard-heartedness might be forgiven him.

But Göinge forest never again celebrated the hour of our Saviour's birth; and of all its glory, there lives today only the plant which Abbot Hans had plucked. It has been named CHRISTMAS ROSE. And each year at Christmastide she sends forth from the earth her green stalks and white blossoms, as if she never could forget that she had once grown in the great Christmas garden at Göinge forest.

The Gold of Bernardino

An ancient legend of Cantabria

Ruth Sawyer

Centuries before the Armada sailed from the bay of Vigo to make war on English ships, there lived high up in the Cantabrian Hills a peasant. He was a strong giant of a man, with gentle hands for creatures and children, a quiet, friendly way of speaking, and an exceedingly simple heart. He lived by himself with the oxen that drew his plough, the goats that gave him milk, and the dog, small and black, that ran bouncingly at his heels.

No churches had yet been built in Spain. But there came one spring a saintly man, a friar, climbing the hills to the peasant's hut, there to dwell with him many days while he told of a new God and of his Son, a holier man than all other men, one who had been born and had died and been born again. Every night, after the day's ploughing, the friar would read out of a small handwritten book about this Son of God, this Jesus the Christ. He had much to tell: a new religion had been called after him — Christianity; and there were many stories not written down which had been passed from mouth to mouth.

"I would become a Christian," said the peasant. "I would follow this Jesus the Christ."

It came naturally therefore that the friar before he left should baptize the peasant. He gave him the name of Bernadino, by which he became known throughout Cantabria. Now, being one who seldom had intercourse with other men, Bernadino was fearful lest he forget all the friar had told him; so he began repeating to the beasts the stories and all that had been read out of the handwritten book concerning the sayings of Jesus the Christ. While the peasant cleared new land and ploughed, he would talk with the oxen, saying: "Slow and gentle ones, it is well

273

that you should hear. Listen then: 'And that same day went Jesus out of the house and sat by the sea ...' "

When he milked the goats at nightfall he would time his words to the dripping in his firkin: "Good my brothers, this is for thy ears, these blessings: 'Blessed are the poor in spirit —' "

And before he slept, with the dog lying beside the hearth, he would tell of the lame, the halt, and the blind, and how they were healed by the laying-on of hands: "Small, faithful one, he was of all men the most holy."

He fitted the story of Jesus the Christ to the seasons, so that with the winter solstice he began with the shepherds, of their watching, of the angels, the star, the manger, and the new-born Babe. " 'Hosanna! Glory to God in the highest!' That is good; but hearken to something better, my beasts: 'On Earth peace, good will toward men!' That is something for beasts and men to carry in their hearts always."

He would tell with wonder, with bitterness, with grief that made his eyes to overflow and sent tears coursing down the furrows of his cheeks only to fall upon the furrows of the earth, all that had to do with the life and death of Jesus the Christ. But always he came back to the winter solstice with a fresh heart, always he began: "Listen, lowly ones, we come again to the birth." Then only did he know joy unbound.

From that first telling of the birth had sprung a great resolve, and this he shared with no man, only the beasts: "I shall go someday to Bethlehem at Christmas-time, when again the Child is born. I, too, shall worship at his manger. You shall see!"

It meant gold for passage, gold for food, and a gift when he should reach the lowly stable. Ships of many countries, from the east, the south, the north, were always making port at the harbour, needing to be revictualled. He would carry half of his harvest each year to the sea and sell it for gold. He would talk with sailors about this place called Bethlehem, in Judea. He would find out from them the length of time for the pilgrimage and the cost.

From the time he made that first journey to the harbour, Bernardino strung a leather pouch about his loins and in it he put his first piece of gold. It would take ten pieces for his undertaking, and a half-year's time. If he started after the autumn equinox he would be back in time for the spring planting. That was good! The beasts would care for themselves; he would have much to tell them when he returned.

Bernardino was a young man when the friar had baptized him; he was at his prime when the pouch was full and the autumn equinox at hand. The gold from this last harvest would provide the gift for the Child. He never doubted he would find Bethlehem, never doubted that the Child would be there, new-born.

His eve of departure came. The clumsy two-wheeled cart was loaded against the morning's journey. Bernardino was stooping over the hearth, putting into the carefully raked embers the oaten-cakes, wrapped in cabbage leaves, which would furnish some of the food he would need. He chanced to look up. A small, struggling figure was weaving its uncertain way up the path to the hut. Before the peasant could regain his feet the figure had stumbled forward and dropped face down not two metres from the door.

Bernadino reached the figure and crouched beside it. It was a lad, his clothes torn from him, his back lashed in places clean to the bone. "Who has dared?" The peasant was angered at what he saw — a lad so small, so young, to be so trod upon. He lifted him with great tenderness, bore him inside, and put him carefully down upon his bed of skins. Then he gathered healing herbs and gum from the trees, making of these a balm to put upon the wounds. Coming to consciousness, the lad would have fled had he not been so weak from loss of blood. It took no strength to restrain him; but it took much gentling of speech, much coaxing, to get him to swallow the warm milk Bernardino held to his lips. Stark terror was in the lad's eyes. "That, too, will take healing," Bernardino thought.

A day came when the lad was well enough to run about. Twice now his lips had broken into a smile when Bernardino had clapped his hands at the lad's quick understanding of a tongue strange to him. The moon had waxed from first quarter to full when a man climbed the hill; he was laced into a leather cuirass and carried a sword. The lad took flight at sight of him and by signs the stranger made Bernardino knew he had come hunting the lad, a slave, to take him back to his ship from which he had fled. In the end the peasant brought out his gold and paid the ten pieces demanded for the lad's freedom.

"It is well," the peasant thought. "Now I will have someone to leave with land and beasts when I go." And he bent his whole strength and heart to teaching the boy to forget fear and understand what freedom meant, and in helping him to a mastery of his tongue — this that he might have human ears in which to pour the stories of Jesus the Christ and all that had been written down in the small book.

Harvests multiplied. Now in the autumn when he and the lad went together to the harbour to sell the grain, the cabbages, the goats' cheese, and sour wine, there were two gold pieces to put into the leather pouch that hung about the peasant's loins. Five years beat themselves out as swiftly as a swallow beats his way across the water, and again came the time for Bernadino's departure. His mind and heart were filled with the joy of going, of forecasting that moment when his feet would cross the threshold of the stable and he would be kneeling there before the Child. "It will all be to tell to you when I come back. Watch for the star. Always I look for it, for who can tell when again it may appear and mark the way."

Night had fallen. The oaten-cakes were done and the lad sat, peeling off the burned cabbage leaves, and laying each cake carefully in the sack Bernardino would carry with him. Suddenly the quiet of the night was cut in twain by a shouting of voices, and out of the darkness came four robed figures — friars, holy men, even such as had once come hither years before. Bernadino rose to welcome them, to give them food and bed them down as best he could, he and the lad going out to the shed to sleep with the beasts. But before he went the friars had a strange thing to tell. All over God's world men were beginning to build churches in which to worship Jesus the Christ. Such a church they had come to build, and a monastery to house their holy order. They would need the help of strong men; they would need all the gold the followers of Jesus the Christ could bring together.

To this strange tale there was but one answer for Bernadino. He must give his gold. Would he ever have heard of the Child, or Bethlehem, had not a holy man brought the tale to him? He would stay and help build this church. It might be the will of the new God that he do his worshipping here, and not in Bethlehem.

So began a new life for Bernardino the peasant. He worked the ground as little as was needful to feed himself, the lad, and the four who had come. From the first coming of light back of the hills to the last shaft of it beyond the sea, he worked at the felling of trees, the shaping of great beams, the curving of them to a vaulted roof. As they worked together the holy men taught Bernardino certain salvés and glorias and chants that had come to be part of the worship. These they sang and the hills gave them back in full echo.

It took years for the building of church and monastery. When all was completed Bernardino had become an old man, having more years than he could remember. There had been times when rebellion and anger filled his heart, when he fought against the work allotted him, and the dying, piece by piece, of his dream of Bethlehem. But these times grew less fearful, less often, and he found much consolation in the worship and prayer in the chapel. There had come from some far distant place a figure of Jesus the Christ upon the cross, with thorns to crown him, and another of Mary his Mother in a blue robe and a golden crown on her head. The brothers called her the Virgin of Light, and Bernardino found much solace in kneeling at matin and complin, telling her all that was in his heart. it was hard to pray to the One upon the cross, for never had he so conceived him. Often he protested this to the brothers: "Why hang him there, year after year? Preach the Crucifixion, yes; and the Resurrection at Easter. But show Jesus the Christ as the Child new-born — always new-born. That is what we must remember. It is the birth we worship, not the death."

The older he grew the oftener he protested: "It is Bethlehem we seek — not Calvary. Come, let us have here the Child, lying within its manger."

But who had ever heard of such a thing put into a consecrated church, built upon ground made holy? "He is getting more ancient than the oldest tree," said one. "Sometimes I think he must have come to Spain with the good Santiago," said another. "He is growing foolish as old men will," said a third. "He will soon die."

But Bernardino did not die. He lived on, far beyond his allotted years. Many friars had come to the monastery; pilgrims climbed the hills to worship there. The brothers gave Bernardino light tasks to perform that would not try his waning strength. But as he drew water, brought faggots from the woods, out of a mind often befogged would come to him that wonder of why he should live on. Why had he not died as those first friars with whom he had worked to build the church? And one day the answer to this came. How could he die until he had seen Bethlehem? Had he not made that promise to worship where the living Christ was born? It was not enough to kneel before a dying Christ; he must find the living One.

There came a winter of great snows and high piercing winds that shook the monastery on the hills and chilled the brothers to their marrow. Bernardino was let bring his goatskins inside and sleep beside the fire in the hall. So it happened that on the Eve of Christmas, when the brothers had withdrawn after complin to their cells to await the celebration of the Christmas Mass, Bernardino lay asleep. And as he slept he dreamed:

Youth had come back to him — strength to his limbs and joy to his heart. He felt again the impending journey to Bethlehem, and raising himself to an elbow he looked upon the hearth to see if the oaten-cakes were cooking there. But the hearth was empty. He felt for the pouch about his loins; no longer did it hang there to hold his gold. Where was it? Where had the gold gone? The winter solstice was at hand; he must hurry to reach Bethlehem in time for the birth.

Of its own accord the doorway of the monastery opened and in there came oxen and goats and a dog, small and black. The noises they made were those of beasts to a loving master. They came, rubbing heads against his limbs, while the dog licked eagerly at his hand and whined. "Good!" said Bernardino, "we go together." Holding fast by the oxen's horns he raised himself, and putting his arms over their necks he walked with them, not to the door, not outside to the winter's night, but across the hall, along the cloisters, to the chapel door.

It did not seem strange that they should enter the church together. Enter and kneel. Nor did it seem strange that where the altar had been there was a manger. The light from tapering candles filled the rude stall to overflowing. It shone upon Mary's face, she kneeling as they knelt. It shone upon the angels' choir, their wings interlaced, their hands raised in salutation. But far more radiant than these it shone upon the face of the Child, lying quietly upon his straw.

"See — we are come, little Holy One. Or is it that thou hast come to us? What matters it? It is the night of the birth — we are here at last to worship." Very tenderly Bernardino held out the forefinger of his right hand and worked it slowly within the small closed fist of the Child. He felt it tighten, a strong tight-holding grip. The Child's eyes opened and there was in them the look of one long-known, long-loved.

But others who had come to worship had brought gifts. Again Bernardino felt for the pouch and found it gone. Then did he look up, wondering, perplexed, and saw an angel's hand extended, and holding a leather pouch. "It is thine, take it. We have but kept it for thee."

When the brothers gathered in the hall, there to form the processional for early Mass, they found the hearth deserted. Gaining the chapel they looked with consternation upon the ancient figure kneeling there, the creatures about him. The Father Superior paused to waken him; and then he saw, as did all the brotherhood, at what lowly place the peasant was worshipping: a manger, although to them no manger was visible; the Child, for only upon a child did the human soul so pour forth such love and adoration. They could have sworn on Holy Writ that, clasped within the ancient wrinkled hand, there lay that of a young child. What they did see was the pouch beside him.

"The gold," they whispered one to another. "It was in such a leather pouch he brought his offering for the church, so the records say." Ten pieces of gold it held when they counted it. "Look, here are now the same ten pieces within."

As the spring drew near, the brothers talked often of Bernardino's going, the time and manner of it.

"He was a good man — none better ever walked the earth."

"He consecrated his life as a true follower of Jesus the Christ. We, ourselves, have done no more."

"That strange idea he had about the manger, the coming to worship there, before all other places!"

It was not strange that out of talk such as this should have come the wish to honour Bernardino's memory. "Of all things he would have liked best," said the Father Superior, "what say you?"

And so it came to pass that thoughout the full green of spring, the sweet lagging of summer, the glowing the plenty of garnered harvest, those brothers who could carve bent all their skill and time upon the making of a manger and figures to kneel about it. When the next Christmas Eve came, the manger was placed full lovingly upon the steps of the altar. There were Mary and Joseph, angels in attendance. And kneeling among the shepherds the brothers had made the figure of Bernardino hold out his offering of gold to the Child.

That was the first Nativity put into a Spanish church. That was the first Christmas Mass sung to the Child. It has made this birth everlasting. And in the kneeling figure of Bernardino has come down the memory of a great and simple man.

The Crib of Bo'Bossu

From Brittany

Ruth Sawyer

Listen, *mes enfants*, this is a tale for Noel — a tale from that part of France called Brittany, known among all people as the Country of Pardons. That is a good name; that tells you something already about the Breton folk, and I could tell you more. Do you know that all summer, along the sand dunes, the Korrigans dance in the moonlight? They are Celtic princesses who have lost their souls because they were born and died before the good tidings of the birth of Our Lord had been brought to them. Brittany is Celtic and the people are of deep faith, of light heart, of gay spirits. They are good workers. They mind their own business, and they expect you to mind yours.

On the Côtes-du-Nord there is the very ancient walled city of Saint-Malo. The Romans walled it, but they did not name it. It was named long afterwards for that good saint who was so gentle, so good, so mindful of lowly creatures, that one day when working in the field he put off his cloak, for the sun's heat was strong, and laid it on the brush. And when at eventide he went to cover himself again he found a wren had built her nest in the fold of the cloak, and rather than destroy the nest and the tiny bird's faith he left the coat to lie until the eggs were laid, the fledglings hatched and raised, while he went cold. That is something good to remember.

The city of Saint-Malo has a cathedral built of grey stone, as rugged, as massive, as eternal to stand as the Côtes-du-Nord itself. And there is something I must tell you of the city and the cathedral. The Breton navigator Jacques Cartier was born here. And in the cathedral, before the choir, he knelt for his last benediction before he sailed for the New World. A tablet tells one, so it must be true.

The Malouins are mostly sailors and fishermen and builders of boats. They are good men and unafraid on land or sea. For long now it has been the custom for them to keep the Eve of Noel with a celebration in the cathedral, before beginning the Christ Mass. This celebration is made that all should remember throughout the coming year the birth of Our Lord, and the placing of Our Lady on the Throne of Heaven. It is not enough that they should be told it happened thus and so, but they must hear again the birth proclaimed and see with their own eyes the manger.

Long before midnight the people of Saint-Malo gather. They come from the quays, from the yards, from the shops and the homes; they come in quiet, for this is a holy night. Long ago they bore torches through the twisted, narrow streets, leaving them outside, to enter in darkness — the whole cathedral dark save for the red eye of the oil lamp burning before the altar. Voices were hushed. No sound save for the brushing of feet against the flagging, the rustle of garments, the long indrawing of the breath in great expectancy.

This is the order of the celebration, *mes enfants,* and it has been changed little in the last three hundred years. In the darkness and the silence, high aloft, a young boy dressed in white, for he is the Angel of Glad Tidings, takes his place. Then out rolls the organ, and with voice high-soaring the angel sings:

> *Annuncio vobis gaudum magnum*
> *Quia natus est hodie,*
> *Salvator mundi,*
> *Alleluia!*

As by some breath of magic a thousand candles burst into flame, and all the children of Saint-Malo, robed in white, join the choir, bursting into jubilant song:

> *Gloria in excelsis Deo*
> *Et in terra pax*
> *Hominibus bene voluntates.*
> *Alleluia!*

Then come the shepherds. The number of them has grown with the long years. Sometimes they bring sheep with them from their folds, and one can hear the soft tinkling of the bells as they move up the long nave. They approach the choir where stands the manger, veiled. They sing their songs of praise, of peace. All hold their breath, for now the veil is drawn, the manger is disclosed, and all may look upon Our Lady, kneeling by the crib wherein lies the Babe, Lord Jesus. So beautiful it is! The children sing:

Alleluia, alleluia!
Christus natus hodie!

The church bells over all the city ring out for midnight. So begins the Christ Mass.

Now in the city there lived a hunchback whom everyone called Bo'Bossu. He worked down by the quays, an apprentice to the boat-builder Penhoël. There were a dozen apprentices like Bo'Bossu, but none so clever with the hands, none so quick to lay a keel, to shape a hull, or to carve with perfection the head or figure that often finished the prow of a large vessel. To Bo'Bossu was given the most delicate of the work; and he was happiest when he held wood or tool in his hands, when he was giving shape to something, could see it turn from a rough-hewn block or beam of oak or fir into a boat or some part of it before his eyes. The "Old One," Penhoël, and the other apprentices treated him kindly. Boys like himself, the apprentices looked up to him as the better craftsman; they watched often to see how he did this or that. The boat-builder gave Bo'Bossu a straw pallet in the corner of the boat-shed to sleep on, and fed him from his own table.

Of a truth Bo'Bossu was happy always at work, but to go abroad, that was another matter. On the streets Bo'Bossu met with jeers too often; and too often other boys, who were straight and strong as boys should be, pelted him with stones or refuse, laughing to see him take to his warped legs. That was funny — to see Bo'Bossu run for cover. And many believed, because the Malouins carry strange notions in their heads, that God's curse rested on the hunchback, that this curse had taken the form of misshapen legs and a hump.

He was a quiet boy, slow to move save when he was harried. He carried abroad always a white, frightened face — a sorry-looking boy. And when folk took time to look at him, which was rare, they thought: there goes one God has smitten. Never enough *potage* to fill his stomach, never enough love to fill his heart. All this was quite true, save that God had nothing to do with it.

Now Bo'Bossu loved the cathedral. He loved the very weight and roughness of its structure, for there was strength as well as beauty in all of it. He loved the quiet hours when few came to pray. Saint Malo was his friend: Our Lady was his mother; the Lord Jesus was his brother; and to these in turn he would bring his aching heart and pour it out in slow, laboured speech. For his tongue had none of the skill that lay in his hands.

Before Our Lady he would kneel most often; he would plead for a small sliver, a shaving of her love, that she might spare him this who knew no kin. That was why he went to the cathedral and bore the agony of his travels there and back, the fear of the stoning, the chasing not the abuse. Truly, to pray, to urburden the heart was worth this burden.

He did not know his own age, did Bo'Bossu. But he knew this much: he was no longer a child and not yet had he become a man. It was a gusty night of spring, he was kneeling after evensong in the cathedral before Our Lady, when the great, the magnificent idea came to him. On the Eve of Noel, now some four months past, he had been very near to the manger when the veil had been drawn, and he had seen for the first time how cheap, how crude was the fashioning of the manger in which the Babe, Lord Jesus, lay. Truly a poor affair to cradle the King of Kings. Had no one thought to make a better one? That was strange, for everything else about the celebration was rich and beautiful. So many candles, such stiff brocade and fine lace as Our Lady wore, and the priests put on their finest copes and stoles, beaded with seed-pearls and sewn with gold. And yet the Babe lay in a poor and roughly made crib.

That was the magnificent idea — that he should spend every precious moment of his spare time and make a fine one for the Blessed Babe. He would carve it, polish it, put all his skill into making it supremely fine. It would be a work of love for all the cathedral, a work to touch the heart.

He began to gather bits of wood left from the boats, good for nothing but to light the fires. He hid these under his straw pallet. When there were enough, he drew roughly with charcoal on the shed wall his design for the crib. It should be like a little boat, but with two prows, each with an angel as figure-head. It should have a wreath of ilex leaves about the gunwale, intertwined with the blossoms of the field lily. With the crib conceived, there remained only to win time for the work. He worked far into the long evenings; he worked at full of moon; he rose an hour before time for morning coffee. His own working hours for the Old One were long enough to tire; but this was work for love and he rested at it.

In the beginning there was no thought to make a bargain with Our Lady. But winter was at hand, he had gone again to pray at evensong and had been abused along the way worse than usual. The hurt in his heart was sharp as he knelt, and there rose to his lips his cry for help: "I am making a crib for thy Son. It is for the coming Noel. It is beautiful. He will lie with comfort in it and be rocked, even as the great sea rocks the men of Saint-Malo. If thou art pleased with it, I pray — oh, I pray — thee to make me straight as other boys. But then — but then — I would lose my fear of the street. I could come with safety here — to thee.''

After that, until the very Eve of Noel, he never knelt before Our Lady that he did not think her eyes were upon his hump, as if She noticed it now and felt for him a great compassion. Even in the dim light of the candles burning before her, Bo'Bossu was certain that he saw compassion growing in her eyes.

As Noel approached, as the crib neared its completion, he forgot hunger, he felt nothing of the cold, though his smock was thin and his breeches worn. A fever burned within him which kept him warm and satisfied. He sang at his work, as he swung the axe, as he smoothed with the spoke-shave, as he shaped and turned and ran in the copper bolts which held the planking. He had a pleasant voice and the other apprentices kept him singing. "Give us another *cantique* for Noel, Bo'Bossu,'' they would cry. He knew them all, that Bo'Bossu. He made of the long hours of the day a scrap of time that was soon gone. One song he always sang besides the carols and that was the song to the Earth which every Breton boy knows:

> When Goodman Winter comes again —
>> Sing to the Earth;
> He covers up his blessed grain —
>> Sing to the Earth.
> Sleep quietly, Jean-the-wheat,
> Till Spring and Winter meet;
>> Sing to the gentle Earth,
> Mother of Bread, Mother of Birth.

A week — that was all there was left — seven days before the Eve of Noel. And there came a man from Dinan with an order for a new vessel for the fishing fleet. It must be ready for launching by early spring when the fleet set off for the Grand Banks, for Le Gran and Le Petit Manan.

That meant work not to be put off. The order came to begin the laying of the keel that day, and until the vessel was finished there must be no let nor hindrance to swift and skilful building.

Behind the straw pallet the crib lay hidden and almost finished; but the angel at one prow was not yet carved, and all had still to have much rubbing. So driven were the apprentices, so tired was Bo'Bossu at the end of the day that he threw himself down on his straw without eating. And so was it the next night and the next. An apprehension mounted in

him with the fourth and fifth day gone. Would he be too spent to finish
the crib? He had made a promise to Our Lady. Would he break it? The
singing was gone from his lips, and the others no longer urged him to
sing. Time had become something terrible; there were a hundred hours
to the day instead of the actual twelve they worked.

The dreams of the hunchback became full of terror and despair.
Should he break this promise to Our Lady it would be no small offence.
Bo'Bossu would wake in the night, crying out his protestations: "I came
with it, but the boys in the streets threw themselves against me and the
crib was dashed to the cobbles and lies there, broken," or: "The Old
One has driven us every little moment and it is dark before I can work
on the crib; and I have no candle to work by, no money to buy one."
He had not even time to go to the cathedral to pray for time, a candle,
some help, that the crib might be ready for the Eve.

On the Eve of Noel, according to the custom of all Malouins,
Penhoël, the builder of boats, stopped work early. The apprentices
went to their homes to dress themselves fittingly, and to smell the good
smells of cooking for the feast that would follow the Mass. The building
yard was deserted save for Bo'Bossu, who latched the door of the shed,
took the crib from the hiding-place, and carried it to the west window
where daylight would be entering the longest. But so little light: the sky
was overcast and it looked as if the snow would be driving in from the
sea by nightfall.

With frenzied fingers the hunchback started his carving. He had made
the angel at the finished prow with a small open O of a mouth, that it
might seem as if it were singing "Alleluia." The fire, that heated the shed
none too well in winter, was out. Bo'Bossu could see his breath rise
upwards in wreaths of cold mist. His hands were lumps of frozen flesh. It
was as if he had never held a tool, never carved skilfully and well.

The day, having made up its mind to depart, went quickly. Between
watching it and dropping the tools, stopping to blow on his fingers,
straightening a little the cramps in his back and legs, the first thing
Bo'Bossu knew was that he could see to work no longer. With deep
weariness, with despair, he put down his tool and leaned his poor
twisted body on the bench. "I can do no more, Holy Mother, I can do
no more!" He made of it a kind of chant, saying it over and over,
making of it an outlet for his suffering.

And so it came about that he did not hear the latch of the shed lift, the
sound of light, sandalled feet walking; nor anything at all, until a hand

touched his shoulder and a voice said: "Give me the chisel. Thou hast worked long. Sleep, I will do it for thee."

The hunchback turned at the speaking. Beside him stood a boy his own age, his own height, had he been straight. He was clothed in a tunic that came almost to his ankles, so that Bo'Bossu thought him at first a novice. But the tunic was blue as the boy's eyes, which were blue as myrtle. A metal belt of strange workmanship held it about the waist. The boy's hair was yellow as a candle-flame; and to Bo'Bossu it seemed to cast light — like a candle. At least the shed seemed not as dark as it had been.

Long they looked at each other, the boy who was whole and the boy who was not. "Canst thou carve?" asked Bo'Bossu. "Canst thou see to work?"

"Surely. There will be light enough to finish. Thou art very weary, sleep."

Amazed that he should trust another with this important and holy thing, the hunchback went stupidly to his pallet, threw himself down, and was at once asleep.

The bells, ringing for the celebration, were what wakened him. He rose drugged with sleep, only to start in a kind of panic to his feet. "It is too late," he cried, and stumbled over to the bench. There he stood in wonder, for without wick or candle there was a wide circle of light about the strange boy, and in that light his hands were giving a last polish to the finished crib. Like rich satin it shone. For a long moment Bo'Bossu could not speak. Greater than the wonder of the light was the marvel of the workmanship. Although the crib was of his planning and his execution it was as if the holy hands of the Creator had touched it, making it perfect. "Who art thou?" asked Bo'Bossu.

The boy put down his cloth. "An apprentice, even as thyself. I work for my father."

The hunchback gave his twisted shoulders a shrug of hopelessness. "It is too late," he said again. "They will already have laid the Holy Babe in his crib. It is not for me to go behind the veil."

"It is not too late," said the boy. "Come, we will go together."

Together they bore the crib that was shaped like a small boat, with two prows and an angel at each prow, that had a garland of ilex leaves with lilies all around the gunwhale, that was so heavy when Bo'Bossu bore it alone he could hardly lift it, but which was now no more than a feather's weight carried by the two.

They entered through the door of the priests and found their way through the darkness to where the manger was waiting. They put down the crib, and the boy nodded at Bo'Bossu and said: "Lift the Little One into thy crib and I will take away the other."

Clumsily the hunchback knelt. Humbly he reached for the little figure of the Blessed Babe and lifted it, smoothing out the long blue swaddling robe, straightening the tiny golden halo about its head. He had put the straw into the boat-crib, and carefully, on this, he laid the Babe.

Then it was that the greatest of all wonders of that holy Eve came to pass for Bo'Bossu. For as he placed the Lord Jesus in the crib the Babe opened his eyes. He smiled. It was a smile Bo'Bossu knew. The Babe's eyes were blue as myrtle. His hair was as yellow as a candle's flame. "Thou art the boy, and yet not grown as he. The boy is truly thee, and yet not small as thou art." The hunchback spoke the words in awe, with little understanding. He raised his eyes and saw that Our Lady was smiling even as the Babe. Not the figure of Our Lady, you understand, but, yes, her own living self, come down to earth for that one holy Eve of Noel; come down to bless Bo'Bossu the hunchback.

From far aloft came the voice of the boy who was the angel:

Annuncio vobis gaudum magnum
Quia natus est hodie,
Salvator mundi,
Alleluia!

He was singing to the very dome of the cathedral — to the very dome of Heaven. Beyond the veil a thousand candles burst into flame and children's voices took up the "Gloria." The veil was drawn. The people of Saint-Malo held their silence for fear of breathing. For there beside the manger knelt Bo'Bossu — and yet not Bo'Bossu. They saw the new crib, a miracle of wonder, wherein lay the Babe so like a living babe that that, likewise, was a miracle.

From that night the hunchback walked the streets of Saint-Malo straight and strong like all Breton boys. The Malouins gave him a new name — the name of Jean, after that favourite disciple of the Lord Jesus. Throughout the singing of the Christ Mass for many years they pointed to the crib that was a small boat, with two prows and an angel at each one. They told the story of Bo'Bossu to their children and their children's children.

Prester John and the Trolls

Anonymous

High up on a mountain ridge that was covered with moss in a lonely and distant part of Norway there lived a long time ago a young minister and his wife. The house in which they lived was actually nothing more than a grey wooden hut with a roof of turf. It was just as mean as all the other houses of the poor village. The only inmates of the stall were the minister's red mare, one single cow, two goats and two sheep; in fact nothing to boast about.

High up in the mountains the fields were poor and small and the minister's family had often nothing else to eat than the hard bread baked with meal mixed with ground bark. But they were young and happy and trusted in God who fed the wild animals and would never let them starve. Whenever the young wife came out into the early summer morning and walked over the dewy grass in front of the hut to go to the stall to feed the animals and milk the cow she would often pause by the great birch tree in the middle of the little compound and look out over the surrounding countryside. In the distance she could see at the foot of the mountain the glistening mirror of the sea and beyond again many blue mountains as far as the eye could reach. Then she folded her hands and prayed that God would keep this beautiful region and would give her husband strength and wisdom to preach the Word of God. Whenever the minister made himself ready on Sunday mornings to go to the church, he whispered in his heart the same prayer. In this way they lived their lives with much toil and hard work but in great love and contentment. And all went well with them.

But in those days the trolls still lived in great numbers in the wide forests round the village. There were old trolls and little trolls, big trolls and an ugly miserable troll-rabble, all with long hairy tails, hairy bushy eyebrows, hairy tufts on their ears and red inflamed eyes that hated the light. They all bore a great black hatred of all that was human, light and

generous. But above all they hated the minister because they knew that all his efforts were directed to persuade people to abandon the shadowy side of life and come over to the sun-filled side where he himself loved to walk. For this reason he visited those people who lived hidden away in evil and spoke gently to them about goodness and forgiveness. Whenever he succeeded in wakening in one of these poor people the desire to grow better, the trolls would grind their teeth, clench their fists, growl, and think how they could trap the minister in their nets, because if he were to go on like this it would make an end of the troll kingdom in that region.

The minister went out regularly to comfort the dying and to help the poor people who lived far away from the church. It often happened that he only reached home when night was falling and many times when he was riding alone through the forest on his little red horse he heard and saw things that no one sees or hears when the sun is shining with its bright light, such as the patter of footsteps and rustling in the under-growth, squeaks and squeals between the tree-trunks, knobbly arms reaching out towards him and malignant troll packs running across the path to frighten the horse. But faithful old Rølla, his mare, did not let herself get upset. She just went on her placid steady way as if she heard and saw nothing. Nor did her master let himself be disturbed. Some-times he could hear in the depths of the wood a mumbling, hissing sound that grew louder and finally turned into a spiteful song. The minister understood the words clearly. The troll-song always began in the same way:

> Prester John of the big white birch,
> Prester John of the old grey church

But he never listened to any more and instead he began to sing a psalm in a loud strong voice so that the forest echoed from it. Thus he always came home singing. When the trolls saw that every year the minister was weakening their power more and more, so that goodness and joy came where before evil and gloom had reigned, they realized that if they did not succeed in getting rid of him, they would be forced to decamp and leave this ancient troll region and look for another piece of country, and this they did not want to do. So they came together one stormy night and took counsel how best to get the minister into their power. Now because they knew that he was a poor man they agreed that the best thing was to deprive him of the little that he had. Then he would be forced to slave away to replace it all, and with that slaving away fear and anxiety would come, and then they would be able to defeat him; at least so they thought.

The next time that the minister came riding through the forest, the squeaking and whistling was worse than ever, and from the darkest clump of bushes he heard again the song:

> Prester John of the big white birch
> Prester John of the old grey church!

Prester John thought: "for once it would be amusing to hear the rest of the song of the troll pack, and so I won't sing a psalm but I'll go on listening."

Shrill and eerie the song sounded in the night:

> Prester John of the big white birch,
> Prester John of the old grey church!
> Two will be drowned,
> Two lame will be found,
> Goldhorn we shall sting.

To despair we shall bring
You, ugh, you of the birch
You, ugh, you of the church!

Then the minister stood up in the stirrups and shook his clenched fist towards the woods.

"You trolls don't know Prester John, nor those who stand behind him," he called out as loud as he could. Then he sat down again in the saddle and began to sing his psalm.

When the minister arrived home his wife was sitting on the doorstep waiting for him, and although the dusk had fallen he could see clearly that she had been weeping and he knew then that the trolls had done their work.

"Is it fire or water, mother?" he asked. "Is it the goats or the sheep?"

Then his wife told him that the two goats had plunged from the cliff-top into the mill-race and had drowned in the water, and then her husband told her what he had heard in the forest.

"But keep up your courage, mother," he said after finishing his story. "The great Father above will not desert us and as long as we have each other and the children we shall not suffer want."

His wife smiled and was comforted, believing what he believed, and so they went to bed.

The next day lightning struck and killed the two sheep, and again the minister's wife shed many tears.

"If only I had the lovely wool," she sobbed, "so that I had something to make clothes for the children this winter. But now the lightning has spoilt the fleeces and every tuft of wool is burnt black."

"Do not grieve, little mother," said Prester John stroking her light gold hair, "The Good Lord will not let our children suffer cold."

The woman dried her tears and believed what he believed, though it was hard for her, for she had so looked forward to the beautiful wool.

On the evening of the third day the minister's wife went into the forest to look for Goldhorn, their only cow. She was very anxious about the cow for however much she called there was no sound from the cow, no lowing, no sound of the cowbell. After searching in vain for a time she at last found the cow lying dead upon the ground and she just caught sight of an adder gliding away in the grass. Then she fell on her knees and threw her arms round Goldhorn's neck and wept bitterly, more bitterly than she had ever done in her life, for apart from her husband and her children she loved nothing more than the old cow.

The two little children came and found her in the place where the adder had bitten Goldhorn, and when they saw their mother weeping they each crept to one side of her and burst into tears while they all stroked their dead friend. That is where the minister found them at last. His eyes misted over but he bent over his wife and raised her up.

"Mother," he said quietly, "Now the trolls have not threatened us with any more evil, and now you must come home and help Prester John to fight against poverty."

So all four of them went silently home.

The winter that came now was hard and difficult for the minister's family, for not only had they lost the five animals but the harvest from the barren little fields had been poor and more than once the minister and his wife had to listen to their children crying in their sleep because they were hungry. That was worse than suffering hunger themselves. But now and again a friendly neighbour would come with a couple of round loaves of bread or a jug of milk, but for the rest they lived mainly on the game which the minister was able to shoot in the forest.

If Prester John had not recognized the importance of the struggle he would have given in more than once, but now he knew that if he gave up working for the Kingdom of Light for even one day, the trolls would conquer him and perhaps dominate the whole region. So his prayers that winter were more fervent than ever, and never had he preached so powerfully as he stood in the little church on Sundays, nor had he ever spoken such strong words of hope to the poor people in the huts. When they saw how he suffered hunger, and how he prayed, and how in spite of all his poverty his eyes shone out more light and his voice became stronger, they understood that it was worth listening to what he had to tell and worth following his example. So the trolls had never before lost so much of their power in those parts than they did that winter.

When spring came there was a new Goldhorn in the minister's stall and two sheep and two goats cropped the light green grass in the clearing in front of the forest. That had been a gift from the poor inhabitants of the village to their minister, and his wife wept tears of joy when she milked the new cow for the first time.

But the trolls gathered together again in the darkest depths of the forest and gnashed their teeth in baneful anger.

"We shall never get the better of this minister by making him poor," said the big troll himself, "We need something stronger if we are going to conquer him."

"Take his horse away, take his horse away," hissed a little troll. "Have you not noticed how he loves the red mare? He strokes her and talks to her as if she were a human being. Ugh! Humans, ugh!"

So the trolls decided together that Prester John should lose his Rølla.

Some time later the minister was riding again through the forest. His old musket hung over his shoulder and his game-bag was full. He was in a happy mood and was whistling a tune as he rode on, sometimes patting his horse's neck with a word of endearment.

It was growing dark early for it was already autumn and the cranberries shone red through the green. Very quickly it was quite dark. The minister heard the familiar squeaking and whistling in the undergrowth and then the shrill song began in the deep forest:

> Prester John of the big white birch,
> Prester John of the old grey church!

What was it going to be this time, wondered the minister and listened.

> Six-legs in the wood,
> Four-legs before the plough,
> Four-legs we shall break,
> Two-legs we shall beat.
> You, ugh, you of the white birch,
> You, ugh, you of the grey church!

The minister heard and understood every word. "No, as true as I am called John," he called, "Six-legs will still go through the forest for a time, and Four-legs will go before the plough, and you won't beat Two-legs as easily as you think. So, on we go Rølla!"

Rølla trotted on, but she was trembling all over and it did not help that her master caressed her and spoke to her lovingly. The trolls were grinning malevolently and the wind blew fiercely over the tops of the trees. The minister did not understand why he felt uneasy as never before. When he tried to sing a psalm he sang with a trembling weak voice which was completely drowned by the mocking laughter of the trolls.

When they came near home and the minister could see the light shining out from the house, Rølla suddenly plunged with a heavy groan to the ground. The rider leaped off and found a deep hole in the ground which had never been there before. Judging by the heavy rasping of the horse he knew that the poor beast would never rise again.

"My Rølla," he said and his grief brought a lump to his throat. "I thank you for all your faithful service, my Rølla."

He put his musket to her head and pressed the trigger, and then it was all over with the old red mare. But the minister could not bear to leave his old friend alone in the wood. He thought that Rølla had the right to demand of him that he should hold wake by her corpse and so he stayed sitting on a stone, stroking her head while the wind howled and the trolls laughed mockingly. He did not know how long he had been sitting there when he heard light footsteps approaching in the darkness. It was his wife. She bent quietly over him and kissed his brow.

"I knew while I was at home what had happened, John," she said, "And now I have come to help you. When Goldhorn was bitten by the adder and we lost our goats and sheep it was you who was the strong one, but now it must be me. Come home with me, John, in God's name."

But the minister went on stroking the old horse's head. "No horse can ever be for me what this animal has been," he said weeping. "I am not mourning for a creature, but for my friend."

"I know that, John," said his wife, "but for the sake of God come home with me now and do not let yourself be defeated."

Then the minister took his wife's hand and together they went into the house, their little hut. And she was such a support to him that the trolls failed to conquer him this time.

As time went by his spirit revived and even more strongly he worked to win the souls of men for the World of Light. Once again all the trolls gathered together to think out some means of getting dangerous John into their clutches.

"Steal the children, steal the children," hissed the old troll with an evil grin. "Human beings love nothing as much as their children. Ugh, humans!"

All the trolls gathered there, except the great troll himself, joined in with a hoarse shout: "Steal the children, steal the children!"

But the great troll only wrinkled his already wrinkled face and he looked more evil than ever.

"You're a stupid pack of trolls," he roared, "Don't you know that we have no power over children? He up there," and the great troll pointed to the sky, and all his underlings trembled with fear and terror, "He up there has placed a strong guard round children, and our sovereignty ends there. Trolls, give me better advice."

All the trolls were silent for a long time, great furrows crossing their ugly faces while they writhed with the effort of thinking. Finally a little ancient old troll-woman came shuffling up to the great troll and whispered something in his ear. He nodded and his face cleared.

"Listen trolls," he said. "The old mother has thought it out. Tell them yourself, old mother."

But the old troll-woman was much too shy too speak before such a big gathering so she whispered to him again and asked him to speak for her.

The great roll coughed and spluttered and then he said: "Trolls, the old mother is more cunning than we. She says that Prester John has nothing dearer than his wife. House and glebe, stock and children, all that he could lose, she says, as long as he can keep his wife. So we must take his wife away from him; then we really have got him."

"Honourable Great Troll," piped up a voice from the back, "It does not lie in our power to take a human life."

The great troll seemed taken aback, for he had not thought that far, but he wanted the others to think the opposite.

But then the old troll-woman stood up quickly and whispered, but loud enough for the whole assembly to hear: "We can fire a troll-shot at her."

Then she went and sat down again quickly and hid her wrinkly face in her hands for now she was terribly embarrassed. But all the trolls yelled and whooped together: "We'll give her a troll-shot, we'll give her a troll-shot."

Then they pulled each other by the hair on their ears which is an expression of the greatest joy among the trolls.

A little while later the minister's wife went walking through the forest. It was almost Christmas and she was smiling to herself because she knew that for once this year she would be able to bake a white flour cake and cast a big thick branched Christmas candle. She was imagining how beautifully the light would be shining from it, when she suddenly felt something stinging in her eye. It was as if something sharp had flown into it and had got stuck in it, and however much she wiped it she could not get it out. A bit later she could not feel it any more and thought no more about it. But she grew strangely gloomy and she was no longer happy thinking about the Christmas candle and the white flour cake. When she got back home she went and sat with her hands folded in her lap and stared out into the darkness.

She did not know how it came about, but everything in the little hut seemed to her to look so poor and grey. The cupboard stood open so that she could see all the familiar utensils. Not a single silver spoon in the minister's house she thought with a sigh. Not even a pewter jug for the Christmas feast. Nothing but wood and earthenware, earthenware and wood, and she ran her hand over her coarse skirt. Grey homespun material, nothing else. And yet there existed such soft materials, velvet and silk, that were so smooth that it was a pleasure to stroke them. Why could she not have clothes of such materials just as well as other people? Was she not still young and beautiful, and should she not also find it a pleasure to go dressed like a high-born lady or like the wives of rich town burghers? When she thought of all this she began to weep hot tears, and they fell on to her folded hands, and where they fell they burned like fire.

Soon she heard the merry voices of her children outside the house, and three pairs of feet, one pair large, and two pairs small, stamped the snow off on the doorstep. It was the minister and the two children coming home, and for the first time in her life she did not stand up to meet them.

When the minister came into the kitchen, which was so low that he could hardly stand upright in it, he saw her right away, although it was almost dark in the house.

"The peace of God, little mother," he said. "Here are three frozen and hungry fellows who need fire to warm them and gruel to fill their stomachs."

The children shouted for joy because they had been called fellows, but the mother hardly raised her head and said gloomily: "What's the use of trying to make a fire with the wet wood, and what kind of pleasure is it to put on the pot when there is nothing else to cook but this miserable gruel?"

When she had said that it was as if a cold wind blew through the hut and the minister felt a chill go through him to his marrow bones. Like a sleep-walker he went to the stove himself, kindled the fire and set on the pot with rye-meal.

The whole evening the woman remained gloomy and silent, so that the children crept frightened into a corner of the room. When she did speak a single word it was only a complaint, and even as she spoke her gloom seemed to increase. At last she went to bed without a word of thanks or wishing the children good night and the children cried themselves to sleep that night. But the minister sat up that night and stared out into the darkness.

He felt that something terrible and inexplicable had come into his house, and the misfortune had caused him so much fear that he was in no condition with his prayers to knock at the door of Our Lord as he had always done.

The next day was grey and cold, and it was like that too in the minister's house. When John saw that his wife, who had been the most contented and sunny being on earth, now only had a sharp word for everything and everyone, he was overcome with great distress. He did try to talk with her now and then with the loving tone which he always used with her, but his words seemed to find no echo and she did not even answer him. So he spoke no more and went about his work.

As the day went on his wife became even more gloomy and discontented. It seemed to her that no one had such a heavy lot to bear as she and she envied everyone. The minister felt his love for her cooling and being quenched, and an even greater fear took hold of him, for he knew that when love is lost, its place is taken by all the evil powers. His work went badly and his words lost their ring when he stood in the pulpit in the little grey church. But the trolls rejoiced for now they realized that they had got the upper hand of John.

Christmas Eve had come, but no Christmas candle was burning in the minister's house and the children had not received a white flour cake. The minister opened the Bible for he wanted to read the holy Christmas Gospel by the light of a burning brand, but he was so downcast that he could only read a few lines. Silent and bent he sat in his chair and stared sadly into the glow of the fire. Outside was rough weather and through the storm he seemed to hear the mocking laughter of the trolls. They now had dared to come so far that they were mocking him right by his own door. Soon they would come bursting into the house he thought, and he felt he had no strength to withstand them.

Prester John did not know how long he had been sitting there, sunk in his sombre thoughts, when suddenly the embers burst into flame. By the bright light he could see that his wife had fallen asleep where she sat on the other side of the hearth. Her head had fallen on to her shoulder, and the minister could not take his eyes off her, for she was now the same as she had been before the trolls had cast their shot into her eye. All that had been hard and bitter and had changed the expression of her face in the last weeks and had made her so old and ugly, that he sometimes thought that she looked rather like a troll herself, all that had gone now, and she was young again, loveable and good as before.

She smiled in her sleep, but with such melancholy, that his eyes filled with tears. He felt all his love returning. Then he fell on his knees and prayed to God as he had never remembered praying before and gradually he felt himself grow more serene and outside he no longer heard the shrill voices of the trolls.

That night the minister had a wonderful dream. There was fluttering and rustling about him as of wings, and he heard voices coming to him, sometimes whispering and sometimes calling: "Prester John, Prester John, sacrifice your sight, sacrifice your own eyes."

When he woke up it was pitch black in the house and he lay for a while thinking about the dream but without realizing its full meaning.

It was time to get up for the early morning service in the church and he woke his wife and asked her to go with him. But she answered grumpily that she did not want to show herself in her ugly old clothes before the church-goers and her husband knew by her voice that her face had grown ugly and repulsive again. He sighed and for the first time on Christmas morning he went to the early service without her.

For two more nights Prester John was on his knees before God praying for help, and each time he dreamed the same marvellous dream. When on the third night he woke up he suddenly understood quite clearly what the voices meant. He understood that if he sacrificed the light of his eyes his wife would receive back her face, the enchantment would be broken and she would be herself again, she would love, and work, and be happy as formerly. But he himself would be blind. The minister struggled hard with himself, but in the end he resolved to carry it through. He stood up, kindled a fire and holding a burning stick aloft he approached the bed where the children slept.

"Once more I wish to see you blessed faces," he said. "Once more, before I enter the great darkness. Once more I wish to see the stars and the sky. But my wife's face I shall keep in my memory as it was on Christmas Eve. It shall be like that again, praise be to God, but I shall never see it."

After that he went out and fell on his knees in the snow under the stars. He commended himself into God's hands and took up his knife to cut out his eyes.

But at that very moment when the cold steel was about to touch his eyes the charm was broken which had taken away his wife's true features and nature. She woke up, felt a great fear catch hold of her, and ran more swiftly than her thoughts outside to where he was. She snatched the knife out of his hands. And God let her know what had happened and what was going to happen.

"John, John," she whispered and her face was more beautiful than a star. "You have conquered again. May God bless you!"

That night the trolls set off in great rancour to the North, for they realized that the minister had been too strong for them.

The Little Angel

Leonid Andreyev

At times Sashka wished to give up what is called living: to cease to wash every morning in cold water on which thin sheets of ice floated about; to go no more to the grammar school, and there to have to listen to everyone scolding him; no more to experience the pain in the small of his back and indeed over his whole body when his mother made him kneel in the corner all the evening. But, since he was only thirteen years of age, and did not know all the means by which people abandoned life at will, he continued to go to the grammer school and to kneel in the corner, and it seemed to him as if life would never end. A year would go by, and another, and yet another, and still he would be going to school, and be made to kneel in the corner. And since, Sashka possessed an indomitable and bold spirit, he could not supinely tolerate evil, and so found means to avenge himself on life. With this object in view he would thrash his companions, be rude to the Head, impertinent to the masters, and tell lies all day long to his teachers and to his mother — but to his father only he never lied. If in a fight he got his nose broken, he would purposely make the damage worse, and howl, without shedding a single tear, but so loudly that all who heard him were fain to stop their ears to keep out the disagreeable sound. When he had howled as long as he thought advisable, he would suddenly cease, and, putting out his tongue, draw in his copy-book a caricature of himself howling at an usher who pressed his fingers to his ears, while the victor stood trembling with fear. The whole copy-book was filled with caricatures, the one which most frequently occurred being that of a short stout woman beating a boy as thin as a lucifer-match with a rolling pin. Below in a large scrawling hand would be written the legend: "Beg my pardon, puppy!" and the reply, "Won't! Blow'd if I do!"

Before Christmas Sashka was expelled from school, and when his mother attempted to thrash him, he bit her finger. This action gave him his liberty. He left off washing in the morning, ran about all day bullying the other boys, and had but one fear, and that was hunger, for his mother entirely left off providing for him, so that he came to depend upon the pieces of bread and potatoes which his father secreted for him. On these conditions Sashka found existence tolerable.

One Friday (it was Christmas Eve) he had been playing with the other boys, until they had dispersed to their homes, followed by the squeak of the rusty frozen wicket gate as it closed behind the last of them. It was already growing dark, and a grey snowy mist was travelling up from the country, along a dark alley; in a low black building, which stood fronting the end of the alley, a lamp was burning with a reddish, unblinking light. The frost had become more intense, and when Sashka reached the circle of light cast by the lamp, he saw that fine dry flakes of snow were floating slowly on the air. It was high time to be getting home.

"Where have you been knocking about all night, puppy?" exclaimed his mother, doubling her fist, without, however, striking. Her sleeves were turned up, exposing her fat white arms, and on her forehead, almost devoid of eyebrows, stood beads of perspiration. As Sashka passed by her he recognized the familiar smell of vodka. His mother scratched her head with the short dirty nail of her thick fore-finger, and since it was no good scolding, she merely spat, and cried; "Statisticians! That's what they are!"

Sashka shuffled contemptuously, and went behind the partition, from whence might be heard the heavy breathing of his father, Ivan Savvich, who was in a chronic state of shivering, and was now trying to warm himself by sitting on the heated bench of the stove with his hands under him, palms downwards.

"Sashka! The Svetchnikovs have invited you to the Christmas tree. The housemaid came," he whispered.

"Get along with you!" said Sashka with incredulity.

"Fact! The old woman there has purposely not told you, but she has mended your jacket all the same."

"Nonsense," Sashka replied, still more surprised.

The Svetchinkovs were rich people, who had put him to the grammer school, and after his expulsion had forbidden him their house.

His father once more took his oath to the truth of his statement, and Sashka became meditative.

"Well then, move, shift a bit," he said to his father, as he leapt upon the short bench, adding: "I won't go to those devils. I shall prove jolly well too much for them, if I were to turn up. *Depraved boy,*" drawled

Sashka in imitation of his patrons. "They are none too good themselves, the smug-faced prigs!"

"Oh! Sashka, Sashka," his father complained, sitting hunched up with cold, "you'll come to a bad end."

"What about yourself, then?" was Sashka's rude rejoinder. "Better shut up. Afraid of the old woman. Ba! Old muff!"

His father sat on in silence and shivered. A faint light found its way through a broad clink at the top, where the partition failed to meet the ceiling by a quarter of an inch, and lay in bright patches upon his high forehead, beneath which the deep cavities of his eyes showed black.

In times gone by Ivan Savvich had been used to drink heavily, and then his wife had feared and hated him. But when he had begun to develop unmistakable signs of consumption, and could drink no longer, she took to drink in her turn, and gradually accustomed herself to vodka. Then she avenged herself for all she had suffered at the hands of that tall narrow-chested man, who used incomprehensible words, had lost his place through disobedience and drunkenness, and who brought home with him just such long-haired, debauched and conceited fellows as himself.

In contradistinction to her husband, the more Feoktista Petrovna drank the healthier she became, and the heavier became her fists. Now she said what she pleased, brought men and women to the house just as she chose, and sang with them noisy songs, while he lay silent behind the partition huddled together with perpetual cold, and meditating on the injustice and sorrow of human life. To everyone, with whom she talked, she complained that she had no such enemies in the world as her husband and son, they were stuck-up statisticians!

For the space of an hour his mother kept drumming into Sashka's ears: "But I say you shall go," punctuating each word with a heavy blow on the table, which made the tumblers, placed on it after washing, jump and rattle again.

"But I say I won't!" Sashka coolly replied, dragging down the corners of his mouth with the will to show his teeth — a habit which had earned for him at school the nickname of Wolfkin.

"I'll thrash you, won't I just!" cried his mother.

"All right! Thrash away!"

But Feoktista Petrovna knew that she could no longer strike her son now that he had begun to retaliate by biting, and that if she drove him into the street he would go off larking, and sooner get frost-bitten than go to the Svetchnikovs, therefore she appealed to her husband's authority.

"Calls himself a father, and can't protect the mother from insult!"

"Really, Sashka, go. Why are you so obstinate?" He jerked out from the bench. "They will perhaps take you up again. They are kind people." Sashka only laughed in an insulting manner.

His father, long ago, before Sashka was born, had been tutor at the Svetchnikovs', and had ever since looked on them as the best people in the world. At that time he had held also an appointment in the statistical office of the Zemstvo, and had not yet taken to drink. Eventually he was compelled through his own fault to marry his landlady's daughter. From that time he severed his connection with the Svetchnikovs, and took to drink. Indeed, he let himself go to such an extent, that he was several times picked up drunk in the streets and taken to the police station. But the Svetchnikovs did not cease to assist him with money, and Feoktista Petrovna, although she hated them, together with books and everything connected with her husband's past, still valued their acquaintance, and was in the habit of boasting of it.

"Perhaps you might bring something for me too from the Christmas tree," continued his father. He was using craft to induce his son to go, and Sashka knew it, and despised his father for his weakness and want of straightforwardness; though he really did wish to bring back something for the poor sickly old man, who had for a long time been without even good tobacco.

"All right!" he blurted out; "give me my jacket. Have you put the buttons on? No fear! I know you too well!"

II

The children had not yet been admitted to the drawing-room, where the Christmas tree stood, but remained chattering in the nursery. Sashka, with lofty supercilliousness, stood listening to their naïve talk, and fingering in his breeches pocket the broken cigarettes which he had managed to abstract from his host's study. At this moment there came up to him the youngest of the Svetchnikovs, Kolya, and stood motionless before him, a look of surprise on his face, his toes turned in, and a finger stuck in the corner of his pouting mouth. Six months ago, at the instance of his relatives, he had given up this bad habit of putting his finger in his mouth, but he could not quite break himself of it. He had blonde locks cut in a fringe on his forehead and falling in ringlets on his shoulders, and blue, wandering eyes; in fact, he was just such a boy in appearance as Sashka particularly loved to bully.

"Are 'oo weally a naughty boy?" he inquired of Sashka. "Miss said 'oo was. I'm a dood boy."

"That you are!" replied Sashka, considering the other's short velvet trousers and great turndown collars.

"Would 'oo like to have a dun? There!" and he pointed at him a little pop-gun with a cork tied to it. The Wolfkin took the gun, pressed down the spring, and, aiming at the nose of the unsuspecting Kolya, pulled the trigger. The cork struck his nose, and rebounding, hung by the string. Kolya's blue eyes opened wider than ever, and filled with tears. Transferring his finger from his mouth to his reddening nose he blinked his long eyelashes and whispered: "Bad — bad boy!"

A young lady of striking appearance, with her hair dressed in the simplest and the most becoming fashion, now entered the nursery. She was sister to the lady of the house, the very one indeed to whom Sashka's father had formerly given lessons.

"Here's the boy," said she, pointing out Sashka to the bald-headed man who accompanied her. "Bow, Sashka, you should not be so rude!"

But Sashka would bow neither to her, nor to her companion of the bald head. She little suspected how much he knew. But, as a fact, Sashka did know that his miserable father had loved her, and that she had married another; and, though this had taken place subsequent to his father's marriage, Sashka could not bring himself to forgive what seemed to him like treachery.

"Takes after his father!" sighed Sofia Dmitrievna. "Could not you, Plutov Michailovich, do something for him? My husband says that a commercial school would suit him better than the grammer school. Sashka, would you like to go to a technical school?"

"No!" curtly replied Sashka, who had caught the offensive word "husband."

"Do you want to be a shepherd, then?" asked the gentleman.

"Not likely!" said Sashka, in an offended tone.

"What then?"

Now Sashka did not know what he would like to be, but upon reflection replied: "Well it's all the same to me, even a shepherd, if you like."

The bald-headed gentleman regarded the strange boy with a look of perplexity. When his eyes had travelled up from his patched boots to his face, Sashka put out his tongue and quickly drew it back again, so that Sofia Dmitrievna did not notice anything, but the old gentleman showed an amount of irascibility that she could not understand.

"I should not mind going to a commercial school," bashfully suggested Sashka.

The lady was overjoyed at Sashka's decision, and meditated with a sigh on the beneficial influence exercised by an old love.

"I don't know whether there will be a vacancy," dryly remarked the old man avoiding looking at Sashka, and smoothing down the ridge of hair which stuck up on the back of his head. "However, we shall see."

Meanwhile the children were becoming noisy, and in a great state of excitement were waiting impatiently for the Christmas tree.

The excellent practice with the pop-gun made in the hands of a boy, who commanded respect both for his stature and for his reputation for naughtiness, found imitators, and many a little button of a nose was made red. The tiny maids, holding their sides, bent almost double with laughter, as their little cavaliers with manly contempt of fear and pain, but all the same wrinkling up their faces in suspense, received the impact of the cork.

At length the doors were opened, and a voice said: "Come in, children; gently, not so fast!" Opening their little eyes wide, and holding their breath in anticipation, the children filed into the brightly illuminated drawing-room in orderly pairs, and quietly walked round the glittering tree. It cast a strong, shadowless light on their eager faces, with rounded eyes and mouths. For a minute there reigned the silence of profound enchantment, which all at once broke out into a chorus of delighted exclamation. One of the little girls, unable to restrain her delight, kept dancing up and down in the same place, her little tress braided with blue ribbon beating meanwhile rhythmically against her shoulders. Sashka remained morose and gloomy — something evil was working in his little wounded breast. The tree blinded him with its red, shriekingly insolent glitter of countless candles. It was foreign, hostile to him, even as the crowd of smart, pretty children which surrounded it. He would have liked to give it a shove, and topple it over on their shining heads. It seemed as though some iron hand were gripping his heart, and wringing out of it every drop of blood. He crept behind the piano, and sat down there in a corner unconsciously crumpling to pieces in his pocket the last of the cigarettes, and thinking that though he had a father and mother and a home, it came to the same thing as if

he had none, and nowhere to go to. He tried to recall to his imagination his little penknife, which he had acquired by a swap not long ago, and was very fond of; but his knife all at once seemed to him a very poor affair with its ground-down blade and only half of a yellow haft. Tomorrow he would smash it up, and then he would have nothing left at all!

But suddenly Sashka's narrow eyes gleamed with astonishment, and his face in a moment resumed its ordinary expression of audacity and self-confidence. On the side of the tree turned towards him — which was the back of it, and less brightly illumined than the other side — he discovered something such as had never come within the circle of his existence, and without which all his surroundings appeared as empty as though peopled by persons without life. It was a little angel in wax carelessly hung in the thickest of the dark boughs, and looking as if it were floating in the air. His transparent dragon-fly wings trembled in the light, and he seemed altogether alive and ready to fly away. The rosy fingers of his exquisitely formed hands were stretched upwards, and from his head there floated just such locks as Kolya's. But there was something here that was wanting in Kolya's face, and in all other faces and things. The face of the little angel did not shine with joy, nor was it clouded by grief; but there lay on it the impress of another feeling, not to be explained in words, nor defined by thought, but to be attained only by the sympathy of a kinded feeling. Sashka was not concious of the force of the mysterious influence which attracted him towards the little angel, but he felt that he had known him all his life, and had always loved him, loved him more than his penknife, more than his father, more than anything else. Filled with doubt, alarm, and a delight which he could not comprehend, Sashka clasped his hands to his bosom and whispered: "Dear — dear little angel!"

The more intently he looked the more fraught with significance the expression of the little angel's face became. He was so infinitely far off, so unlike everything which surrounded him there. The other toys seemed to take a pride in hanging there pretty, and decked out, upon the glittering tree, but he was pensive, and fearing the intrusive light purposely hid himself in the dark greenery, so that none might see him. It would be a mad cruelty to touch his dainty little wings.

"Dear — dear!" whispered Sashka.

His head became feverish. He clasped his hands behind his back, and in full readiness to fight to the death to win the little angel, he walked to and fro with cautious, stealthy steps. He avoided looking at the little angel, lest he should direct the attention of others towards him, but he felt that he was still there, and had not flown away.

Now the hostess appeared in the doorway, a tall, stately lady with a bright aureole of grey hair dressed high upon her head. The children trooped round her with expressions of delight, and the little girl — the same that had danced about in her place — hung wearily on her hand, blinking heavily with sleepy eyes.

As Sashka approached her he seemed almost choking with emotion.

"Auntie — auntie!" said he, trying to speak caressingly, but his voice sounded harsher than ever. "Auntie, dear!"

She did not hear him, so he tugged impatiently at her dress.

"What's the matter with you? Why are you pulling my dress?" said the grey-haired lady in surprise. "It's rude."

"Auntie — auntie, do give me one thing from the tree; give me the little angel."

"Impossible," replied the lady in a tone of indifference. "We are going to keep the tree decorated till the new year. But you are no longer a child; you should call me by my name — Maria Dmitrievna."

Sashka, feeling as if he were falling down a precipice, grasped the last means of saving himself.

"I am sorry I have been naughty. I'll be more industrious for the future," he blurted out. But this formula, which had always paid with his masters, made no impression upon the lady of the grey hair.

"A good thing, too, my friend," she said, as unconcernedly as before.

"Give me the little angel," demanded Sashka, gruffly.

"But it's impossible. Can't you understand that?"

But Sashka did not understand, and when the lady turned to go out of the room he followed her, his gaze fixed without conscious thought upon her black silk dress. In his surging brain there glimmered a recollection of how one of the boys in his class had asked the master to mark him 3* and when the master refused he had knelt down before him, and putting his hands together as in prayer, had begun to cry. The master was angry, but gave him 3 all the same. At the time Sashka had immortalized this episode in a caricature, but now his only means left was to follow the boy's example. Accordingly he plucked at the lady's dress again, and when she turned round, dropped with a bang on to his knees, and folded his hands as described above. But he could not squeeze out a single tear!

---

* In Russian schools 5 is the maximum mark.

"Are you out of your mind?" exclaimed the grey-haired lady, casting a searching look round the room; but luckily no one was present.

"What is the matter with you?"

Kneeling there with clasped hands, Sashka looked at her with dislike, and rudely repeated: "Give me the angel."

His eyes, fixed intently on the lady to catch the first word she should utter, were anything but good to look at, and the hostess answered hurriedly: "Well, then, I'll give it to you. Ah! What a stupid you are! I will give you what you want, but why could you not wait till the New Year?"

"Stand up! And never," she added in a didactic tone, "never kneel to anyone: it is humiliating. Kneel before God alone."

"Talk away!" thought Sashka, trying to get in front of her, and merely succeeding in treading on her dress.

When she had taken the toy from the tree, Sashka devoured her with his eyes, but stretched out his hands for it with a painful pucker of the nose. It seemed to him that the tall lady would break the little angel.

"Beautiful thing!" said the lady, who was sorry to part with such a dainty and presumably expensive toy. "Who can have hung it there? Well, what do you want with such a thing? Are you not too big to know what to do with it? Look, there are some picture-books. But this I promised to give Kolya; he begged so earnestly for it." But this was not the truth.

Sashka's agony became unbearable. He clenched his teeth convulsively, and seemed almost to grind them. The lady of the grey hair feared nothing so much as a scene, so she slowly held out the little angel to Sashka.

"There now, take it!" she said in a displeased tone; "what a persistent boy you are!"

Sashka's hands as they seized the little angel seemed like tentacles, and were tense as steel springs, but withal so soft and careful that the angel might have imagined himself to be flying in the air.

"A-h-h!" escaped in a long diminuendo sigh from Sashka's breast, while in his eyes glistened two little tear-drops, which stood still there as though unused to the light. Slowly drawing the little angel to his bosom, he kept his shining eyes on the hostess, with a quiet, tender smile which died away in a feeling of unearthly bliss. It seemed, when the dainty wings of the little angel touched Sashka's sunken breast, as if he experienced something so blissful, so bright, the like of which had never before been experienced in this sorrowful, sinful, suffering world.

"A-h-h!" sighed he once more as the little angel's wings touched him. And at the shining of his face the absurdly decorated and insolently glowing tree seemed to be extinguished, and the grey-haired, portly dame smiled with gladness, and the parchment-like face of the bald-headed gentlemen twitched, and the children fell into a vivid silence as though touched by a breath of human happiness.

For one short moment all observed a mysterious likeness between the awkward boy who had outgrown his clothes, and the lineaments of the little angel, which had been spiritualized by the hand of an unknown artist.

But the next moment the picture was entirely changed. Crouching like a panther preparing to spring, Sashka surveyed the surrounding company, on the look-out for some one who should dare wrest his little angel from him.

"I'm going home," he said in a dull voice, having in view a way of escape through the crowd, "home to Father."

III

His mother was asleep worn out with a whole day's work and vodka-drinking. In the little room behind the partition there stood a small cooking-lamp burning on the table. Its feeble yellow light, with dificulty penetrating the sooty glass, threw a strange shadow over the faces of Sashka and his father.

"Is it not pretty?" Asked Sashka in a whisper, holding the little angel at a distance from his father, so as not to allow him to touch it.

"Yes, there's something most remarkable about him," whispered the father, gazing thoughtfully at the toy. And his face expressed the same concentrated attention and delight, as did Sashka's.

"Look, he is going to fly."

"I see it too," replied Sashka in an ecstacy. "Think I'm blind? But look at his little wings! Ah! Don't touch!"

The father withdrew his hand, and with troubled eyes studied the details of the little angel, while Sashka whispered with the air of a pedagogue: "Father, what a bad habit you have of touching everything! You might break it."

There fell upon the wall the shadows of two grotesque, motionless heads bending towards one another, one big and shaggy, the other small and round.

Within the big head strange torturing thoughts, though at the same time full of delight, were seething. His eyes unblinkingly regarded the little angel, and under his stedfast gaze it seemed to grow larger and brighter, and its wings to tremble with a noiseless trepidation, and all the surroundings — the timber-built, soot-stained wall, the dirty table, Sashka — everything became fused into one level grey mass without light or shade. It seemed to the broken man that he heard a pitying voice from the world of wonders, wherein once he had dwelt, and whence he had been cast out for ever. There they knew nothing of dirt, of weary quarrelling, of the blindly-cruel strife of egotism, there they knew nothing of the tortures of a man arrested in the streets with callous laughter, and beaten by the rough hand of the night-watchman. There everything is pure, joyful, bright. And all this purity found an asylum in the soul of her whom he loved more than life, and had lost — when he had kept his hold upon his own useless life. With the smell of wax, which emanated from the toy, was mingled a subtle aroma, and it seemed to the broken man that her dear fingers touched the angel, those fingers which he would fain have caressed in one long kiss, till death should close his lips for ever. This was why the little toy was so beautiful, this was why there was in it something specially attractive, which defied description. The little angel had descended from that heaven which her soul was to him, and had brought a ray of light into the damp room, steeped in sulphurous fumes, and to the dark soul of the man from whom had been taken all: love, and hapiness, and life.

On a level with the eyes of the man, who had lived his life, sparkled the eyes of the boy, who was beginning his life, and embraced the little angel in their caress. For them present and future had disappeared: the ever-sorrowful, piteous father, the rough, unendurable mother, the black darkness of insults, of cruelty, of humiliations, and of spiteful grief. The thoughts of Sashka were formless, nebulous, but all the more deeply for that did they move his agitated soul.

Everything that is good and bright in the world, all profound grief, and the hope of a soul that sighs for God — the little angel absorbed them all into himself, and that was why he glowed with such a soft divine radiance, that was why his little dragonfly wings trembled with a noiseless trepidation.

The father and son did not look at one another: their sick hearts grieved, wept, and rejoiced apart. But there was a something in their thoughts which fused their hearts in one, and annihilated that bottom-less abyss which separates man from man and makes him so lonely, unhappy, and weak. The father with an unconcious motion put his arm round the neck of his son, and the son's head rested equally without conscious volition upon his father's consumptive chest.

"*She* it was who gave it to you, was it not?" whispered the father, without taking his eyes off the little angel.

At another time Sashka would have replied with a rude negation, but now the only reply possible resounded of itself within his soul and he calmly pronounced the pious fraud: "Who else? Of course she did."

The father made no reply, and Sashka relapsed into silence.

Something grated in the adjoining room, then clicked, and then was silent for a moment, and then noisily and hurriedly the clock struck one, two, three.

"Sashka, do you ever dream?" asked the father in a meditative tone.

"No! Oh, yes," he admitted, "once I had one, in which I fell down from the roof. We were climbing after the pigeons, and I fell down."

"But I dream always. Strange things are dreams. One sees the whole past, one loves and suffers as though it were reality."

Again he was silent, and Sashka felt his arm tremble as it lay upon his neck. The trembling and pressure of his father's arm became stronger and stronger, and the sensitive silence of the night was all at once broken by the pitiful sobbing sound of suppressed weeping. Sashka sternly puckered his brow, and cautiously — so as not to disturb the heavy trembling arm — wiped away a tear from his eyes. So strange was it to see a big old man crying.

"Ah! Sashka, Sashka," sobbed the father, "what is the meaning of everything?"

"Why, what's the matter?" sternly whispered Sashka. "You're crying just like a little boy."

"Well, I won't, then," said the father with a piteous smile of excuse. "What's the good?"

Feoktista Petrovna turned on her bed. She sighed, cleared her throat, and mumbled incoherent sounds in a loud and strangely persistent manner.

It was time to go to bed. But before doing so the little angel must be disposed of for the night. He could not be left on the floor, so he was hung up by his string, which was fastened to the flue of the stove. There it stood out accurately delineated against the white Dutch-tiles. And so they could both see him, Sashka and his father.

Hurriedly throwing into a corner the various rags on which he was in the habit of sleeping, Sashka lay down on his back, in order as quickly as possible to look again at the little angel.

"Why don't you undress?" asked his father as he shivered and wrapped himself up in his tattered blanket, and arranged his clothes, which he had thrown over his feet.

"What's the good? I shall soon be up again."

Sashka wished to add that he did not care to go to sleep at all, but he had no time to do so, since he fell to sleep as suddenly as though he had sunk to the bottom of a deep swift river.

His father presently fell asleep also. And gentle sleep and restfulness lay upon the weary face of the man who had lived his life, and upon the brave face of the little man who was just beginning his life.

But the little angel hanging by the hot stove began to melt. The lamp, which had been left burning at the entreaty of Sashka, filled the room with the smell of kerosene, and through its smoked glass threw a melancholy light upon a scene of gradual dissolution. The little angel seemed to stir. Over his rosy fingers there rolled thick drops which fell upon the bench. To the smell of kerosene was added the stifling scent of melting wax. The little angel gave a tremble as though on the point of flight, and — fell with a soft thud upon the hot flags.

An inquisitive cockroach singed its wings as it ran round the formless lump of melted wax, climbed up the dragon-fly wings, and twitching its feelers went on its way.

Through the curtained window the grey-blue light of coming day crept in, and the frozen water-carrier was already making a noise in the courtyard with his iron scoop.

The Guest

by Nikolai Leskov

This story tells of a true event which took place in Siberia on Christmas Day: Christ himself came to one of the exiles as his guest and revealed his commandment to him. I heard this story from an old Siberian who was present when this happened, and I will relate it in his own words.

We live in Siberia in a colony of exiles but our district is not poor as a good deal of trade is carried on there. My father came to our village at the time when there were still serfs in Russia. I myself was born in Siberia. Our family had some property, enough to enable us to live in the way we had been used to. Even now we are not poor.

We share the simple faith of the Russian people. My father was well-read and from him I learnt to love books. I always considered a man who loved knowledge as the most valued of friends for whom I would be ready to go through fire and water. Now the Lord in his goodness once gave me such a friend: Timofei Ossipovich, the same who was graced to witness the miracle which I am going to describe.

Timofei Ossipovich came to us when he was still a young man. I myself was then eighteen years old and Timofei in his early twenties. He lived the best of lives and nobody knew why he had been condemned to live in exile. In our situation one avoids being inquisitive but there was a rumour that a relative had brought about his ruin. This uncle had been the guardian of the young orphan and he had partly squandered and partly embezzled nearly all the property of his ward. When still very young Timofei Ossipovich had once lost his temper and stabbed his uncle in a quarrel. Thanks to God's mercy the man had not been killed but had only had his hand pierced through. Because of this and because of his youth Timofei had not been fined too heavily. Being a member of a rich tradesmen's guild he was sentenced to exile in our district.

Although he had lost nine-tenths of his wealth Timofei could still live on the remaining tenth. He built himself a house in our colony and lived there quietly, but his heart was burning with anger and indignation. He could not forget the wrong he had suffered and he did not want to see anyone except his two servants, a manservant and his wife. Day after day he would sit at home, always reading books and by preference the more pious ones.

At last we came to know each other just because of the books. I started to visit him and he readily accepted me, so that soon we realized that we had become very attached to each other.

At first my parents were not pleased with this new acquaintance of mine. They did not know what to think of him. "No one knows who he is or why he hides from everyone. May you never learn evil from him!" they said.

I listened to my father and mother but I could answer in all truth that an evil word was never to be heard from Timofei and that we met simply to read books to each other and to talk about the faith. We were seeking together to find the will of God and to learn how man could live without disgracing and disfiguring the image of his Creator. So my parents soon agreed that I could visit Timofei as often as I liked. My father even went to see him himself, and after this Timofei also came to us.

My parents soon recognized Timofei's nobility of soul. They took a liking to him and they grew more and more concerned about his frequent spells of depression. For it was so that whenever he was led to think about the past, about the wrong which he had suffered, or when his uncle happened to be mentioned with but a single word, he would turn pale and his hands would become limp. At once his mind seemed disturbed, and his heart downcast and all his courage and strength gone. Then he could not face reading any more and anger would burn in his eyes in place of their customary kind expression. He was a man of absolute integrity and keen intelligence, yet because of his gloomy state of soul he was unable to undertake any sort of enterprise.

But soon the Lord cured Timofei's melancholy. He fell in love with my sister and married her and from then on ceased to lament the past. He started to take an active interest in life; he began to make money and within ten years he had become a wealthy man. He built a spacious house which he furnished well. There was enough of everything and he came to enjoy the respect of all those around him. He had a good wife and healthy children. What more could he wish for? One might well imagine that every past grievance had been forgotten once and for all. Yet still Timofei brooded over the great wrong he had suffered.

One day when riding together in a small carriage we had a heart-to-heart talk.

"Brother Timofei, are you really contented now?" I asked.

"What do you mean?" he asked in reply.

"I mean, have you regained all that you lost in your old home country?"

At once Timofei turned pale, answered not a word and kept the reins in his hands in utter silence.

I had not wanted to hurt him. "Oh brother Timofei," I pleaded, "please forgive me for asking, but I thought that you had suffered that wrong so long ago that it was over and done with and quite forgotten."

"That it happened so long ago," he answered, "makes no difference: I simply cannot forget it."

I was worried about my friend, not because he had lost a fortune but because of the darkness in his soul. How could it be that he knew the Gospel so well and spoke about the faith with pious words and yet persisted in resenting the wrong he had once suffered? It meant quite clearly that the word of God held no true blessing for him. I had to ponder deeply about this. I had always considered him much further than I in faith and wisdom, and I had conversed with him in order to help my own spiritual development. But now I saw that he still could not overcome his old bitterness of heart about that great wrong he had once suffered.

Timofei noticed that I was deep in thought and he suddenly asked me what I was thinking about.

"Oh, whatever happens to cross my mind," I answered.

"No, you are thinking about me."

"Yes, that as well."

"And what are you thinking about me?"

"Please, brother, don't be angry with me if I do tell you my thoughts. I was thinking that although you know the Gospel your heart is not at peace but full of anger instead, rejecting the will of God. As matters stand I cannot see what good you derive from Holy Scripture."

Timofei was not angry but the expression on his face became sad and withdrawn. "You do not know the Bible well enough," he said, "to appeal to its authority."

"Of course you are right," I said. "I am not deeply enough versed in Holy Scripture."

"You are also not experienced enough," he continued, "to know how great and manifold are the wrongs of the world."

I agreed with him in this too, and then he pointed out that there were wrongs which no one could possibly forgive. He explained that he did not reproach his uncle so bitterly about the money but about another matter he would never be able to forget.

"I thought my lips would be sealed about this for all eternity," he said, "but now I will tell it to you as my friend."

"Tell me if you feel that it will help you," I answered. Timofei then revealed to me that already as a child he had heard his uncle insult his father and that his mother's death had been brought about by all the sorrow his uncle had caused her. Finally, his uncle had slandered Timofei and, old as he was, had succeeded in persuading certain people by flattery and threats to give him for his wife the very girl whom Timofei had loved since childhood and whom he had always wanted to marry.

"Can anyone forgive all this?" demanded Timofei. "I will certainly not do so as long as I live." "There is no doubt that you had to suffer grievous wrongs," I replied, "but it is still true that Holy Scripture is of no help to you."

Again he started to explain to me that I did not know the Bible as well as he and that I should remember the holy men in the Old Testament who knew no pity towards evil doers, even slaughtering them with their own hands. This was how my poor friend tried to justify his inability to forgive. But I replied to him in my simple way.

"Timofei," I said, "you are a clever man, well read and very knowledgeable. I cannot refute your words about Holy Scripture. I must confess that I have not grasped all that I have read, for I am but a sinful man. But I must tell you that I find much that is written in the Old Testament ancient and obscure, whereas the message of the Gospels is much clearer. There shines a light, a leading star: 'Love and forgive!' This light is more precious than any other. It throws its rays into every darkness; it lights the way we ought to go. But what are the offences which we must forgive? Only the small ones? Or could it be rather the most grievous wounds our enemy has inflicted on us?"

He remained silent and I prayed: "O Lord, may it be your will that through my mouth your word can reach into my brother's soul."

Then I tried to put before my friend the image of the Christ. He who had neither hearth nor home was persecuted all his life and even in the end was beaten, abused and spat upon. Yet hanging on the cross still had forgiveness for his enemies.

"O Timofei," I pleaded, "you would do better to follow Christ's example than the old laws of revenge."

But once again he sought to justify his attitude by lengthy explanations of the Scriptures. He argued that by forgiving certain misdeeds one would multiply the evil in the world.

I could not refute this but could only say simply: "You Timofei, be watchful and direct the sword against yourself. While you persist in thinking of the evil you have suffered this evil remains alive. If you could let it die, your soul would begin to live in peace."

Timofei listened to the end, he pressed my hand and stopped justifying his hatred with clever words. He simply said, "I cannot do this. Please do not mention it again. It weighs too heavily on my heart."

From that day on I held my peace for I realized that he was still suffering. It was quite obvious that if he had been free and had met the uncle he would most certainly have fallen prey to the devil of revenge, forgetting all his knowledge of the Bible.

But after a long time it came about that I saw God's hand at work in Timofei. It was still only one finger that showed itself but I was full of confidence that one day we would see the whole hand. I firmly believed that the Lord could redeem my friend from the sin of wrath and from his thirst for revenge. And then it really happened and in a most miraculous way...

Timofei had now been living with us in exile for sixteen years. He was about thirty-seven or thirty-eight years old. He had three children and lived in comfortable circumstances. He had a special love for flowers and roses in particular; he grew very many of them in his garden, underneath the windows and along the wooden fence. His front garden was filled with roses whose scent wafted into the house.

Now Timofei had a certain custom. As soon as the sun was low he would go out and spend the rest of the day in his garden. He pruned his roses and then sat down on the bench to read. And I feel sure that he often prayed there.

One day he came out with the Bible in his hands. After he had cared for his rose bushes he sat down, opened the holy book and started reading. It chanced that he read how Christ came as a guest into the house of the Pharisee and how he was not even given water to wash his feet. Timofei suddenly felt that this offence done to our Lord was quite unbearable. He felt such a deep compassion and suffered so severely in

Christ's place that he began to weep over the treatment Christ had suffered from his host.

This was the moment when the miracle began that changed Timofei's heart. Timofei related it to me in the following words: "After I had read this story I looked around me and suddenly I thought, 'I can live so well and have plenty of everything and yet our Lord walked on earth so poor and ill-used.' Tears filled my eyes and however hard I tried I could not stop weeping. But as I wept everything around me became tinged with rose-coloured light. Even my tears were roses! Nearly fainting I cried, 'O Lord, if only you would come to me I would serve you, body and soul!' Then in the rose-coloured light an answer sounded, breathed by a gentle wind: 'I will come'."

After this Timofei had come in haste to me. Trembling, he asked, "What do you think of it? Is it possible that the Lord will visit me?"

"This, brother," I replied, "is beyond my understanding. Should we not rather seek the answer in the Holy Bible?"

But Timofei answered, "It is the same Christ, who was and who is and shall be evermore. I dare not doubt his promise."

"You had better believe it then," was all I could say.

Timofei continued, "I will see to it that a place is laid for him at every meal."

I shrugged my shoulders. "Don't ask me any more. You must find out for yourself what will please him most. But I don't think he will be offended if you prepare a place for him. One has of course to consider whether it is not pride to do so."

"But it is written: 'This man accepts sinners and sits down to meals with tax-collectors'."

"But it is also written: 'Lord, go out from me, for I am a sinful man.' These words seem also apt."

"You don't understand this," answered Timofei.

"Well, that is quite possible," I said.

From that day on Timofei made his wife lay an extra place. When they sat down for meals, the five of them — he, his wife and three children — there was always a sixth place laid, the place of honour at the end of the table, and before it was placed a big armchair.

His wife would have liked to know whom this chair was waiting for but Timofei kept his secret. To her and to others he only explained that it had to be done like this because of a vow he had made. He only added that the place was kept for "the most important of guests." But nobody knew who this guest was meant to be — apart, that is, from himself and me.

Timofei hoped that the Lord would come the day after the voice had been heard in his rose garden. Then he expected him on the next day and again on the third. Then he waited for the Sunday. But his hopes were in vain. Nevertheless Timofei kept on waiting month after month. Whenever a Sunday or Holy Day came round he expected the visit of the Lord. He was exhausted and restless but never for a moment did he lose his faith that Christ would keep his promise and come to him.

One day Timofei confessed to me, "I pray every day with the words, 'Come, O Christ!' I wait and hope for the answer, 'Yea, I will come soon.' But I never hear these words."

I did not know what to say. Often I thought that pride had possessed my friend and that this temptation had received and confused him. But God's providence was working otherwise ...

Christmas drew near. It was a hard winter. Timofei visited me on Christmas Eve and said, "Dear brother, the Lord is sure to come tomorrow."

I had given up arguing with him about this matter long ago. I only asked, "How can you be so sure of this?"

"I had hardly finished saying grace today," my friend replied, "when my heart began to beat with strong emotion. Then out of its inmost depths an answer sounded like a trumpet call: 'I will come soon!' Tomorrow is his holy festival. Will he not wish to see me on this day? Please come to me then, dear brother, and bring your whole family, for otherwise my heart will never stop trembling with fear."

"Timofei," I answered, "you have seen that I do not know what to make of all this. As for me, sinner that I am, how can I expect to see our Lord? But we have accepted you into our family, you are one of us, so we will come. But for your part, if you are really expecting such a great guest, do not think simply of inviting your own friends but rather bring together such people as he would be pleased to see."

"I understand," he replied. "I will send my servants immediately and also my son. They shall go through the whole village and whosoever among the exiles is suffering from need or distress shall be invited to the meal, so that if the Lord will grace me with his presence he shall find everything prepared in accordance with his commandments."

Even these words did not sound humble enough to me. "Timofei," I said, "who could possibly prepare everything exactly as the Lord commands? One thing you may not understand, another you may forget, a third may prove impossible to fulfill, but if all this is stirring and sounding in your soul you should simply do whatever seems right to you. For if the Lord should come he will add what is missing and if you have forgotten to invite someone he would wish to see, he is sure to lead him into your house."

On Christmas Day we went to Timofei with the whole family. We arrived somewhat later than usual for dinner as Timofei had asked us to do so. He waited to begin the meal only after all the expected guests had arrived. We found his spacious house full of our kind of people: exiles in Siberia, men women, young people and children, people from every walk of life and from different regions and countries, not only Russians but Poles and Estonians. Timofei had invited all those poor settlers who had not yet managed to establish themselves.

The tables were large and furnished with all that was needed. The maids were running to and fro setting down kvass and dishes of meat pie. Outside dusk was deepening and no more guests could be expected as all the servants sent out to fetch the invited guests had long since returned. Moreover a snowstorm had blown up and soon grown into a blizzard through which thunder sounded as if the Day of Judgment itself had come. Even Timofei had to admit to himself that no further guest would be able to find his way there.

He walked about and sat down in turns. One could see that he was going through an agony of unrest. All his faith was about to be shattered, for now it seemed certain that the special Guest would not come.

Another minute passed. Timofei uttered a deep sigh, looked at me and said, "Now, my dear brother, I can see that it is either God's will to make me the laughing stock of all the people or that you are right and that I did not manage to bring together all those whom the Lord wanted to meet here. But God's will be done. Let us say grace and sit down."

He walked to the corner and began to pray in front of the Icon. After the Lord's Prayer he cried out,

"Christ is descending from heaven, praise him!

Christ is coming to earth, proclaim it!

Christ is born at this hour ..."

Suddenly as he was uttering these last words a terrible blow struck the wall outside. The house shook and a noise like thunder resounded in the passage. All at once the door sprang wide open by itself.

All the people present shrank back into the corners of the room, many fell down and only the bravest ones dared to look at the door. On the threshold of the open door stood an old man, old as the hills and clothed in poor rags. With trembling hands he gripped the doorpost, to prevent himself from falling down. From the passage behind him which had not been lit before a miraculous rose-coloured light shone forth, and above the shoulder of the old man a snow-white hand could be seen. This hand stretched forward into the room holding an earthenware oil lamp, oval and ancient such as we know from the pictures of Jesus and Nicodemus. A golden flame burnt quietly on this lamp. Outside the snowstorm raged but the flame did not waver or flicker. It shed its calm light right into the face of the old man and on to his hand which was gripping the doorpost. On this hand an old wound scar caught the eye for it had become quite white with cold.

Timofei had hardly seen the man before he cried, "O Lord, I recognize him and I will receive him in thy name! But thou, O Lord, do not enter my house for I am an evil and sinful man." With these words Timofei bent down deeply, his face touching the floor.

And I, too, fell on my knees with him, filled with awe and tremendous gratitude and also with great joy because true Christian humility had touched my brother's heart. I exclaimed for all to hear, "Let us be aware that Christ is in our midst!"

"So it is in truth!" they all answered.

Light was brought. Timofei and I rose from the floor and looked up. The white hand had disappeared but the old man was still standing in the open doorway. Timofei took him by his hands and led him to the place of honour.

Now you will perhaps be able to guess for yourself who this old man was with the white scar on his hand. He was Timofei's enemy, the uncle who had completely ruined him. In a few words he related how nothing was left of all his wealth or family. He had been walking through Siberia for a long time seeking his nephew in order to ask his forgiveness, longing to find him but at the same time fearing his anger. That day he had lost his way in the snowstorm and nearly fainting from the cold he had expected nothing but death. He continued, "Suddenly a stranger lit my way and said to me, 'Go, warm yourself in my place and eat from my bowl.' He took me by the hand and led me. So I reached this house not knowing what way I came."

Timofei raised his voice before all the people.

"O uncle," he exclaimed, "I know who your companion was! It was the Lord, the same Lord who said, 'If thine enemy be hungry, give him bread. If he thirst, give him to drink.' Therefore, I pray you, sit down at the best place and eat and drink. You shall stay with me for the rest of your life. Enjoy to your heart's content all that the Lord through his grace has provided me with."

From that time on the old man stayed with Timofei and when the time came for him to die he gave Timofei his blessing. Timofei had found peace of heart at last.

Just as this simple man was taught to prepare his heart for the Christ who came to earth, so can every man's heart be made ready to receive his Saviour if only he fulfils Christ's commandment: "Love your enemies, bless them that curse you, do good to them that hate you and pray for them which despitefully use you and persecute you."

Into such a heart Christ will enter as a guest enters the house prepared for him and surely he will live therein.

Yea, come, O Lord, come soon!

Tamara, the Moorish Angel

Hans Berghuis

After a journey of some days I came to the village of Rocas Altas just before Christmas. I had left the South of Spain in order to spend the Christmas days in a more northerly part. I did not wish to sit in the sun, I longed for a rugged landscape and I was homesick for the fresh cold of the North. Already I had half a mind to go back to my own country, but at the last moment a friend had said to me: "You must go to Rocas Altas. It is a village on the north-east coast of Spain. At this time of the year it is rainy and stormy there. But besides that, in Rocas Altas there is a marvellously beautiful Moorish church, and in Rocas Altas you will find the strangest Christmas crib that you have ever seen."

I always allow myself to be persuaded to do things that I myself would never have done on my own initiative, and so off to Rocas Altas I went. First a day and a night on the boat, and then half a day in the train, and the last bit of the journey I did in an old donkey-cart. It was just as if I had been travelling for weeks when I finally arrived with my donkey-driver in the little square of Rocas Altas.

"And what now?" asked the man.

"Nothing more. I am where I want to be," I replied. I paid him, he unloaded my bag and slowly turned his cart round. He hesitated. Perhaps he thought that I had made a mistake and that I should want to go back with him right away to the civilized world of the city. But I was not thinking of that. Here I was in Rocas Altas and here I intended to stay, come what may.

The donkey-driver was still hesitating.

"Que vaya con Dios," I called to him, — "Go with God." That was a command. He did not look round any more, but led his donkey away along the steep track to the coast.

There I stood abandoned in the little square. After a few steps I noticed something strange about the village of Rocas Altas. In every town and in every village in Spain the church stands in the midst of the community of white houses. But in Rocas Altas the church was missing. In the square there were only little shops, wine-cellars and a fountain. But a church was nowhere to be seen.

I thought I should be able to lodge with the village priest, and that is why I had simply sent the donkey-driver back down to the plain. But now I was sorry that I had not asked the man's advice. As there was no church in Rocas Altas where could the priest's house be?

Rocas Altas seemed to be a very remarkable village. On one side of the square the streets went steeply uphill in steps to a ruined castle, while on the other side of the square they went down also in steps to a strong wall that enclosed the square like a medieval fortress of the Middle Ages. First I climbed up to the castle. It was a ruin, but the round forms of the gateways and towers made me think that the fortress must be very old, probably from the time of the Moorish dominion. Then I descended to the wall on the other side of the village. I climbed up on to the wide parapet and before my eyes extended a wonderful view.

Sea, sea, sea as far as the eye could reach. The blue Mediterranean, not as in summer — a flat ornamental lake full of sunshine — but now as in winter; deep blue, with waves raised by the North wind, rolling in to the coast, thundering against the rocks below; deep blue in its depths but with white-capped waves. It was a glorious sight. But far below the walls was a little beach lying enclosed in a semicircle with the sea on one side and on the other the high wall of the village of Rocas Altas, the rock on which the village was built. And on that little beach was the church. Usually churches are built on the highest point of the village or town, but here in Rocas Altas the church lay in the deep bowl between the village and the sea. I leaned over to look at it better.

"Do you want to jump down?" asked a friendly voice behind me.

I straightened up with a jerk. It was my donkey-driver.

"What are you doing here?" I asked him.

"Well you see, strangers usually need some help when they come into a strange village. I left my cart in a side-street and followed you. You obviously don't know what kind of a village you've landed up in."

"Oh, and you do?" I said sharply.

"Yes, indeed," he replied, "of course I know. I have brought a whole lot of strangers to Rocas Altas. And they always wander about through the village and they always come to the wall and they always stand looking out to sea and they always find the church of Rocas Altas down there below. Do you know how far down it is to the shore and the church?"

"A hundred and fifty feet?" I asked.

"No, two hundred!"

"That's quite a jump," I said laughing.

"Yes," he answered, "but anyone jumping down would be killed."

"Of course," I said, "anyone jumping down would be dead on the spot."

"Unless he were to become an angel," answered the donkey-driver.

"Have you many of those angels here?" I asked jokingly.

"No," he replied very seriously, "here we have only one angel."

"And what's that angel called?"

"That angel," said the Spanish donkey-driver, "that angel is the Moorish maiden Tamara."

Now of course I had to ask how the Moorish maiden Tamara could be an angel. That is how a story always starts in Spain. First the story-teller tells a few strange things about a village or a town. As soon as the visitor asks curiously how all that could have happened, only then comes the whole story.

And so, following the custom of the country, I said: "Won't you tell me how Tamara became an angel?"

"Yes I will," he replied, "But first come away from that wall. Not everyone who falls off it will become an angel."

I went back with the donkey-driver to the inn in the square. We ordered a dish of *arroz a la marinera,* and with a bottle of red wine of the country we slowly got the better of the rice with fish and lobster. Then the donkey-driver lit his brown Spanish cigarette and began his story. A thousand years ago up in the castle there lived a Moorish count called Tarik. His forebears came from the land of the Berbers and his family had ruled for more than two centuries over Rocas Altas under the Great Caliph. Count Tarik was a good Moorish count and the people of Rocas Altas were well content under his rule.

But they had only one complaint. Tarik's father had forbidden the people of Rocas Altas to build a church in the middle of the little town. They might indeed build a church for God, but outside the walls of Rocas Altas, in the deep bowl of the shore beneath the walls. It is the same church that you have seen from the walls. Now the people of Rocas Altas found it irksome that they had to walk so far when they went to church, because they could not reach it along the wall, nor could they descend the steep cliffs to get to the beach where the church stood. They had to go up through the highest gate of Rocas Altas and along a long winding mountain path that took them more than two hours to walk before they reached the church. But on the other hand they found the site of the church very convenient: because it was such a long way off and the path was quite dangerous they did not feel obliged to go down to the church every day. Once a week was enough for them, indeed once a year for some of them. And of course they did not blame their own laziness, but the command of the Moorish count. People always look for excuses to justify themselves before God.

Now the Moorish Count Tarik had a sixteen-year-old daughter who was called Tamara. She was the most beautiful maiden in Rocas Altas, but not only was she beautiful, she was very devout. Even though her father was a Muslim, young Tamara went down every day to the beach to pray in the church of the Christians. Not every Sunday like the inhabitants of Rocas Altas, but every day. That annoyed the people of Rocas Altas. Why did that Moorish maiden have to go to the church every day? People always get annoyed when other people are good.

Then it came to Christmas. It was the year 999. Tamara had slept late and when at last she awoke in the castle up there, the church bells below were already ringing. She dressed hastily and left her father's castle. When she reached the village square she noticed that the whole village was forsaken. Everyone had gone off to the church where the birth of the Child was to be celebrated. And Tamara had so wished to be present. She would so have like to see the Child in the Manger. In despair she ran to the gate of the town. But the inhabitants had shut the gates.

Tamara did not know what to do. She ran to the wall above the beach, climbed up on to the parapet of the wall and looked down full of longing. In the depths of the bowl lay the little church. From the windows shone the light of the candles.

"Child of the God of the Christians," prayed Tamara then in her despair, "how I wish I could fly down to see thee lying in the manger. How I should love to be an angel so that I might come and be right beside thy stable. How I wish I had wings to be able to fly down from this high wall. For it is a festival in thy house, and where thy festival is, there I would be. Help me, O God of the Christians, to be at thy festival."

And young Tamara the Mooress sprang from the high wall down the two hundred feet. To her astonishment she landed safe and sound on the beach. Full of joy she ran to the church, and full of joy she told the

Christians of Rocas Altas that an angel had borne her over the precipice to the manger of the Child. She cried with joy and told everyone who would listen about the miracle. But the Christians of Rocas Altas grew angry. Already they had been annoyed at the Moorish maiden Tamara for a long time. And they could not bear it that God had done a miracle for a Moor. Miracles do not exist, said the inhabitants, because they themselves no longer believed in God's miracles.

Angrily they told Tamara, "If it is true that an angel from heaven has borne you over the precipice to the manger, then the angel will do it again, so that we can all see it. Go back up to the wall with us and jump down again!"

The priest of Rocas Altas was a god-fearing man and he tried to restrain his believers from such a rash act.

"Miracles only happen once," he said. "Do not try to force God to repeat his miraculous deeds in order to convert you from your unbelief. Let Tamara be; she is a better Christian than all of you."

But the inhabitants of Rocas Altas were stubborn in their wrath

"God shall judge," they said to the old priest. "Why should you meddle? Tamara shall jump from the wall again and we shall see whether she is a Christian or a heathen."

"Count Tarik will punish you!" warned the priest still.

But the villagers laughed and said that God would protect them from the wrath of a Moorish dog. Then they led Tamara back along the mountain path to Rocas Altas. They brought her to the wall and set her on the parapet.

"Jump down," they commanded the Moorish maiden. "Jump!"

Tamara looked down. The lights were extinguished. Tamara was courageous, proud and happy because she had seen the child in the manger. Once again she prayed to the God of the Christians.

"O God, these people are thy faithful ones, but they have lost their faith in thee and in thy words. This time bring me not to a festival among men, but to a festival in thy heaven. Save me not from my fall into the depths. I have seen and felt thy wonder. That is enough for me. I am so happy with the miracle of this night, that I have no desire to live longer among these unbelieving Christians."

"Jump, Tamara," screamed the villagers of Rocas Altas.

Tamara looked at the menacing crowd. "Your God is better than you," she called.

"Witch," shouted the villagers.

Then Tamara leapt and fell crushed on the beach below.

"Ah, did we not say so," said the villagers joyfully. "God is just. Tamara was a witch, she was an enchanted heathen. God has let us see that she was a witch. We have been saved from the snares of the Devil."

Then, satisfied with the judgment of God they went back down the cliff to celebrate the Birth of the Child. But when they had arrived at the church after two hours walk the doors were shut. No one could open them. They fetched a smith, but neither could he force the locks. They brought ladders to climb through the windows to get in, but the ladders fell down as soon as any one set his foot on the bottom rung.

Suddenly there was a cry in the Christmas night. Count Tarik came riding down with the Moorish guards from his castle. In panic the inhabitants of Rocas Altas tried to flee, but they were hemmed in on one side by the stormy sea and on the other by the high cliffs and walls of the town. The only way out was blocked by the Moorish soldiers of the count.

Without a word Count Tarik rode to the spot where his daughter Tamara lay dead in the wet sand. He dismounted. Count Tarik held his dead daughter in his arms when he rode away out of the bowl. Full of horror the inhabitants watched him.

At the foot of the cliff Count Tarik turned and faced the crowd.

"For what you have done I ought to kill you all, unbelievers of Rocas Altas," spoke the Count, deeply moved. "But I shall not kill any Christian dog. All your lives are worth less than that of my beloved daughter Tamara. She was the only true believer in this town. Fear not my sword then, you cowards. Fear your God, who shall punish you for what you have done. Never shall a church be built up there in the town, never as long as Rocas Altas remains. Until eternity shall your church remain below in the valley by the sea. And until eternity each one of you, every man, every woman and every child of Rocas Altas shall descend below to pray for my daughter Tamara. Whosoever breaks this command shall lose his life. Have you heard what I have commanded you? Every day, every day, everyone of you shall go down. Every day you shall do penance for your misdeed."

Count Tarik rode back to his castle with his dead daughter Tamara in his arms. And from that day the inhabitants of Rocas Altas descended by the steep mountain path to the church on the beach to do penance for the misdeed done on that Christmas night. But the church remained shut however much penance they did.

Once again it was Christmas in Rocas Altas. A whole year of penance had gone by. On Christmas night all the men, women and children went down from the village to the church on the beach. The doors of the church stood wide open and from within streamed the light of the candles. Count Tarik too had come because it was a year since the villagers had killed his daughter. The open doors and the light welcomed the people to come in, but no one dared set a foot inside.

Count Tarik rode to the fore. "Why do you not go into the church?" He asked.

"We dare not," answered the villagers.

"Do you not see that your God has forgiven you?" asked Count Tarik.

"You go in first, Count Tarik," prayed the villagers. "When you go in we shall know that not only God but you also will have forgiven us."

"You are still unbelieving," said Count Tarik. "The first thing you ask for in this night is a fresh sign from God. Therefore you say that I must be the first to go in. Well, I shall do it. Perhaps your God wills that you shall be finally converted by the example of one of Allah's faithful."

Count Tarik dismounted from his horse and was the first to enter the little church of Rocas Altas. Hesitantly the villagers followed him. Right to the front of the church strode Count Tarik, and the inhabitants of Rocas Altas followed him to the front. And when they were all inside, again a cry was heard on that Christmas night, a cry of joy and gratitude. For this time the inhabitants of Rocas Altas saw something which they had never seen before in their church.

Suddenly the donkey-driver stopped in his story. He took a sip of black coffee and stood up as if he would go out and leave me alone in the inn.

"What did the people of Rocas Altas see then?" I asked him quickly.

"Come with me." He answered. "It is quite late now and the darkness of Christmas Eve has fallen. I'll take you to the church. Isn't that why you came?"

"Yes," I replied. "That's why I came. But tell me first what the people of Rocas Altas saw on that second Christmas night."

He gave me no answer and left the inn. Behind him I walked along the winding mountain path which led down to the beach with the church. Just as a thousand years ago, it was still a walk of two hours. When we reached the beach the church doors stood wide open and the windows were lit. I entered the church with the donkey-driver and with all the other people of Rocas Altas. And just as a thousand years ago, we all went forward to the crib. When I was near the crib I saw what the inhabitants of Rocas Altas must have seen. Mary and Joseph and the Child were white as snow. The shepherds and the shepherd boys with

330

sheep and lambs were white as wool. But the angel of Rocas Altas was quite a different angel from those that usually stand by the crib. The angel of Rocas Altas was a Moorish maiden of sixteen with sparkling eyes, jet black hair, a Moorish countess' tiara on her head, and a smile on her mouth as only a Moorish angel can smile.

"Look carefully," whispered the donkey-driver beside me. "The angel at the crib is our angel Tamara!"

"Yes," I whispered back, "it is the most beautiful Christmas angel that I have ever seen."

"Even the Christ-Child in the manger is looking at Tamara," whispered the donkey-driver.

"Of course," I replied. "Why not? The Christ-Child naturally wants to tell us, 'Whosoever of you has so great a love as once the Moorish maiden Tamara, shall not die and everlasting death'."

"Do you really believe that?" asked the donkey-driver.

"Certainly," I answered. "Certainly I believe that. Or is the angel Tamara still the only believer in Rocas Altas?"

"No," said the donkey-driver quickly, "no, we are all believers since that night a thousand years ago. You are right. I do believe it too."

I looked at the Angel Tamara. She was smiling. But it may be that I am mistaken, for there was the candle-light shining over the face of the Moorish angel Tamara and perhaps Tamara was not smiling towards me but to the Child in the manger.

A Christmas Story

Maxim Gorki

My Christmas story was finished. I threw down the pen, stood up from the desk and paced up and down my little room, three quarters of which lay in darkness.

It was night and outside in the storm the snow swirled through the air. Strange noises, a soft whispering and sighing, coming from the street and penetrating the walls reached my ears. It was the snow driven by the wind against the walls and window panes. A light white unrecognizable object flew past my window and disappeared, and a cold shiver troubled my soul.

I walked over to the window, looked out into the street and laid my head, heated from the effort of concentration and imagination, on the cool window pane. The street lay in abandoned stillness. Now and again the wind tore transparent clouds of snow from the pavement and let them fly like delicate white veils through the air. Opposite my window a street light was burning. Its flame trembled and flickered in its struggle with the wind. The ray from the lamp cast itself like a broad sword in the air, and the snow blown from the roofs of the houses into this beam of light glowed for a moment like a glistening garment of sparks. My heart grew sad and cold watching this play of the wind. I undressed quickly, blew out the lamp and lay down to sleep.

Once the light was out and darkness filled my room the noises could be heard more clearly, and the window stared at me like a great white patch. The ceaseless ticking of the clock signalled the passage of the seconds. Sometimes its energetic onward march was drowned by the rustle and swish of the snow, and then again I could hear the faint ticking of the seconds as they passed away into eternity. At other times its sound was as clear and exact as if the clock stood inside my skull.

I lay in bed and thought about the story which I had just finished and wondered whether it would bring me any success.

This story was about two beggars, an old blind man and his wife, whose lives, constantly exposed to fear and humiliation, were spent in quiet and timid isolation. On the morning of Christmas Eve they had left their village in order to go begging in the neighbourhood so as to be able to celebrate the Birth of Christ on the next day in a festive manner.

They wanted to visit one more village and then be back for the early service, with their bags full of the crumbs which they had been given for the sake of Christ.

Their hopes (so my story went on) were of course not fulfilled. They only received a few gifts, and it was already very late when the couple, tired out from the days efforts, finally decided to return to their cold deserted mud hut. With their light bundles on their shoulders and with pain in their hearts they dragged themselves over the snow-covered plain; the old woman went ahead and the old man, holding on to her girdle followed her. It was a dark night. Clouds covered the sky and for two ageing people the way to the village was a long one. Their feet sank into the snow and the wind whisked it up and blew it into their faces. Silent and shivering with cold they tramped on and on. Tired and blinded by the snow the old woman had lost the track and now they were wandering aimlessly through the valley over the open fields.

"Are we near home? Mind we don't miss the early mass," mumbled the old man behind the weary shoulder of his wife.

She said they would soon be home, and a fresh shiver ran through her body. She knew that she had lost her way, but she did not dare tell her husband. Sometimes it seemed that the wind brought the sound of dogs barking and she set off in the direction from which the sound came: but soon she heard the barking coming from the other side.

In the end her strength failed her and she said to the old man, "Forgive me little father, forgive me in Christ's name. I have lost the way, and I can go no farther. I shall have to sit down."

"You will freeze to death," he replied.

"Just let me rest for a moment. And even if we do freeze, what does it matter? Our life on earth is not a happy one."

The old man sighed and consented.

They sat down in the snow, back to back, and they looked like two bundles of rags for the wind to play with. It blew snow clouds against them, covered them with sharp-pointed crystals, and the old woman who was more thinly dressed than her husband, suddenly felt herself embraced by a strange delicious warmth.

"Little mother," called out the blind man, who was trembling with cold, "stand up, we must go on."

But she had fallen asleep and in her sleep she murmured half intelligible words. He wanted to pull her up, but he lacked the strength.

"You will freeze," he shouted, and then he called loudly over the fields for help.

But she felt so warm and comfortable. After some vain endeavours the blind man sat down again in the snow in numb despair. He was now firmly convinced that all that was happening to him was clearly the will of God and for him and his aged wife there was no escape. The wind swirled and danced in unrestrained hilarity round them, cheerfully covering them with snow and played happily with the strips of clothing that covered their old bones, bones grown weary from their long existence in poverty and need. A feeling of delicious comforting warmth came over the old man too.

Suddenly the wind brought the sound of a lovely solemn, melodious sound of bells to his ear.

"Little mother!" he called, starting up. "The bells are ringing for mass. Quick, come on."

But already she had departed to the realm from which there was no return.

"Do you hear? The bells are ringing, I'm telling you. Get up. Oh, we'll be too late."

He tried to stand up, but found that he could not move. Then he realized that he was near his end, and he prayed softly: "Lord, be gracious to thy servant's soul. Forgive us, Lord. We have both sinned. Have mercy on us."

It seemed to him that a radiant temple of God came floating over the field, wrapped in a brightly sparkling cloud of snow, a magnificent, wonderful temple. It consisted entirely of flaming human hearts and was itself like a heart, and in the midst stood Christ himself on a pedestal. At this vision the old man arose and fell on his knees before the temple. He received back his sight and saw his Redeemer and Saviour. From where he stood above him Christ spoke to him in a gracious sweet-sounding voice.

"Hearts that glow with compassion are the founders of my temple. Enter my temple, you who have thirsted for compassion in life, you who have suffered misery and oppression, enter into your eternal peace."

"O Lord," said the old man who having regained his sight was weeping with joy, "It is truly thee, O Lord"

And Christ smiled down kindly on the old man and on his life's companion who had woken to life again through the smile of the Redeemer.

Thus the two beggars froze to death outside in the snow-covered fields.

I recalled to memory the various details of the story and wondered whether I had succeeded in making them good and moving enough to arouse compassion in the reader. It seemed to me that I could answer the question positively, for I believed that the story would undoubtedly have the desired effect.

With this thought I fell asleep, very pleased with myself. The clock went on ticking, and in my sleep I heard the storm growing wilder and stronger. The lantern of the street-lamp had been blown out. The storm kept on bringing new sounds out there. The windows rattled. The branches of the trees near the door knocked against the gutters of the roof. There was a sighing, groaning, howling, roaring, whistling which all combined into a melancholy melody filling the heart with sadness, a soft gentle lilting tune like a cradle song. It had the effect of a fantastic story putting the soul under a spell.

But suddenly, what was that? The dim patch of the window flamed up in a bluish, phosphorescent light, and the window grew bigger and bigger, until it spread right over the whole extent of the wall. In the blue light filling the room, there suddenly appeared a dense white cloud in which sparks glowed as from innumerable eyes. The cloud swirled and puffed as if driven by the wind, and began to dissipate, becoming thinner and thinner and splitting up into tiny particles and pouring an icy coldness into my body that made me afraid. Something like malcontented, angry murmurs came out of the wraiths of cloud which took on more determined and recognizable shapes becoming familiar to my eye. Behind in the corner I became aware of a crowd of children, or rather the shadows of children, and behind them along with several female forms there appeared a grey-bearded old man.

"Where do these shadows come from? What do they want?" Those were the questions running through my head while I fearfully watched these strange apparitions.

"Where we come from and whence we are?" replied a stern and earnest voice solemnly. "Do you not know us? Reflect!"

Silently I shook my head. I did not know them. With rhythmical movements they glided through the air, as if they were dancing solemnly to the sound of the storm. Half transparent, without sharp outlines, they wavered lightly and soundlessly round me, and suddenly in their midst I recognized the old blind man holding on to the girdle of his aged wife. Bent low they hobbled past me directing a reproachful gaze at me.

"Do you recognize them now?" The same earnest voice asked.

I could not tell whether it was the voice of the storm or the voice of my conscience, but it had a commanding tone which allowed of no argument.

"Yes, there they are," went on the voice, "the poor protagonists of your successful stories. And all the others are also the characters of your Christmas stories — children, men and women, whom you have allowed to freeze to death to amuse the public. See how many there are, and how wretched they look, the offspring of your imagination."

A movement went through the wavering figures, and two children, a boy and a girl appeared in the foreground. They looked like two snow-flowers or like the disc of the moon.

"These children," said the voice, "you allowed to freeze to death under the window of that opulent house in which a bright Christmas tree was lit. They were looking at the tree — do you remember — and they froze to death."

Soundlessly my two poor characters glided past me and disappeared. they seemed to dissolve in the blue misty light. In their place a woman appeared with a careworn emaciated face.

"This is the poor woman who was hurrying home to her village on Christmas Eve in order to bring her children a few cheap Christmas presents. Her too you have allowed to freeze to death."

Full of shame and fear I gazed at the shadowy woman. She also vanished and new figures appeared in turn. They were all sad, silent apparitions with an expression of indescribable yearning in their gloomy looks.

And again I heard the earnest voice with measured emphasis saying: "Why did you write these stories? Is there not enough real, tangible and visible misery in the world that you have to invent more distress and sorrow, straining your imagination in order to write even more emotional and realistic stories. Will you rob men and women of the joy of life, will you take from them their last drop of faith in the good by showing them only the evil? Why do you allow children, men and women to freeze to death year after year in your Christmas stories? Why? What do you think to achieve by that?"

I was upset by this remarkable accusation. Everybody writes Christmas stories according to the same pattern. You take a poor boy or a poor girl or something similar and let them freeze to death beneath a window where there is usually a Christmas tree shining out to them. That has become the fashion, and I was just following the fashion.

With this in mind I answered: "When I allow these people to freeze, I do it for the best possible reason. When I describe their death-struggles I mean to waken in my readers human feelings for the unfortunate ones. I wish to move the hearts of my readers. That is all."

A strange movement went through the crowd of figures, as if they were going to raise mocking objections to my words.

"See how they laugh." said the mysterious voice.

"Why do they laugh?" I replied almost inaudibly.

"Because you are talking nonsense. With your descriptions of imagined misery you wish to arouse noble feelings in the hearts of people, while real misery and suffering is for them nothing else than a daily spectacle. Think for how long many people have tried to waken noble feelings in the hearts of others, consider how many men have applied their gifts to this purpose, and then look at real life! Fool that you are! If reality will not move them, and their feelings are not touched by cruel and merciless penury and the bottomless abyss of real evil, how can you hope to make them better through the creations of your imagination? Do you really think you can move a person's heart by telling him about a frozen child? The sea of misery beats against the breakwater of heartlessness, it thunders against it and you would assuage it by throwing in a few peas."

The figures accompanied these words with their silent derision and the storm sent out a burst of mocking laughter. But the voice went on inexorably. Every word that it spoke was like a nail driven into my head. It was unbearable, and I could no longer stand it.

"That is all lies, lies!" I cried in a towering rage. As I sprang out of bed, I fell head over heels in the darkness, and faster and faster and deeper and deeper I dropped into the yawning chasm that suddenly opened before me. The piping, howling, roaring and laughter followed me down, the figures chased me through the darkness, grinning in my face and mocking me.

In the morning I awoke with a fierce headache and in a very bad mood. The first thing I did was to read my story of the blind beggar and his wife through again, and then I tore the manuscript into tiny shreds.

From Christmas to Epiphany

The Adoration of the Magi

From the Gospel of Matthew

Now when Jesus was born in Bethlehem of Judea during the reign of King Herod, Magi from the East arrived in Jerusalem, and they said, "Where is the one who is born King of the Jews? We have seen his star in the East, and have come to worship him."

When he heard this, King Herod was disturbed, and with him the whole of Jerusalem. Having assembled the chief priests and the scribes of the people, he asked them where the Christ should be born.

And they told him, "In Bethlehem of Judea, as the prophet has written,

> 'And you Bethlehem in the land of Judah
> are not in any way least among the leaders of Judah,
> because from you will come a leader
> who will shepherd my people Israel'."

Then Herod called the Magi secretly and made careful enquiries about the time when the star appeared. He sent them to Bethlehem, and said, "Make searching enquiries about the child, and when you have found him bring me news, so that I myself may also come and worship him."

When they heard the King they continued on their way. And now the star which they saw in the East led them until it came to stand over where the child was. On seeing the star they rejoiced with the greatest joy. When they came to the house they saw the child with his mother Mary, and they fell down and worshipped him. They opened their treasures and offered him gifts: gold, frankincense and myrrh.

As they had been warned in a dream not to return to Herod, they took another road and departed to their country.

When they had gone, an angel of the Lord appeared to Joseph in a dream and said, "Get up! Take the child and his mother, and go away into Egypt. Stay there until I tell you, as Herod is now going to search for the child to destroy him."

So he got up and took the child and his mother at night, and went away into Egypt. He was there until Herod's death to fulfil what the Lord had spoken through the prophet, saying, "Out of Egypt have I called my son."

When Herod saw that the Magi had scorned him, he was full of fury. He sent out and killed all the boys in Bethlehem and in the surrounding districts who were two years old or less, according to the time which he hade carefully enquired from the Magi.

Then what was said through Jeremiah the prophet was fulfilled:

"A voice was heard in Rama,
weeping and sorrowing;
Rachel weeping for her children
and would not be comforted
because they are no more."

When Herod had died, an angel of the Lord appeared in a dream to Joseph in Egypt and said, "Get up! Take the child and his mother and go into the land of Israel because the people are dead who wished to take the child's life."

So he got up and taking the child and his mother he went into the land of Israel. But when he heard that Archelaus was ruling over Judea in place of his father Herod he was afraid to go there and being warned in a dream he turned away into the region of Galilee and went to live in a town called Nazareth.

So that what was spoken through the prophets was fulfilled: "He shall be called a Nazarene."

The Little Match-Seller

Hans Christian Andersen

It was terribly cold. Snow was falling and soon it would be quite dark; for it was the last day in the year — New Year's Eve. Along the street, in that same cold and dark, went a poor little girl in bare feet — well, yes, it's true, she had slippers on when she left home; but what was the good of that? They were great big slippers which her mother used to wear, so you can imagine the size of them; and they both came off when the little girl scurried across the road just as two carts went whizzing by at a fearful rate. One slipper was not to be found, and a boy ran off with the other, saying it would do for a cradle one day when he had children of his own.

So there was the little girl walking along in her bare feet that were simply blue with cold. In an old apron she was carrying a whole lot of matches, and she had one bunch of them in her hand. She hadn't sold anything all day, and no one had given her a single penny. Poor mite, she looked so downcast as she trudged along hungry and shivering. The snowflakes settled on her long flaxen hair, which hung in pretty curls over her shoulder; but you may be sure she wasn't thinking about her looks. Lights were shining in every window, and out into the street came the lovely smell of roast goose. You see, it was New Year's Eve; that's what she was thinking about.

Over in a little corner between two houses — one of them jutted out rather more into the street than the other — there she crouched and huddled with her legs tucked under her; but she only got colder and colder. She didn't dare to go home, for she hadn't sold a match nor earned a single penny. Her father would beat her, and besides it was so cold at home. They had only the bare roof over their heads and the wind whistled through that although the worst cracks had been stopped up with rags and straw. Her hands were really quite numb with cold. Ah, but a little match — that would be a comfort. If only she dared pull

343

one out of the bunch, just one, strike it on the wall and warm her fingers! She pulled one out ... ritch! ... how it spirted and blazed! Such a clear warm flame, like a little candle, as she put her hand round it — yes, and what a curious light it was! The little girl fancied she was sitting in front of a big iron stove with shiny brass knobs and brass facings, with such a warm friendly fire burning ... why, whatever was that? She was just stretching out her toes, so as to warm them too, when — out went the flame, and the stove vanished. There she sat with a little stub of burnt-out match in her hand.

She struck another one. It burned up so brightly, and where the gleam fell on the wall this became transparent like gauze. She could see right into the room, where the table was laid with a glittering white cloth and with delicate china; and there, steaming deliciously, was the roast goose stuffed with prunes and apples. Then, what was even finer, the goose jumped off the dish and waddled along the floor with the carving knife and fork in its back. Right up to the poor little girl it came ... but then the match went out, and nothing could be seen but the massive cold wall.

She lighted another match. Now she was sitting under the loveliest Christmas tree; it was even bigger and prettier than the one she had seen through the glass-door at the rich merchant's at Christmas. Hundreds of candles were burning on the green branches, and gay-coloured prints, like the ones they hang in the shop-windows, looked down at her. The little girl reached up both her hands ... then the match went out; all the Christmas candles rose higher and higher, until now she could see they were·the shining stars. One of them rushed down the sky with a long fiery streak.

"That's somebody dying," said the little girl, for her dead Grannie, who was the only one who had been kind to her, had told her that a falling star shows that a soul is going up to God.

She struck yet another match on the wall. It gave a glow all around, and there in the midst of it stood her old grandmother, looking so very bright and gentle and loving.

"Oh, Grannie," cried the little girl, "do take me with you! I know you'll disappear as soon as the match goes out — just as the warm stove did, and the lovely roast goose, and the wonderful great Christmas tree".

And she quickly struck the rest of the matches in the bunch, for she did so want to keep her Grannie there. And the matches flared up so gloriously that it became brighter than broad daylight. Never had

Grannie looked so tall and beautiful. She took the little girl into her arms, and together they flew in joy and splendour, up, up, to where there was no cold, no hunger, no fear. They were with God.

But in the cold early morning huddled between the two houses, sat the little girl with rosy cheeks and a smile on her lips, frozen to death on the last night of the old year. The New Year dawned on the little dead body leaning there with the matches, one lot of them nearly all used up.

"She was trying to get warm," people said. Nobody knew what lovely things she had seen and in what glory she had gone with her old Grannie to the happiness of the New Year.

The Thistle

Elisabeth Klein

Long is the way to Egypt. Far the holy family had to travel on their flight to Egypt. For many months they were on the way and still King Herod sent pursuers after the child. Many were the dangers the holy family met, and always the Child had been miraculous saved.

Once when Mary looked back with worried eyes she saw a little cloud of dust moving forward quickly, and soon helmets and flowing capes could be seen. Broad fields lay beside the road, and beyond were three little houses but no protecting woods. Where could Mary and Joseph hide themselves quickly? The soldiers would surely search the houses first. The horsemen were already approaching fast and it was time to act quickly.

Beside the road lay a large field with many flowers, which were cultivated for seed. Hastily Mary dismounted from the donkey. She took the sleeping child in her arms and ran out a little way into the field and hid the child there among the flowers. Even though she was in such a hurry she still found time for a short prayer. "Lord in heaven and you flowers of the earth protect and guard the child."

Meantime Joseph had mounted the steps of the house. The door stood open. The fire on the hearth was burning and soup was cooking. Plates were on the table. But there was no one to be seen. The inhabitants of the house were working in a distant field.

Now Mary came in and with beating heart stood by the hearth and began to stir the soup, while Joseph sat at the table and began to carve a piece of wood which he had found half finished on the low shelf.

In their haste they had not been able to bring the donkey into the stable. He was peacefully cropping the grass in the field in front of the house.

Soon the sound of horses' hooves could be heard.

346

"Here is the donkey!" a harsh voice called. "They'll be hiding in this house. This time they won't escape us."

Quick footsteps sounded and the soldiers entered.

"Where have you hidden the couple with the child who have just arrived on the donkey in front of your house?" the leader of the group demanded. When Mary did not answer he shook her shoulder roughly. Never, not even in her greatest need, did a lie pass over Mary's lips.

"We are the only people in the house," she answered softly.

"You're lying," barked the leader, "What's the donkey doing then in front of the house?"

"He's our donkey," answered Mary truthfully. "He's just feeding out there in the field."

The soldiers searched the house from top to bottom with much noise and swearing, but of course they found nobody else. They were hoping for the great reward which King Herod had promised for the capture of the family.

They soon searched the other two houses as well. There the soldiers asked about the number living in each house. But they learned nothing new, for in the house in which Mary and Joseph had sought refuge there really lived just one couple.

The soldiers were at their wits' end.

"There's something strange about that donkey," said one of them. "They could have hidden the child in the field and fled themselves. It's our duty to have a look."

The leader had already reached out his hand to look under the flowers. But he quickly withdrew it with a cry of pain.

"Oh, the stuff there has got sharp thorns," he said annoyed.

"Don't let's waste any more time," said the second. "No child can be hidden under these prickly plants."

"Didn't I say so already," said a third. "I saw the two of them in that other direction. Let's get after them quickly. It's still not too late."

Mary and Joseph heard with joy the hoof-beats of the horsemen charging off.

They went out of the house, and saw what had happened. God had heard Mary's prayer. He had transformed the soft flowers into prickly thistles. The flowers had kept their shape but they had become hard and thorny and so the child had been saved.

But when Mary went to get the child the flowers made way reverently and she could pick up her child who was lying among the flowers sleeping peacefully.

Ever since that day there have been thistles.

But the little donkey who had been eating the flowers in the beginning had taken part in the miracle. For it just went on eating happily when they were transformed into thistles. Indeed it seemed to him that he had never tasted anything better than the prickly flowers. In memory of that moment thistles are still the favourite food of donkeys.

New Year's Eve

Dan Lindholm

It was the last day of the year. The snow lay deep over everything. A little boy was walking along. He was wearing new shoes, a grey scarf and a red cap with a tassel. His name was Hans. On his back he carried a little knapsack with a Christmas cake and a Three Kings' candle which his mother had packed in it. She had given him plenty of good admonition, for he was to visit his grandmother and grandfather; he was not to forget to greet them properly and to wish them a Good New Year with blessings. Yes he was going to do that all right.

The winter days were short. Snow clouds hung in the air. Soon the snow-flakes were falling, silent and thick, like the down from a feather bed. When Hans had gone a little way it occurred to him that he could follow a short-cut through the forest. The snow was falling thicker and thicker, and soon it began to grow dark between the trees. Before Hans knew night was upon him and the snow had obliterated the path completely.

If only he had had some matches with him, he would have lit the candle, so that he could follow his own footsteps back to the road. As it was he could think of nothing better than to sit down under a tree and to wait till the stars or the moon should come out.

How long he had been sitting there only the darkness knew. He was almost completely snowed up when suddenly he saw a light in the distance. He pulled himself together and went towards the light, and soon he was standing by a fire. Never had he seen one that was burning so brightly. Round the fire twelve tall men in white cloaks were sitting, silent and solemn, gazing into the fire. They rather looked like kings. Some of them had crowns of ice on their heads, others wreathes of fir-cones, others had green branches, flowers or golden ears of corn on their brows. The one who seemed to be the oldest held a stick in his hand and was poking the fire. Slowly he turned his head. "Do you know us?" he asked.

"I think so," answered Hans, for he thought that he had the twelve months of the year in front of him. The oldest who was holding the stick was surely December; that is why he was wearing such a dark cloak.

"Then tell us," the old man encouraged him. And Hans said this verse as his grandfather had taught him.

> January sends the ice and frost
>> In the snow-drifts don't get lost.
>
> February's light is growing
>> Even though it still is snowing.
>
> March is bringing in the thaw
>> And the wind is cold and raw.
>
> April brings the rain and sun,
>> Sometimes both and sometimes one.
>
> May brings in the cuckoo's call
>> And the sun light over all.
>
> June is full of lovely posies
>> Fills the air with scent of roses.
>
> July is bountiful and good,
>> Cool and leafy is the wood.
>
> August bends down ears of corn,
>> Soon the fields will all be shorn.
>
> September gives the ripening apple
>> While the leaves begin to dapple.
>
> October makes the barn-yard full
>> Now the housewife spins her wool.
>
> November's storms set trees a-shaking
>> While indoors we're presents making.
>
> December's days are short and cold,
>> Advent candles gleam with gold.

The old man with the stick nodded his approval.

"Because you know us," he said, "we know you too. You have come at the right time, for tonight when the Old Year is finished we can really use your help. Do you see how small the fire has grown? Watch carefully what is going to happen when I pass the stick on to brother January. Slip under his cloak quickly and you will see how the New Year comes down from the stars. Then hasten and bring us a fresh light for our fire with your candle. For very soon the Old Year will pass away."

After the old man said that, the air resounded as if huge bells were ringing. The sound came from far and near and seemed to pass over all the countries and kingdoms of the earth. December stood up, lifted the stick and called out in a loud voice:

Now pass the staff from hand to hand
While bells do ring across the land.
May God who thrones in heaven high
Bless all that here on earth does lie.

While he was speaking Hans had crept under January's cloak which covered him like a great white mist. Up above the stars were shining and sparkling through it, down below all the seeds were stirring and a crowd of dainty little people came along with lanterns in their hands.

"Here we come with the New Year," they said, and as Hans watched, little faces peeped out from all the roots. It was as if the wee folk and elves were celebrating a wedding. Hans was so filled with astonishment that he almost forgot what he had been told to do. But then he noticed that the Three Kings' candle was already burning. One of the little men had lit it for him. Hans held his hand before the flame to protect it and came out from under the cloak. There was only a little glow from the fire of the Old Year. Now December handed his staff over to brother January, who took the light which Hans was holding in his hand and lit the fire with it.

The flames shot up high, the light became so strong, that Hans had to hold his hands before his eyes to protect them. When he came to himself again the fire and the twelve months were no longer there. The weather, however, had cleared and over the tree tops the moon stood round and full. Hans went on his way. In the moonlight it was easy to find his tracks back and there only a short way back stood his grandparents' house. In the darkness he had passed by the fence.

"A Happy New Year," said Hans in greeting as he passed through the doorway into the warm room. The old people had been wondering and were glad, for Grandfather had wanted to go out into the forest and look for Hans. Grandmother had warm milk and candy sugar on the stove, but Hans was so tired that he could hardly swallow it. Then Grandmother said it would be better if he went to bed.

"I think that the Christmas cake is still whole, but not the Three Kings' candle, for with it I fetched new fire for the twelve months," he murmured.

And straight away he fell fast asleep.

The Miraculous Corn

Nienke van Hichtum

The day was over and the road still stretched a long way forward into the distance. The donkey was flagging with his head hanging. Beside him, Joseph walked with heavy feet. Mary started out of a slight doze and pressed the Child under her cloak closer to her body. Then she cast her eyes forward a little. The shadows of night moved over the cold frozen earth. There was nowhere a village or a house to be seen. The trees of a wood in the distance were surrounded by a grey mist that was swirling already in long damp wisps over the plain.

Mary shivered.

It is going to be a cold night, she thought. Then she looked at Joseph and saw his weary tread. She saw too the resigned nodding of the donkey. They must be even more tired than I am, she thought. Again she looked into the distance. The mist was coming towards her like a silent calm sea.

"We'll have to rest, Joseph," she said.

The donkey heard her words and immediately stopped. He just turned his head to the woman on his back, then he let it hang again with drooping ears.

"Yes," said Joseph. "Rest. You must be tired."

"You too."

"I can still go on."

Joseph bent down and put a sack, which he had been carrying, carefully on the ground. Then like Mary he looked out across the country. "Rest, yes," he repeated softly. But the highway to Egypt went on into the darkness, empty and forsaken. How many more days? he thought, how many days? He was anxious for Mary and the Child.

"We had better go on a bit further," he said a little louder. "The night is going to get cold and damp. Already we have slept twice under the open sky. You and the Child won't stand another night like that."

"We shall have to put up with more than that," thought Mary, but she said nothing. The mist swept over them now and they shivered. In the distance they suddenly heard the cry of a wild animal. Joseph was startled. That must be a wolf. He looked at Mary with concern. Mary smiled tiredly back at him.

"Do not fear, Joseph, the Lord protects the Child. We are safe in his care."

Joseph nodded. "I know," he said softly. But he had to think of the trial which Simeon in the temple had prophesied, and of the pain that should cut through her heart concerning the Child.

He bent down again with difficulty, picked up the sack and laid it over his shoulder.

"Come, Greyling," he said.

But the donkey did not move and pricked up his ears now.

"He hears something, Joseph!"

Mary straightened herself up in the saddle. Again the tired smile spread over her lips.

The two of them listened carefully for a few moments. The chilly mist drifted over them but they did not notice it any more. All their attention was on a faint and regular clip, clap that came to them from the distance: clip, clap, clip, clip clap. They looked at each other.

"That is the sound of flails threshing," said Joseph.

"Where they are there will be people too," laughed Mary gratefully.

"And a roof!"

"Yes, a roof for the Child!"

"And for you!"

"And for you too!"

Once again Joseph urged the donkey on: "Come on Greyling!"

There was something melodious in his voice and the donkey started to move. In the distance the faint clapping of the flails could still be heard.

"A farm, Mary! A good lodging!"

Mary nodded and smiled at the Child, sleeping peacefully, wrapped in her cloak.

Again the wolf howled in the wood and the mist seeped clammily into their clothes. Quickly now they went on along the great long road.

"The sound is coming from the right, Joseph!" warned Mary after a while. Just then Joseph pointed to a side track that led away into the mist.

"That will lead us to the farm, Mary," he said cheerfully. "Come on Greyling, come on my boy, over there a well-earned rest awaits us."

Gratefully he looked at Mary. She was now sitting quietly on the donkey, with her eyes cast down, her face as white as a sheet.

"Mary," whispered Joseph softly, "Mary."

The clapping grew clearer. The donkey was now walking along the winding side-track quicker than he had ever done during the three days journey. Joseph patted him affectionately on the neck.

"Good animal, good boy!" he praised.

"Clip, clap, clip," went the flails enticingly in the distance. It was even clearer now. They were getting nearer. It seemed to Joseph as if they had now escaped all the dangers which threatened from the wicked King Herod. But he knew that that was really not the case.

"Clip, clap, clip, clip, clap, clip."

"We're getting nearer, Mary!"

"God is leading us, Joseph, for the sake of the Child."

"He shall not fear who puts his trust in him."

"No, he shall not fear."

Above the mist there rose up darkly against the night sky the roof of a barn or a house. Hens clucked softly. A chain rattled. A dog began to bark loudly.

"We've got there, Joseph."

Now they stood in front of the farmhouse. Joseph left the donkey standing and walked up to the door. Mary watched him in silence. She sat quite still in the dusk on the donkey. Her heart was beating peacefully. She was sure that this would be a good night. Joseph knocked at the door.

No one came. A late bird flew past between Joseph and Mary. They could hear the whirr of its wings. Then it disappeared.

Joseph knocked again, louder this time.

A woman appeared in the doorway. Her old dim eyes peered at him suspiciously. The dog in his kennel barked angrily. She made him be quiet. Then she greeted the strangers and asked what they wanted and where they came from. Joseph answered that they came from Bethlehem and were on the way to the Land of Egypt, he and the two on the donkey; his wife and the Child. The woman clapped her hands in astonishment at the length of the journey. Then she went in quickly to call her husband.

The farmer came and stared at the travellers for some moments in silence.

"You come from Bethlehem?" he asked finally.

"Yes," said Joseph.

"And you're going all the way to the Land of Egypt?"

"Yes, friend. This is our third day. Two nights already we have slept under the open sky. I am afraid for my wife and child if that should happen again. The nights are cold and the chill of the mist pierces right to the bones. Please let us spend the night in your barn."

"You are welcome," answered the farmer. "This is a difficult time to be travelling. Come in."

"We are very grateful to you." said Joseph.

He helped Mary and the Child down from the donkey who was then led away by a farm-hand to the stable. Everyone went into the house. In the room a fire was burning.

They ate together. Then Joseph was shown the best seat by the fire while the farmer's wife took the exhausted Mary and the Child to the room where they could sleep.

"We are very grateful to you, good friend," said Joseph to the farmer, while he held out his hands to the fire. "I should like to pay you."

He thought of the sack which he had been carrying, in which he kept the gifts from the three wise men from the East. Those gifts were worth a lot. On this journey they would assure Joseph that he would not have to beg for anything for Mary and the Child.

But the farmer refused all payment. He said: "We shall treat you as we should like to be treated ourselves if our lot made us go on a journey through strange parts."

"Then God will reward your hospitality," said Joseph.

The farmer bowed his head at this blessing. After that they sat for a while in silence staring into the fire.

"Your wife looks very tired," the old farmer began to say, "You should let her have a day's rest and stay here two nights."

Joseph considered this.

"She is indeed very tired," he admitted. "The days were hard. We were in a hurry to get on. And the nights in the open fields do not bring enough rest."

"So you'll stay another day."

"I'm very sorry. Two more mouths to feed, that all counts in this difficult time."

The farmer laughed. "Where there is food for six there's food for eight. And the child has the precious food of his mother."

Again they sat for a considerable time in silence together. The wife came and sat with them. The farmer threw some more logs on to the fire and the flames greedily licked at them; yellow tongues shot crackling up into the chimney. Joseph asked the farmer how his winter corn was doing.

The farmer looked at him in astonishment and asked if he had not seen it. "Stranger, you came straight through my fields. Did you not see any corn?"

Joseph shook his head. "The mist lay over everything," he said, "and night came on too early. We didn't see your fields. We had it hard enough to keep to the road. We were following the sound of your flails. Otherwise we should not have taken this side-road and should not have found your house. Do not take it amiss that we did not notice your corn."

The farmer looked at Joseph for a long time. It seemed as if a shadow crossed his face. Then his expression cleared again. He laughed softly and sympathetically.

"There's no need to excuse yourself, stranger," he said. "You could *not* have seen our corn. For the seed which we sowed was blighted. It never sprouted. Your way took you through bare fields. It threatens to be a bad harvest next year."

"And you're feeding us all the same?" demurred Joseph.

The farmer shrugged his shoulders.

"We give as long as we live," he said simply.

Joseph was troubled and exclaimed. "We must not abuse your kindness," he said. "Tomorrow we must continue our journey. God will give us strength and guidance."

"You mean to continue along the high road?" asked the farmer.

"Yes, tomorrow," said Joseph decidedly.

The farmer shook his head. "Then you are making a mistake," he admonished Joseph. Joseph looked at him questioningly.

"You can take the high road in the summer," the farmer explained, "but in winter it won't do. The high road dips down into a deep valley which is flooded over in winter."

"Yes," the farmer's wife agreed, "In winter the high road is impassable. Then you have to take this by-way."

"Does this by-way also go to Egypt?" asked Joseph, doubtfully.

"To be sure," affirmed his host. "This is the only way that can be used in winter."

Joseph murmured thoughtfully. He looked into the fire for a long time. Anxiety crossed his face. At last he turned his head towards the farmer. "Do you think that King Herod's soldiers know that?" he asked.

Again the farmer shrugged his shoulders. "Perhaps they do, and perhaps they don't," he answered slowly. "Here in winter we hardly ever see anyone from Herod's army."

It seemed that he wanted to say something more, but he hesitated. His gaze went over Joseph's figure searchingly. Then he looked straight ahead and the stillness returned. The farmer's wife looked anxious.

"Sometimes soldiers do come this way. They guard the frontier." She said after a pause. "But stranger, why do you ask about them?"

Joseph nodded. "I was expecting that question," he said, "and because of your hospitality you have a right to an answer. I asked about Herod's soldiers because the King has been sending out after the child which has now found rest in your house. Herod does not want the child to live."

The farmer sprang up in consternation, and his wife gave a smothered cry.

"Stranger!"

The farmer laid his hand heavily on Joseph's shoulder. There was fear in his gaze.

"Stranger, are you bringing misfortune over our house?"

Joseph shook his head and smiled.

"Have no fear, my friends," he said. "I bring you good fortune. This child ... In time you will know all. There was a singing of angels when he was born. In the East wise men saw his star in the heavens. They followed it and they found him and greeted him as a king. Glory to God in the highest sang the angels' voices, peace on earth for men of good will."

"Is he a royal child?" asked the wife, much moved.

"To be sure," answered Joseph.

"A king of peace?" asked the farmer.

"To be sure," answered joseph.

"He had such a peaceful lovely little face," said the farmer's wife.

"I cannot remember ever having seen a child who made me feel so happy," said the farmer almost in a whisper.

"The donkey bowed when the woman came in with the child." said the farmer's wife. "I'm quite positive that I saw it."

"Great things are happening," said the farmer, staring into the fire, "Great things. Glory to God in the Highest."

After a while they stood up to get ready for the night.

"Tomorrow," said Joseph, "we shall go on our way. Now you understand why we may not stay here any longer."

The next day the sun rose over the Land of Palestine. The sky was a cloudless blue. The frost on the fields glistened in the early morning sun. The farmer brought the donkey. Joseph helped Mary with the Child on to it. All the people of the farm stood by. The farmer pointed out the land round about to Joseph. The fields lay hard and bare.

"It's a disaster," he said sorrowfully, "a disaster."

Then he mastered himself and bade them a hearty farewell.

Mary pressed the Child to her breast. "God bless you for your hospitality, friends," she said. "We thank you, and for the Child."

"The peace of God be with you," came the answer.

Then the people stepped back.

Finally Joseph spoke to the farmer. "Your fields," he said, "I am sorry about your fields. Have you any seed left of the winter corn?"

The farmer nodded. "Yes, we have, but God has blighted it. It is no good for sowing, stranger."

"It *is* good for sowing, friend! Sow it, sow it!"

There was such a warm, firm sound to Joseph's voice and on his face such a wonderful smile, while the woman on the donkey sat so holy and still, that all the people were moved.

"Sow it!" said Joseph once more. "Sow it this very morning. Sow it from the highway to your house. Sow it from your house to the wood, sow it from field to field, sow it on all the paths and borders, sow it on the byways, everywhere, and speedily! Go quickly to work! At noon today, when the sun stands at its highest you shall understand why I say this. Have thanks and farewell, good friends"

"Go on Greyling," said Joseph, and the donkey started off.

"Farewell, good strangers," they heard the farmer call after them. "We shall do what you say. Peace be with you in the land of Egypt."

They sowed the corn that very morning. Many hands scattered the seed. They sowed it from field to field, from the highway to their house, from their house to the wood, everywhere they sowed it, on all the paths and borders, also on the farm-road, as they had been told.

And the miracle happened. After their footsteps the green sprouts shot up: the fields clothed themselves after their footsteps. Life sprang from the dead bareness, everywhere, everywhere. And when the sun had risen to its highest at noon, the farmer's winter corn stood higher and more luxuriantly than any other in all the countryside: a green expanse lay full of promise around the hospitable dwelling which had housed the Child.

Then in the afternoon along the great highway came the soldiers of wicked Herod. They were hunting the Child like wolves after their prey. There were frontier guards there who knew these parts well. They were hard on the heels of the refugees, that they knew. Only a little time and they would find the Child. King Herod's reward should fill their sacks.

They stopped by the spot where shortly before the side-road had been.

"We must turn off to the right here," one of them told the captain, who laughed out loud at him.

"Straight through the corn, you dog's foot?" he asked jeeringly

"Yes sir, that's where they will have gone. This is where the winter road to Egypt branched off. I know it with certainty."

"Straight through the corn, you dog's foot? Is that where you think they've gone? Straight through the corn, right up to the farmer's house? To be set on by the dogs? What farmer allows anyone to trample through his standing corn? Not one. Don't you know that, you town-pig? And have they left any tracks? Do you see any? Do I see any? Forward men, keep on the highway. We'll soon catch this booty. King Herod will soon reward us. Forward men!"

The sun shone on the waving corn. Was there a secret softly whispering in the fresh young shoots? The winter-corn waved. The farmhouse lay in the midst of it. The winter-corn waved from the highway to the wood. On the other side of the wood a small path led on through the wide land towards the distant Land of Egypt. That afternoon there were fresh prints of donkey's hooves and those of a man.

The Three Gifts

Jane T. Clement

Joseph woke sharply. He lay in the dark, staring, wide-eyed, out of the cave entrance to where in the night sky a shimmering seemed to fade and vanish among the stars; the thudding of his heart slowly quieted and the roaring in his ears died away. He listened. He could hear the slow breath of Mary and the little murmurs of the Child, on the pallet in the sheltered corner beyond the workbench. Then fear and the memory of this second visitation forced him to his knees on his own heap of straw, and to his feet, and he slipped quietly out into the yard. There by the door was the bench where Mary would sit with her Babe on her knees in the soft winter sun, and there he sank, and buried his face in his hands.

So now, here it was again, the hand of God, laid on him, Joseph, poor carpenter, who, past his first youth, had chosen a simple maid for wife, because the purity and kindness of her face, the clearness of her eyes, had spoken to his heart — and then had come task so great he still had named it to no one. Not even to Mary had he told the visitation of the Angel — nor the words so awesome they filled his soul with terrible trembling.

He had only said to her, "When your son is born, His name will be Jesus." And she had looked at him with gratitude but made no answer. So he had served her, protected her, yearned over her, feared for her. And now the Child was here, so lovely and quiet, so filled with life he feared to touch him with his rough finger or take him on his arm.

Then had come the wonder of the bright star; the golden voices in the dazzling night he would have thought had been a dream if the shepherds had not come seeking, and bringing little gifts, and smiling at the Baby with tears on their dusty cheeks, full of holy joy at the Child so new, so unspotted and fresh from God.

And near the khan in this peaceful cave he had decided they would stay, where he had made things more comfortable, and had begun to make a foothold as carpenter in this, David's city. He had hired out by the day, brought home work to do, while Mary regained strength and the Child grew, and the day of Purification drew near. So they had gone up to Jerusalem.

Then there had come another wonder, for among all the multitude in the Temple court there had been one, an old rabbi trembling and frail, who had started up with joy when they drew near, and with a light about his face had stretched out his arms for the Child, uttering praise and blessings, while the Child smiled into his eyes. And the old man had spoken words he, Joseph, could not comprehend: "a light to the Gentiles," "the salvation of God," "this Child is set for the rising and falling of many in Israel." And Mary, white-faced, stood listening with her hands on her heart, until the old man gave her back the Child and blessed them. And at that instant came the aged woman, who also sprang forward with a cry, as if she knew all, and the longing of her heart was now answered. And she, too, blessed them in a loud voice, and uttered praise, and declared to all that redemption had come. Then they had gone wordlessly home.

And then this third wonder, just this past night, the coming of the Three. Never, never would he forget the sight — how at the stir in the yard he had gone to the cave door, and there had seen, in the glimmering star-light, three great white shapes folding themselves down on their haunches, three camels, three attendants at their heads, and three robed figures stepping down and standing, hesitant, before the door. And then the tallest had come forward and had spoken. "We have come to worship him, who was born King over Israel. We have followed his star and surely he lies within."

Then Joseph had moved aside and the three had entered. Mary rested by the low stone manger where the Child lay. Above her a tiny oil lamp stood in a niche in the wall, throwing a flickering light upon their faces, but there was a golden shimmer in the room, and a sweet fragrance. Their donkey tipped his big ears forward as the three came in, and the light caught their jewels. The rustle of their garments as they knelt was like the rustle of a great wind; their dark eyes were filled with wonder and with joy, though weariness lay upon their faces.

And then the first had laid a small bronze coffer on the earthen floor before the manger. "Myrrh, in praise to the one God of Gods." And then the second had set beside it a small faience vial, sea-blue and scarlet, with a golden stopper. "Frankincense, in praise of God Most High." And the third, the tallest, stooped and laid beside the other gifts the last one, a bag of golden mesh, through which gleamed golden coins. "Gold, in praise of the Lord of Hosts." Then Mary, tears on her face, bent over the manger and lifted the Child; she set him on her lap, where all could see, and he slept untroubled while the three gazed and gazed, even as had the simple shepherds. Then at last they had roused and raised themselves and bowed, and with a last look had turned and left. And out in the courtyard they had mounted, and the three great shapes heaved themselves up, and with stately tread went away in the night.

And Joseph had gone inside. Mary was busy with the Child, but he had stared for a long time at the glittering gifts before he dared to touch them. Then he had placed them one by one in the leather sack where he kept his tools, wrapping them first carefully in strips of old leather. And then he had pinched out the lamp, and he had at length drifted into fitful sleep.

And then the dream — clearer than waking, clearer than the brightest day. The voice, not of this earth, speaking to him, to Joseph, and to none other. "Rise, take the Child and his mother, and flee to Egypt, and there remain until I tell you; for Herod is about to search for the Child, to destroy him."

At last Joseph in the dark before the cave leapt to his feet. What God had declared to him, that he must do. What the end would be — that was hidden, not for his eyes. He could only do this next thing, weak as he was. And they must go now, before the dawn, before the khan awoke and the courtyard was astir. Even now he feared a faint lightening in the east. He went inside swiftly, and in the starlight stooped over Mary. At his touch upon her shoulder she instantly awoke. With few words he told her what they must do, and unquestioning she rose to gather together the things they might need, and to prepare the Babe. Joseph fed the donkey and led him out before the door; over his back he strapped the pallet and hung the saddlebag. He helped Mary to mount and laid the Child in her arms. Last, at his own side he hung his leather sack.

She looked at it and asked, "Is it not too heavy?"

"The gifts. And I need my tools."

A faint smile came over her face. "Our trust must be in God, not in gold. We are in his hand," she said.

Then they moved off before the coming dawn.

II

Joseph had chosen the ancient road to Hebron of his forefathers, then into the more level desert of Beer-sheba. The swifter and more traveled highway near the coast he had feared, feeling Herod's men would hunt there first. Once across the desert he went up to the sea road, for he would be out of Herod's realm by then, beyond the reach of his men.

Now, on the twelfth day, they came into Raphia as evening drew on. From the blazing sun and the cheerless sand they had glimpsed from afar the ancient palms and the white roofs of the town, and in the westering light a cool wind had come from the distant sea. Mary's face had lifted; she had thrown back her head-covering and uncovered the Child's face. The donkey's steps quickened. Joseph's breath had come more easily, and the little knot of fear about his heart slowly eased as they passed into the town. The strange faces, the strange streets did not trouble him. Not many glances fell on them, as travelers were a common sight. On through the town they went, until at length the huddled houses thinned a bit, the winding street widened, and they came to the last well. It lay in a grove of palms, and near it sat an old man leaning against a tree. For utter weariness Joseph stood still, and the donkey with a great sigh stopped, and Mary slid from his back. The breeze had freshened, and the shadows were falling. Joseph went forward to the well, carrying their water jar. He paused near the old man, who turned his head to Joseph. Then Joseph saw he was quite blind, his old eyes filmed over. But his face smiled.

"Peace, father," said Joseph. "We are travelers, and seek water here, and rest for the night." He watched the old man to see if he could hear and understand. The old face smiled still more, the wrinkled hands gestured in the air.

"Welcome, my son. The water is the Lord's and he gives it to all men." He kept his face turned to them then, as Joseph leaned on the stone well rim and let down the skin bucket and hauled it up, first filling the stone trough for the tired and thirsty beast, and then filling their jar and holding it for Mary. The water was cool and sweet. At the sound of the bucket dropping into the well a second time the old man spoke again.

"Where do you journey?"

Joseph did not answer, but stood wordless, pondering. And while he waited, wondering what to say, the Child began to cry, a small, clear little cry. Then the old man turned his face to Mary, and slowly over it came a glow as if the sinking sun shone on it, and he held out his hands.

"You journey down to Egypt, surely," he said softly. "And on this night my poor house is blessed to shelter you. I am a swineherd and my house is shunned by many. But God has been merciful to me." And trembling in his ancient haste, he dragged himself up and seized his staff.

"Yonder —" he pointed his staff through the trees, "you will be welcomed by my son who brings home a wife in two days' time — a fair and pure little maiden — and he has made the house ready." He went on as he hobbled before them through the trees. "And the neighbours, the kind-hearted ones, brought anise cake and wine, melons and dates —"

After one look at Mary, Joseph unquestioning led the donkey after the old man, who still talked on, breathless and full of joy. They came to the edge of the tall palms and found the house, white and low, with a small court and a bake oven near the door. The old man thumped his staff on the ground as he hurried on a young man leapt to the door. He had a thin brown face and dark anxious eyes. He came out at once at his father's call.

"Wayfarers, my son, who seek the night's lodging with us."

Then the young swineherd turned to Joseph and said with dignity, "You are welcome to all we have, such as it is." He turned to Mary. "And you will find no other womenfolk here — not for two days' time. But then," and a little smile lit his somber face for an instant, "then a woman will again tend the hearth my mother loved. Come, go ye in. And we will care for the beast and prepare supper while you rest yourself."

So Mary passed through the door into the cool, bare room. She stood and looked around. Her eyes took in the neat pile of pallets in the corner, the kneading bowl, scrubbed clean, on the ledge of a few clay dishes, a cooking pot; and in the corner a small carved chest. By it leaned a corn broom. And in a niche in the wall there was a clay lamp. Two water jars stood by the door. The room was spotless, empty, expectant. She smiled, thinking of the hurry and bustle to come, the modest feasting, the young bride so soon to bring the room to life, to give joy to the days of the old swineherd and his son. And then she busied herself with the Child. She heard the old swineherd outside. "Bring melons and bread from the storeroom, my son. This night we are blessed of God." And she heard Joseph murmur, "Keep it for the wedding feast," and the young man firmly, "Nay, it will be richer for having fed the travellers in God. She who is my betrothed would joyfully welcome you. Share our feast now. The Lord has given it."

Then Joseph stood in the door. He looked at her and his eyes came at last to the Child. His tired face softened.

"Indeed God cares for us," he whispered.

In the early light the donkey stood before the door. The old swineherd leaned upon his staff, his face sad now that they would go. Joseph slung the pallet over the beast's back. He fastened the saddlebag, and made ready for Mary to mount. But she stood and looked into his face. Then she spoke, "Joseph, there is a wedding at this house. And we have left no gift."

He stared at her. Then, "Take thou the Child," she whispered, and laid the swaddled Babe in his arms. She stooped to the ground where there lay Joseph's leather sack, and the water jar. With quick fingers she undid the thongs, and her hands searched inside. She pulled out a small bundle. Swiftly she unwrapped it, and in the early sunlight there glowed between her hands the vial of frankincense. A fragrance rose, faint and sweet. Then she turned to the door and went inside. The young swineherd was laying the last pallet away. He turned at her step and his eyes grew round with wonder. She set the vial on the ledge, where it gleamed blue and scarlet and gold in the shadows. Then she spoke to the young man,

"Frankincense, in praise of God — that in the holy joy of marriage we may glimpse the mystery of his Unity and his promise for all men."

And they rode out of Raphia, on the shoreward path. The white dunes rippled in the sun, and the sapphire sea glistened beyond. White gulls dipped and flew and circled around them, calling, and the wind was cool. There was purity everywhere. And the leather sack hung lighter at Joseph's side.

III

Tanis — alien city, yet strangely home. For had not these bricks, generations ago, perhaps the very bricks of this small house, been shaped and set by their forefathers — in bondage, enslaved, under false gods? Yet now here they sought asylum, here they were safe from the new tyrant, here they kept the promise sent from God, the little Flame that would light the whole world.

Here too they had found welcome, a hand held out to them, bread for their need, and the voices of friends — nay, more than friends.

When they had come into the city, those weeks ago, and had stood in the crowded market, amid the strange smells, the foreign cries, the strange wares — for the very fruits were new — a tall, dark man with skull cap and forelocks came up to them quietly and greeted them with the accents of home. In the name of the Lord he had asked them if they would accept his shelter, and had led them out of the noise and hustle, through narrow ways, to the tiny, ancient Jewish quarter.

There, in Simon the Potter's house, they were given a small room off the court, and there Joseph went out to his trade, finding work now and then — not much, but enough to bring a bit home to pay for their bread. Simon had a slim, dark-eyed wife, Rachel, and one small pale child, little Benjamin, with eyes like brown stars and long lashes. Benjamin loved Mary, but most of all he loved the Child. He would sit by his cot hour after hour, waiting for him to stir and wake, and stand entranced, scarcely breathing, when the Child woke and clutched Benjamin's slender finger in his tiny fist. Rachel would pause in the doorway to gaze at her own child, her small face careworn yet aglow with love. Or she would stop her work at the handmill to watch the Child kicking on a pallet in the cool courtyard, while Benjamin dangled a small green bough above him, laughing. Then she would say to Mary, "What life he brings us, and what joy. Blessed the day Simon brought you home." Or she would say, "Benjamin has been too much alone. That is why he thrives so slowly." But her face would shadow and grow pinched.

Sometimes in the evening, when the whir of Simon's wheel was still and the shutters of the shop were closed, they would all sit in the courtyard and watch the faint stars grow closer, brighter, until they seemed just above the rooftops to be plucked. And they would talk, not much nor many words from Joseph. But heart spoke to heart. And Mary, with the Babe on her lap, would speak with longing of the land that they had left, the land of her childhood.

"When we return, I will show him the Sea of Tiberias all asparkle in the sun — and let him watch the shining fishes in the nets the fishermen draw up upon the shore — and show him the heron wading in the shallows. And I shall pick him scarlet anemones — all his hands can hold." And Rachel would droop her head over her frail little son who lay asleep on her knees, listening to his shallow breathing, and her fingers would stroke his hot little brow, and the tears would glisten on her cheeks. Joseph, sitting in the deep shadows, would watch and listen. He was waiting for he knew not what, a sign from God, a word that would come.

So the days passed, and the weeks. As the Baby throve and grew strong, so little Benjamin faded. Fever glowed upon his cheeks, and his breath came short. He went now only from his own small cot to lie with his small face propped upon his hands beside the Child's pallet, his eyes shining with joy as he gazed and gazed at the small one, who smiled and smiled upon him in return. And Mary, a helpless aching in her heart, felt a wordless mystery between the two. She watched in awe. Joseph, coming home, would stand in the door, watching also, silent, his eyes shadowed and sad, yet a strange joy within him, as at a secret promise soon to be revealed.

Then there came a day when Benjamin lay flushed upon his cot and could not rise. His lashes lay dark upon his cheeks. His little hands were still but his heart beat like a small wild bird. Rachel was past tears. Upon her knees she bathed and tended him but her face was like a mask, nor could she speak. Mary, at her side, gave all the aid she could, and as night fell, together the two women watched as the little life flickered on.

Joseph, in their room off the courtyard, slept fitfully. The night was very still, the stars hanging low and brilliant. Before the dawn there came a faint stirring of the wind, a fragrance carried on the air, a golden shimmering — and Joseph woke, his heart pounding. Again the voice — again the summons not to be withstood. "Rise, take the Child, and go to the Land of Israel. For those who sought the Child's life are dead." He waited until his heart slowed, then obediently he rose and stood in the dimness, his mind already busy with what they must do. He heard the quiet breathing of the Babe — and then a small, stifled outcry from the farther room. Ah — Benjamin! Why must they leave now. He went with haste across the court and stood on the threshold of the farther room. As he paused, his hands gripping the door frame, he saw in the flickering lamplight the two figures of Mary and the mother, bending over the small face bathed in sweat and deathly pale — and as he looked the great eyes opened for the last time, the white lips smiled, and the watchers heard faint but clear and joyful the one word "Jesus." Then the eyes closed and the last breath faded, and a stillness lay upon them all.

At noon the donkey stood tethered beyond the courtyard, by the house door in the narrow street. Marty, within, with tear-stained face, packed their last belongings. Beyond, beside the small bier in the farther room, could be heard the lamentations of the women. Joseph took down his leather sack from a peg upon the wall and began to gather up his tools. His heart felt numb. He only knew he was in the grip of something so great he must only stand before it helpless and unquestioning, taking the next step, laying his hand to the next task.

Then Mary's small hand lay upon his own, as he began to fasten the leather thong upon the sack, and she looked at him. "The myrrh." she whispered, "Fetch me out the gift of myrrh." He stared at her a moment. The frankincense and now the myrrh! But at the look upon her face he did not hesitate. His hands undid the sack again, and his fingers sought the small square bundle. He laid it on the floor and unwrapped it carefully. The dull rich gleam of copper met their eyes; the small coffer was embossed with a row of little fishes leaping around the rim, and the latch was shaped like a star. Mary took it gently in both hands, then turned and went swiftly from the room, across the court, and into the room of mourning, where a silence fell at her step. The lamentations ceased, all heads were lifted, and, behind her in the doorway. Joseph heard her speak.

"Rachel, beloved sister, I give thee this gift for the anointing of thy child. For know that this day he truly lives. For a promise is now given us from God that death can rule no more but must go down to everlasting defeat, and the day of the Lord shall dawn upon the earth, even as it has already dawned in heaven. Then shall we all truly live, and all sorrowing shall pass away."

Then she knelt and laid the coffer in the trembling hands of the mother, and kissed her once upon the brow. Turning, she went past Joseph with resolute face, and gathered up the Child where he slept. Without words they laid the last things upon the donkey, and Joseph helped her mount. Then they made their way through the narrow lanes and at last set their feet upon the road to El Qantara, the crossing that would take them to the highway leading them back to Israel. And in Joseph's sack were now only his tools, besides the mesh bag of golden coins.

IV

Along the dusty highway, in the morning light, went many travelers, some from Esh Shan, from Aleppo in the far north, come down the sea road to trade in slaves, to carry spice and amber down into Egypt, to barter purple dye for ivory and peacock plumes. Some traveled from the south, with gems and gold, with cotton spun like gossamer. Some went in chains, whipped if they stumbled. Others went in litters borne of the soulders of enormous bondsmen richly clad. A wagon rumbled by, laden with wineskins. And weary donkeys trod the dust, heads down, ears forward, eyes half-closed. Out of Gaza, lying just behind, or into Gaza, lying just ahead, unending lines of wayfarers met and passed. The ancient ruined temple beside the road gave scant shade, as the sun already blazed with a foretaste of noon. Going north, to the right lay the desert brown and parched; to the left dunes and a hint of sea beyond — somehow a stir in the air, a sparkle, half mirage, half reality.

Joseph walked beside the donkey's head. His face was brown from the sun, like an old leaf, lined with care. Mary's veil was drawn close, and the Child well covered from the dust. He slept untroubled and in peace. So they came to the city gates and passed within, where the clamour hit them like a blow, and the alien air swept over them so strong that Joseph's hand tightened on the donkey's lead; the little group stopped, and with indrawn breath Joseph waited, watched, and at length drew off to the left, where a narrow street seemed more quiet. There was no friendly face, no Simon to come up to them and ask them home. Tall, harsh-featured men brushed by; there was a stench of old fish, sweat, rotted vegetables, uncleanliness. Joseph led them on till the way widened, small shops appeared, and an old, neglected khan stood at a corner, its courtyard emptied of the night's trade, but still unswept. A half-grown boy shoveled at the piles of dung, and an old woman stood beside the wall feebly shaking the straw and dust from a worn pallet. Joseph stopped, and Mary pushed aside her shawl. The woman ceased her shaking, and let the pallet slip from her old hands. She looked at them.

"We seek a place to rest from the noon's heat," said Joseph quietly. "Then we journey on."

She jerked her head over her shoulder toward the court. "All's fit to lie in is that first hole in the wall. You can rest there if you want, and have five coppers to pay for it."

"Water?" said Joseph. "Our jar is nearly empty."

"Slave market, next street. There you'll find a well. If you can stand the stink."

Out of the tail of his eye he saw Mary clutch the Child closer, and heard her sigh. His hand tightened on the halter, and he led the donkey in. The little room was dark and bare, but passably clean, and was sheltered from the noise and heat. He laid his cloak over the straw in the corner, then went out to take the Child from Mary's arms and help her down. She drooped from weariness and he was glad to see her stretch herself upon the straw and close her eyes, the Baby quiet at her side. He stood gazing down at them, his eyes dark with care, his mind heavy with dread and the question whether they yet were safe. Herod was dead. That much was sure. All men spoke of it, but also of Herod's son — and with the same fear and forboding. Like father, like son, they muttered, and shook their heads darkly. Would this new ruler, Archelaus, not also seek out the Child, to slay him? So they had slipped through Raphia, not daring to stop where they had stopped before, and spent the night at Yunis; and there again this past night the voice had come, warning that they must not return to Bethlehem, but must journey farther on.

So now Joseph stood and gazed at Marty and the sleeping Babe, and the worry gnawed at him again. They could return to Nazareth, he told himself. There they were not strangers, and there he could set up his shop. His mind eased a bit, and already he felt hungry for a sight of the Galilean hills, the peaceful valleys green and cool. He was weary to the bone. There he could rest. And he still had the gold. With that he could without trouble even build a little house, and buy more tools and wood and start his trade in comfort and in peace. He sighed, and passed his hand across his brow. It would not be so hard after all, to start afresh.

Outside the door the patient donkey snuffled in the heat and stamped his hoof. Joseph remembered that they must have water, so he turned and slipped out, into the court, and then beyond, into the street. In the noonday dazzle he stopped, to get his bearings. The boy now sat upon the wall, and watched him idly. Joseph asked, "Which way to the well?" and the boy motioned with his scrubby finger to the left. With his empty water jar and his leather sack over his shoulder, Joseph went. It was not far, and then he came to a turning, and there the narrow way opened into a small square, in its center a large stone block, and beside it a well, with worn stone rim. The square was fairly empty, two or three tattered tents set up where clusters of humanity sprawled in the shade; an urchin or two loitered at the well rim, and a mongrel dozed beside the block. The stink of human filth and degradation hit him like a wave, and he stopped in his tracks. Even as he stood, wondering if he would have courage to draw from that well, from the dark street opposite emerged the figures of two men, one tall and dark and straight, the other short and fat, between them a laden donkey. They came slowly across the square to the well rim. Then Joseph saw the tall man, dark of skin, was chained at the wrists and at the ankles, so his steps were slow. The fat man, who wore a well-woven cloak bordered in blue and a loose head covering of white linen, untied a skin bucket from the donkey and leaned over the well, lowering it quickly and hauling it up slowly with grunts and curses. He held the bucket under the nose of the beast, who slobbered and drank in great gulps. Then the fat man drew the bucket away and said loudly, with a sneer to the slave, "Parched? Dying of thirst? Take that!" and he flung the dregs into the man's face. But the man stood unmoved, his eyes closed, while the drops of dirty water slid one by one down into his beard. Then he opened his eyes, and across the soiled cobbles and the shimmering heat his gaze met that of Joseph.

Their eyes met and held, and to Joseph, time seemed to stop. What he wrestled with he could not have said — but he fought and struggled in his heart, the blood thundered in his head, and for what seemed eternity he stood, rooted to the spot, a tempest in his breast. Then at last the tall Negro turned his face away and gazed into the dust; and Joseph came to himself and found his hands gripped tight upon his leather sack as if he could never loosen it, and underneath his fingers he could feel the gold. But he knew, as if the voice had spoken, what he must do.

He watched while the fat man led the donkey and the slave off beside the little huddle of tents, and began to drag out a shelter of sorts, to keep himself, at least, from the blazing sun and the night's chill, until market opened on the morrow. Then Joseph walked slowly across and stood there before the fat man, who stopped his puttering and looked up.

"How much?" said Joseph, quietly, nodding toward the slave.

"How much?" The fat man's voice was half amazed half mocking. "Why should the likes of you ask?"

"Perhaps I have the command of a great lord laid upon me to purchase a slave. How much?" said Joseph.

"This is no mere slave. A king's ransom alone will purchase him," jeered the man.

"How much?" persisted Joseph.

"I take him down into Egypt, to sell to the Pharaoh perhaps. He came from a slave ship out of the dark lands, where he was king. I got him in Tyre, with a fortune. Now who is your master, that he can purchase him?"

"How much?" said Joseph. "Tell me how much and I go to fetch the scribe."

"Fetch the scribe, fool," sneered the man. "Twenty gold denares alone will purchase him."

Joseph turned and went swiftly across the square to where the scribe's booth huddled against an ancient wall. Inside, a wizened little man dozed, pens and scrolls beside him. Joseph nudged him gently with his foot and he roused at once and looked up sleepily.

"Will you write a bill of sale for a slave, now, on the instant?"

The man shuffled to his feet and gathered up his gear. He followed at Joseph's heels, blinking in the sun, across the square, to where the fat man waited, dumbstruck. The slave still stood motionless and straight beside the donkey. The scribe squatted in the shade and arranged his little desk. He set out his ink horn, and then looked up, his stylus poised.

"Let me see your gold," hissed the fat man.

"Not till it is writ fair and clear, then you give me the man as I give you the gold."

Greed, doubt, bewilderment, all played across the face of the trader. But at last, "What's to lose!" he muttered, and began to dictate to the scribe, who wrote with care and flourishes, and held up two documents, and his pen, and pointed here, and here for them both to make their scrawl. Then, and only then, did Joseph with trembling fingers undo the thong of the leather sack, and fumbled inside for the mesh bag. This he drew out slowly and held it for an instant in his cupped fingers. Again the faraway night came back to him, the dim stable in the starlight, the great kings kneeling, the wonder and the awe, and the lovely Child sleeping while they gazed. Then he reached out for the document of purchase with one hand, and with the other he held out the gold. The breath hissed in the fat man's throat. His eyes bulged and his jaw fell.

"But — but — it is too much even," he stammered.

"It is to free the slaves of all the world," whispered Joseph. "Take it!"

For an instant a look of terror swept over the man; he trembled and went pale. Then he grabbed the gold.

"Go, go!" he muttered. "Take him. Go! Out of my sight!"

"The key," said Joseph.

The man fumbled wildly in his wallet and pulled out a copper key. Joseph seized it and knelt at the Negro's feet, unlocking his chains. Then he stood and unlocked the chains about his wrists. He flung key and chains into the dust.

"Come," he said to the freedman, laying his hand on his shoulder, and turning him toward the well. The man's unshackled feet moved slowly, then more freely, as Joseph guided him across the cobbles. At the well he lowered the bucket quickly, hauled it up, and poured the water into their water jar. This he held to the man's lips and his hands trembled a bit as the man drank deeply. Then he touched the man's shoulder again, and together they went across the square, into the narrow street. Joseph led him swiftly, not stopping at the khan where Mary lay, on to the gate of the city, out to the highway. There he stopped. He turned and faced the dark man.

"This road leads down to Egypt and beyond to your own lands, perhaps. In Raphia, stop at the swineherd's house on the far side. There you will find shelter in the Lord's name. In Tanis ask for Simon the Potter, in the Jewish quarter, and tell him Joseph ben Jacob sent you. He will give you aid. Here are tools, so you may earn your way." He undid his leather sack. "And my tunic." He undid his outer garment. He held out both to the man, whose eyes glistened with tears. Only then did Joseph wonder ... were his very words not strange, in a foreign tongue? But the man then suddenly clasped Joseph's outstretched hands, and spoke, truly in an alien tongue and yet Joseph knew them as if they were in his own, "Blessed be his name forever."

And Joseph cried out, "It is spoken by God."

Then the man turned quickly and went southward on the highway. And Joseph stood half-naked, empty handed, in the road, watching him. But such a joy flooded him he thought his heart would burst.

And Joseph answered, "For one who serves the Word of God, what need has he of gold or tools?"

And the travellers streamed by him eyeing him as if he were crazed. But he cared not. And finally he turned to go back to Mary and the Child and to Journey on to Nazereth.

The Little Lights Blown Out

Karl Paetow

Old, weathered and bent by the winds, a farm-house stood remote in the high mountains. There every year on the night of the Three Kings, which in that place was also called Berchta's Night, Frau Berchta herself passed by, and her little crickets accompanied her on her way. It was also the custom there, and it was done as an ancient duty, that the farmer's wife should set a table with food and drink on the sunken track along which the nocturnal procession took place. Then Frau Berchta would bless the gifts and the giver, taste the food and drink, and was then well-disposed towards the fields, the stock, and the whole family. But there was a strict law that no one should go out of the house on that evening to spy or to eavesdrop, so that Frau Berchta would not be disturbed by idle curiosity when she would partake of the refreshment.

On one of those special evenings after the farmer's wife had carefully set the table in the gorge and the moon was rising over the mountain forest, the youngest maid of the household was plagued with doubt and curiosity. So she stole out of the house and hid in a woodshed, and peered at the festive table on which the white noodles were still steaming. There she waited impatiently to see what would happen, moving from one foot to the other. But nothing happened. No hare sprang across the fields of snow, no bird perched in the iced-up branches of the birch-tree, which was bending over the table sparkling like a glass tree in the moonlight. The stillness of waiting began to lull her, and the girl no longer believed what the old folk had told her.

Finally there arose a gentle chirping and singing from the mountain forest like someone singing and the plucking of strings. Nearer and nearer, with tripping steps in the white snow, came the procession of the blessed crickets. At their head strode Frau Berchta herself, and round her the moonshine crystallized in splendour. The little ones hung around her and slipped beneath her flowing robe like chicks under the

374

hen's wings. Others were humming and singing to the zither and fiddle with silver voices. At the tail of the procession some of these children were tugging at a heavy plough that was sliding over the fields. The little ones were also carrying little jars filled with dew. Some of the dew slopped over and worked its way through the snow into the slumbering ground. Now Frau Berchta stopped in thought by the gift-table and said to one of these children: "I see two little lights. That is too many. Go and blow them out."

The maiden behind the wooden doors felt the cold breath on her eyebrows, and the moonshine went out. Like a black sack she felt darkness come over her. The lovely sounds were turned to wails and woe. In a fright she pushed the door open. But even out there she was caught in her lightlessness. The moon was dead. Weeping, she groped her way back to the farm and looked into the fireplace for the usual light of the fire. But the fire in the hearth only bit her skin and singed her eyebrows, for her sight was lost. Blind she was, and blinded she remained, and no spell was of any help to her.

There lived however an old spaewife on that farm. She belonged to the ancient world. At all hours she sat by the hearth, spun in the smoke and smelled the invisible. She had knowledge of ancient times, and she knew more of the change and course of things than ordinary folk. Sometimes as she was busy spinning she would stop her spinning-wheel, rub her withered hands on her lap, look as it were into the far distance and sigh with happy memories: "Ah, those were the days when Frau Berchta spun!" then her old eyes would shine as if the person named were present.

Now the maid who had formerly been so industrious had to sit and spin beside the old woman in the ingle-nook, breaking flax, hackling or doing such work as a blind person may. But she sat there stiff and stubborn beside the fire, for her young soul was frozen with bitter resentment. Thus she remained in her obduracy over the winter, and no word of comfort from the old woman could rouse her from her bitterness.

When at last spring burst forth from all the bushes, and the first bird-song came from the flower-garden, the young soul thawed out again, and the blind girl cried out in sudden joy: "Do you hear Old Mother, just listen how that bird is calling! What does it know? What does it want? Oh, whoever knows the language of animals what would he all hear?"

The spaewife smiled in her goodness and said, "I have long been waiting for this song. So now I will tell you from old lore what I have heard about that time when Frau Berchta worked her good fortune among men.''

She joined a new thread to the old one and told of the deeds of the Forest-woman, the Aunt of the Spinning-Room, the Mistress of the Rose Garden and The Mother of the Crickets. More and more new stories did the blind girl cajole from her and the maid's dark year was thus brightened until once again the twelve Holy Nights came. Already the house was fragrant from honey cakes and sweet spices; already the promise of the Child was spreading over the whole earth; already the sunken sun was preparing to be born again from the darkness of the solstice night. Often the maid would lie in her bed listening, thinking over all that the old woman had told her. She saw herself as in a mirror which had opened her inner eye to her. All these things she had felt and suffered as if they were her own self. And now as she lay listening in the night of nights she knew that fulfilment stood at hand.

So she lay and waited for the hour of grace. She was aware of a strange activity coming from the byre. She heard the bull scratching his horns on the crib. Then she heard clearly from his mouth as he chewed the cud the enigmatic words: "Do you know," asked the bull of the cow, "that Frau Berchta will forgive the blind maid?"

And the cow answered, "Do you know that Frau Berchta is going to remove the blindness from that maiden?"

"How is that going to be?" asked the bull in a muffled voice.

The cow answered, "It will come about as Frau Berchta will tell the spaewife."

This all happened to the lass as in a dream, and she could not move a limb, and the night was full of confused voices and dark wraiths. In the morning she told the spaewife what the animals had announced to her. Then the old woman said, "Last night I saw Frau Berchta travelling over the mountains. She looked like my dear mother who has died and she greeted me intimately and gave me a message that you should set the table in the ravine for her on Berchta's Eve and she will appear to you once again. One word supports the other and so it may well all come to be."

The sun sank on the twelfth night. The spaewife took the girl by the hand and staggered up to the path through the ravine with her. There under the birch-tree the young maiden set up the table, spread a white linen cloth over it, smoothed it down carefully and placed the dishes and jugs in their right places. From her groping hands the picture of the previous year rose up in her mind, and she remembered how when she looked upon the gifts her sight had been overcome by eternal night. Now her eyes became two living fountains, and the salt tears seeped into the white linen.

Then she heard a kind voice asking near her eyes:

> The moon that shines,
> Who weeps and whines?

"Oh," cried the maid, confessing her guilt, "I wanted to see Frau Berchta with my eyes, and that was against her command. I did not believe it, and I lost the moon, the sun and the light of everything."

Then Frau Berchta said, for it was she herself who had come again with her crickets: "That must be true. Last year I put out two eyes in this place and for them I lit two inner lights. So now have double sight, go hence and forget not the best!"

And she blew upon the maiden's dead eyes so that light blossomed forth again with all its stars. And all around her was like in the year before. The moon was shining too, and the table was laid under the sparkling birch-tree, but Frau Berchta with her crickets was long since away over the hills. From the distance it still sounded like singing and the harping of strings.

As the guilt now was wiped away and as the new light entered the extinguished eyes the lass became aware of the wonder and a great joy overcame her. For where those eyes had only seen the skin and the outside of the body, now it was as if she could see right into things as in amber or in rock crystal. And on that night she realized the ancient wisdom in all its depths:

> Who God would find
> Must to this world be blind.

The Three Kings Ride

A tale of many centuries

Ruth Sawyer

The Roman, Aelius Antoninus, had been a soldier, boy and man, all his life. He had known nothing else but fighting. He had served under Hadrian while he was praetor, and later when he was Emperor. At the end of his service he had been promoted to Senior Centurian and had been sent at last to that legionaries' camp city of Italica in Spain which was founded by the first Scipio Africanus. Here he lived comfortably. The baths were the best, the fighting in the arena as good as a Roman could ask. The fiercest beasts were brought from Africa, the Libyan desert, the highlands of Asia; they gave the gladiators good combat.

But as he grew old Antoninus grew tired and slightly bored with comfortable living. Life had been good, campaigning. What had he not seen? What had he not done? Whom had he not fought? He had led his cohorts well under Hadrian, and it had been a lusty, stormy, outstriding life, knowing something of defeat but more of victory. The gods had been good to him, and he had not done ill by them. But time came when he grew restless watching one more lion fighting his last fight. He found himself spending more and more time in the baths, yawning away good hours of a still good life.

Restlessness drove him to the road. He travelled up and down the ancient river Baetis, that he might see all of the Roman province. He found children along the way; and as there were few in Italica, as he had had none of his own, they interested him, especially the lads. He spent much time at Hispalis, which is now the city of Seville, loitering in the public square, watching the boys playing with their small javelins, throwing their discuses. He picked out a certain one named Flavius, a boy of ten; and him he bound in a growing friendship because of the tales he had to tell, the wonder and variety of them. He told of the

Britons on their island across from Gaul. He told of the far Rhine, of the Parthians, of what he had seen in Asia Minor, of Antioch amd Athens, Thebes and the Nile. And he told of that far-away city of Jerusalem and the strange tribes of the Jews, whom the Romans had conquered.

It happened on a day in early April that Antoninus brought the lad Flavius to Italica to see the yearly festival for the Great Mother of the Gods. In the arena were to be games and chariot races, and slaves throughout the empire were coming to wrestle.

"Who is this Great Mother?" asked the lad. "I do not rightly know her."

"In truth she is not a Roman goddess — not as we claim Ceres and Juno. But we, the army, worship her with great honour. The Sibylline Books have prophesied of her, Like Mithra, we have found it well not to slight her. She is over the winds, the sea, the earth, and all creation. She gave us victory over the Mauretanians without a doubt."

"I will take Mars and Vulcan," said the lad contentedly. "What can they not do? And for a goddess — give me Minerva, O Antoninus."

"It is well to pray and make sacrifices to all. We slaughtered a six-year-old bull to the Great Mother this day at dawn. The smoke of it filled the heavens, the blood propitiated the ground well. We should have a fine harvest."

"There are too many gods," said the lad wearily. "I cannot remember them all, and who has the olive branch and who the pine, and what they best like for sacrifice. It would be better if they all went but Father Jupiter, and he alone took care of us."

"Mind thy tongue, boy. Even now the gods may be listening!"

The chariot races had begun. They watched the winner crowned, and Flavius, still confused over the Great Mother, plied his questions further: "Is she mother over Jupiter?"

"I have told you, she is mother over all the gods. The only one ..." A look of perplexity passed over the big soldier's face, then a smile broke the grim line of his mouth. "I have told thee of Jerusalem and the Jews. I was with the Emperor there when he ordered the city rebuilt and saw many shows in the arena. It is not as it is here — the fights. There the gladiators combat prisoners; and the lions, the leopards, and the tigers fight with a strange people called Christians.

"I have never heard of them," said Flavius.

"'Tis as well." The centurion shrugged his shoulders as if to dismiss all thought save that which bore upon the festival. A great procession was forming in the arena. The music of flute, tympan, and cymbal, lute

and tambourine sounded. Those who marched were garlanded, and
there were many dancers. And then a dark blot of dun colour in the
midst of the saffrons, blues, crimsons, and greens of the tunics caught
the eye of the Roman centurion, and he laid a compelling hand on the
lad beside him. "Look. There are Christians. Those towards the end of
the procession, chained together. They have brought them here from
Rome, no doubt to force them to do honour to the Great Mother.
A good joke." And Antoninus threw back his head and bellowed
laughter.

But the lad understood nothing of this joke. "Tell me, O Antoninus,
why is it so funny?"

"Because the Christians have a great mother of their own. I heard of
her in Jerusalem. It will go against the spleen of those four to worship
another."

The dancing had begun. Swaying, singing, shouting, playing, the
procession advanced until the chained men had come directly below
the centurion and the lad. "There is nothing fierce in them," Flavius
said as if disappointed. "Is it such as these who fight the lions?"

Again Antoninus bellowed. "They fight not. It is against their belief.
They stand like stuffed sacks and let the beasts slaughter them."

Without knowing it the lad sighed. "At that rate, there will soon be no
more of them."

The big soldier patted him approvingly: "Thou hast some of thy
Minerva's wisdom. They cannot last out the empire."

"And this mother that they worship — what is her emblem? What
sacrifices to her do they make? Where have they set up her altar?"

The centurion's laughter was running low; he mixed it with his words:
"Sacrifices! Altar! Rome would tear it down had it found one. They
worship in secret. It is strange that any worship could have come out of
such a simple, everyday affair. She was the mother of a man born in
Judea, a Jew. They crucified him — the Roman governor ordered it
because the Jews, his own people, demanded it. It happened little more
than a hundred years ago. I talked with a Roman legionary whose
grandsire had seen the crucifixion. The man had set himself above the
priests as a kind of prince and saviour of the world; mayhap he called
himself the son of a god, I forget. So when he was crucified all looked
for some heavenly omen or deed to be enacted, for Jehovah, the
god of the Jews, to come down and take this one, his son, from the
cross."

"Did nothing happen?"

"Nothing. They buried him. His mother wept. A few of his followers took his body to a tomb. That was all."

"What was her name?"

"I have forgotten, if I ever knew." He pulled at the lad's sleeve. "Look — look at the Christians now. They will whip them till they kneel in worship before the Great Mother. I doubt not they will whip them till they die." And Aelius Antoninus, the senior centurion, threw back his great head, pounded his chest with delight, and bellowed his laugher again so that all heard. It rang across the arena and one of the chained and flogged men in dun-coloured robes turned his eyes towards him, raised one shackled hand, and pointing lean fingers upwards he made the sign of a cross. A cross in the air between himself, the laughter, and the man who had made it.

The lad watching shivered. "I feel cold," he said. "The air is sharp for April."

A great harvest was reaped in Baetica that fall. All remembered how tremendous was the festival celebrated for the Great Mother of all the gods and doubted not that having Christian blood to mix with bull's blood had propitiated well the goddess.

Winter came cold for the south of Spain. December was far gone and the time approached from the ending of the Saturnalia, the last day of the revels. The Roman centurion departed early for the camp for Hispalis. He rode along the river-front, with night coming on. There was a young crescent moon in the sky and all was clear and fair. The spirits of Aelius Antonius rose. By years he might be a man growing old, but in feeling he was still young, strong, full of the good lusty appetite for life and all it held. He was thinking that he might live to see the rounding of the century. That would be something.

The padding of soft feet behind him roused him from his reverie. He drew up to see who these were, overtaking him. His horse under him began to shake like aspen, and for one who had been a Roman legionary he felt a strange cold gripping about the heart. For coming towards him on three gigantic camels were men the like of which he had never seen in all his marching with the Roman army of conquest.

The pale thin curve of the moon's light picked out every detail of their splendour. Their robes were richer than any emperor's. Jewels of great brilliance caught them together at throat and belt. Each rider wore a crown — the magnificence of these crowns surpassed anything Antonius had seen in Egypt, in Persia, in Greece, in the far reaches of the Euphrates.

The camels were caparisoned with rich cloths and harness. As they drew abreast, the Roman could see that each King — or so he took them to be — carried in his hand a jewelled casket. Albeit a great man himself, and his horse a mount of no mean stature, he had to look well up to see their faces. One was dark, one black as a Nubian, one as fair as a Greek. "Who are ye? Whence come ye? Whither go ye?" the Roman asked with the voice of Roman authority.

"I am Melchior, a king from Nubia and Arabia, wherein lies gold. Behold I bring it as my gift." He held up the jewelled casket.

"I am Balthasar, King from Tarsis and the Isle of Egriswilla, wherein grows myrrh."

"I am Gaspar, a King from India and Saba, land of spices. I bring frankincense. Together we ride to Bethlehem in Judea."

"On camels!" Antoninus let out prodigious laughter. "Ye will be in your graves before ye reach there." And then his mouth snapped together, making a grim line. The words he next spoke were those of a Roman Soldier. "Come ye to make trouble? Know this: the Roman Empire allows no interference. Our power is supreme. What business takes ye into Judea?"

Antoninus's quick eyes caught the look that passed from King to King, a secret look. It angered him. "Speak up, ye Kings from the East. What business takes ye to Judea?"

"To bear gifts. Look — I bring gold."

"And I, frankincense."

"And I, myrrh, to the King of Kings."

Again each King held up his jewelled casket.

A look of greater bewilderment covered the face of the Roman. "What mean ye — the King of Kings? The birth of such a one was prophesied in Herod's time — to be born in Judea. But he was crucified a hundred years ago. The man is dead, forgotten."

Again the secret and wise look passed from King to King. Melchior spoke. "And what is a hundred years? God himself hath said a thousand years shall be even as a day. We ride tonight to the manger where Jesus lies, even as we rode when he was born. We bear those gifts we first brought him. So shall it always be. Until the world grows too old to bear men longer on its surface, we, Three Kings, ride to worship him, our Lord Jesus."

Here was a joke the magnitude of which Antoninus had never in his entire life experienced before. Three kings riding to worship a new-born baby who had grown to manhood, been crucified, died, and was buried over a hundred years ago. Three Kings still riding! Here was a joke to regale the camp with when he returned on the morrow. Suppressing his mirth the Roman said: "He has been a man dead these many years, and yet he becomes a babe that you may have him to worship. Your Christian god works miracles and this is one no doubt. Our Roman gods can do much — much — but once born and grown they do not become babies again. Venus does not go back to her sea-shell; Hercules does not go back to his cradle to strangle the serpent. Ha-ha-ha-ha, ho-ho-ho-ho!" His laughter shattered the air.

They let him have his fill of it; then Melchior spoke again: "That is thrice thou hast laughed, Aelius Antoninus the Roman! The counting has been made against thee. Thou shalt live until thou hast expiated each laugh. Thou shalt live until thou too shalt kneel beside the Babe and worship him."

The Kings rode on into the night. The Roman watched them go, sobered for the moment, then amazed. That last night of the Saturnalia had no flavour for him. The next day he told of his preposterous encounter to his familiars at the camp but the joke tasted foully to him, and the veterans insisted he had been deluded by too much strong wine.

Years passed. Aelius Antoninus began to mark their toll, which was nothing for him. Others, those who had been retired at Italica with him and were of the same age, he watched grow feeble, and at last be carried to their graves. Yet time aged him not at all. He watched Flavius grow into manhood, reach prime, age, and be buried; yet his own body remained unstooped, his stride vigorus, his muscles sound. It was incredible. It was a curse! A kind of terror slowly filled him which lingered even in his sleep.

The soldiers in the camp had long since avoided him. The new governor coming from Rome, where Marcus Aurelis was now Emperor, had stricken his name from the records as one long since dead. Hearing this he left Italica and became a wanderer on the face of the earth. Every temple he passed — to whatever pagan god it had been erected — he stopped to make sacrifice and prayer. He sought out those cities which were beseiged and joined the attacking army, thrusting himself into the front ranks, praying that some lance, some stone from a cross-bow might end his life. He visited those cities stricken with the plague. He helped to nurse the sick, to bury the dead; he drew in great draughts of the death-infested air, hoping one breath would bring him to his end. Yet all these things he survived.

A hundred years passed. Homesickness drove him back to Baetica, to the camp, to find the might of Rome weakening. He rode again upon the river road that last night of the Saturnalia. Would they come — would they ride, those Kings? Throughout the hundred years he still scoffed at all save pagan gods. Even with death withheld, he doubted that the Kings would come again.

But even as before he heard the padding of camels' feet behind him. He turned to meet again the splendour of the Kings, to see each carrying the golden casket in his hands, come as before. The Kings hailed him "Peace be with thee brother."

Anger mounted hot within him. He thrust his chin at them in fierce scorn: "And still ye ride?"

"As we shall always ride."

"And the babe is born again?"

"As he shall always be re-born this blessed season."

"A fig for your babies!" And the Roman laughed again long and hard, but with a hollowness that struck his heart. He watched them ride into the night and turned his horse back to the camp, but having no longer a place within he rode on northwards.

How can I tell you all that befell the Roman, Aelius Antoninus? He journeyed into Britain and watched the Druids worship their god, the sun. He found the gods of the Gauls much the same as his own. He took passage to Africa to see where old Carthage had been. The boat was shipwrecked and all lost save himself. He came back to Spain to find the Vandals ruling it; and met again the Three Kings and laughed and laughed so that the wind caught up his laughter and seemed to carry it throughout the world.

When next he came he found the Goths overrunning Spain. The Boldmen, they were called, mighty, barbaric, and conquering, good warriors but without the culture that Rome had brought. He became a ghost which went about visible to all, pointed out for the ancientness of his armour, and for the mystery which clung to him. Wherever he went his speech was forever betraying him. The Boldmen brought him into their halls, bade him to their feasting, made him welcome until unwittingly he spoke of Hadrian, of the campaign against the Britons; and then a silence fell and even Alaric the King was seen to draw away from him in a kind of fearful amazement.

Like the swinging of a great pendulum the centuries went on. He came again to Spain and found the Goths gone and the Arabs everywhere. They had set up a strong kingdom in the south, had made of the Roman city Hispalis a Moorish one. He learned of a new god, his name was Allah, and of his prophet Mohammed. When he met the Kings upon the road he threw these names at them. "By Jupiter, ride into the city — look at their mosques — here them calling to their god from the high towers, and then tell me if you keep on to Judea?"

"We ride," said the Kings.

"So ye still worship that Jesus, even while a new King has come to claim the world. Fools — fools — fools!" And he shook his fists in a mighty anger at them.

Five centuries, six centuries, and still Aelius Antoninus grew not one year older. He saw the Jews come into trade and grow rich. He stopped a certain important one named Isadore in the street and asked: "Have you heard of one of your own people by the name of Jesus?"

"There are many called by that name."

"This one was born in Bethlehem, lived, and was crucified. Tell me is he a King?"

The Jew shook his head. "He claimed to be a King, even the Messiah, but he was false."

That year the Roman waited long upon the road for the Kings, to fling this thing a Jew himself had said concerning Jesus. But night after night passed. Instead of coming at the end of the old Saturnalia, it was twelve days afterwards before he heard the padding of camels' feet on the road behind him, and in a surge of victorious scorn he blocked their way. "I salute you in the name of Jupiter, Hercules, Mars, Mithras, Allah-yea, even Jehovah, but never in the name of Jesus." He spat upon the ground. "Even his race denies him. Hear what the Jew Isadore saith!" And he told. "Now whither ride ye?"

"To Bethlehem, in Judea."

"But ye are late. Ye will get there only to find him crucified." And the Roman laughed.

"We will find him a babe of thirteen days. Already the church celebrates our day — the Day of the Three Kings — the day we reach Bethlehem. So it shall be upon the day we henceforth ride, not upon the eve of His birth." And they passed on into the night.

Seven centuries — he saw Charlemagne and the Franks marching against the Arabs. He saw the establishing of a Christian kingdom following a Mohammedan one. He watched churches being built upon the mosques, bell-towers above minarets, Mass said instead of the muezzin call to prayers, *prie-dieux* instead of prayer-rugs. And now, behold, the very images of Jesus filled the churches — Jesus and his Mother. Christians were on the streets, Christians on the seas, Christians marching, marching, marching, everywhere.

The name of Díaz of Bivar, the great Christian warrior, was heard on every lip; the name of the Blessed Santiago was whispered wherever a Christian army marched, and the battle cry "For God, Jesus, and Mary!" rang out through Spain. Ferdinand the Saint had come to rule. Nearly twelve hundred years had gone since that first night the Kings rode. Aelius Antoninus waited again upon the road. He now knew the name of this night on the Christian calender — it was called the Eve of the Epiphany. So long had it been since he had heard the names of the ancient gods spoken that he could recall them only with great difficulty. No temple was left standing to them, all worship of them had crumbled. He had stood outside the doors of some of the churches and heard something of this new worship. Strange words took form — Love — Peace — Mercy — Life — Justice. He heard low mumblings of sacrifice, but could not understand the nature of it. No longer were creatures slaughtered on the altar, no bringing of young lambs or cocks. Now there was talk of giving away all one had to the poor, of forgiving an enemy, of laying down a life for a friend. Strange teachings!

But he would have more of it. This time he would question the Kings.

They came, and again there hung in the western sky a young crescent moon. He heard the padding of the camels. He drew to the side of the road, dismounting to wait for the kings to stop. But the Kings rode on. "I salute ye!" he cried, running beside the camel of Melchior. "Stop! I command! I would have speech with ye!"

"We cannot stop. Tonight we make haste. Tonight we keep tryst with our Lord Jesus yonder."

But Antonius caught at the bridle. "Wait, I must have speech with ye. Another hundred years and I shall be mad. Hark ye, I cannot live longer. Confusion has come upon me. My body is a curse; my heart has withered. I would lie down and sleep in eternal death."

"There is no eternal death."

"You mean there is Olympus for the brave?"

"We mean there is a heaven, call it what you will, for souls who find their salvation."

"But ye have cursed mine."

"Thou hast laughed the curse upon thyself. Thou must bear it till —"
The words were lost to the Roman. His breath was coming in choking gasps. It seemed as if the camels were outstriding the air itself. But he

would not let go of the bridle; he would not lose the Kings, not again. He would run beside them till he dropped, till death took him.

They came to the bridge spanning a great muddy river. And on the bridge were massed such a crowd as had never filled the square of the city for the feast of Saturn, or for the Great Mother, or for Father Jupiter himself. Rich and poor, noble and peasant. Torches flared to heaven. Musicians lined the way. Children cast flowers on the bridge — white jasmin, claveles, roses. And as the Kings came there arose such a shouting as shook the very stars and made them fall: "Melchior, Gaspar, Balthasar! The Kings ride!"

They rode to the church which had been an Arab mosque. As the great doors swung open, a hush so profound caught up the crowd and held it that one could hear a new-born babe sigh, that one could hear an angel bending low from heaven's own gate to listen, that one could hear the curving of Mary's lips in a smile. So was it.

The Kings entered first; Aelius Antoninus the Roman strode hard upon their heels. They traversed a Christian nave between what had once been a line of Moorish arches supporting the roof. They came to the high altar, lighted by towering candles, and there was built the coarse, rude stall — the like of which might be found in any eastern stable. An ox stood there, a small grey donkey. A man leaned upon his staff, his heavy beard of black half covering his face. A woman in a robe of blue knelt beside the ox's manger, filled with hay. And there within lay the Babe, now thirteen days of age. All living — all everlasting.

The Kings knelt. The Roman knelt, unknowing what he did. He heard the Kings give salutation: "Peace be unto thee, blessed Mother of Jesus; and peace unto thy Son.

He heard the low, sweet voice of this Great Mother: "Peace be unto ye, O Kings."

Then came the salutation to the Babe: "Peace be unto thee, Emanuel, now and forever more. As thou art now so thou shalt always be — King of all Kings, Saviour of all Saviours — Prince of Peace!"

Drawing himself closer upon his knees, Aelius Antoninus the Roman found himself giving the salutation: "Peace be unto thee, Jesus of Bethlehem. I salute thee above Jupiter — above Mithras, above Allah, above all gods. May thy reign be eternal and supreme."

And so did Aelius Antoninus find death at last. Yet abroad, on the face of many countries, in the memory of many people, he left a legend. The legend of a Roman centurion, ageless and a wanderer, seen in this country and in that, upon the mountain fastnesses, and upon the seas, marked throughout so many centuries that the counting has not been kept absolute. But of all places Spain knew him best. And so God rest his soul!

Babushka

A Russian legend

Once upon a time, deep in the heart of Russia there lived an old peasant woman whose name was Babushka. Babushka lived by herself yet she was happy and wanted for nothing. She had a fine cabin made of logs cut from the best fir trees in the forest, and a good garden in which to grow vegetables.

"I am a fortunate woman," Babushka would say to herself. "Have I not food in the cupboard and a good fire in the big black stove."

Her hospitality was known throughout the forest where she lived, for when a tired traveller passed by the old woman would call, "Friend, stop and rest in my cabin," and indeed they would.

One day, at the time when Mother Snow covers the great forests with her white mantle and Father Frost goes dancing from tree to tree decorating the branches with glittering icicles, old Babushka was outside, busily clearing away the snow from her path, when three travellers came up to her gate. They were richly dressed in fine furs and each one carried a leather bag.

"Good day, Mother," they called.

"Good day to you, gentlemen," replied Babushka, a little breathless, for clearing snow is no easy task for an old woman. "Can I help you?" asked Babushka.

"Indeed you can, good Mother," said the first stranger, "for we have travelled far and have need of food and warm beds to sleep in."

"Then come inside," she answered. "I have black bread made this very morning and hot tea on the stove. As for beds, there is only one, for I live on my own, but it's large enough for three."

When the three travellers had eaten and drunk so that their stomachs no longer felt empty, they settled down in the old woman's bed, thanked her for her kindness and went to sleep. While the travellers slept Babushka baked more black bread for the next day. But as she baked, the more she thought about the three strangers. "Is it not so," thought Babushka to herself, "that all good men sleep by night and travel by day? When they rise I shall ask them why they travel so."

As Mother Evening came creeping over the forest, speading her grey veil behind her, the three travellers awoke and started to make ready to depart.

"Kind sirs," Babushka said, "why is it that you journey by night and sleep by day? For surely it is hard to find your way in the darkness of the night."

"Good Mother," said the first man, "we are three Kings who have travelled far from the lands of the East."

"We search for the Christ Child," said the second King. "Many years we have been waiting for a mighty star to appear in the heavens and now it has. For it is told that beneath that star the Christ Child will be born. It will guide all who wish to pay homage to the new-born child."

"We travel by night," said the third King, "so that we may follow the star. Each of us carries a gift to give the Christ Child. The first King gold, the second King myrrh, and I take frankincense."

"Oh, how I would like to go with you," said Babushka, in wonderment at what the three Kings had told her. "I have no rich things to give, but I could take my black bread, for they say it is the finest in the forest."

"Then come, good Mother," replied the first King, "but you must follow us now, or we shall lose sight of the star."

"That is impossible," cried poor Baboushka, "for I must first clean my cabin and see that all is put away. Can you not wait for me just a little longer?"

The Kings shook their heads sadly, saying that they could not lose a moment longer, but told the old woman to hurry her work and follow after them. This Babushka said she would do, and bidding the Kings goodbye started to clean her cabin.

When at last Babushka had finished her work, she wrapped her great winter cloak around herself and taking her black bread opened the door of her cabin. But as old Babushka looked up into the night sky to find the great star, she felt her heart break. For the star had gone. Babushka had taken so long to clean her cabin that night had given way to dawn. Even the Kings' tracks had been covered up by the newly fallen snow.

"How silly I was to see to my home, I should have left with the Kings," sobbed the old woman. "No matter, I shall travel on. Surely there must be someone who has seen the Kings. They will tell me which way they went and I will follow."

And so Babushka trudged through the snow asking all she met, "Have you seen three Kings? Which way were they going?" but each answer was the same: "No."

Days turned into weeks and weeks turned into months, while Babushka, footsore, tired and hungry, looked in vain for the Christ Child. After many months Babushka met a traveller sitting by the roadside.

"Have you see three Kings who go to see the Christ Child?" asked Babushka.

"Three Kings I have not seen, old woman," said the traveller, "but I have been told of a child who will one day be King. He was born not far from here; they call the town Bethlehem. But stay awhile, you look too ill to travel on, old woman."

"I must," said Babushka, "I have travelled far and cannot stop now that I am so near the Christ Child's birthplace."

At last Babushka came to Bethlehem.

"Where is the one they call the Christ Child?" she inquired of a woman washing at a well.

"If you believe that story," laughed the woman, "you will believe anything. Well, if you want to know, the Child and the family have gone. They stayed in a stable; it's at the top of that hill. Look, you can see it from where we are standing."

Babushka thanked the woman and made her way up the hill to the stable. Inside Babushka found it empty, except for one ox and an ass, who snorted and brayed in greeting.

"Ah me," sighed Babushka, "I am too late, but I shall lay my black bread in the manger, then the Christ Child will know I came. I shall sleep here for the night and start home in the morning. Come, ox and ass, we shall sleep side by side tonight, for it is cold outside."

Soon Babushka fell into a deep sleep only to be awakened by a beautiful golden light, which came from the far corner of the stable.

"Babushka, Babushka, I am here. Come rise and greet me," said a child's voice.

"Who are you?" cried Babushka in fright.

"Do you not know, have you not been looking for me? I am the one they call the Christ Child."

"O Child, I have waited so long to see you."

"Then walk into my light, Babushka, and let us hold hands," said the voice softly.

And Babushka did so.

The next day they found old Babushka dead, curled up on the straw, with only the ox and ass to watch over her.

But that is not quite the end of my story. For every Christmas Eve children all over Russia hang up their stockings in the hope that they will be full in the morning. And so they are, with toys and games, and right at the bottom in coloured paper is a piece of black bread. The old ones who know nod their heads and say Mother Christmas has been there. "See, Babushka has left some black bread. Just as she did for the Christ Child all those years ago."

The Secret King

Georg Dreissig

Every few months Uncle Stephanos would turn up in our house — usually without warning, but always joyfully welcomed by us children. In the first place we loved him because he always brought us a bag full of sweets, and in the second place because he knew countless stories to tell. Most of what he told he had experienced himself. But mother said that Uncle Stephanos had never been along with pirates, nor had he met polar bears at the North Pole, and the Red Indian dances which he said he had learnt as a young man from the Redskins themselves he could no longer dance, not because he was plagued by gout, but because he had never been anywhere near the Indians. It was funny when Mother said that, then we also believed that Uncle Stephanos was rather making up his stories and was not very strict about the truth. But when he was sitting again in front of us and began: "Yes, it was in those days when I was a mounted courier of the Tsar ..." then we could no longer doubt that he had experienced everything exactly as he told it.

Many of his stories I have long since forgotten. One however has remained deeply imprinted on my memory, perhaps because it was only after we had long pleaded with him that Uncle Stephanos told us, and perhaps because as a child there was much that I did not understand and only today come to understand it more. Uncle Stephanos, our pirate and mounted courier, was in ordinary life a grocer. But everyone who asked him what his trade was received unfailingly the answer: "Imperial merchant and secret king."

We children were mightily impressed with the "imperial merchant" until we learned that it just meant "a glorified grocer". But what made us particularly curious and incited us to fresh questions was his second calling: "secret king". And it is about the story of the secret king that I must always think when the thought of Uncle Stephanos comes into my mind, for I was so impressed by what after long hesitation he finally told us.

He had a rather gruff voice, our uncle had, and he spoke rather more loudly than was necessary in our playroom, "because on deck under sail you have to shout to be understood," as he explained to us. Mother however said that it was because he was a bit hard of hearing. But the story of the secret king he told us very softly almost as if he were talking to himself alone, or as if what he was telling were too great a pity to be heard.

"Yes, it was at that time," he began as he always did his stories, "when I had finished my apprenticeship in Munich and I came back home to Oberndorf. How small, how very tiny and wretched my own village seemed to me then with the few cabins which seemed to hide under their big overhanging roofs for protection from the high towering mountains all around. Life there, which went on in the same way as in great-grandfather's time, seemed to me empty and boring. How different was the activity in the city, the variety, the excitement and the dangers! To be sure I was not completely surprised by the impression, for I had not expected anything different. It was not homesickness that had brought me back into the mountains, but — Maria."

Uncle Stephanos hesitated for quite some time before he spoke the name, and when he now was silent, his gaze, which seemed to go right back into the past, was so compelling that we watched the man whom we so loved, and we kept still and waited for him to take up the thread of his story.

"Maria was the same age as myself. She came from the same village. We went to the same school, looked after the same goats and milked them together. Indeed we had grown up as brother and sister, and it was only at the time when I was accepted for apprenticeship in Munich that I realized that Maria had become more than a sister to me, that I loved her. Everything in me had yearned to be out of the narrowness and simplicity of that little mountain village, and only now that it was certain that I should leave it did I notice how hard that would be for me — because of the girl. The days before my departure were numbered, and everything that went on between us, everything that we felt for each other, had to be told quickly if the other were still to hear it. But we who had never had secrets from each other suddenly felt shy. The unusual words stuck in our throats, and instead of acknowledging our secret love, we could only mutter a 'Well,' or 'It'll be alright,' or some such.

"Why I am convinced that Maria at that time returned my love, I cannot say. She never said so much in words. But there is much that can be left unsaid because the heart has heard. At all events I departed with a lump in my throat even though I seemed outwardly brisk, perhaps too brisk, and I did not dare look round, because I felt she was watching me go, until I was over the saddle of the mountain.

"Did I write? To Maria of course not. In my parents' letters however I searched eagerly for news of her, but they only wrote good wishes and told about the weather, the births and deaths in the village. Of the girl not a word — which might mean good or bad.

"For three years I did not see my village. In those days you hardly got a day off, and money was so tight that a short visit was not to be thought of. It was three years in which I became more and more of a stranger to my village, I went dancing, sometimes I drank too much, and did not keep in the best of company. I just wanted to be like the others, a city-dweller, not someone who smelled of the byre.

" 'Do you still go to church?' my mother had once asked with presentiment in one of her letters, and I had written in reply telling her this and that about the priest of the Holy Cross Church near which I stayed. The priest was a man whom I hardly knew even by sight and whom I had never seen in a service. My mother forgave me these lies later more quickly than I did myself.

"As I gradually began to forget about my life in Oberndorf so too I gradually began to forget Maria; never completely, but other things were closer to me; whether they were more important I cannot say. But when at last I was on the way home, city life fell from me like a heavy curtain, and the girl stood before my mind's eye just as I had seen her when we parted and I had loved her. Suddenly I could not wait to get home, though, as I have said, I had no illusions about the village. When at last I saw it appear beyond the hill I had to hold myself in check so as not to start running. Of course I went home first, and was genuinely glad to see my parents again, who seemed to me not to have altered at all in the years I had been away, as if time there had just stood still.

"But it was a real agony to be sitting at the polished oak table in the kitchen, watching Mother getting supper ready, and answering my parents' questions concerning my doings in Munich, while in me only the one question was burning: how is Maria? My patience was put to a severe test that evening. I soon heard about the inmates of our goat-shed, heard that we had acquired some new cows, and that a golden wedding was being celebrated in our neighbour's house. But at last I dared to ask the questions myself: 'And the young folk? How are the young folk doing?' Two had also left the village, and the others were still there. 'It all turns out as it must' and suddenly both parents were silent, and something dark came over their features so that I felt afraid.

" 'And Maria?' Now I had put the question. A long silence, then Father answered curtly: 'She went after her geologist.' Further information had to be squeezed out of him, which I did in spite of the questioning look and the reluctant manner of answering. I wanted to know, I had to know. What I then found out was not very heartening. An educated man, a geologist, had come to the village and had taken up lodgings with Maria's parents and soon had turned the girl's head. So far so good. But when he went away again after a few months he left a most unfortunate lassie behind him in Oberndorf. She appeared pale and wretched, grieved and only yearned for him who perhaps was not at all interested that she should hang on him. It was pure tragedy. They all tried their best with her, tried to cheer her up, but all in vain. One morning they found a note on her bed: 'I had to follow him. Do not look for me. Maria.'

"What then had happened I could imagine: The people had clamped their teeth and tried to forget the girl who had brought shame on them. No one spoke of her any more.

"When I came to lie again in my little room under the great roof, I had a strange uneasy feeling and could not sleep. 'I must go after him,' Maria had written, my Maria, and 'Do not look for me!' That went round in my head like a millstone. At last I got up quietly, dressed in the dark and slipped outside. A little above the village I sat down on the grass and looked up to the stars. 'Do not look for me.' It was a clear night. Up above in the sky the stars were shining like golden ducats. Away over there above the Doppelhorn stood a really bright one — it must have been Jupiter — shining like a little sun. In its light I thought I could make out the alm-hut in which we had often spent the night when we wanted to climb the Doppelhorn the following morning early. It was an old cabin, unused for a long time, more like a shed than a house, but for us children extremely snug and adventurous at the same time. 'Do not look for me.' And suddenly it came to me with absolute certainty; She is up there. Suddenly my wildly thumping heart told me more: She needs you!

"In any case I had not been able to sleep that night, now however I was wide awake. As long as Jupiter was in the sky I should be able to find my way up there, I thought. Haste was necessary. As quietly as my urgency would allow I slipped back into the house and in the dark I got together everything that I wanted to take with me: this and that, bread and cheese, a knife, the table-cloth — yes even the table-cloth, why that I did not know! A little later I was on my way. I realized that it was not as light as I had thought. I could not make out the alm-hut at all. But my resolve remained firm, and as in any case everything that was done that night was not thought out, but came from an intuition, I could not hold back in the darkness now.

"What a long time since I had climbed up to the alm-hut! but my feet seemed to know the way, felt for themselves their sure footing, and all the time up and up I went, on and on. My whole attention was now so concentrated on the path that I no longer could look up at the stars in the sky. But it did not seem to be necessary, for I felt Jupiter shining down on me, and its light gave me an unshakable confidence. I must have climbed for hours in this way but I felt that I had covered the ground in a very short time.

"Only when I had reached the meadow of the alm, did the question strike me: what if she is not there at all? One glance at the sky showed me that Jupiter had long since disappeared behind the Doppelhorn — and yet I had felt its gleam all the time — but a whimpering from the hut told me that I had not come in vain. I ran across quickly and entered the dark doorway. 'Maria?' I called hesitantly. Quite near me she answered in a calm if rather flat voice, 'So you've come, Ernst.' The gentle whimpering showed me clearly that she was not alone. I felt my way surely through the room and found the fireplace which was laid, and soon the flames shot up giving light and warmth.

"Then I saw Maria. I need not describe how she looked. She had been up here alone for days, and it stood ill with her. But her face that was quite pale and transparent shone mysteriously. In her bosom she held the baby, only a few hours old, that had shown me with its whimpering that they were there. I knelt beside her to look more closely at the tiny creature.

" 'He's a boy,' whispered Maria to me.

" 'Has he got a name?' I asked in my turn without looking up.

" 'Ernst,' said Maria without hesitation.

"Then I had to look up. Was she trying to joke? She seemed to smile a little as she calmly returned my gaze and added by way of explanation. 'After the king who has found the way to him.'

" 'King? — that's a good one!' I muttered, while I remembered at the same time that I really had brought all sorts of gifts in my bag, even the table-cloth.

" 'Yes you really are a secret king, Ernst,' said Maria with certainty.

"That she always maintained even when I later told her how I had thought I saw the alm-hut in the light of Jupiter, and so the thought had come to me that she might be up there. Even today she maintains firmly that I saved their two lives. Well, indeed, alone she could never have come down the mountain. She had gone up there to make an end. But the baby had revived her life-spirits. For the sake of the child she came back with me in the end; whatever people might look or say. Yes, and that was how it was too."

Uncle Stephanos now thought he had told enough, but we still wanted to hear the end the story, so we plied him with questions. What happened to Maria and the baby afterwards? Did he ever marry her? Did he know any other secret kings, or was he the only one?

Uncle Stephanos obviously did not want to answer, but he did nevertheless. No, he did not marry Maria; didn't we know that he wasn't married? No, no, Maria and Little Ernst had found their way to the real father and now lived near Munich, and Little Ernst had in the meantime become a geologist himself and gave to his own children the sweets that Uncle Stephanos brought him on his infrequent visits.

But secret kings, oh well he knew a whole lot!

"How many?" we wanted to know, for we thought it would be three again, like in the story of the three Kings.

But Uncle Stephanos answered — and the answer gave him visible pleasure: "I can't give you a number, but will it do if I tell you exactly?" And grinning at our astonished faces he said, "As many as I know people."

That was away above us. We had to exert ourselves to understand what he had said. Finally my elder brother solved the riddle.

"You think, Uncle Stephanos," he asked slowly, "that every person you know is a secret king?"

"I don't just think it, I am certain!" came the answer promptly. As we were thinking this one out he went on, "You know, I had to think about it for a long time how I was made out to be a secret king, and at first I thought it was because Jupiter had led me. But Jupiter could have done nothing unless my heart had so beaten and insisted: 'She needs you,' so you see, a true heart in one's breast, that is what makes one a secret king. And the other thing that belongs to it is that each of us really carries a treasure with us — it does not need to seem very precious to ourselves — a treasure that we can give away when someone is in need, like that time when I brought the table-cloth for a baby's napkin. Our hearts must be open for what is needed, otherwise we do not notice that we have got the treasure."

Imperial merchant and Secret King Ernst Stephanos, our surprise-uncle. You meant much to us in our childhood days with your visits, your stories and your sweets. The older we grow, the clearer we realize what you have opened up for us; our own wealth, our own treasure, that you have revealed the secret of the hidden kingliness of all people. yes that is what we want to be: of some trade or profession and — a secret king.

The Story of the Other Wise Man

Henry Van Dyke

You know the story of the Three Wise Men of the East, and how they travelled from far away to offer their gifts at the manger-cradle in Bethlehem. But have you ever heard the story of the Other Wise Man, who also saw the star in its rising, and set out to follow it, yet did not arrive with his brethren in the presence of the young child Jesus?

Of the great desire of this fourth pilgrim, and how it was denied, yet accomplished in the denial; of his many wanderings and the probations of his soul; of the long way of his seeking, and the strange way of his finding, the One whom he sought — I would tell the tale as I have heard fragments of it in the Hall of Dreams, in the palace of the Heart of Man.

The Sign in the Sky

In the days when Augustus Caesar was master of many kings and Herod reigned in Jerusalem, there lived in the city of Ecbatana, among the mountains of Persia, a certain man named Artaban, the Median. His house stood close to the outermost of the seven walls which encircled the royal treasury. From his roof he could look over the rising battlements of black and white and crimson and blue and red and silver and gold, to the hill where the summer palace of the Parthian emperors glittered like a jewel in a sevenfold crown.

Around the dwelling of Artaban spread a fair garden, a tangle of flowers and fruit trees, watered by a score of streams descending from the slopes of Mount Orontes, and made musical by innumerable birds. But all colour was lost in the soft and odorous darkness of the late September night, and all sounds were hushed in the deep charm of its silence, save the splashing of the water, like a voice half sobbing and half laughing under the shadows. High above the trees a dim glow of light shone through the curtained arches of the upper chamber, where the master of the house was holding council with his friends.

He stood by the doorway to greet his guests — a tall, dark man of about forty years, with brilliant eyes set near-together under his broad brow, and firm lines graven around his fine, thin lips; the brow of a dreamer and the mouth of a soldier, a man of sensitive feeling but inflexible will — one of those who, in whatever age they may live, are born for inward conflict and a life of quest.

His robe was of pure white wool, thrown over a tunic of silk; and a white, pointed cap, with long lapels at the sides, rested on his flowing black hair. It was the dress of the ancient priesthood of the Magi, called the fire-worshippers.

"Welcome!" he said, in his low, pleasant voice, as one after another entered the room — "welcome, Abdus; peace be with you, Rhodaspes and Tigranes, and with you my father, Abgarus. You are all welcome, and this house grows bright with the joy of your presence."

There were nine of the men, differing widely in age, but alike in the richness of their dress of many-coloured silks, and in the massive golden collars around their necks, marking them as Parthian nobles, and in the winged circles of gold resting upon their breasts, the sign of the followers of Zoroaster.

They took their places around a small black altar at the end of the room, where a tiny flame was burning. Artaban, standing beside it, and waving a barsom of thin tamarisk branches above the fire, fed it with dry sticks of pine and fragrant oils. Then he began the ancient chant of the Yasna, and the voices of his companions joined in the beautiful hymn to Ahura-Mazda:

> We worship the Spirit Divine,
>   all wisdom and goodness possessing,
> Surrounded by Holy Immortals,
>   the givers of bounty and blessing,
> We joy in the works of his hands,
>   his truth and his power confessing.
>
> We praise all the things that are pure,
>   for these are his only Creation;
> The thoughts that are true,
>   and the words and deeds that have won approbation;
> These are supported by him
>   and for these we make adoration.
> Hear us, O Mazda!
>   Thou livest in truth and in heavenly gladness;

Cleanse us from falsehood,
    and keep us from evil and bondage to badness;
Pour out the light and the joy of thy life
    on our darkness and sadness.

Shine on our gardens and fields,
    shine on our working and weaving;
Shine on the whole race of man,
    believing and unbelieving;
Shine on us now through the night,
    shine on us now in Thy might,
The flame of our holy love
    and the song of our worship receiving.

The fire rose with the chant, throbbing as if it were made of musical flame, until it cast a bright illumination through the whole apartment, revealing its simplicity and splendour.

The floor was laid with tiles of dark blue veined with white; pilasters of twisted silver stood out against the blue walls; the clerestory of round-arched windows above them was hung with azure silk; the vaulted ceiling was a pavement of sapphires, like the body of heaven in its clearness, sown with silver stars. From the four corners of the roof hung four golden magic-wheels, called the tongues of the gods. At the eastern end, behind the altar, there were two dark-red pillars of porphyry; above them a lintel of the same stone, on which was carved the figure of a winged archer, with his arrow set to the string and his bow drawn.

The doorway between the pillars, which opened upon the terrace of the roof, was covered with a heavy curtain of the colour of a ripe pomegranate, embroidered with innumerable golden rays shooting upward from the floor. In effect the room was like a quiet, starry night, all azure and silver, flushed in the east with rosy promise of the dawn. It was, as the house of a man should be, an expression of the character and spirit of the master.

He turned to his friends when the song was ended, and invited them to be seated on the divan at the western end of the room.

"You have come tonight," said he, looking around the circle, "at my call, as the faithful scholars of Zoroaster, to renew your worship and rekindle your faith in the God of Purity, even as this fire has been rekindled on the altar. We worship not the fire, but him of whom it is the chosen symbol, because it is the purest of all created things. It speaks to us of one who is Light and Truth. Is it not so, my father?"

"It is well said, my son," answered the venerable Abgarus. "The enlightened are never idolaters. They lift the veil of the form and go in to the shrine of the reality, and new light and truth are coming to them continually through the old symbols."

"Hear me, then, my father and my friends," said Artaban, very quietly, "while I tell you of the new light and truth that have come to me through the most ancient of all signs. We have searched the secrets of nature together, and studied the healing virtues of water and fire and the plants. We have read also the books of prophecy in which the future is dimly foretold in words that are hard to understand. But the highest of all learning is the knowledge of the stars. To trace their courses is to untangle the threads of the mystery of life from the beginning to the end. If we could follow them perfectly, nothing would be hidden from us. But is not our knowledge of them still incomplete? Are there not many stars still beyond our horizon — lights that are known only to the dwellers in the far south-land, among the spice-trees of Punt and the gold-mines of Ophir?"

There was a murmur of assent among the listeners.

"The stars," said Tigranes, "are the thoughts of the Eternal. They are numberless. But the thoughts of man can be counted, like the years of his life. The wisdom of the Magi is the greatest of all wisdoms on earth, because it knows its own ignorance. And that is the secret of power. We keep men always looking and waiting for a new sunrise. But we ourselves know that the darkness is equal to the light, and that the conflict between them will never be ended."

"That does not satisfy me," answered Artaban, "for, if the waiting must be endless, if there could be no fulfilment of it, then it would not be wisdom to look and wait. We should become like those new teachers of the Greeks, who say that there is no truth, and that the only wise men are those who spend their lives in discovering and exposing the lies that have been believed in the world. But the new sunrise will certainly dawn in the appointed time. Do not our own books tell us that this will come to pass, and that men will see the brightness of a great light?"

"That is true," said the voice of Abgarus; "every faithful disciple of Zoroaster knows the prophecy of the Avesta and carries the word in his heart. 'In that day Sosiosh the Victorious shall arise out of the number of the prophets in the east country. Around him shall shine a mighty brightness, and he shall make life everlasting, incorruptible, and immortal, and the dead shall rise again'."

"This is a dark saying," said Tigranes, "and it may be that we shall never understand it. It is better to consider the things that are near at hand, and to increase the influence of the Magi in their own country, rather than to look for one who may be a stranger, and to whom we must resign our power."

The others seemed to approve these words. There was a silent feeling of agreement manifest among them; their looks responded with that indefinable expression which always follows when a speaker has uttered the thought that has been slumbering in the hearts of his listeners. But Artaban turned to Abgarus with a glow in his face, and said:

"My father, I have kept this prophecy in the secret place of my soul. Religion without a great hope would be like an altar without a living fire. And now the flame has burned more brightly, and by the light of it I have read other words which also have come from the fountain of Truth, and speak yet more clearly of the rising of the Victorious One in his brightness."

He drew from the breast of his tunic two small rolls of fine linen, with writing upon them, and unfolded them carefully upon his knee.

"In the years that are lost in the past, long before our fathers came into the land of Babylon, there were wise men in Chaldea, from whom the first of the Magi learned the secret of the heavens. And of these Balaam, the son of Beor, was one of the mightiest. Hear the words of his prophecy: 'There shall come a star out of Jacob, and a sceptre shall arise out of Israel'."

The lips of Tigranes drew downward with contempt, as he said:

"Judah was a captive by the waters of Babylon, and the sons of Jacob were in bondage to our kings. The tribes of Israel are scattered through the mountains like lost sheep, and from the remnant that dwells in Judea under the yoke of Rome neither star nor sceptre shall arise."

"And yet," answered Artaban, "it was the Hebrew Daniel, the mighty searcher of dreams, the counsellor of kings, the wise Belteshazzar, who was most honoured and beloved of our great King Cyrus. A prophet of sure things and a reader of the thoughts of God, Daniel proved himself to our people. And these are the words that he wrote." (Artaban read from the second roll:) " 'Know, therefore, and understand that from the going forth of the commandment to restore Jerusalem unto the Anointed One, the Prince, the time shall be seven and three-score and two weeks'."

"But, my son," said Abgarus, doubtfully, "these are mystical numbers. Who can interpret them, or who can find the key that shall unlock their meaning?"

Artaban answered: "It has been shown to me and to my three companions among the Magi — Caspar, Melchior, and Balthazar. We have searched the ancient tablets of Chaldea and computed the time. It falls in this year. We have studied the sky, and in the spring of the year we saw two of the greatest stars draw near together in the sign of the Fish, which is the house of the Hebrews. We also saw a new star there, which shone for one night and then vanished. Now again the two great planets are meeting. This night is their conjunction. My three brothers are watching at the ancient Temple of the Seven Spheres, at Borsippa, in Babylonia, and I am watching here. If the star shines again, they will wait ten days for me at the temple, and then we will set out together for Jerusalem, to see and worship the promised one who shall be born King of Israel. I believe the sign will come. I have made ready for the journey. I have sold my house and my possessions, and bought these three jewels — a sapphire, a ruby, and a pearl — to carry them as tribute to the King. And I ask you to go with me on the pilgrimage, that we may have joy together in finding the Prince who is worthy to be served."

While he was speaking he thrust his hand into the inmost fold of his girdle and drew out three great gems — one blue as a fragment of the night sky, one redder than a ray of sunrise, and one as pure as the peak of a snow mountain at twilight — and laid them on the outspread linen scrolls before him.

But his friends looked on with strange and alien eyes. A veil of doubt and mistrust came over their faces, like a fog creeping up from the marshes to hide the hills. They glanced at each other with looks of wonder and pity, as those who have listened to incredible sayings, the story of a wild vision, or the proposal of an impossible enterprise.

At last Tigranes said: "Artaban, this is a vain dream. It comes from too much looking upon the stars and the cherishing of lofty thoughts. It would be wiser to spend the time in gathering money for the new fire-temple at Chala. No king will ever rise from the broken race of Israel, and no end will ever come to the eternal strife of light and darkness. He who looks for it is a chaser of shadows. Farewell."

And another said: "Artaban, I have no knowledge of these things, and my office as guardian of the royal treasure binds me here. The quest is not for me. But if thou must follow it, fare thee well."

And another said: "In my house there sleeps a new bride, and I cannot leave her nor take her with me on this strange journey. This quest is not for me. But may thy steps be prospered wherever thou goest. So, farewell."

And another said: "I am ill and unfit for hardship, but there is a man among my servants whom I will send with thee when thou goest, to bring me word how thou farest."

But Abgarus, the oldest and the one who loved Artaban the best, lingered after the others had gone, and said, gravely: "My son, it may be that the light of truth is in this sign that has appeared in the skies, and then it will surely lead to the Prince and the mighty brightness. Or it may be that it is only a shadow of the light, as Tigranes has said, and then he who follows it will have only a long pilgrimage and an empty search. But it is better to follow even the shadow of the best than to remain content with the worst. And those who would see wonderful things must often be ready to travel alone. I am too old for this journey, but my heart shall be a companion of the pilgrimage day and night, and I shall know the end of thy quest. Go in peace."

So one by one they went out of the azure chamber with its silver stars, and Artaban was left in solitude.

He gathered up the jewels and replaced them in his girdle. For a long time he stood and watched the flame that flickered and sank upon the altar. Then he crossed the hall, lifted the heavy curtain, and passed out between the dull red pillars of porphyry to the terrace on the roof.

The shiver that thrills through the earth ere she rouses from her night sleep had already begun, and the cool wind that heralds the daybreak was drawing downward from the lofty, snow-traced ravines of Mount Orontes. Birds, half awakened, crept and chirped among the rustling leaves, and the smell of ripened grapes came in brief wafts from the arbours.

Far over the eastern plain a white mist stretched like a lake. But where the distant peak of Zagros serrated the western horizon the sky was clear. Jupiter and Saturn rolled together like drops of lambent flame about to blend in one.

As Artaban watched them, behold, an azure spark was born out of the darkness beneath, rounding itself with purple splendours to a crimson sphere, and spiring upward through rays of saffron and orange into a point of white radiance. Tiny and infinitely remote, yet perfect in every part, it pulsated in the enormous vault as if the three jewels in the

Magian's breast had mingled and been transformed into a living heart of light.

He bowed his head. He covered his brow with his hands.

"It is the sign," he said. "The King is coming, and I will go to meet him."

By the Waters of Babylon

All night long Vasda, the swiftest of Artaban's horses, had been waiting, saddled and bridled, in her stall, pawing the ground impatiently, and shaking her bit as if she shared the eagerness of her master's purpose, though she knew not its meaning

Before the birds had fully roused to their strong, high, joyful chant of morning song, before the white mist had begun to lift lazily from the plain, the other wise man was in the saddle, riding swiftly along the high-road, which skirted the base of Mount Orontes, westward.

How close, how intimate is the comradeship between a man and his favourite horse on a long journey. It is a silent, comprehensive friendship, an intercourse beyond the need of words.

They drink at the same wayside springs, and sleep under the same guardian stars. They are conscious together of the subduing spell of nightfall and the quickening joy of daybreak. The master shares his evening meal with his hungry companion, and feels the soft, moist lips caressing the palm of his hand as they close over the morsel of bread. In the grey dawn he is roused from his bivouac by the gentle stir of a warm, sweet breath over his sleeping face, and looks up into the eyes of his faithful fellow-traveller, ready and waiting for the toil of the day. Surely, unless he is a pagan and an unbeliever, by whatever name he calls upon his God, he will thank him for this voiceless sympathy, this dumb affection, and his morning prayer will embrace a double blessing — God bless us both, and keep our feet from falling and our souls from death!

And then, through the keen morning air, the swift hoofs beat their spirited music along the road, keeping time to the pulsing of two hearts that are moved with the same eager desire — to conquer space, to devour the distance, to attain the goal of the journey.

Artaban must indeed ride wisely and well if he would keep the appointed hour with the other Magi; for the route was a hundred and fifty parasangs, and fifteen was the utmost that he could travel in a day. But he knew Vasda's strength, and pushed forward without anxiety, making the fixed distance every day, though he must travel late into the night, and in the morning long before sunrise.

He passed along the brown slopes of Mount Orontes, furrowed by the rocky courses of a hundred torrents.

He crossed the level plains of the Nisaeans, where the famous herds of horses, feeding in the wide pastures, tossed their heads at Vasda's approach, and galloped away with a thunder of many hoofs, and flocks of wild birds rose suddenly from the swampy meadows, wheeling in great circles with a shining flutter of innumerable wings and shrill cries of surprise.

He traversed the fertile fields of Concabar, where the dust from the threshing-floors filled the air with a golden mist, half hiding the huge temple of Astarte with its four hundred pillars.

At Baghistan, among the rich gardens watered by fountains from the rock, he looked up at the mountain thrusting its immense rugged brow out over the road, and saw the figure of King Darius trampling upon his fallen foes, and the proud list of his wars and conquests graven high upon the face of the eternal cliff.

Over many a cold and desolate pass, crawling painfully across the wind-swept shoulders of the hills; down many a black mountain-gorge, where the river roared and raced before him like a savage guide; across many a smiling vale, with terraces of yellow limestone full of vines and fruit trees; through the oak groves of Carine and the dark Gates of Zagros, walled in by precipices; into the ancient city of Chala, where the people of Samaria had been kept in captivity long ago; and out again by the mighty portal, riven through the encircling hills, where he saw the image of the High Priest of the Magi sculptured on the wall of rock, with hand uplifted as if to bless the centuries of pilgrims; past the entrance of the narrow defile, filled from end to end with orchards of peaches and figs, through which the river Gyndes foamed down to meet him; over the board rice-fields where the autumnal vapours spread their deathly mists; following along the course of the river, under tremulous shadows of poplar and tamarind, among the lower hills; and out upon the flat plain, where the road ran straight as an arrow through the stubble-fields and parched meadows; past the city of Ctesiphon, where the Parthian emperors reigned and the vast metropolis of Seleucia which Alexander built; across the swirling floods of Tigris and the many channel of Euphrates, flowing yellow through the corn-lands — Artaban pressed onward until he arrived, at nightfall of the tenth day, beneath the shattered walls of populous Babylon.

Vasda was almost spent, and he would gladly have turned into the city to find rest and refreshment for himself and for her. But he knew that it was three hours' journey yet to the Temple of the Seven Spheres, and he must reach the place by midnight if he would find his comrades waiting. So he did not halt, but rode steadily across the stubble-fields.

A grove of date-palms made an island of gloom in the pale yellow sea. As she passed into the shadow Vasda slackened her pace, and began to pick her way more carefully.

Near the farther end of the darkness an access of caution seemed to fall upon her. She scented some danger or difficulty; it was not in her heart to fly from it — only to be prepared for it, and to meet it wisely, as a good horse should do. The grove was close and silent as the tomb; not a leaf rustled, not a bird sang.

She felt her steps before her delicately, carrying her head low, and sighing now and then with apprehension. At last she gave a quick breath of anxiety and dismay, and stood stock-still, quivering in every muscle, before a dark object in the shadow of the last palm-tree.

Artaban dismounted. The dim starlight revealed the form of a man lying across the road. His humble dress and the outline of his haggard face showed that he was probably one of the poor Hebrew exiles who still dwelt in great numbers in the vicinity. His pallid skin, dry and yellow as parchment, bore the mark of the deadly fever which ravaged the marsh-lands in autumn. The chill of death was in his lean hand, and as Artaban released it the arm fell back inertly upon the motionless breast.

He turned away with a thought of pity, consigning the body to that strange burial which the Magians deemed most fitting — the funeral of the desert, from which the kites and vultures rise on dark wings, and the beasts of prey slink furtively away, leaving only a heap of white bones in the sand.

But, as he turned, a long, faint, ghostly sigh came from the man's lips. The brown, bony fingers closed convulsively on the hem of the Magian's robe and held him fast.

Artaban's heart leaped to his throat, not with fear, but with a dumb resentment at the importunity of this blind delay.

How could he stay here in the darkness to minister to a dying stranger? What claim had this unknown fragment of human life upon his compassion or his service? If he lingered but for an hour he could hardly reach Borsippa at the appointed time. His companions would think he had given up the journey. They would go without him. He would lose his quest.

But if he went on now, the man would surely die. If he stayed, life might be restored. His spirit throbbed and fluttered with the urgency of the crisis. Should he risk the great reward of his divine faith for the sake of a single deed of human love? Should he turn aside, if only for a moment, from the following of the star, to give a cup of cold water to a poor, perishing Hebrew?

"God of truth and purity," he prayed, "direct me in the holy path, the way of wisdom which thou only knowest."

Then he turned back to the sick man. Loosening the grasp of his hand, he carried him to a little mound at the foot of the palm-tree.

He unbound the thick folds of the turban and opened the garment above the sunken breast. He brought water from one of the small canals nearby, and moistened the sufferer's brow and mouth.

He mingled a draught of one of those simple but potent remedies which he carried always in his girdle — for the Magians were physicians as well as astrologers — and poured it slowly between the colourless lips. Hour after hour he laboured as only a skilful healer of disease can do; and at last the man's strength returned; he sat up and looked about him.

"Who art thou?" he said, in the rude dialect of the country, "and why hast thou sought me here to bring back life?"

"I am Artaban the Magian, of the city of Ecbatana, and I am going to Jerusalem in search of one who is to be born King of the Jews, a great Prince and Deliverer of all men. I dare not delay any longer upon my journey, for the caravan that has waited for me may depart without me. But see, here is all that I have left of bread and wine, and here is a potion of healing herbs. When thy strength is restored thou canst find the dwellings of the Hebrews among the house of Babylon.

The Jew raised his trembling hand solemnly to heaven.

"Now may the God of Abraham and Isaac and Jacob bless and prosper the journey of the merciful, and bring him in peace to his desired haven. But stay; I have nothing to give thee in return — only this: that I can tell thee where the Messiah must be sought. For our prophets have said that he should be born not in Jerusalem, but in Bethlehem of Judah. May the Lord bring thee in safety to that place, because thou hast had pity upon the sick."

It was already long past midnight. Artaban rode in haste, and Vasda, restored by the brief rest, ran eagerly through the silent plain and swam the channels of the river. She put forth the remnant of her strength, and fled over the ground like a gazelle.

But the first beam of the sun sent her shadow before her as she entered upon the final stadium of the journey, and the eyes of Artaban, anxiously scanning the great mound of Nimrod and the Temple of the Seven Spheres, could discern no trace of his friends.

The many-coloured terraces of black and orange and red and yellow and green and blue and white, shattered by the convulsions of nature, and crumbling under the repeated blows of human violence, still glittered like a ruined rainbow in the morning light.

Artaban rode swiftly around the hill. He dismounted and climbed to the highest terrace, looking out toward the west.

The huge desolation of the marshes stretched away to the horizon and the border of the desert. Bitterns stood by the stagnant pools and jackals skulked through the low bushes; but there was no sign of the caravan of the wise men, far or near.

At the edge of the terrace he saw a little cairn of broken bricks, and under them a piece of parchment. He caught it up and read: "We have waited past the midnight, and can delay no longer. We go to find the King. Follow us across the desert."

Artaban sat down upon the ground and covered his head in despair.

"How can I cross the desert," said he, "with no food and with a spent horse? I must return to Babylon, sell my sapphire, and buy a train of camels, and provision for the journey. I may never overtake my friends. Only God the merciful knows whether I shall not lose sight of the King because I tarried to show mercy."

For the sake of a little child

There was a silence in the Hall of Dreams, where I was listening to the story of the Other Wise Man. And through this silence I saw, but very dimly, his figure passing over the dreary undulations of the desert, high upon the back of his camel, rocking steadily onward like a ship over the waves.

The land of death spread its cruel net around him. The stony wastes bore no fruit but briers and thorns. The dark ledges of rock thrust themselves above the surface here and there, like the bones of perished monsters. Arid and inhospitable mountain ranges rose before him, furrowed with dry channels of ancient torrents, white and ghastly as scars on the face of nature. Shifting hills of treacherous sand were heaped like tombs along the horizon. By day, the fierce heat pressed its intolerable burden on the quivering air; and no living creature moved on the dumb, swooning earth, but tiny jerboas scuttling through the parched bushes, or lizards vanishing in the clefts of the rock. By night the jackals prowled and barked in the distance, and the lion made the black ravines echo with his hollow roaring, while a bitter blighting chill followed the fever of the day. Through heat and cold, the Magian moved steadily onward.

Then I saw the gardens and orchards of Damascus, watered by the streams of Abana and Pharpar with their sloping swards inlaid with bloom, and their thickets of myrrh and roses. I saw also the long, snowy ridge of Hermon, and the dark groves of cedars, and the valley of the Jordan, and the blue waters of the Lake of Galilee, and the fertile plain of Esdraelon, and the hills of Ephraim, and the highlands of Judah. Through all these I followed the figure of Artaban moving steadily onward, until he arrived at Bethlehem. And it was the third day after the three wise men had come to that place and had found Mary and Joseph, with the young child, Jesus, and had laid the gifts of gold and frankincense and myrrh at his feet.

Then the other wise man drew near, weary, but full of hope, bearing his ruby and his pearl to offer to the King. "For now at last," he said, "I shall surely find him, though it be alone, and later than my brethren. This is the place of which the Hebrew exile told me that the prophets had spoken, and here I shall behold the rising of the great light. But I must inquire about the visit of my brethren, and to what house the star directed them, and to whom they presented their tribute."

The streets of the village seemed to be deserted, and Artaban wondered whether the men had all gone up to the hill-pastures to bring down their sheep. From the open door of a low stone cottage he heard the sound of a woman's voice singing softly. He entered and found a young mother hushing her baby to rest. She told him of the strangers from the far East who had appeared in the village three days ago, and how they said that a star had guided them to the place where Joseph of Nazareth was lodging with his wife and her new-born child, and how they had paid reverence to the child and given him many rich gifts.

"But the travellers disappeared again," she continued, "as suddenly as they had come. We were afraid at the strangeness of their visit. We could not understand it. The man of Nazareth took the babe and his mother and fled away that same night secretly, and it was whispeered that they were going far away to Egypt. Ever since, there has been a spell upon the village; something evil hangs over it. They say that the Roman soldiers are coming from Jerusalem to force a new tax from us, and the men have driven the flocks and herds far back among the hills, and hidden themselves to escape it."

Artaban listened to her gentle, timid speech, and the child in her arms looked up in his face and smiled, stretching out its rosy hands to grasp at the winged circle of gold on his breast. His heart warmed to the touch. It seemed like a greeting of love and trust to one who had journeyed long in loneliness and perplexity, fighting with his own doubts and fears, and following a light that was veiled in clouds.

"Might not this child have been the promised Prince?" He asked within himself, as he touched its soft cheek. "Kings have been borne ere now in lowlier houses than this, and the favourite of the stars may rise even from a cottage. But it has not seemed good to the God of Wisdom to reward my search so soon and so easily. The one whom I seek has gone before me; and now I must follow the King to Egypt."

The young mother laid the babe in its cradle, and rose to minister to the wants of the strange guest that fate had brought her into her house. She set food before him, the plain fare of peasants, but willingly offered, and therefore full of refreshment for the soul as well as for the body. Artaban accepted it gratefully; and, as he ate, the child fell into a happy slumber, and murmured sweetly in its dreams, and a great peace filled the quiet room.

But suddenly there came the noise of a wild confusion and uproar in the streets of the village, a shrieking and wailing of women's voices, a clangour of brazen trumpets and a clashing of swords, and a desperate cry: "The soldiers! The soldiers of Herod! They are killing our children."

The young mother's face grew white with terror. She clasped her child to her bosom, and crouched motionless in the darkest corner of the room, covering him with the folds of her robe, lest he should wake and cry.

But Artaban went quickly and stood in the doorway of the house. His broad shoulders filled the portal from side to side, and the peak of his white cap all but touched the lintel.

The soldiers came hurrying down the street with bloody hands and dripping swords. At the sight of the stranger in his imposing dress they hesitated with surprise. The captain of the band approached the threshold to thrust him aside. But Artaban did not stir. His face was as calm as though he were watching the stars, and in his eyes there burned that steady radiance before which even the half-tamed hunting leopard shrinks and the fierce blood-hound pauses in his leap. He held the soldier silently for an instant, and then said in a low voice:

"I am all alone in this place, and I am awaiting to give this jewel to the prudent captain who will leave me in peace."

He showed the ruby, glistening in the hollow of his hand like a great drop of blood.

The captain was amazed at the splendour of the gem. The pupils of his eyes expanded with desire, and the hard lines of greed wrinkled around his lips. He stretched out his hand and took the ruby.

"March on !" He cried to his men, "there is no child here. The house is still."

The clamour and the clang of arms passed down the street as the headlong fury of the chase sweeps by the secret covert where the trembling deer is hidden. Artaban re-entered the cottage. He turned his face to the east and prayed:

"God of truth, forgive my sin! I have said the thing that is not, to save the life of a child. And two of my gifts are gone. I have spent for man that which was meant for God. Shall I ever be worthy to see the face of the King?"

But the voice of the woman, weeping for joy in the shadow behind him, said very gently

"Because thou hast saved the life of my little one, may the Lord bless thee and keep thee; the Lord make his face to shine upon thee and be gracious unto thee; the Lord lift up his countenance upon thee and give thee peace."

In the hidden way of sorrow

Then again there was a silence in the Hall of Dreams, deeper and more mysterious than the first interval, and I understood that the years of Artaban were flowing very swiftly under the stillness of that clinging fog, and I caught only a glimpse, here and there, of the river of his life shining through the shadows that concealed its course.

I saw him moving among the throngs of men in populous Egypt, seeking everywhere for traces of the household that had come down from Bethlehem, and finding them under the spreading sycamore-trees of Heliopolis, and beneath the walls of the Roman fortress of New Babylon beside the Nile — traces so faint and dim that they vanished before him continually, as footprints on the hard river-sand glisten for a moment with moisture and then disappear.

I saw him again at the foot of the pyramids, which lifted their sharp points into the intense saffron glow of the sunset sky, changeless monuments of the perishable glory and the imperishable hope of man. He looked up into the vast countenance of the crouching Sphinx, and vainly tried to read the meaning of the calm eyes and smiling mouth. Was it, indeed, the mockery of all effort and all aspiration, as Tigranes had said — the cruel jest of a riddle that has no answer, a search that never can suceed? Or was there a touch of pity and encouragement in that inscrutable smile — a promise that even the defeated should attain a victory, and the disappointed should discover a prize, and the ignorant should be made wise, and the blind should see, and the wandering should come into the haven at last?

I saw him again in an obscure house of Alexandria, taking councel with a Hebrew rabbi. The venerable man, bending of the rolls of parchment on which the prophecies of Israel were written, read aloud the pathetic words which foretold the sufferings of the promised Messiah — the despised and rejected of men, the man of sorrows and the acquaintance of grief.

"And remember, my son," said he, fixing his deep-set eyes upon the face of Artaban, "the King whom you are seeking is not to be found in a palace, nor among the rich and powerful. If the light of the world and the glory of Israel had been appointed to come with the greatness of earthly splendour, it must have appeared long ago. For no son of Abraham will ever again rival the power which Joseph had in the palaces of Egypt, or the magnificence of Solomon throned between the lions in Jerusalem. But the light for which the world is waiting is a new light, the glory that shall rise out of patient and triumphant suffering. And the kingdom which is to be established forever is a new kingdom, the royalty of perfect and unconquerable love.

"I do not know how this shall come to pass, nor how the turbulent kings and peoples of earth shall be brought to acknowledge the Messiah and pay homage to him. But this I know. Those who seek him will do well to look among the poor and the lowly, the sorrowful and the oppressed."

So I saw the other wise man again and again, travelling from place to place, and searching among the people of the dispersion, with whom the little family from Bethlehem might, perhaps, have found a refuge. He passed through countries where famine lay heavy upon the land and the poor were crying for bread. He made his dwelling in plague-stricken cities where the sick were languishing in the bitter companion-ship of helpless misery. He visited the oppressed and the aflicted in the gloom of subterranean prisons, and the crowded wretchedness of slave-markets, and the weary toil of galley-ships. In all this populous and intricate world of anguish, though he found none to worship, he found many to help. He fed the hungry, and clothed the naked, and healed the sick, and comforted the captive; and his years went by more swiftly than the weaver's shuttle that flashes back and forth through the loom while the web grows and the invisible pattern is completed.

It seemed almost as if he had forgotten his quest. But once I saw him for a moment as he stood alone at sunrise, waiting at the gate of a Roman prison. He had taken from a secret resting-place in his bosom the pearl, the last of his jewels. As he looked at it, a mellower lustre, a soft and iridescent light, full of shifting gleams of azure and rose, trembled upon its surface. It seemed to have absorbed some reflection of the colours of the lost sapphire and ruby. So the profound, secret purpose of a noble life draws into itself the memories of past joy and past sorrow. All that has helped it, all that has hindered it, is transfused by a subtle magic into its very essence. It becomes more luminous and precious the longer it is carried close to the warmth of the beating heart.

Then, at last, while I was thinking of this pearl, and of its meaning, I heard the end of the story of the Other Wise Man.

A pearl of great price

Three-and-thirty years of the life of Artaban had passed, and he was still a pilgrim, and a seeker after light. His hair, once darker than the cliffs of Zagros, was now white as the wintry snow that covered them. His eyes, that once flashed like flames of fire, were dull as embers smouldering among the ashes.

Worn and weary and ready to die, but still looking for the King, he had come for the last time to Jerusalem. He had often visited the holy city before, and had searched through all its lanes and crowded hovels and black prisons without finding any trace of the family of Nazarenes who had fled from Bethlehem long ago. But now it seemed as if he must make one more effort, and something whispered in his heart that, at last, he might succeed.

It was the season of the Passover. The city was thronged with strangers. The children of Israel, scattered in far lands all over the world, had returned to the Temple for the great feast, and there had been a confusion of tongues in the narrow streets for many days.

But on this day there was a singular agitation visible in the multitude. The sky was veiled with a portentous gloom, and currents of excitement seemed to flash through the crowd like the thrill which shakes the forest on the eve of a storm. A secret tide was sweeping them all one way. The clatter of sandals, and the soft, thick sound of thousands of bare feet shuffling over the stones, flowed unceasingly along the street that leads to the Damascus gate.

Artaban joined company with a group of people from his own country, Parthian Jews who had come up to keep the Passover, and inquired of them the cause of the tumult, and where they were going.

"We are going," they answered, "to the place called Golgotha, outside the city walls, where there is to be an execution. Have you not heard what has happened? Two famous robbers are to be crucified, and with them another, called Jesus of Nazareth, a man who has done many wonderful works among the people, so that they love him greatly. But the priests and elders have said that he must die, because he gave himself out to be the Son of God. And Pilate has sent him to the cross because he said that he was the 'King of the Jews'."

How strangely these familiar words fell upon the tired heart of Artaban! They had led him for a lifetime over land and sea. And now they came to him darkly and mysteriously like a message of despair. The King had arisen, but he had been denied and cast out. He was about to perish. Perhaps he was already dying. Could it be the same who had been born in Bethlehem thirty-three years ago, at whose birth the star had appeared in heaven, and of whose coming the prophets had spoken?

Artaban's heart beat unsteadily with that troubled, doubtful apprehension which is the excitement of old age. But he said within himself: "The ways of God are stranger than the thoughts of men, and it may be that I shall find the King, at last, in the hands of his enemies, and shall come in time to offer my pearl for his ransom before he dies."

So the old man followed the multitude with slow and painful steps toward the Damascus gate of the city. Just beyond the entrance of the guard-house a troop of Macedonian soldiers came down the street, dragging a young girl with torn dress and dishevelled hair. As the Magian paused to look at her with compassion, she broke suddenly from the hands of her tormentors and threw herself at his feet, clasping him around the knees. She had seen his white cap and the winged circle on his breast.

"Have pity on me," she cried, "and save me, for the sake of the God of purity! I also am a daughter of the true religion which is taught by the Magi. My father was a merchant of Parthia, but he is dead, and I am

417

seized for his debts to be sold as a slave. Save me from worse than death."

Artaban trembled.

It was the old conflict in his soul, which had come to him in the palm-grove of Babylon and in the cottage at Bethlehem — the conflict between the expectation of faith and the impulse of love. Twice the gift which he had consecrated to the worship of religion had been drawn from his hand to the service of humanity. This was the third trial, the ultimate probation, the final and irrevocable choice.

Was it his great opportunity or his last temptation? He could not tell. One thing only was clear in the darkness of his mind — it was inevitable. And does not the inevitable come from God?

One thing only was sure to his divided heart — to rescue this helpless girl would be a true deed of love. And is not love the light of the soul?

He took the pearl from his bossom. Never had it seemed so luminous, so radiant, so full of tender, living lustre. He laid it in the hand of the slave.

"This is thy ransom, daughter! It is the last of my treasures which I kept for the King."

While he spoke the darkness of the sky thickened, and shuddering tremors ran through the earth, heaving convulsively like the breast of one who struggles with mighty grief.

The walls of the houses rocked to and fro. Stones were loosened and crashed into the street. Dust clouds filled the air. The soldiers fled in terror, reeling like drunken men. But Artaban and the girl whom he had ransomed crouched helpless beneath the wall of the Praetorium.

What had he to fear? What had he to live for? He had given away the last remnant of his tribute for the King. He had parted with the last hope of finding him. The quest was over, and it had failed. But even in that thought, accepted and embraced, there was peace. It was not resignation. It was not submission. It was something more profound and searching. He knew that all was well, because he had done the best that he could, from day to day. He had been true to the light that had been given to him. He had looked for more. And if he had not found it, if a failure was all that came out of his life, doubtless that was the best that was possible. He had not seen the revelation of "life everlasting, incorruptible and immortal". But he knew that even if he could live his earthly life over again, it could not be otherwise than it had been.

One more lingering pulsation of the earthquake quivered through the ground. A heavy tile, shaken from the roof, fell and struck the old man on the temple. He lay breathless and pale, with his grey head resting on the young girl's shoulder, and blood trickling from the wound. As she bent over him, fearing that he was dead, there came a voice through the twilight, very small and still, like music sounding from a distance, in which the notes are clear but the words are lost. The girl turned to see if some one had spoken from the window above them, but she saw no one.

Then the old man's lips began to move, as if in answer, and she heard him say in the Parthian tongue:

"Not so, my Lord: For when saw I thee an-hungered and fed thee? Or thirsty, and gave thee drink? When saw I thee a stranger, and took thee in? Or naked, and clothed thee? When saw I thee sick or in prison, and came unto thee? Three-and-thirty years have I looked for thee; but I have never seen thy face, nor ministered to thee, my King."

He ceased, and the sweet voice came again. And again the maid heard it, very faintly and far away. But now it seemed as though she understood the words:

"*Verily I say unto thee, Inasmuch as thou hast done it unto one of the least of these my brethren, thou has done it unto me.*"

A calm radiance of wonder and joy lighted the pale face of Artaban like the first ray of dawn on a snowy mountain-peak. One long, last breath of relief exhaled gently from his lips.

His journey was ended. His treasures were accepted. The Other Wise Man had found the King.

The Dream Song of Olaf Åsteson

A Norwegian Folk Song

I

Now hearken all you and give heed
    To you I'll sing a song
About a young and nimble youth
    Called Olaf Åsteson,
        Of him I'll sing to you.

On Christmas Eve he went to rest
    A deep sleep held him fast,
And never once awakened he
    Until the thirteenth day
When folk to church had passed.
    I sing of Olaf Åsteson
        Who once did sleep so long,
        Of him I sing to you.

He went to rest on Christmas Eve
    And long he slept that tide,
Nor ever once could he awake
    Until the thirteenth day,
The bird its wing spead wide.
    'Twas Olaf Åsteson
        Who once so long did sleep,
        Of him I sing to you.

And Olaf never once awaked
    Until the thirteenth day.
The Sun shone o'er the mountains high
    His fleetest horse then saddled he,

And fast to church made he his way.
 'Twas Olaf Åsteson
   Who once so long did sleep,
   Of him I sing to you.

Before the altar stood the priest
 And Mass he chanted loud
As by the church door Olaf sat
 And told to all the dreams
   That through his soul did crowd
   In that long sleep of days.

And all the folk both young and old
 Heedful they heard the fiery words
In which his vision Olaf told.
 'Twas Olaf Åsteson
   Who slept so long a tide,
   Of him I sing to you.

II

I went to rest on Christmas night,
 A deep sleep held me fast,
Nor ever once awakened I
 Until the thirteenth day,
   When folk to church had passed.
   Bright shone the moon,
   And far the road did wind.

Upborne was I to cloud wrapped heights,
 And flung in depths of sea
No happy thing befalleth him
 Who thinks to follow me.
   Bright shone the moon
   And far the road did wind.

Thrust was I into turbid swamp,
 Upborne to cloud wrapt height.
Hell's horrors opened wide to me,
 And gleam of heaven's light

Bright shone the moon,
And far the road did wind.

And fare must I to deeps of earth
Where streams of gods outpour;
To look I neither could nor dare,
Yet heard their fearful roar.
Bright shone the moon,
And far the road did wind.

My black horse did not neigh,
My hound it did not bay,
The morning birds they did not sing,
O'er all a wonder lay
Bright shone the moon,
And far the road did wind.

Now must I fare to spirit land
The far field's thorny heath,
Torn and rent was my scarlet cloak,
And the nails of my feet beneath.
Bright shone the moon,
And far the road did wind.

Then came I to the Gjaller Bridge,
It hangs in a windy height,
Lofty, adorned with fine red gold,
And nail points sharp and bright.
Fair shone the moon,
And far the road did wind.

Stung was I by the spirit snake,
The bull stood in the way;
Bright shone the moon
Of evil fearful kind.
Three creatures of the bridge are they,
Bitten was I by the spirit hound,
And far the road did wind.

Snap full soon will the spirit hound,
   Sting full soon will the snake,
   Bellows the bull most mightily;
None o'er the bridge their way may take,
   That do not truth revere.
      Bright shone the moon,
      And far the road did wind.

I have o'er passed the swinging bridge,
   So small and high in air,
Into the marshes now I wade
   Behind me lie they there.
      Bright shone the moon,
      And far the road did wind.

I have o'er passed the swinging bridge,
   In marshes must I wade,
No ground there seems beneath my feet,
   Earth I feel in my mouth now laid,
   As dead men in the grave.
      Bright shone the moon,
      And far the road did wind.

To water then I came wherein,
   Like glittering flames of blue,
   The iceberg masses glancing shone,
By God mine eyes were guided true,
   That I direction found.
      The moon shone bright,
      And far the road did wind.

To Winter's path I bent my steps,
   It lay upon my right,
I looked as into paradise,
   Clear rayed its beams of light.
      Bright shone the moon
      And far the road did wind.

And in the radiant heavenly light,
 God's Mother did I see,
To Brooksvalin to wend my way,
 So did she counsel me,
There, where men's souls shall judgment find.
  Bright shone the moon,
  And far the road did wind.

III

In other worlds I sojourned then
 Full many long nights through,
And only God himself can tell
 What stressful troubled souls I knew,
  In Brooksvalin, where souls
  World judgment find.

A young man there I first beheld,
 A small boy had he slain,
For ever must he carry him
 Within his own arms twain.
Deep in the mire and slime he stood.
  In Brooksvalin where souls
  World judgment find.

And there an old man did I see,
 A cloak he wore of lead,
When on the earth a miser he,
 And this his penance dread.
  In Brooksvalin where souls
  World judgment find.

Men who a fiery raiment wore
 Appeared in heavy woe,
Dishonesty thus weighted down
 These poor souls so,
  In Brooksvalin where souls
  World judgment find.

And children also saw I there,
   Who walked on glowing coals,
They worked their parents ill in life,
   Afflicted were their souls,
      In Brooksvalin where souls
      World judgment find.

And now towards that house of ill
   To go I was constrained,
Where sorcerers their work performed
   With blood that they in life inflamed,
      In Brooksvalin where souls
      World judgment find.

By Princes of Hell outstrode,
From the north, the evil host
   In wild troop banded rode,
      In Brooksvalin where souls
      World judgment find.

Evil, above all things that are,
   There came from out the north,
In front rode he, the Prince of Hell,
   Upon his coal black horse,
      In Brooksvalin where souls
      World judgment find.

But from the south, in holy quiet
   There came another band,
Foremost there rode St Michael great
   By Jesus Christ's right hand,
      In Brooksvalin where souls
      World judgment find.

The souls with sin o'erladen,
   Must tremble now with fear,
The tears ran down their cheeks like rain,
   As they their deeds must hear,
      In Brooksvalin where souls
      World judgment find.

In majesty St Michael stood
 And weighed the souls of men,
 In cosmic balance for their sins,
And judging thereby then,
  There stood the world judge, Jesus Christ,
   In Brooksvalin where souls
   World judgment find.

IV

How blessed he, who in earth life,
 Shoes to the poor hath given,
He wanders not in thorny paths
 With naked feet and riven;
  So speaks the balance tongue,
  And world truth then
Resounds in spirit lands.

How blessed he, who in earth life,
 Bread for the poor hath found,
No harmful wound, in yonder world
 To him shall give the hound,
  So speaks the balance tongue,
  And world truth then
  Resounds in spirit lands.

How blessed he, who in earth life,
 Grain gives now to the poor,
When o'er the Gjaller Bridge he treads,
 The sharp horns of the bull, to him
 Shall never threatening lower,
  So speaks the balance tongue,
  And world truth then
  Resounds in spirit lands.

How blessed he, who in earth life,
 Clothed the poor shall see,
In Brooksvalin, he by iceberg's mass,

Shall never frozen be.
    So speaks the balance tongue,
    And world truth then
    Resounds in spirit lands.

And folk, both young and old,
    They listened spellbound to the words,
    In which his visions Olaf told.
Long, full long, hast thou slept this tide,
    Awake now, Olaf Åsteson.

Acknowledgements

Thanks are due to the following authors and publishers for permission to reprint copyright stories in this work.

Dan Lindholm "Why God Created Man" translated by Polly Lawson from *Wie die Sterne entstanden*, by permission of Freies Geistesleben, Stuttgart.

Eberhard Kurras "The Search for the Secret King" translated by Polly Lawson from *Die Christengemeinschaft*, December 1939, p. 206.

Selma Lagerlöf "The Legend of Santa Lucia's Day", by permission of the Estate of Selma Lagerlöf.

Gerhard Klein "Andrey" and "Blind Peter", translated by Polly Lawson from *Beim Schicksal zu Gast*, by permission of Urachhaus, Stuttgart.

Jakob Streit "The Star-Rider" from *Der Sternenreiter*, Novalis, Schaffhausen.

"The Birth of John the Baptist", "The Annunciation to Mary" and "The Birth of Jesus in Bethlehem" from the Gospel of Luke translated by Kalmia Bittleston (Floris Books, 1989).

Dan Lindholm "The Shepherd Boy's Flute" translated by Polly Lawson from *Wie die Sterne entstanden*, by permission of Freies Geistesleben, Stuttgart.

Georg Dreissig "Jonas, the Shepherd in the Stable" translated by Polly Lawson from *Die Christengemeinschaft*, December 1981, p. 395-97.

Elizabeth Goudge "The Well of the Star" and "The Legend of the First Christmas Tree" from *The Reward of Faith*, by permission of Gerald Duckworth, London.

Ruth Sawyer "The Shepherds", "A Candle for Saint Bridget", "The Wee Christmas Cabin of Carn-na-ween", "Schnitzle, Schnotzle, and Schnootzle", and "Fiddler, Play Faster, Play Faster," from *The Long Christmas*, by permission of Viking, New York, and Christofoor, Zeist.

Willem Brandt "The Candle" translated by Polly Lawson from *De Kaars*, by permission of Christofoor, Zeist.

Edzard Schaper "Semyon" translated by Polly Lawson from *Stern über die Grenze*, by permission of Christofoor, Zeist.

Jakob Streit "Rösli from Stechelberg" and "The First Christmas Tree" translated by Polly Lawson from *Der erste Weihnachtsbaum*, by permission of Christofoor, Zeist.

C.E. Pothast-Gimberg "A Christmas Story from the Mountains" translated by Polly Lawson from *De Kerstschoof*, by permission of Christofoor, Zeist.

Karl Paetow "Frau Holle and the Glassblower", "The Miner and his Wife", and "The Lady's Coach" translated by Polly Lawson from *Volkssagen und Märchen um Frau Holle*, by permission of Christofoor, Zeist.

Selma Lagerlöf "The Christmas Rose" translated by Velma Swanston Howard, published in *Christ Legends and other Stories*, Floris Books 1978.

Ruth Sawyer "The Gold of Bernardino", and "The Crib of Bo'bossu" from *The Long Christmas*, by permission of Viking, New York, and Christofoor, Zeist.

Elizabeth Klein "The Thistle" translated by Polly Lawson from *Geschichten von Tieren und Pflanzen, Steinen und Sternen*, by permission of Mellinger, Stuttgart.

"The Adoration of the Magi" from the Gospel of Matthew translated by Kalmia Bittleston, Floris Books 1988.

Dan Lindholm "New Year's Eve" translated by Polly Lawson from *Wie die Sterne entstanden*, by permission of Freies Geistesleben, Stuttgart.

Nienke van Hichtum "The Miraculous Corn" translated by Polly Lawson from *Groot 'Sagenboek*, by permission of Christofoor, Zeist.

Jane Clement "The Three Gifts" from *Behold that Star*, by permission of Plough Press, New York.

Karl Paetow "The Little Light Blown Out" translated by Polly Lawson from *Volkssagen und Märchen um Frau Holle*, by permission of Christofoor, Zeist.

Ruth Sawyer "The Three Kings Ride" from *The Long Christmas*, by permission of Viking, New York.

Georg Dreissig "The Secret King" translated by Polly Lawson from *Die Christengemeinschaft*, January 1985, pp. 24-27.

"The Dream song of Olaf Åsteson" translation by Maud Surrey reproduced by permission of Winifred R. Porter.